ROUGH RIDE

Also by John Francome

Stud Poker
Stone Cold

And by John Francome and James MacGregor

Eavesdropper
Riding High
Declared Dead
Blood Stock

ROUGH RIDE

John Francome

HEADLINE

First published in 1992
by HEADLINE BOOK PUBLISHING PLC

10 9 8 7 6 5 4 3 2 1

British Library Cataloguing in Publication Data

Francome, John
Rough Ride
I. Title
823.914 [F]

ISBN 0–7472–0566–3

Phototypeset by Intype, London
Printed and bound in Great Britain by
Richard Clay Ltd, Bungay, Suffolk

HEADLINE BOOK PUBLISHING PLC
Headline House
79 Great Titchfield Street
London W1P 7FN

ROUGH RIDE

Prologue

I was nearly home when the headlights of my old Mercedes picked out a small, plain stock lorry trundling down the hill towards me. I knew it shouldn't have been there. At a quarter to five on a black March morning, neither of my neighbouring farmers would be leaving for market.

The lane that led up to their farms and my ramshackle house had deep drainage ditches on either side. It was not wide enough for two vehicles to pass. One of us would have to yield and reverse to the nearest gateway. Traditionally, it is the smaller vehicle which gives way. This time, it was not going to be.

Leaving my headlights on and the motor still running, I got out of my car and walked towards the lorry. As I passed through the lights to his side, the driver saw me. The lorry's engine revved, and the gears crashed as he tried to find reverse in a hurry. Before he had, I was pulling his door open. I could see his face. I did not know him, but it was clear from his startled look that he knew me; and he had not been expecting to see me.

Without stopping to formulate the thought, I knew that my best horse had been kidnapped; someone was stealing Caesar's Consul – my first-class ticket to the Amateur Riders' Championship. My temper, not my most admirable trait, jumped straight into the red.

The driver, still fumbling with the gear-stick, tried to swing a feeble blow with his right hand. He missed. I reached up, grabbed him by his unzipped waxed jacket, and yanked him out of the cab. The man, who landed with a thud and a grunt on the ground behind me, was at least fifteen stone, judging by the effort it took to get him out of the cab. I followed the well-founded rule about fighting people bigger than yourself – you hit them first. Before

1

he had time to recover, I thrust my right foot firmly between his legs. Bellowing, he curled up like a hedgehog and I aimed a passing kick at his exposed back.

I leaned into the lorry cab and fumbled for the ignition keys. I tugged them out and flung them towards the ditch ten yards down the road.

With the lorry's engine stopped, I could hear the Mercedes spluttering quietly. I turned to the driver, moaning by the side of the road. I clutched his shirt-collar, lifted his head and hit him on the chin as hard as my inexperienced fist would allow. He fell back limp and yielding and I heaved him into the ditch. I ran to my car, turned off the engine and took the keys out.

By the new light of a misty half-moon, I ran round to the back of the lorry and knocked out the clips which held the ramp in place. It was a filthy old cattle truck. The ramp was covered in fresh cow slurry. I slithered up in my leather-soled shoes and groped around inside for the Consul. I could smell him and hear him, up at the cab end of the box.

I worked my way along the sides until I found the gelding tethered but standing unsupported. There was no straw on the slippery floor. Thank God they had not gone far; he would have been down on his side – or worse, his back – before travelling a few hundred yards more like that.

I fumbled with the headcollar rope, which had been tied to the side in a granny-knot, while I patted the horse's neck and spoke to him to calm him. After what seemed like an infuriatingly long struggle, I undid the rope and warily led the Consul to the back of the lorry and the top of the skiddy ramp. I had no idea if I had hit the driver hard enough to keep him quiet for long. I hoped I had, but now what mattered most was to get my horse home.

The Consul could not wait to get out of the dark box that reeked of cattle. He trotted down the ramp, dragging me on the end of his rope. I caught the tip of my shoe under a loose board and fell with a crash, hitting the side of my head at the edge of the lane. The rope was gone from my fist and I could hear the horse clattering back up the lane towards his stable. I had already fallen badly three times that season, and I was getting used to it; but not onto tarmac. My face felt badly scraped and bruised; my head throbbed and sang as I lay in a daze for a moment, trying to get my breath back.

I heard the rustle behind me vaguely and too late.

There was a crack on my head that produced instant vivid fireworks; then nothing.

If I had been capable of feeling anything in this comatose condition, I suppose it would have been relief. I needed a short rest from the bizarre events and frantic activity that had sprung into my life less than two weeks before.

It is hard to pinpoint the day that I first became aware of the threat that Clive Drury posed to my disorderly but generally peaceful existence.

It had all started innocently enough with a not entirely unexpected fall on a normal Saturday afternoon's point-to-point racing. The meeting had been held on Drury's land at Gazeley Park.

Chapter 1

I lifted my head until my chin was an inch or two off the ground, and took in the view with dazed detachment.

Fine pasture, which had been grazed by fifty generations of well-bred sheep, swept up between parkland oaks and cedars towards a handsome stone mansion.

The designer of this classic piece of eighteenth-century landscape would not have approved of the white running rails and large, steeple-chase fences which had turned the park into one of the best-looking – though not best-riding – point-to-point courses in Britain.

I sucked a deep breath through my nostrils. The smells brought me sharply back to earth. My eyes focused closer, on the long blades of lush, wet grass on which I lay, and a large, evil-looking cow-pat a foot in front of my face.

The ragged thundering of ten sets of aluminium-shod hooves was fading now. I hoped that the great brown idiot of a horse with whom I had just parted company would stay with the bunch until they reached the home straight where the lorries were; it was probably too much to hope that Georgie, my self-appointed groom, would manage to catch the beast.

And I wondered if I had been deliberately ridden into a two-foot gap at the edge of the fence.

I groaned, more out of frustration than pain.

What a way to enjoy yourself!

I moved a few limbs. They all seemed to work. I raised myself on to my hands and knees and took a few more long breaths to get some air back into my lungs. I was on my feet before the St

John's ambulance, bucking and jerking its way straight across the park, had reached me.

When it pulled up, Georgie leaped out and ran towards me, her eyes brimming with concern and compassion. Feeling like an undeserving, ungrateful bastard, which I was, I could not bear to meet them.

'For God's sake, Georgie,' I said testily, 'what have you done about the bloody horse? He'll be halfway to Hereford by now.'

'It's okay. Someone caught him. But what about you, Archie? It looked a horrible fall from up there.'

Georgie was beside me now. She clutched my arm through the sodden, muddy silk. I forced a light-hearted smile to reassure her.

'I'm fine, but we may as well get a lift back in the ambulance, so they don't have a wasted journey.'

I walked towards the vehicle, trying not to wince from a nasty bruise on my hip. Once in, I was glad of the lift. Georgie was wedged in beside me, still tentatively fingering my arm.

'God, what a day,' she said. 'And it started so well.'

'It's finished okay,' I said quickly. 'I'm still ahead in the championship this season, and with luck no one will catch me up now.' Why was it, I wondered, that this thoughtful and very good-looking girl seemed to bring out the arrogant animal in me?

'But are you sure you're all right? Will you still be able to come to Mum's party tonight?'

I nodded. 'Yes, I'll come.' I turned my head to glance at the glow of relief in her bright, speedwell-blue eyes, and sighed to myself.

'Do you want me to come back and help you put the horses away?' Georgie asked as we climbed out of the ambulance.

'No,' I said, a little too quickly, 'Thanks, but I can manage. Then I need a long bath with a few Scotches, and I won't need my back scrubbed. I'll be at your parents' place by eight.'

She accepted this with a small downturn of her mouth. I was not being deliberately unkind, but I always preferred to be on my own after a day's racing, at least for a few hours while I wound down.

The big brown horse, Cocoa – or 'Bill's Flutter', as he somewhat tastelessly appeared on Weatherby's Register – had been caught and was standing calmly now, tethered to a ring on the side of my lorry. Someone had put a sweat rug on him and he was munching from a hay net. Amateur racing people tend to be very supportive of one another.

A grey horse, Caesar's Consul, with whom I had won the Open, two races earlier, was already in the box where I had put him. Like the star that he was, he was cool and dry now. I hobbled up the ramp and swapped his string vest for a heavy quilted rug and poured him a drink from the tank on the Luton. He nuzzled my back for a treat and I delved into a bucket for his favourite, a bright green Bramley the size of a turnip. His big lips sucked it off my palm and he munched with noisy relish.

'Well done, son. It'll be Cheltenham soon.'

The horse gave what I considered a confident nod, and I limped out of the lorry to deal with Cocoa.

I was thankful that I had already had my two rides for the day – the Open and the Maiden – and I had no particular interest in the Restricted Open which was the last race. I loaded Cocoa, trying not to be unreasonably impatient with him, clambered into the cab, summoned up a farewell smile for Georgie, and lurched slowly down the track towards the Hereford road.

Three hours later, I left my house. I turned the key to lock the back door and walked round to the stable yard to take a quick look at the horses in their boxes. Cocoa looked at me mournfully, with his neck resting in the V of his anti-weaving grille, and I cursed the day Bill Beecham had ever given the animal to me.

I clambered into my eighteen-year-old Mercedes 450, and turned the ignition key as I made encouraging noises and nursed the car into life.

A long bath and a couple of large malt whiskies were all the medication I had needed after my fall, and I set off from the farmhouse in the East Herefordshire hills feeling reasonably content with my day's work. Even the thought of Georgie's slightly smothering attentions did not seem so bad now, and the parties at Temple Ferris were famous. I was looking forward to experiencing one at first hand.

Georgie – that is to say, The Honourable Georgina Henry – was the adopted daughter of Lord Walford, her mother's heiress and their only child.

I think it was that, as much as anything, that made it hard for me to respond to her. That her father was a Peer of the Realm, and her mother the ninth generation of a family of eighteenth-

7

century bankers, while I was the posthumous bastard of a 1950s Fleet Street hack, was completely immaterial to me; that I had watched my mother strive to bring me up on her meagre novelist's earnings, sending me to Eton, helping me through Oxford and the first few years afterwards as I tried to set up my picture business, was not. Everything that my mother and I had struggled for, Georgie could have had for the price of the breath it took to ask her doting parents. That was not her fault, of course, but it must surely have given her such a different perspective on life that it seemed unlikely we could be truly compatible.

But I could not deny that there were times when her enthusiasm for me gave a leg-up to the self-esteem.

That morning she had turned up at my place and persuaded Sharon, the groom, to let her take her place for the day. Sharon had yielded all too easily, and Georgie had told me she specially wanted to see me ride at Gazeley Park. She had spent some of her childhood holidays there, before her grandfather sold the estate to Clive Drury.

To be fair, she had prepared both horses beautifully. She had proudly accepted her groom's prize of ten pounds for the best turned out in the Open, and she had caused quite a stir in the paddock, leading Caesar's Consul round. I had been amused to see Clive Drury himself, almost looking the part in a bowler and trench raincoat, eyeing her up lasciviously, until he suddenly realised who she was. I had asked her to introduce me to Drury after the race.

Pushing the old Merc across the Severn Valley, between the dinosaur's back of the Malverns and the wooded escarpment of the Cotswolds ahead, I thought of Drury; he was going to be at Lady Walford's party tonight, Georgie had said.

I was grudgingly impressed by the big man. He must be in his sixties now, but obviously still in good shape. He was at least six foot three, and bulky with it. But for all his eighteen stone, he gave the impression of still being nimble on his feet. His movements were quick and decisive; his voice deep and fast. His dark brown eyes, I had noticed, were permanently on the move, inspecting everyone within his field of vision as well as whomever he was speaking to at the time. He was also handsome. Even from my perspective as a younger man who still resented the idea of women finding older men attractive, I could imagine that he had little difficulty in keeping women interested. He was one of the few people I had ever met who really did exude power and a kind of animal magnetism. It was impossible to ignore him, and hard not to defer to him. He also had just the kind of self-satisfied smugness that I loathed, and I had instinctively marked him down as a challenge.

It was chance that I had not met Drury before. He had an obnoxious son of twenty-one, Damian, against whom I had frequently ridden for the last two years. Drury had bought Damian a forty-thousand-pound chaser, ten years old, with the experience and speed to win any members' race doing the proverbial handsprings. The animal had not fallen in five years. Drury still seemed to think that his son was in some way responsible for the success he had in his first season. In fact, all that Damian had needed to do was to mount the horse, sit on it trying not to flap his elbows too much, and get off when the race was over.

I knew that Drury often arrived at the most obscure little point-to-point courses to witness his son's glories, but always left in a chopper or a Bentley as soon as his race was over.

Lord and Lady Walford's Temple Ferris House was set into a gentle south-facing cleft of the Cotswolds. Lights blazed from thirty windows, and the floodlit front gave the impression of being elegantly carved from honey-coloured fudge. The lighting was a little flashy for my taste, and I was surprised that the fiercely traditional Lord Walford had succumbed to this suburban treatment. But it also suggested that the champagne being served inside would have the right name and date on it.

I parked among a few dozen expensive cars and the odd tatty Land Rover and walked up a broad path of well-worn flagstones to the front door.

There were a lot of people in the vast front hall, but I saw Clive Drury at once. He saw me too and unexpectedly nodded in recognition across the sea of heads which separated us. I took a glass from a table by the door, and was going to look for my hostess when I felt a gentle squeeze on my behind. I turned round, but not too quickly.

A pair of lusty, dark brown eyes smiled up at me.

'What a lovely firm pair of buttocks.' The girl had a husky, Mayfair-receptionist sort of voice and her cheeks dimpled as she spoke.

'How do you know?' I asked. 'You've only felt one of them. I might be like the man from Devizes.'

The girl reached her arm behind me and squeezed again. 'No,' she said with certainty, 'you're not from Devizes. You're Archie Best, aren't you?'

'I'm afraid so,' I admitted, conscious of her hand still kneading my buttock. 'Are you a professional masseuse?'

'I wouldn't charge you.' She gave a final squeeze and withdrew her hand. 'I won quite a lot of money on you today.'

'Then you must have put a lot on. I think I started odds-on.'

The girl answered with an enigmatic smile. 'I know a winner when I see one.'

'Do you know a bit about horses, then?'

'No, but I know a lot about men.'

I could not help smiling. 'I can imagine that you might. Who are you?'

'Amanda Drury. We've met once before. I'm a friend of Georgie's.'

I had to assume that she was connected in some way to Clive of the same name. Second, third wife? I opted for daughter.

'It must have been very dark. I'm sure I'd have remembered,' I said.

'I don't think you were entirely sober at the time,' Amanda said. 'You certainly look in better shape now. Did that fall do any damage?'

'I've a couple of sore spots that could do with a massage.'

'I bet you have. If they're still bothering you later, let me know.'

I was about to firm up on this arrangement when Georgie joined us.

'Hi, Mandy. My stepfather would really like to see you. He's in the drawing room.'

'Randy old bugger,' Amanda laughed. 'Okay, I'll go and perk him up.' I could not help being aroused by the concupiscent smile she flashed at me before she wove her way through the party with a voluptuous swing of her silk-clad hips.

'Not very subtle, your friend Mandy. No VPL,' I remarked.

Georgie looked blank.

'Visible Panty Line,' I said.

Georgie laughed. 'You're right. When I was sharing a flat with her, the men always used to call her Nicholas. I suppose she was chatting you up.'

'Just a bit. Is the Drury you introduced me to at the races her father?'

'Yes,' Georgie nodded. 'And I should warn you that the Mandy Drury fan club isn't very exclusive,' she added, dismissing the subject lightly. 'Anyway, you seem to have impressed her father, too.'

'Oh, yes?' I said without much interest. 'He probably sees me as an obstacle to the racing success of the precious Damian. I won't tell him that if I win the championship this season, I'm going to pack it in.'

'Good Lord, are you?'

'Yes. Now that I can see I've got a real chance of doing it. Mind you, if I don't, I'll carry on until I do.'

'Why are you so obsessed with this championship? Don't you just enjoy the riding?'

'Yes, of course I do. But the championship is something I have to get out of my system; that and winning the Foxhunters at Cheltenham. There are a couple of bastards whom it will give me a great deal of satisfaction to beat.'

'That doesn't sound like you, Archie. You're not a vindictive person, are you?'

'Perhaps not, but this goes back a long way.'

I could see that she wanted to push me for details, but I was ashamed of my reasons and she would not have understood them anyway. She had never known what it was like to be the poorest boy among a group of rich, spoilt schoolboys.

'I must find your mother,' I said. 'I haven't seen her since I arrived.'

'Yes, do,' said Georgie. 'You're one of her favourites. She was really glad I'd finally got you here.'

I wondered about that as I made my way across the hall, which was still filling up with designer-clad and scented women with their bland, bored-looking men. This lot, if they were typical of Lady Walford's guests, did not present much competition.

Before I reached the double-doors that gave onto the drawing room, I was hailed at close quarters by the beaming, bulky figure of Clive Drury.

'Hello, Archie. You look a little cleaner than you did earlier today,' he boomed.

'I always change and wash before coming to parties,' I answered flippantly.

Drury's eyes hardened with a quick wince. He was obviously unused to back-chat, as I had guessed but could not resist testing.

'That horse is only fit for the knackers anyway. Why do you bother to ride rubbish?' he asked with less bonhomie than before.

'Because I haven't got a rich father to buy ready-made animals for me. If someone gives me a horse, I don't look it in the mouth.'

'Bill Beecham *gave* it to you? That old lush needs all the money he can lay his hands on.'

'You know Bill, do you? He's a very old friend of mine, and I was grateful to him. I admit that I didn't feel much gratitude lying among the cow-pats this afternoon, but if you think he's so hard up, it must have meant a lot to give it to me so I'll definitely persevere with the animal.'

I nodded, and carried on through the drawing room doors.

Lady Walford, who was as thoughtful and genuine a society hostess as I had ever come across, did seem pleased to see me.

She chatted about my prospects in the Championship, and seemed unconcerned about my lack of prospects in more serious areas. And she certainly did not seem opposed to the idea of a relationship between me and the Hon. Georgina.

I tried somehow, without being rude, to convey the fact that Georgie and I had not even slept together and were unlikely ever to become more intimate. But Georgie had evidently issued an exaggerated version of our relationship, which her mother was happy to buy. I supposed that her daughter was so rich in her own right that a future husband's income was not relevant.

Well, it might not have been to her.

Despite my non-committal answers, I found myself accepting an invitation to stay for a weekend in early March. I was planning to go to a large house sale near Stow on the Friday before and I dislike cooking for myself, so I decided it would suit me. Anyway, I guessed there would be a houseful, so I would not have to spend the whole weekend trying to avoid offending the blameless Georgie.

This flattering conversation was interrupted, I was surprised to see, by the once again beaming Clive Drury. He made no apologies for breaking into one of Susan Walford's breathless sentences.

'Hello, Sue. I just wanted a quick word with Archie here before I go.'

'Oh, are you going already, Clive? Is everything all right? Rollo will be sorry,' Lady Walford gushed.

'Yes, yes. Everything's fine, but I've left a few guests back at Gazeley who'll be offended if I don't see them at all, and there's a lot of money involved.' He turned to me. 'I'd like you to come over and look at my sporting pictures, Archie. That's your field isn't it? I may have an order for you.'

The man had hit both my weak spots in one: my fascination with any good old pictures – his were famously good – and my constant need to top up the funds required to pay for my expensive habit; the more prizes you win as an amateur race-rider, the more the whole business seems to cost.

I was tempted to stay longer than I did at Temple Ferris that evening. Mandy Drury's unsubtle charms had aroused an unsubtle response in me. She was not, in any strict sense of the word, a beautiful woman, but she was wickedly, invitingly sexy.

Nevertheless, I resisted. Georgie had invited me that evening and, though she would do her best to suppress any outward sign, she would be very miffed if Mandy and I went absent together. I decided to compromise and, having eaten a fair dinner's worth of vol-au-vents, angels-on-horseback and various concoctions of avocado and seafood, left before most of the guests.

I woke next morning with a little soreness in my hip but no hangover. It was a crisp sunny day, just the sort of day that had made me choose to live among these small, quiet hills and I did not want to waste it by lying about in bed.

I dressed, forgot about shaving and went out into my tidy stone stable-yard. Of the six boxes, three were currently occupied by Caesar's Consul, Cocoa and Jasper, my thirteen-year-old hunter. The rest were empty.

The two racehorses had both galloped three and a half miles the day before and would not need much exercise. Jasper, on the other hand, was on his toes and longing for a bit of action. I gave the other two a bucket of breakfast – some rolled oats and damp beet – filled their hay nets and tacked up the hunter. As usual, he would not stand still, in anticipation of our outing. I tried to calm him by telling him that we were not going hunting, which he refused to accept.

But when we rode out of the yard instead of clambering into the lorry, he understood and settled for a long solo hack up across the Suckley Hills. It was one of those faultless mornings, when thrushes were in their first, early spring song; pheasants, relieved by the sudden absence of human predators, honked through the woods, and lambs danced around their shaggy mothers' dirty behinds. It was on a morning like this, high on the hill-tops, hundreds of miles from any concentration of humans and all their detritus that in my more misanthropic moments I would have been quite happy to stop the clock.

But, this time, my reverie was persistently interrupted by thoughts of the father and daughter I had met the day before.

What Amanda Drury wanted from me was obvious; what her father wanted was less so. I was certain he had not invited me to Gazeley to see his pictures that afternoon simply because he liked the look of me. As far as I could judge, Clive Drury did not like the look of anyone. He must have had a dozen people, far more eminent in the field than I, waiting around for the opportunity to purchase his pictures for him.

But, whatever his reasons, he was adamant that he wanted to talk business with me, as well as show off his paintings to someone who could barely have afforded a decent frame.

Mandy, I decided, was probably best steered clear of. I had the impression that she was a woman who liked to get her way, in everything, and was capable of kicking up rough if denied; and that would not suit me. So, with a sigh, I consigned that potential source of entertainment to my mental out-tray, and found myself pondering Georgie.

I may have given the impression that I did not find Georgie attractive, but that would be wrong. She was about five foot eight, with a pair of cat-walk legs. Her hair was a rich brown-black, recently bobbed and framing a near-perfect set of features, of which her blue eyes and luscious lips were the most striking. She was a much better-looking example of young English womanhood than Amanda, for example. But her attainability, straightforward and honest as it was, presented no challenge, and much though I tried to overcome my caveman instincts, I found the lack of that unexciting. Of course, Mandy did not look as though she'd put up much of a chase either. What she purported to offer was a great deal of uncomplicated, no-holds-barred sex.

As to the real worth of the two, there was no contest and, feeling slightly guilty about my cavalier treatment of Georgie, I rode back into the yard to find her car parked there.

When she heard the sound of Jasper's hooves, she came out of the back door from the kitchen. She looked fresh and lovely and I was almost pleased to see her.

'Morning, Archie,' she said brightly. 'Have you had any breakfast yet?'

'Nope,' I grunted as I swung my leg over the back of the saddle.

'That's lucky, because I've just made it, though there's not much in your fridge,' she added censoriously.

'I've been having a bit of trouble doing the weights recently, so there hasn't been much point in stuffing it full of temptation.'

'Oh, Lord. Will you want breakfast? It's a real fry-up.'

'As a matter of fact, I'd love it. Apart from nibbling bits and pieces from trays at your house last night, I haven't had a thing since the day before yesterday, and I haven't got another ride for a week.'

I was untacking the horse now, and Georgie came over to lead Jasper into his box.

'How long have you been out?' she asked.

'An hour or two.'

'Jasper must be fit. He's as dry as a bone.'

'All my horses are fit,' I said with unfair impatience, and relented. 'Unfortunately one of them can't jump.'

'How are your bruises, then?'

'Nothing serious,' I smiled truthfully.

Together we installed the horse, checked his water and filled his haynet before going into the house.

I seldom bothered with more than a piece of toast and a mug of Gold Blend in the morning. The smell of fresh coffee, bacon and eggs that greeted me in the kitchen was very welcoming. I said as much to Georgie, and sat down to demolish the breakfast while she sipped a cup of camomile tea.

'Shall we go out to lunch?' I asked her between mouthfuls, such was my gratitude.

She shook her head mournfully. 'I can't. We're having a big crowd for lunch and they'll expect me there.'

I knew that being an only child placed extra responsibilities on one's shoulders, and was prompted to think that perhaps I should make the effort and visit my own mother down near Cirencester. Clive Drury had asked me to come at about six that evening – presumably to have a few drinks while I admired his paintings – so I would have time to do both. I wondered what Georgie could tell me about the man.

'Drury has asked me over to Gazeley this evening. He says he wants me to find some pictures for him. I'm not sure that I believe him.'

'Why not? He's always buying them, and Dad . . . my step-father's told him how marvellous you are.'

'How the hell does he know that I'm so marvellous?'

'Because I told him, of course.'

'He must be bloody gullible, but thanks all the same. I suspect Drury is after something else. Still it'll be entertaining to find out what. How well do you know him?'

'Not very. He's not the sort of man one gets to know. Dad's been chairman of his group for ten years, so we see him quite often. I used to find him absolutely terrifying, until I realised he scarcely notices anyone even when he's talking to them.'

'Unless, presumably, he's going to make some money out of them.'

'Well, yes. That seems to be all he's interested in, besides his pictures, of course, and his horses.'

'What about your friend, Amanda?'

'He's never taken much notice of her, that's why she's like she is. I feel rather sorry for her.'

'Yes, you're right. She'll end up a mess.'

Georgie poured some more coffee.

'I think that Clive Drury could be a dangerous man,' she said. 'Sometimes there's a foul, cold look in his eyes. Of course, he must be one of the richest men in England now, and in with a good chance of a knighthood soon. But I remember when he first asked Dad to be chairman, my mother was very against it.' She stopped as if that was all she was going to say.

But I prompted her for more.

'I don't know a lot more,' she said. 'He's come up from nowhere. Nobody seems to know how he got started in Lloyd's. At the time he was first a broker, your old school was a lot more important

16

than your ability. But he was obviously making money for people and they tolerated him. Then he bought into Beecham's.'

For a moment there was an awkward silence between us. Beecham's had once been Bill Beecham's family firm. Bill Beecham, at sixty-five, still hopeless, feckless and a promising candidate for both Alcoholics and Gamblers Anonymous, was, by me at least, a much-loved old family friend. He was also Georgie's natural father and her mother's first, disastrous husband.

It had come as something of a shock when I had first discovered the relationship. Bill and Susan, Georgie's mother, had split up twenty-odd years ago, before I was really conscious of that sort of event, and my mother had never told me about it. It was only a few weeks before, when I happened to mention to Bill that I was getting a bit of assistance at the races from Georgie, that he had told me that his ex-wife had taken their daughter with her, and married Rollo Walford.

He had quickly sunk into a shamelessly maudlin state of self-disgust after imparting the information, and begged me not to mention it to Georgie. It was, he felt, up to her whether or not she should own up to such disreputable parentage.

'Beecham's that, er, Bill used to be in?' I asked.

Georgie nodded. 'The old family firm.'

'I hadn't realised that. No wonder Drury said he knew him. It must have been Drury who threw him out of the firm, then?'

'It was. When I was living with Amanda, she once hurled it at me out of spite.'

'Out of spite?' I asked, as if I did not know what she was talking about.

'Archie, don't tell me you didn't know he was my father.' She did not present it as a question.

As it happened, I still found it hard to believe that he was. I had got to know Georgie, quite independently of her father, as the daughter of Lord and Lady Walford. She had been only two when Lord Walford had formally adopted her, and, as far as most of the world was concerned, he was her father.

But now, I nodded. 'As a matter of fact, I did. Bill told me, a few weeks ago.'

'I know. He wrote and told me.'

I might have guessed. This was how Bill's curious code of ethics

17

worked. It made life tricky for his friends.

I did not know where to take the conversation next, so I came back, briefly, to Drury.

'I mentioned Bill to Drury yesterday,' I said. 'He was very scathing about him. I'm afraid a lot of people are these days. Poor old Bill's been buried by gambling and booze, but he's still a very knowledgeable man – at least, about pictures. Did you know, he was an old friend of my father's? And he's been a sort of surrogate father to me, on and off. I'm very fond of him and I've always found him good company. The only thing I've got against him is Cocoa. He gave me the bloody horse, though how he bought him, and why on earth he named him Bill's Flutter, God knows.'

Georgie kept quiet while I stumbled through this monologue.

'I could hardly believe it when he told me you were his daughter,' I finished lamely.

Georgie gave me a quick, understanding smile.

'I'm very fond of him too,' she said. 'But I don't see him often. It seems to upset him, and, truthfully, I grew up thinking of my stepfather as Dad. But I know Bill thinks a lot of you. Although, when I first met you, I couldn't think for the life of me why.'

It seemed that we both wanted to leave the subject alone after that but Georgie stayed for another hour. While she helped me muck out the horses and make their beds, we talked about other things, only tacitly acknowledging the subtle change that had now taken place in the status of our relationship.

Later, when I drove out of the yard behind her, I watched her car's disappearing tail with less than my normal impatience. Then our ways split: hers to her parents' stone mansion; mine to my mother's tiny timber-framed, wattle-panelled cottage.

Chapter 2

My mother, Monica Best, had lived in her small house by the Coln, near Bibury in Gloucestershire, since before I was born. Her father had given it to her before dying deep in debt a few years later.

My father, she told me, had come out from London by train and bicycle every weekend to woo her, while she tried to establish herself as a novelist.

I was living proof of his successful wooing, but I had never met him. He had died six months before I was born, and a week before he was due to marry my mother.

Then, in the early sixties in quiet rural communities, illegitimacy was still a cause for shame. But my mother had trusted to the good will of the local people, and her trust had not been misplaced. It was partly out of gratitude for their loyalty that she felt she could never leave, and partly because, though it had been the place of her grief, before that it had been a place of intense happiness for her.

Although I had never met my father, I felt that I knew him intimately. I had had his mannerisms and characteristics lovingly described to me in vivid detail. I had read his poetry and his beautiful prose descriptions of his travels in Greece in the early fifties. I had even read some of the love letters he had sent my mother when his job as an up-and-coming investigative journalist had taken him away for weeks at a time. One day, while dashing across a quiet street just off the King's Road with a handful of last-minute invitations to their wedding, he had been hit by a car and bowled headlong down the road. His skull had cracked on a cast-iron kerbing, and he had died before the vehicle that hit him had reversed and driven away. Two witnesses had testified to the event, but neither driver nor vehicle had ever been traced.

My mother had never stopped loving him. He had gone at the peak of her passion for him, and was irreplaceable. And he left her nothing but me.

Then, as now, only a few people made a decent living from novel-writing, and my mother was not one of them. But by supplementing her income with rural despatches for women's magazines, she had managed to feed and clothe us both; but that was about all. I started at the village school, but she had higher ambitions for me. By working harder and tightening her belt still further, she sent me off to prep school, then, like her brothers, to Eton. But there was not a penny left for anything else. If I wanted something, I had to go out and earn it during my school holidays.

This had left me with curiously mixed memories of childhood. I had loathed my penury at school and developed an aggressive chippiness while I flung myself at my books to make up for it. But I had loved my holidays, working for a gentle and talented old furniture maker and spending every penny I earned on saving for, then keeping, my first ugly little Welsh cob of a pony.

Ugly he may have been, but he meant a great deal to me, and from him I learned nearly all that I ever learned about horses. After I had schooled him to win his first hunter trials with my heels barely a foot off the ground, I trained him to harness, and bought myself a small thoroughbred from a rich but understanding neighbour.

All through this time, and afterwards, when I had managed a modest exhibition to a modest Oxford college, my mother had encouraged and supported me. She had devoted her life to the memory of my father; and me. Which was why now, quite uncharacteristically, I tried hard with my filial duties.

I had telephoned that Sunday morning before I set off, and felt a twinge of guilt that I had left the arrangement to the last minute.

'I tell you what,' I had said, 'as I've given you no warning, I'll take you out to lunch.'

'But can you afford it, Archie?'

'Sure,' I lied, thinking that I was already five hundred quid over my overdraft limit.

In the hour it took to drive to my mother's, I briefly considered the state of my finances.

The mortgage on my house and twenty-five acres, and Sharon the groom's wages were my largest outgoings. Or at least they should have been. But somehow keeping my old but thirsty car, a lorry and three horses on the road seemed to use twice as much.

And the more time I spent with my horses, the less time I had to make any money to pay for them. Up until a year ago, I had been managing to keep one jump ahead, but the property price collapse of the late eighties had driven a stave through the rotten and corrupt body of the art market, and it was becoming hard to sell anything at any price. Spenders were very thin on the ground now, and when one, like Drury, gave even a hint of wanting to throw some business my way, I was not about to make him pass a morality test before accepting his commission.

I found my mother in her small back garden, where it bordered the gushing winter stream. Her slight body was wrapped in an army greatcoat, and a long woollen scarf framed her finely boned face. She looked up with pleasure from the task of pruning an ancient pear tree.

'Archie, how lovely to see you.' She walked briskly across the lawn to greet me, and immediately spotted the slight limp the previous day's fall had caused me. Her forehead puckered. 'You haven't hurt yourself again, have you?'

'Not badly. Just a very ordinary, unspectacular sort of a fall.'

'Do you think you should still be doing it, Archie? After all, you're not so young now.'

'For God's sake, Mother, I'm only thirty! Anyway, I'm in with a chance of the championship this year. Caesar's going like a train, and I've been offered some very tasty rides next month. But I promise, if I win this season, I'll retire gracefully.'

My mother chided me with a shake of her head. 'I don't know why you still care about beating those frightful Prideaux-Jameses.'

'I think you do.'

'I know how foul they were to you, but that was so long ago. You've proved yourself a dozen times since then. What does it matter now?'

'It matters because for years I lay awake thinking of trouncing them on their own terms. I promised myself that one day I'd make them eat such a large helping of humble pie they'd choke on it. If I broke the promise now, I'd always feel I'd let myself down.'

'Dear old Archie. You always did take other people's views of

21

you so seriously. You'll find in the end it's the inner you, not anyone else's perception of you, that matters.'

'Yes, well, I dare say you're right, but until then, I won't be satisfied until I've taken the trophy from them and rubbed their faces in it.'

My mother laughed. 'I think you're mixing your metaphors a bit, and that's something I really won't tolerate. Anyway, come on in. It's horribly cold out here. Let's go and have a drink.'

In the small and warmly elegant drawing room, a fire was blazing. I thought of the times when even coal fires had to be eked out in this household, and recognised it as a sign of my mother's affection. I poured two gins and tonic, and we sat down to talk about my horses and her work.

When she steered the conversation around to picture-dealing and my own finances, I was determined not to give her an excuse for offering me help. I thought of positive things to say.

'I'm seeing a potential new punter this evening; a big one.'

'Who's that?' my mother asked, pleased.

'A particularly gross example of the unacceptable face of capitalism: Clive Drury.'

'Oh,' my mother said without enthusiasm, 'I know about him.'

'You would, though he doesn't feature much on the arts pages of the *Guardian*. He says he has an order for me.' I shrugged. 'And one can't be proud.'

'Yes, it must be very difficult at the moment. I read that several gallery owners have got into terrible trouble.'

'But don't worry about me, Mother. My straits are not all that dire yet.'

'You'd tell me, wouldn't you, if they were?'

'Of course,' I said.

We ate lunch at an over-decorated, over-priced restaurant nearby, and I left my mother at the front door of her house, content with her son's condition, physical, moral and fiscal.

On the way back to Herefordshire, I psyched myself up, as I might before a big hunter-chase, for whatever confrontation with Clive Drury awaited me.

The first quarter of an hour at Gazeley with Drury turned out to be more of a love-in than a confrontation.

I was plied with expensively dated Krug and treated to the

proud owner's monologue on his famous paintings. Drury almost took my hand as he led me round the ugly, Victorian appendage which was Gazeley's picture gallery, where one of the finest private collections of eighteenth- and nineteenth-century sporting pictures hung. My opinion was sought and savoured. My views on bloodstock were deferred to.

A climax was reached when my services in procuring a pair of obscure, missing Fernleys were requested; a deal which he and I knew could be worth seventy or eighty thousand to me. I wondered when the sting was coming.

It did not take long.

As we walked down a long, gloomy corridor from the gallery to the drawing room, Drury quickened his pace, then spun round on his heel to block my path. His eyes hardened and his mouth assumed a small tight smile. He tapped my chest with a sharp forefinger as he spoke.

'There's something else you must do for me if you accept this commission.'

I held my breath and tried not to blink.

'You must sell me Caesar's Consul.'

The unsteady vision before my eyes of seventy thousand mortgage-slaying pounds faded as fast as it had appeared.

Drury's cold, iron-hard eyes did not.

Especially when I laughed.

'You seriously think I'd sell Damian the championship for seventy grand?'

'Fifty,' Drury hissed. 'I'll allow you to make fifty on the deal.'

I side-stepped and carried on walking past Drury.

'Where the hell do you think you're going?' he shouted after me.

I did not look back. 'Home,' I said.

I could almost hear the effort the angry man made to control himself. 'Hang on, Archie.' He gave a bluff boom of a laugh. 'I still want the Fernleys. Let's have another drink and talk about it.'

I did not believe him, but, I shrugged to myself, it would be entertaining to see what he tried next. I turned. 'It'll take more than a few bottles of Krug to persuade me to sell the Consul, but I'm quite happy to let you try.'

Drury gave me a fine exhibition of his famous chameleon-like charm. His eyes and mouth beamed convincingly. He caught up with me and we carried on down the corridor.

In the drawing room, we stood by blazing logs in a fine Adam fireplace. Drury rang for a nervous Filipino and ordered more champagne while he filled two glasses from a bottle that was already there. He handed me a glass, and put a large forearm around my shoulders.

'Damian's so desperate to win the championship,' he shrugged, 'You can't blame me for trying. At least,' he laughed, 'give me credit for knowing you simply wouldn't sell the animal. I must admit I thought fifty thousand would tempt you.'

'It did, but not for long.'

'The thing is, Damian's got a better chance this season than both the Prideaux-Jameses. You're the man to beat. And there are very few horses qualified for the Foxhunters at Cheltenham *and* Aintree.'

'I'm well aware of that,' I answered. 'Most people thought I was mad to take the Consul hunting this year. But he gave me a few very good days.' To qualify for the Aintree Foxhunters, a horse had to have hunted regularly that season and this can be risky – for horse and jockey – with a fit, hot-blooded chaser.

'I'm afraid Damian didn't want to hunt The Twister,' Drury said, not disguising his disparagement.

'I'm not surprised,' I said. 'That horse isn't an easy ride. But he could have got one of the grooms or someone else to qualify him.'

'He could have, but quite frankly, the horse is a bloody liability out hunting and no one would take him.'

I thought that was likely. If I had been a groom at Gazeley, having seen a hint of Clive Drury's ill-temper, I would not have risked getting the blame for putting the forty-thousand-pound chaser out of action.

'Maybe next year,' I shrugged.

'Next year!' Drury snorted. 'No one ever won anything by waiting till next year. You may be aware that I run a company worth hundreds of millions. I created it from the wreck of a business that was run by people who were always prepared to wait for next year. When I want results, I want them now. I've piled a lot of money into Damian's racing, and I want to see a result.'

'He's done pretty well so far,' I said. 'He'll probably beat both the Prideaux-Jameses. That's something I've been trying to do for ten years, and I'm not giving up now.'

'The only way Damian's got as far as he has is because I bought him the best horses in the country for the job.'

'You haven't bought him the best. And what's more, you're not going to.'

The Filipino sidled in with the champagne. Drury nodded at him to open a bottle and pour two more glasses, then turned back to me with angry eyes. I wondered why he was so anxious to see his son succeed.

When we were alone again, he said quietly, 'Of course, it's not important.' He gulped the contents of his glass and slammed it down on the marble top of a chiffonier. He strode towards the door of the room. He did not look back. 'Help yourself to champagne,' he said. 'And let me know when you've changed your mind about the horse.'

It was probably fortunate that before I could ask him if he still wanted the pictures, he had left the room. He was not a man to chase for a deal.

I picked up one of the bottles, sat in a large sofa by the fire, with my back to the door, and contemplated the proposition that finally seeing my boyhood enemies getting their come-uppance was going to lose me at least fifty thousand – a lot of money for a quick sip from the sweet cup of revenge.

I sighed. Of course, it was not just that.

There was also straightforward, personal vanity, which is a famously expensive beast to maintain.

'Hello.' A woman's voice, low and warm.

I resisted the urge to turn and see who had come into the room; I had guessed anyway.

'Have you been annoying my father?'

I stood and turned to greet Amanda. She walked up to me and leaned forward to offer a dimpled cheek for a kiss.

'I hope so,' I answered.

'You did. He's just stormed off in a helluva mood. Odd really. He normally only gets like that if money's involved. And I shouldn't have thought you had enough to worry him.'

'As a matter of fact, he was trying to give me money.'

'Of course. He was trying to buy a horse from you?'

'Together with a large inducement: a commission to acquire a couple of very expensive pictures.'

25

'He must think a lot of you. That's remarkably subtle for him.'

Amanda took a glass from the drinks table and poured herself some champagne.

'I'm sorry he left so abruptly. Can I make up for his bad manners by offering you dinner?'

I had drunk a bottle and a half by now. Tomorrow morning's exercising was too distant a prospect to intrude on the short struggle between the forces of vice and virtue. Vanity and lust won; easily.

'I should say that's the least you could do,' I answered.

'It probably will be,' she said.

Dinner, in a small sitting room near the kitchen, was not of great gastronomic significance. In the absence of the master of the house and any other guests, the staff had disappeared to their flat in a distant wing of the house. Amanda volunteered to make an omelette, into which, besides half-a-dozen eggs, she hurled spices, mushrooms, chillis, pieces of ham and anything else that seemed appropriate. The eating of it was enhanced by some top-of-the-range Burgundy, and her own, undivided attention.

She did not want to talk about herself. She said she wanted to know all about me; my racing and my work.

I told her a bit about the picture trade. The last thing I wanted was her sympathy, so I tried to give a positive version of my current activities within it.

'But you're skint,' she said simply. 'I heard my father telling Damian, and he's never wrong about that sort of thing. He can check anyone out.'

'Not everything's checkable,' I said enigmatically.

'He certainly thought you'd sell Caesar's Consul for the right money. It was Damian who said he'd have to wrap it up in some other deal.'

'He was almost right,' I admitted.

'Poor Damian,' his sister said. 'He's not that interested in the whole thing. I don't think he even particularly likes horses.'

'So why does he do it?' I asked, though I thought I already knew.

'You may have noticed that despite the effort he makes, my father's still a bit short on social cachet. He's so rich and makes money for so many grand, snotty people that they pretend not to notice. But that doesn't fool him. He thinks the only way he'll be regarded as a gent is if he's prepared to lose a lot of money for the sake of some old-fashioned sport. And Damian doesn't have much talent for anything else, so that's become his task; to give the Drurys a bit of class. It's rather pathetic, isn't it?'

'And Damian goes along with it?'

'You've seen him. He hasn't got much choice.'

'I feel rather sorry for the poor little tit.'

'I wouldn't. Anyway, my father is not very sporting in his pursuit of sporting success, so don't imagine you'll get away with refusing him. He's an utter bastard, and he wouldn't know a scruple if you shoved one up his arse with a sledgehammer.'

'I'll remember not to try that, then,' I said. 'And what do you know about scruples?'

'I don't know much about scruples,' she said with a slow smile, 'but I know a bit about screwing.'

An hour or two later, I discovered that this was something of an understatement.

With Amanda for RSM, no soldier standing to attention on a three-hour parade would have had any inclination to faint.

Her skill in maintaining interest was remarkable. She knew about erogenous zones I never knew I had. Her whole body seemed made for making love. Her lips were greedy, but giving. Her hips thrust eagerly, shuddered, melted and thrust again. Her fingers searched with tingling tips, caressed and excited every square inch of my skin. Her warm, damp breasts, big-nippled with the texture of ripe plums, were above me, beneath me and beside me. Her buttocks were tense, then yielding and her legs wound themselves around my torso, my waist, and, finally, my back as her hands grasped my thighs and we brought the act to a quivering, mind-numbing finale.

We lay in her high, broad bed, in easy satisfaction with mutually received pleasures.

I could feel her beside me; calm, fulfilled and, for the moment, secure.

Wouldn't life be simple – I thought – if it could always be like this?

A rattling window woke me. A February wind howled outside,

27

and shook the oaks in the park. A bedside light was still on. I glanced at my watch beside the bed. Five o'clock. I would have to go.

Amanda was breathing deeply, and the slight smile on her sleeping face made it calmly beautiful in a way her waking face was not. I did not want to disturb her, so I crept around the room to gather my clothes where they had been scattered in the first frenzy of love-making.

It was only then that I saw the picture. I froze and stared, stark naked, clutching my underpants, at a Stubbs that should not have existed. It had been destroyed, along with the rest of the contents of Mount Fitzherbert, when the house in County Kildare had been burned to the ground by Nationalists in 1922.

I tiptoed across a fine Afghan rug to inspect it more closely. In the dim light, it looked, if it was not the real thing, one of the best fakes I had ever seen; and I had seen plenty.

It was a fine painting of Highflyer, the great eighteenth-century stallion, and I feasted my eyes on it for a few moments longer. It seemed an extravagant picture for a despised daughter's bedroom, and I wondered if Amanda could tell me anything about it. But I was not going to ask. I turned back to look at her. She had not moved a muscle since I had left the bed. I dressed with scarcely a sound and, clutching my tie and shoes in one hand, managed to open the door with only a gentle creak. I looked for a back staircase, where intruder-detecting devices, if any, were likely to be less heavily deployed.

I reached the bottom of the staircase without triggering anything, and tried to guess my way to a back door. The surveillance equipment must have been concentrated in the parts of the house where the most desirable and pinchable objects were. I found a small door, bolted and locked, but with its key in the lock, which I opened cautiously. It swung back without a squeak, and, more importantly, without any bells ringing, to reveal a small back courtyard. I let myself out, and crept out into the windy night.

When I found my car, I climbed in and prayed that it would not offer its usual resistance to starting. My prayers were answered, and with a gentle throb of the big motor, it cruised down the long sweeping drive, and out through the same gates by which I had left after racing the day before.

Four hours later, I had dealt with the horses, scraped a razor over my chin, gulped three cups of coffee and was steering the Merc down the scenic, back route to London.

Before leaving the farm, I had rung Bill Beecham. I could feel his hangover down the telephone line. I did not tell him why I wanted to see him, but persuaded him that it would be worth being out of bed to greet me around midday. He grumbled, but agreed.

On the way to London, I could not help my mind straying back to the sensations of the night before. Amanda was no beginner; in fact, she could probably have got a good degree in male anatomy without revising. But along with the sensual memories came worries about how widely, and where, she had been practising. And the idea of a re-match became more alarming than alluring. I pushed these negative thoughts from my mind, and turned my attention to the purpose of this trip. By the time I had reached White City, I had decided that it would not be such a good idea to tell Bill about Drury's Stubbs; but at least I could sound him out a little on its owner.

My mother had always been a bit cagey about Bill Beecham's early life. The truth was that she did not approve of him, but had felt obliged to keep in touch because he had been a friend of my father's since his university days. When I was about ten, Bill had started turning up from time to time in Gloucestershire. He was already then a somewhat raffish figure, and there had evidently been some kind of row or difficulty over my father, hence the delay in his first appearance in my life.

But it was the very absence of my own father and the close connection that Bill had had with him that drew me towards Bill. So, despite my mother's misgivings, he became almost a surrogate father to me. As a child I was blind to many of his most obvious failings, and developed a great affection for him. We would spend hours walking and talking and going to the races together. He knew a great deal about horses, and more about the paintings of them, and it was through him that my own interest had first been spawned.

Now he spent most of his time drinking with Soho low-life, swapping spurious racing tips and gossip from the lesser picture sale-rooms. At night he mysteriously found his way back to a crumbling house in Redcliffe Gardens where he had a squalid three-roomed flat.

I freely cursed the usual lack of parking spaces in the wide Victorian thoroughfare until I found a gap between a semi-abandoned VW Kombi and a builder's skip.

The gloom of this as yet ungentrified stretch of the street almost persuaded me once again to abandon the visit, but I persevered. I did not want to let Bill down if he had got out of bed especially for me. Besides, in the end, I always enjoyed seeing Bill, and I felt somehow responsible for him these days.

I rang a bell next to which was a sticky-backed note bearing the message, 'Bill, where are you, you fucking piss-artist? I waited two hours in Finches. Jeff.' Judging by the grime that had gathered on the paper, it had been left some time ago. I shook my head and pressed the bell again.

After a while, I heard someone descending the stairs inside, and Bill's voice asked, 'Who do you want?'

'It's okay, Bill. It's Archie. We've a date, remember?'

The door was heaved open, and Bill Beecham's face peered round it.

'Hello, Archie,' he said, unenthusiastically. 'I've been expecting a few rather offensive callers.'

'Who?' I asked, stepping over the worn threshold. 'Your landlord? Your bookie? The bailiffs?'

'Yes,' Bill nodded. 'And a few others.'

He shut the door behind me and waved me up the first flight of stairs.

'Why are they seeking your company?'

'Why the hell d'you think?'

'I presume they imagine you owe them money; but you must have some; your telephone is still connected.'

'Don't worry, that'll be the next thing to go.'

'Why has this sudden crisis occurred? I thought you always kept a jump ahead.'

We had reached the landing. The door to Bill's lair was open and he ushered me into its fetid atmosphere.

'Bent jockeys,' Bill muttered.

'Oh dear.' There did not seem anything more constructive to say.

In the pale grey light which penetrated his sitting room, I could see that Bill was more harassed than usual. His untidy, mouse-grey hair fell across his forehead in a lank curtain. His complexion, never healthy, was a pale eau-de-nil and deeply lined. His eyes, a little close together, peered warily from what had once been quite a handsome face. Over a well-made but well-worn sea island cotton shirt, he wore a shapeless tweed jacket, leather-patched at elbows and cuffs. His long, thin legs were clad in cavalry twill which had probably seen the tailor's scissors thirty years before. The only smart things he wore were a pair of brightly polished, heavyweight brown brogue shoes.

'It's all right,' he said, suddenly optimistic. 'I've been in the shit before, and look, I'm still here.'

I looked at him. 'Only just.'

'Thanks,' he said. 'Let's have a drink.'

Despite his lack of funds and his excess of thirst, he was able to find a bottle of gin, almost full.

'Gin and tonic? No ice or lemon, I'm afraid. Actually, no tonic either. You'll have to have it with water.'

'Great,' I said, and made myself a space to sit between several piles of old *Sporting Life*s on what had once been a good Gillows sofa.

Bill handed me a grimy glass of gin with a splash of Thames water and poured himself a scotch.

'So, what were you so anxious to see me about?'

'I've been asked to do a bit of business for a man you might be able to tell me something about.'

'Always glad to help you if I can,' Bill said with a sweeping gesture of generosity. 'Who's the fellow?'

'Clive Drury.'

Chapter 3

Bill showed no reaction at first.

He gazed at me for a while. Then he glanced guiltily at his tumbler and slowly swilled the large whisky he had poured himself.

He stood up and wandered over to look out of the window. After a few moments, he turned round.

'I could tell you a great deal about Clive Drury, but I'm not going to, beyond saying that he is not a man to get involved with. Basically, he's a crook, and he's dangerous. My advice is, have nothing to do with him.'

'A crook? That's a bit strong. You've got to tell me more than that,' I protested.

'As a matter of fact I intend to, some day, but for the time being, take my advice.' He sat down again on a rickety Georgian carver. 'And that's all I'm prepared to say about Clive Drury.'

'Come on, Bill! You can do better than that. It's obvious that Drury's a major shit, but I must know more before you can expect me to be warned off. He's put a very tasty proposition to me. Sure, there must be more to it, but I haven't anything to go on.'

Bill Beecham pursed his lips in a characteristically petulant way. 'Don't try and bully anything out of me. You should know by now that I mean what I say. I'll tell you nothing more; it would only tempt you into trouble if I did. And if you insist on badgering me, you can leave now.'

I was used to Bill being testy and difficult. I did not mind it; I understood it was a device to give his existence a little more significance in the eyes of others. It did not work, of course, but I was fond enough of him to tolerate traits I would not have put up with in many other people.

But this display was more intense than usual. He appeared to be genuinely upset, even scared by the idea of talking about Drury; and I knew I had to pursue it.

'Of course I won't leave now!' I went on the offensive. 'Georgie told me about the old connection between you and Drury. And you owe me an explanation about Georgie too. First you make me promise not to tell her I know she's your daughter, then you go and tell her that you've told me anyway.'

Bill flopped back down into his chair and regarded me with a guilty, hangdog look; another device.

'I'm sorry about that. After you'd left last time, I thought it wouldn't be fair on her if I didn't tell her.'

'Jesus Christ, Bill, that only made it worse that *I* hadn't told her. Anyway, never mind about that; it's out in the open now, and it hasn't created any problems; I told you it wouldn't. But she did tell me that Drury bought into your family firm, then eased you out of it a few years later. I can press her for more, or I can go and inspect the records, but I'd far rather have the story from you.'

After a moment of staring truculently at me, he nodded.

'All right, but you won't like it; it involved one of the less laudable periods of my life.'

I held my breath, not to put him off.

'When Drury came on the scene,' Bill told me, 'I was the only remaining member of the family in the firm. And I was only there because nobody could think what else to do with me. I'd gone along with it, because that was the only way the allowance would keep coming. I was a terrible gambler then – I didn't have a clue. Both my parents were dead and the rest of the family were worried shitless. My so-called inheritance was all held in trust, and I had to go with a begging bowl to a bunch of pompous old farts every time I wanted a halfpenny. When Drury bid to buy the firm, the family jumped at the chance. They were all running short of capital anyway and wanted to high-tail off to sunny climes, mostly around Cannes. They made a kind of half-hearted provision for me to continue being employed by Drury, took the money and ran.

'Drury was a very unknown quantity at that time. He had a reputation for being a red-hot, natural underwriter. I suppose he'd started as a clerk for someone; nobody quite knew where he'd come from. He was a flash young East-end yobbo but he began to make a lot of money for his clients, so they sneered about him behind his back and held out their hands for their divis each year.

'Beecham's was an old-established Lloyd's agency, and there was a bit of a fuss when Drury bought it, but that didn't last long. When he became my boss, he made it very clear what he thought of people like me working in the firm. As far as he was concerned, I was a totally dispensable passenger. And he had a pretty good idea of how little interest the family took in my welfare. I could see that my days were numbered, so I took the view that my best chance was to suck up to Drury, and make myself available for any dirty work that needed doing. At first he didn't take me seriously, but he came round to the idea that having one of the firm's old family members around might add a bit of credibility to some of his schemes. And did he have schemes!

'He was aware that Lloyd's provided an almost bottomless pit of money floating around, in the form of tens of millions of pounds in premium income, which, for a period of time, he could do almost what he liked with. His names still received a perfectly satisfactory return on their capital, but our Clive helped himself to some gargantuan bonuses. It also put him in touch with a large number of very rich, quite stupid and averagely greedy men who were always ready to look for more ways of making money by doing nothing. He found schemes and subtly aimed them at these punters. When they got into trouble, he was always on hand to bail them out, like a fairy godmother. That's how I met Sue, Georgie's mother. I was instructed by Drury to buy Gazeley for him from her father, for a song, because Drury had loaned him some money for one of these idiotic schemes which Sue's dopey parent had sunk everything into. Trouble was, her father never looked at the terms of Drury's loan. It was my task to break the news to him that Drury could call the loan any time, and if it wasn't forthcoming, he could foreclose on the family acres. Mind you, Drury did something very smart then. He gave the family a ten-year lease on the place, so that they could go on living there for a while, and leave when they were ready without too much loss of face. They were pathetically grateful.

'I felt a real cad at the time, but I couldn't help admiring Drury's methods. His systems were foolproof, and, on the whole, legal.

He must have taken a while to hone them into shape. I suspect that he was in and out of every grimy little fraud before he pitched up, semi-respectable, at Lloyd's. As a matter of fact, I did once try and do a bit of research on that. I found out some promising stuff about his earlier life, but nothing specific that could be pinned on him.

'Anyway, I married Sue, and everyone was pleased about that, except her parents; but they weren't in too good a position to do anything about it. Sue had already had her inheritance before the rest of the family went belly up, so she was quite independent. Mind you, she was pretty tough with me; can't blame her really, but it meant that I still needed to bolster my income. I'd been doing a bit of successful picture dealing at the time. The market was just beginning to grow into something big about then, and I had the idea of talking Drury into using this as a means of shifting money around the world, taking profits or losses between a chain of companies, here and abroad, as appropriate. It worked very well, but I'm afraid I got a bit too greedy for Drury's liking, and he slung me out of the firm. In the circumstances, I couldn't really object. But Sue did. Georgie was barely a year old when Sue walked out and left me to the mercies of my trustees. Frankly, when she met and married Rollo Walford, I was very relieved for Georgie, though it did hurt when I heard Rollo wanted to formally adopt her.

'Anyway, I was up shit creek. I thought of trying to shop Drury then. I wish now that I'd had the guts, but I was frankly terrified of him, and I was implicated in most of his recent scams; I didn't want Georgie to have to live with that.'

Bill stopped and put his face in his hands. He rubbed his eyes hard with the backs of his wrists.

'But, Bill,' I asked, 'didn't anyone else ever know what was going on?'

After a while, he lifted his head and looked at me. His eyes were reddened from the vigorous massage he had given them, but there was also in them a look of such deep, wretched remorse that I could barely face it.

Bill coughed a short, bitter laugh. 'Oh yes, he was investigated a few times; by the tax people, Lloyd's itself, and a few, foolhardy journalists. But he easily fobbed most of them off – I told you; he made his scams watertight. Those who got a little too close to the truth had a habit of . . . disappearing.'

He continued to look bleakly at me. It was as if there was much more inside him, fighting to come out. But whatever it was, he held it in. I was aware of this, but, at the same time I was so staggered by what he had just said, that I did not look for any significance.

'Are you saying,' I asked croakily, 'that he had them . . . got rid of?'

'I don't know what I'm saying,' Bill said dismissively. 'There were some people who were on to him that I haven't seen since, that's all. Anyway,' he went on quickly, before I could ask more, 'I ended up crawling back to Drury to do a few more deals for him. I haven't done much with him for years now, but he still has me on a piddling retainer – rather less than I'd get if I were on the dole, I suspect.' Bill, who had concentrated his gaze on the threadbare arms of his chair for the last part of this history, glanced up at me with a look of mortified self-disgust. 'What price pride, eh? Do you wonder I don't tell people about Georgie?'

He seemed to want a reaction from me.

'Does she know about the extent of your involvement with Drury?' I asked.

'Good God, no. Everything I've told you is in strictest confidence. I mean that this time. I had planned at some stage to tell you some of this, but I don't want Georgie ever to know how weak and cowardly her father really was. Not that she could think any less of me. Just look at the state I'm in.' His eyes bleared over, and I began to regret that I'd pushed him into this confession.

'I certainly won't tell her about it, Bill,' I reassured him. 'I told her how helpful and patient you've been with me over the years, and how grateful I am to have had someone to take an interest in me when I was a spotty adolescent. And, believe me, Bill, she's very fond of you. I don't think knowing what you've just told me would change that. As far as I can tell, she's never actually put you on a pedestal.'

Bill gave a croak of a laugh. 'She still comes to see me, you know. Not often, but, my God, I'm proud of her when she does. So don't you ever do anything to hurt her, will you?'

'I'm sure she won't give me the chance,' I said in guilty haste.

Bill looked at me sourly for a few moments. 'You'd better

bloody not. Now,' he changed his tone abruptly, 'what did Drury want from you?'

'He really wanted to buy the Consul for his son.'

'Did he?' Bill murmured. 'Yes, he would. Don't you dare sell him. And if you want to learn from my mistakes, you won't have any more dealings with Clive Drury.' His manner made it clear that he had exercised as much humility as he was going to that day, and the topic was now closed. 'And how's Bill's Flutter?'

I accepted the new subject.

'We don't call him that in the yard. We call him Cocoa.'

Bill laughed. 'I'm not surprised.'

'How on earth did he become Bill's Flutter?'

'I won him as a yearling, on a bet. I sent the animal to the first honest trainer I could think of, and told him to get on with the formalities. Unfortunately he doesn't have a very sophisticated sense of humour, and didn't ring me to ask about a name. Anyway, how is he? I see you fell off on Saturday.'

'Silly bugger put in a short one at a plain fence, hit the top and pecked badly. He nearly came down, then tipped me out of the side door.'

'A professional wouldn't blame the horse.'

'He'd have blamed this one. But the horse is fine. I think I might make something of him. He'll stay three and a half miles easily, and he's got a hell of a jump in him when he feels like it.'

'You'd better make something of him. I could have got fifteen grand for him at Ascot, but I reckoned he'd got all the makings of a staying chaser, and I'd rather see you win on him than anyone else.'

'Thanks, Bill. Provided he doesn't kill me first, I will, I promise. But if you're in such dire straits now, couldn't I give him back so that you can sell him? He'd still fetch good money.'

'Ask someone to return a gift! I may be down, but I haven't sunk that low. Now tell me about the Consul.'

We talked horses for a while longer. I tried to draw him on his own current difficulties, but he sidestepped. I did not mention Drury again, but, on a hunch, I threw another topic into the conversation.

'By the way, there was something else I wanted to ask you. I've got an American punter who's come up with a fairly specific request. He wants a picture of Highflyer, a good contemporary one. Stubbs did one; it's in the catalogue, but it was lost in a fire in Ireland in the twenties. Do you know if anyone else painted the horse?'

A sudden gleam appeared in Bill Beecham's bleary eyes.

'Not everything that was supposed to have been lost in those Anglo-Irish houses was lost. An awful lot was got out before the blaze had taken a hold, either by the families, or by the boyos. It just so happens I may well be able to get my hands on the real thing.'

I looked astonished. 'What, the original Stubbs?'

Bill nodded with a grin.

'But,' I shook my head, 'that's incredible. Surely, though, there would be some doubts about its authenticity?'

'Not to an expert. The difficulty is that there could be some discrepancy over title to the painting. It could never be sold in the open market. Would your punter mind that?'

'No, he's an obsessive collector,' I improvised hurriedly. 'He wants to own it and look at it himself. He has paintings of nearly all the best sires in the bloodlines of his own most successful horses. He collects them like stamps.'

'The best sort of collector,' Bill nodded. 'You can satisfy him that it's real all right, but he won't be able to ask too many questions about how you came by it.

'That'd be fine, I'm sure.'

'Well, you're in luck, because I intend to get my hands on the very picture in the near future. My only concern was finding a suitable home for it.' He stood up with an empty glass. 'I think we'd better drink to this.'

I left shortly afterwards, claiming a lunch date, and feigning astonishment over the coincidence of the picture. I was surprised that this had not struck Bill, but it was clearly the answer to a current problem, and he did not want to question it.

I pulled a parking ticket off the windscreen of my car, and drove towards the West End to see if any dealers I knew were free for lunch. As I crawled through the snarled-up traffic, I wondered how the hell Bill thought he was going to get the picture. He certainly was not up to pinching it himself, even though – my experiences earlier that morning had shown – it did not seem all that well protected. Maybe the fact that it did not officially exist was why it hung in Amanda's room, and not in the gallery, which was full of anti-theft devices.

Besides the physical difficulties of taking the picture, there was Bill's obvious fear of Drury to consider. Despite his attempt to water down his first statement that people who had got too close to Drury tended to disappear, I had little doubt that he thought Drury had taken the initiative in these disappearances.

Conjuring up a mental picture of the offensive tycoon, I found that this was not hard to believe. I hoped that I had not encouraged Bill into doing anything foolish.

I also pondered Bill's reluctance to talk about Clive Drury and the flash of guilt in his eyes when I had first mentioned Drury's name.

And besides the guilt, there had been burning hatred.

I spent the next two days schooling Cocoa, exercising the others, and reading up anything I could find on the missing Stubbs. I found a couple of nineteenth-century prints of the picture in a Tate catalogue, with the unequivocal caption, 'Original destroyed by fire'.

There was no further communication from Drury. But I was sure, from what Amanda had said, that there would be in time.

Nor did I hear anything from Bill Beecham, so, on Thursday morning, I rang him but there was no reply.

I came in from an hour's hack and a short gallop on Caesar's Consul to find my telephone answering machine winking at me.

I put a kettle on the Aga, and rewound the tape. It took a while; evidently there were several people wanting to talk to me. I wondered if any wanted to buy pictures.

The first message was delivered in the voice of a woman I did not know.

'Hello, Mr Best. This is Mr Drury's secretary. Could you please ring him as soon as you return.' She gave a London number and hung up.

After a bleep, the next message started. Once again, an unfamiliar voice, this time a man's.

'Good morning, Mr Best. Could you please ring DS Robinson at West End Central Police Station immediately upon your return.' This was followed by another London number.

I searched my conscience. I could only think of Monday's

'I often went to see him.'

'Yes, but you live in Herefordshire, so you wouldn't have just been dropping in.'

'If I was in London, I often used to drop in and talk about horses or pictures.'

'What were you talking to him about on Monday?'

'Horses and pictures. He gave me a chaser last year, and I wanted to tell him how it was getting on.'

'A chaser?'

'A horse that he'd owned. It hadn't done much after three years in training, so he gave it to me.'

'That was very generous of him.'

'Yes,' I agreed.

'And what pictures did you talk about?'

'None in particular. Just the state of the trade in general.'

'And what is the state of the trade just now?'

'I should have thought you were well placed to know that, with all those galleries just round the corner.'

'I don't often go into them, sir. But I understand things aren't too good at the moment.'

'The market's more or less on the floor, frankly.'

'And how do you make your living, Mr Best?'

He obviously knew.

'I'm a picture dealer.'

expensive hobby? Horses, stables, grooms,

at the moment.'

parking ticket. DS Robinson could wait.

The machine bleeped again, and I heard my mother's voice, breathless and distressed.

'Oh Archie, where are you? Something ghastly has happened to Bill Beecham. The police want to talk to you. I'll stay in until you ring back. Goodbye, darling.'

I turned the machine off with a shaky hand. My heart was thumping.

Shit! I thought, what the hell was going on?

I was conscious of guilt, and the absurd conviction that, whatever had happened, it had something to do with my visit to Bill.

The lid was rattling on the kettle now, and water was splashing, hissing on to the hot plate. I lifted it off and rang my mother.

She answered at once.

'Thank goodness. I thought you might be out all day.'

'What's happened?'

'Bill Beecham was killed last night.'

Although I had guessed this was what I was going to hear, I felt sick with shock.

'Christ!' I muttered. I could not bring myself to say more for a moment. My mother understood. She waited until I went on. 'Where? How?'

'In Soho, after he left the pub. He had been lying in an alley for several hours before anyone reported it. People must have thought he was a drunk, poor old Bill.' I could hear a sob in her voice, too.

'But how did he die?' I asked, not wanting to hear.

'He was stabbed,' my mother whispered.

'Fucking hell!' I gasped before I could stop myself. 'Why?'

'I don't know. The police don't know; or at least they say they don't. That's why they rang. They found our name in his address book. They wanted to know when we last saw him. Have you been to see him recently?'

'Yes. On Monday.'

'You'd better ring the police right away.'

'Yes. They've already left a message here, before yours. I'll have to go down and see them. Do you want me to come to you first?'

'No, no. You go to London. That's more important. Poor old Bill. I was always so unkind to him.'

'For God's sake, Mother, you weren't. We were his only close friends. He understood that you found it hard to tolerate him. He didn't mind; he loved you for trying.'

'He and your father were such great friends. He took it very badly when he died. I have that much in common with him.'

'I'll come and see you, on my way back from London.'

'I'd be glad of that. I imagine we'll have to arrange his funeral. I don't think he's seen any of his relations for years.'

'Okay. I'll ring you later.'

We said goodbye, each understanding the other's reasons for sadness at the death of this weak, hopeless man. There would not be many other people who would mourn him.

I telephoned DS Robinson, told him that I had heard about Bill Beecham's death from my mother and arranged to meet him at the Savile Row police station in three hours' time.

I locked the house, scribbled a note to Sharon and drove to London.

At first meeting, DS Robinson looked and sounded as if he had been sent straight from central casting. He was the same height as myself, with neat, dull brown hair and a trim moustache. He wore a brown leather blouson and grey trousers. His every phrase and mannerism was straight out of the Ham Actors' Guide. But after a while I decided that he was playing the part; he was more astute than he appeared. He met me in the bleak marble lobby of London's busiest police station, and led me to a drab, bare room which smelt of cigarettes and sweat. We sat either side of a tubular-framed table.

'Good of you to come, sir. You're the only person who has, so far.'

'You must have spoken to some of the people he was drinking with last night?'

'Tracking them down is like going on safari. The best way to find them is to wait until they come to their watering hole to drink in the evenings. Most of them are probably still in bed, but we've got someone over there to intercept them. Now, first of all, could you tell me how long you'd known Mr Beecham?'

'All my life, though I saw more of him from when I was about ten. He was an old friend of my father's.'

'And you'd be thirty, now?'

'Well guessed.'

'It wasn't a guess, Mr Best. One of my colleagues follows the point-to-points. We looked you up in the book. I gather you're in with a chance of the championship this year.'

I put my head to one side and shrugged, modestly. 'Maybe.'

'Mr Beecham had an interest in the horses, didn't he?'

'Yes. He's owned a few in his time.'

'And he used to punt a bit?'

I nodded.

'In fact, judging by the betting slips, and correspondence with various bookmakers we found in his flat, he was an utterly committed compulsive gambler.'

'Yes,' I said, 'he used to bet a lot.'

'And do you think he drank because he liked drinking, or just to forget that he was always losing?'

'He didn't always lose.'

'Maybe not, but more often than he won, like all but the most professional gamblers.'

'Look, Sergeant Robinson, I'm as anxious as you to find out who killed Bill, but how's this character assassination going to help?'

'Obviously, we need to build up a picture of the man and his habits if we're to know where to look. But we'll come back to that later. We're having some difficulty finding any relatives. There are one or two Beechams in some of his old add__ they are all deceased or gone abroad__ might contact?'

leaning back in my chair and folding my arms. He went on. 'If you didn't do it, you shouldn't have any worries about answering my questions, should you? First of all, you can tell me where you were last night.'

'At home, in Herefordshire, in bed.'

'Anyone who can corroborate that?'

'As you'll already have discovered, I'm not married, and I live on my own.'

'It isn't unheard of for unmarried people not to sleep alone, but you're saying that last night you did?'

'That's right.'

'So you don't have an alibi.'

'No.'

'And you could have a motive.'

'Like what?'

'That's what I was trying to find out.'

I rose to my feet, beginning to get angry. Robinson put his hand out, palm down in a calming gesture. 'All right, don't get tricky. I've already told you, there's no reason why you shouldn't answer my questions, is there? And I have to ask them. You can understand that, can't you, Mr Best?'

'Yes, I suppose so.' I sat down again.

'Now I won't ask you any more for the time being. If you'll come downstairs with me, we'll take a look at him.'

Bill's face, previously always excitable and truculent, was white and peaceful now. He had been cleaned up a bit, and I was not shown anything below his neck. I gagged when he was pulled out of his shelf, but I managed to nod. 'That's him.'

'Thank you, sir,' Robinson said. 'Now, if you wouldn't mind coming upstairs again and telling me where I can reach you, that'll be all for now.'

'But, hang on! I've got a few questions I'd like to ask you,' I blurted in frustration.

'I dare say you have, sir. But I'm afraid they'll have to wait until next time we meet. I understand you'll want to know more details about your friend's death, but if I told you, that might jeopardise my investigations.'

'You mean you still think I might have had something to do with it?'

We were back in the front lobby of the station now.

'Not necessarily. Thank you very much for your time, Mr Best. I'll be in touch.'

He held out a hand. I looked at his face and guessed I would get no further with him now. I shook his hand briefly, turned and left the building.

I stopped for a moment on the pavement at the bottom of the steps of the police station and wrapped my long cashmere coat more tightly around myself against the cold, damp air. I was considering my next move when a small man in a fawn raincoat approached me from the railings where he had been standing.

'Excuse me. Mr Archie Best?'

The man looked like a journalist.

'Who are you?' I asked.

'My name is Fisher. I represent Perlman and Preiss.'

He handed me a card. Perlman and Preiss, it appeared, were a firm of solicitors with offices in Lincoln's Inn Fields. I glanced at the man.

'What do you want?'

'You are Mr Archie Best?'

'What do you think?'

'Well, I've seen your photograph, and Sergeant Robinson told me he was expecting you here, so I am confident of your identity.'

'I wish I were sometimes,' I said flippantly. 'Anyway, what do you want?'

'Would you mind if we went somewhere to talk?' He gestured at the street in general.

'Sure,' I said. 'That cafe?'

We sat at a formica table, he with a cup of tea, and I with a large cappuccino.

'I presume this has something to do with Bill Beecham?'

'Yes, it has. Mr Beecham has been a client of ours for thirty years. We will be the executors of his will.'

'I don't imagine that'll be a very profitable job.'

'That's not for me to say, but I can tell you that he was very eccentric and was a man of far greater substance than he appeared.'

I was frankly astonished, and said so.

'His assets were all held in trust until the day he died. However,' said Mr Fisher, 'that isn't why I had to see you. Several years ago, Mr Beecham lodged an item with us, which we lodged with the bank for safekeeping. His instructions were that if ever he were to, er, decease in circumstances that were in any way suspicious, we must immediately pass this item on to you.'

'What is this item?'

'It's a small picture, an oil painting.'

'How extraordinary. But surely it comprises part of his estate?'

'No. It is a gift that was made technically at the time of his instruction, which was more than five years ago. Anyway, I don't believe it's a particularly valuable painting. There's also a sealed envelope addressed to you which accompanies it.'

I was excited and intrigued. Bill had always liked to surround himself with a faint aura of mystery. I could not wait to see the picture.

'So? What do I do?' I asked.

'If you wouldn't mind coming with me to my office. We have arranged to collect the painting from the bank. We will want you to sign a receipt for it, and then you may take it.'

I collected my car from the car park in Cork Street and drove Mr Fisher to his office. There I was formally handed a package, wrapped in plain brown paper, and an envelope with my name on it in Bill's writing. I almost ran back to the car, wanting to open them both at once, but I thought that this should be done somewhere private. I drove to the offices of my own lawyer, an old university friend with a small, new practice in the West End.

He came out of his private room to greet me, and I briefly explained what had happened, showing him the package.

'Sounds like something out of a Sherlock Holmes story. Use our partners' meeting room. It's empty all afternoon. I'll join you in a minute if you like.'

He showed me into the small room which contained nothing but a table and eight chairs. There were not even any pictures on the wall yet, so young was the practice.

I thanked him. He left, and I put the package on the table.

I decided to open the envelope first.

There was a single piece of writing paper inside, hand written by Bill.

Redcliffe Gardens, May '84.

Dear Archie, Please accept this small gift. I have left the pitiful rump of my estate to your mother, who was the finest

47

woman I ever knew. I'm afraid yours is a somewhat indifferent painting, though of a fine horse.

Please restore it immediately, and do it yourself.

With my warmest wishes for your happiness,

Bill Beecham.

I could not help tears seeping into the corners of my eyes; so much affection had Bill squeezed into those few lines.

I read the letter three times more, before turning my attention to the package. I carefully undid the string and the Sellotape that bound it.

Battered gilt Victorian gesso framed a murky canvas two feet by eighteen inches on which a deformed-looking horse had been painted in an unlikely pose with an ill-executed, tomato-faced groom.

The legend on the lower edge of the frame claimed that the animal was Lord Jersey's Bay Middleton. It could have been any horse; it looked like none that I had ever seen. The artist, with well-founded modesty, had failed to sign the work. I laughed to myself. Bill's description, 'somewhat indifferent', was an understatement.

I turned the picture over. It appeared to have the original lining, though it had been tampered with. I guessed that the purpose of the gift lay behind it.

I decided that the task of restoration had better be done at home.

'Immediately', Bill had instructed.

I wrapped up the picture, and went out into the reception area of the offices. I left a message of thanks to my lawyer friend and almost ran down the stairs and out to my car.

My old stone farmhouse faced due west, five hundred feet above sea-level. When I arrived home early that evening, it was stolidly withstanding an almost full-frontal battering from a blistering north-westerly.

Inside, I was grateful to the Aga, stoked up that morning and still radiating heat in the large, low kitchen. The seven-foot scrubbed deal table in the centre of the room was covered, as normal, with old newspapers, entry forms, bank statements, sale catalogues and unwashed coffee cups. I swept everything to one side and placed my package on the table.

I pulled off the wrapping once more and, scarcely looking at the terrible painting, turned it face down to extract it from its frame.

A few minutes' careful work revealed that I had been right.

Neatly placed under the lining were a few sheets of paper, slightly discoloured from their confinement with the old picture. I took them out and laid them on the table in front of me.

The first was a photocopy of a marriage certificate, dated August 1951, detailing the nuptials that had taken place in Lewisham Register Office between Arthur Clive Duckett and Doreen Sandra Baker.

Beneath it were two birth certificates, for a boy, John Arthur, dated December 1951, and a girl, Diane Marlene, born a year later.

With growing excitement, and some bafflement about the significance of what I thought I was being told, I turned to the next sheet. It did not come as a surprise.

It was a copy of the change of name by deed-poll of Arthur Clive Duckett to Clive Drury.

I stared at it, and wondered just what Bill was trying to tell me. I lifted it. There was one remaining sheet of paper, a page torn from a small note-book.

Bill had written on it.

Archie,

If you're reading this, I'm dead, and I didn't nod off for a terminal doze in front of the snooker, or suffer a perfectly normal heart attack in a betting shop. I don't suppose too many will weep for me, but the only person who would want my premature departure to that great Tote hall in the sky is one Clive Drury.

Don't tell the police, or my family but, if you can, make Drury pay. The best punishment would be public humiliation.

The documents enclosed will help you on your way. I hope you'll forgive me for what you may discover. I'm bitterly ashamed of nearly everything I've done in my life, and I can't see that changing between now, when I'm writing this, and a future time when you might be reading it.

But you and I have always been friends; you're the only

person I can think of who might see that justice is done.
Best of luck and be careful.
Bill.

Chapter 4

I stared at the scrap of paper until it became a blur.

I shook with guilt and anger.

Anger at myself, for I was sure I had provoked the circumstances which had driven Drury into finally disposing of a man who had always known too much about him; anger at Bill for putting himself in that position, and anger at Clive Drury for depriving me of my cantankerous, bloody-minded, dear old friend.

Quaking with hopeless rage, I got to my feet and crashed through the dark hallway to the drawing room to find a bottle of Scotch. I brought it back to the kitchen, sat down and poured myself an injudiciously large slug.

I studied Bill's letters again, and the scanty ammunition with which he had provided me. How was this small piece of knowledge going to help me deal with a man like Clive Drury? It was fortunate that I had extracted what information I had from Bill only a few days before. Just knowing Drury had changed his name and his wife was not going to help me much. Or was it? Maybe Bill was right to identify Drury's Achilles' heel as a craving for social acceptability; it seemed absurd for someone who now wielded as much financial muscle as he did, but he would not be the first self-made millionaire who had that aspect of life out of all proportion to others.

But what the hell could I do about it? And, God knew, I had enough other problems of my own to deal with.

I stood up, grasping my whisky glass, and paced wildly around the kitchen.

What a sordid, horrific mess!

51

I had no choice but to be involved in it.

I drained my glass, slammed it on the table, and resolved that Clive Drury would pay for the death of Bill Beecham, and every other death for which he might have been responsible.

Then I sat down, calmed myself and tried to sort out my reactions.

I thought that I knew Bill well. I had not lied when I told Robinson that I had known him all my life, and yet, there were large parts of his history and background about which I knew next to nothing. His first marriage, for instance. It was only when I had met Georgie that he had chosen to tell me about her. There must have been many other things he had not revealed.

Mr Fisher's assertion that Bill was, in fact, quite a wealthy man had come as a complete surprise, and yet it explained why, no matter how much he gambled, and however much he complained, he had never quite gone bust.

Even when his hard-luck stories had reached their sporadic crescendos, the telephone bill and the rent were always paid. And he always had enough to pay for an evening's drinking. It was a sign, I supposed, of my own self-preoccupation that I had never really given Bill's circumstances much thought; that and the fact that he never appeared to hit rock bottom.

The one person I felt that I could talk to about Bill was my mother and, with a twinge of guilt, I remembered that I had said I would call in and see her on my way back from London.

That had been, of course, before I knew anything about Bill's extraordinary bequest to me. But that was something I did not want to tell my mother about.

I picked up the telephone, and noticed for the first time since I had come in that it was flashing. The messages could wait. I dialled my mother's number.

'Hello?' she answered.

'Hello, Mum. I'm at home. I had to get straight back. I'm sorry I didn't ring you before.'

'That's all right dear. I was a bit worried, though. Was everything all right with the police?'

'Yes. I had to identify Bill, which wasn't much fun, though I must say, he looked fitter than usual.'

'Oh, Archie. How can you?'

'I'm sorry, I've been very upset too. Look, I'd better not come

52

over now, but can I come and see you in the morning? I want to talk to you about Bill.'

'Yes, do. I've been feeling terrible about him. I feel that I could have done so much more.'

'I don't think there's a thing you could have done to stop what happened. Don't blame yourself for anything. I'll see you at midday, then.'

'All right, Archie. Look after yourself.'

We said goodbye, and when I replaced the receiver, the answering machine still flashed at me censoriously. I wound the tape back and played it.

'Hello Archie. It's me.' It was Georgie. 'I just wanted to confirm that you're coming here for the weekend after next. Mum wasn't certain. I'll probably see you before then, but could you let me know? Bye.'

From her tone, I knew that she had not heard the news about Bill. I wondered how upset she would be when she did. Though she had never seen a lot of Bill, it had been clear from her attitude when we discussed him that she regarded him with deep and genuine affection. I cringed at the prospect of telling her, and hoped that it would not be me who had to.

Other than that, I was surprised how pleased I was to hear her voice; more pleased than I would have been to hear Amanda Drury's.

There was another message. It was not Amanda; it was her brother, Damian.

'Uhm. Archie, this is Damian Drury. If you're racing at Easton on Saturday, could we meet for a quick drink? Uhm, my father won't be there.' There was a pause. 'Don't bother to call me back. I'll see you in the changing room . . . if you're there.'

That was interesting. I wondered if Damian had rung on his own initiative. I thought it likely. Perhaps he saw a way of achieving something his father had not. Poor little shit. He was in luck, though; I was riding Bill's Flutter at the Shropshire point-to-point course in a Restricted Open, and I would have more than a drink with Drury Junior: I wanted a long conversation with him too.

The tape carried on and broke into the message my mother had left that morning. I switched the machine off, and dialled Temple Ferris.

A housekeeper said she would go and look for Georgie.

'Hello?'

'Hello, Georgie. It's Archie. How are you?'

'I'm fine,' she answered as if she meant it.

She had not heard about her father. My heart sank, but I side-stepped the issue once more.

'I got your message, and, yes, I'm coming for that weekend. I'm going to a sale in Stow on the Friday, and I'm not riding the following day.'

'Great! There's a good crowd coming; all my friends, not my parents'. I think you'll get on with them really well.'

'I usually find when people tell me that, I never do, but I'll do my best. I wondered whether you'd like to come grooming again this Saturday.'

'Sure. Who are you riding?'

'Just Cocoa. I'm running the Consul next Wednesday,'

'How are they all?'

'They were all right when I last saw them this morning. If you come here first on Saturday, we can both go up in the lorry. Is that okay?'

'Yes, fine.'

'Okay, see you then.'

I put the phone down, trusting that someone else would have broken the news to her by then.

I was woken next morning at seven by the energetic clattering of Mrs Prater, my weekly daily, who came every Friday to deal with my washing and the usual accumulation of domestic chaos. I sometimes tried to do it myself, but Mrs Prater became so offended that I had begun to feel guilty if I did not leave a real mess for her to cope with. She was not going to be disappointed today.

The wind and rain of the previous day had cleared, and it was a fine, still morning which made Bill's death easier to cope with.

I shaved and turned on the radio to listen to the progress of the Gulf War. It put my own problems into perspective. I went downstairs feeling well able to cope with the several challenges I had set myself.

Mrs Prater greeted me with a large mug of watery tea. As I drank it, I told her about Bill. She had met him a few times when he had come to stay with me for Cheltenham races. He had always been on best behaviour then, and he had become one of her favourite guests. She expressed her sadness at some length; then, in return, she brought me up to date with local gossip.

Sharon, she told me with disapproval, had dropped her nice, solid tractor-driver boyfriend from the village, and had been spotted in Hereford with a tanned, muscle-bound SAS squaddy.

'As long as he doesn't make her late for work, it doesn't worry me,' I remarked, and as if to reassure me, I saw Sharon's battered old Ford lurch into the yard on the dot of seven-thirty.

She bounded into the kitchen, looking as bright and bouncy as I had ever seen her. One could rely, it appeared, on the 22nd Special Air Service Regiment for more than just dealing with terrorists.

After the first ritual cup of coffee, Sharon and I went out into the yard to do the waiting horses. I fed my hunter while Sharon tacked up the others. We rode out of the yard together to warm up the two racehorses with a brisk trot along a sunken green lane to a large level field that my neighbour was happy to let me use, and which provided a good rectangular gallop of three-quarters of a mile. Both horses pricked their ears and were still pulling like traction engines after two circuits.

'How's the Consul?' I yelled at Sharon.

'Hardly puffin',' she yelled back. I could see that there was scarcely a sign of sweat on him. Beneath me, Cocoa seemed ready to go round several more times before coming off the bit.

Afterwards we schooled them over my run of three rickety steeplechase fences. To my delight, Cocoa took them all with big, bold leaps. I was well pleased with both horses and we hacked back feeling bullish about their imminent performances.

'Why don't you run the Consul at Easton with Cocoa?' Sharon asked.

'I think he'd win the open there, but I'm certain he'll win at Gazeley again on Wednesday. And this year, winning's all that matters.'

Sharon smiled. That was what she liked to hear. It was heartening to see her dedication to our campaign. I thought with gratitude that it would take more than an SAS man to put her off her job.

When we got back to Stone House Farm, Mrs Prater told me with great curiosity and excitement that a detective had phoned and was on his way to see me.

'It must be about that poor Mr Beecham,' she added.

'Probably. Did he give a name?'

'Yes, I wrote it down.' She tried to read her own writing on the message pad. 'Robinson,' she said.

'When's he due here?'

'About half past eleven, he said.'

'Oh, shit,' I swore, to Mrs Prater's horror. 'I'll have to ring my mother and tell her I'll be late.'

DS Robinson, like most other people coming for the first time, had underestimated the journey time from London. He arrived after midday.

He climbed out of his red Sierra and picked his way across the muddy yard. I had been wondering how he had justified his trip out here, but his first words cleared that up.

'Good morning, Mr Best. In fact, it's a beautiful morning, and when I was about to leave to drive into London, I thought, what a day for a drive in the country. And there are a few more questions I'd like to ask you about your friend Mr Beecham.'

'Don't forget, you promised you'd answer a few of mine too,' I replied.

The detective nodded, and I showed him into the house. I asked Mrs Prater to bring coffee into the drawing room and keep the noise of hoovering to a minimum.

Robinson and I went through to the drawing room, which had just been cleaned, but which was cold and slightly damp from lack of use.

'If you're going to be here for a while, Sergeant, I'll light a fire,' I said, nodding towards the cavernous open hearth, and the pile of logs stacked beside it.

'That'd be nice,' he answered. He was more deferential than when I had last seen him. I could not tell whether this was because I was now cleared of suspicion, or because he was away from his home ground.

While we waited for Mrs Prater to come and go, I got the fire blazing with a pile of kindling, and placed two bone-dry apple logs on top.

Robinson seemed in no hurry, so I took the initiative.

'How are your investigations going?'

'Not too well.'

'Why's that?'

Robinson took a moment to answer. 'Mr Beecham was stabbed, as far as we can tell, with a perfectly normal kitchen knife, but he was stabbed by somebody who knew exactly what they were doing. Apart from that, there was no sign of anything being stolen from him. He had about fifty quid on him. So it definitely wasn't a mugging. Frankly, Mr Best, we've got no chance of finding the killer unless we can establish a motive.' Robinson paused, and looked into the fire where the large logs were begin to flame. 'That's why I came to see you. I thought you might have a few ideas.'

'Me? I haven't a clue. What ideas have you got?' I said.

Robinson considered this for a moment.

'Well,' he said slowly, 'it's either gambling, or dodgy pictures. The old fella had run up a few debts with two or three bookies, but,' he shrugged, 'they weren't big debts, and anyway they'd have taken what money he had on him. But they don't collect debts like that these days. There's no point. They said he often ran up bigger accounts, but they always got paid in the end, and I can believe that. You went to Mr Beecham's solicitors' office after you saw me yesterday, didn't you? They probably told you that Mr Beecham was quite a wealthy bloke. But the money was all in trust and he couldn't get his hands on it too easily.'

I nodded. 'Yes, it's extraordinary. I had no idea.'

'You even picked up a little bequest he'd made.'

'Not exactly a bequest. It was a gift he made some time ago, apparently.'

'I see. I understand that your mother will be the principal beneficiary of his estate.'

'So I was told,' I agreed.

'And you never knew anything about this before?'

'Absolutely nothing.'

'And your mother?'

'Not as far as I know, but you'll have to ask her yourself.'

'I've spoken to her on the phone. I don't think a visit's necessary, though no doubt I'll see her at the funeral.'

'I take it you don't still think I or my mother was in any way responsible for killing him?'

'It's early days yet, Mr Best. We're keeping all options open. I'm inclined to think it must have something to do with pictures.'

Robinson looked at me knowingly. I said nothing and he went on. 'Thirty years ago, Beecham was involved in several dodgy but not strictly illegal deals. D'you know a gentleman by the name of Clive Drury?'

'Yes.' I answered guardedly, 'I've met him a couple of times. His son rides against me in point-to-points.'

'Mr Beecham used to work for Drury, after Drury took over the family business, but they fell out, in about sixty-two. Did you know about that?'

'Not much. I only really saw anything of Bill ten years after that. But what could Clive Drury have to do with it? He's a big man at Lloyd's and he has a lot of other big business interests. It seems highly unlikely that he'd be involved in anything with Bill now.'

'It may seem unlikely, but though he has friends in a lot of high places, my colleagues down in the City have always considered Clive Drury a bit tricky. He probably pulled a few strokes before he became respectable. And as events have shown recently, other people have found the insurance market can provide very tasty illegal profits without breaking any bones.'

'I certainly don't know anything about that side of Drury. I don't think he's a particularly pleasant man; in fact, he turned quite nasty when I wouldn't sell him a horse he wanted for his son.'

'Why wouldn't you sell it? Didn't he offer you enough?'

'It's not for sale,' I shrugged. 'I've wanted to win the two big hunter-chases, and the amateur riders' championship for a long time and Caesar's Consul's my best chance. Drury's welcome to bid me for the horse when I've won them.'

'You'd sell it to him then?'

I laughed. 'If he's prepared to pay me a lot more than the animal's worth.'

'I wonder if you'd bear in mind what I've said about Drury. We have no good reason for interviewing him over this murder, whatever hunches we might have, and we can't get near him. But if you ever come across anything which you think might be relevant, you'll let us know, won't you.'

'Of course, though I don't think that's likely.'

Robinson stood up. 'I dare say you're right, sir. So I won't keep you any longer.'

'I'm afraid you've come a long way for not much, Sergeant Robinson.'

'I wouldn't say that. It's been a beautiful drive. I must come out this way with my wife some time. She loves a bit of old-fashioned countryside.' He had obviously decided to go, and though there was more I would have liked to ask, I did not at this stage want to demonstrate more knowledge than I had to. I showed him to the seldom-used front door and shook hands with him before watching him reverse and drive carefully out of the yard.

It was clear from the redness of my mother's eyes that she had been weeping.

'Has it upset you a lot, then?' I asked.

We were sitting in the small cosy kitchen where I had spent many childhood meals with her; where she had comforted all the hurts, physical and emotional, real and imagined that afflict young, lonely boys.

She shook her head. 'I don't know really. In a funny sort of way, Bill was my last contact with your father. He used to talk about him as if he were still alive. They'd been on a lot of trips together, when they were students, and afterwards. Bill spent three months in the Peloponnese with Edward, and they both used to talk as if it was the best part of their lives. Bill was useless and selfish in most things, but he was clever, and witty, and I think your father felt somehow responsible for him.'

'Bill wasn't so bad. I always liked him. He could be fairly difficult with other people, but he never was with me.'

'You're very like your father, not only in looks, in temperament too. I think that's why Bill was so fond of you. I almost got the impression sometimes that he was trying to make up for something,' she mused.

'Did you know about this trust of his?' I asked.

'I always knew he had a bit of money. He came from a wealthy family, and I assumed he must have come into some money. But they always kept him on a very tight rein. When they discovered he was gambling at school at the age of fifteen, I think they decided that he was incurable and incapable of managing his own affairs and that's partly why he was so moody. It wasn't not having the money, but the fact that he was being treated as a permanent child. I believe the terms of the trust were very stringent and his trustees stuck to them rigidly.'

'Poor old bugger. Anyway, the police haven't got far with their enquiries. They're certain it wasn't a mugging, because he still had some money on him, and they don't think it was anything to do with his gambling. Maybe it was someone he goaded a bit further than he should have done.'

'But surely no one would murder him for that?'

'I don't know. He had some very iffy boozing pals. I've met some of them with him, but' – I gave a gesture of ignorance – 'I just don't know. What's happening about a funeral?'

'I've been in touch with the police about that. They don't want to release his body,' she winced at the word, 'just yet. They said probably at the end of next week. I spoke to his solicitors too. They suggested that a cremation would be best and they very kindly gave me the name of some undertakers. Apparently they've not been able to contact any other relations, though there are some in the South of France. They gave me the address.'

'Are you going to want any help making the arrangements?'

'No, that's all right. It'll keep me occupied, and I expect you've got plenty of other things to get on with.'

My mother was more right than she realised, I reflected. Seven days before, I had never set eyes on Clive Drury; now my life seemed to be inextricably linked with his. He had offered me a chance to do the biggest deal I had ever done. He had tried hard to buy my horse. He had threatened me. I had slept with his daughter. I had given Bill Beecham a reason to acquire from him an important and very valuable painting, and Bill, I reckoned now, had tried to acquire it by blackmail. Drury had murdered Bill and Bill had posthumously charged me with meting out justice.

And I still wanted to win every race that would bring me closer to the championship.

I could not explain all this to my mother, but I had to talk about it to someone; and I had Georgie all to myself for two hours in the lorry next day.

Georgie arrived looking fresh and warm as she always did. She was wearing a pair of loose-cut jeans that managed to accentuate her long legs and nectarine-shaped bottom.

She smiled as if she did not have a care in the world, and I groaned at the thought of having to spoil her day, but not just yet, I decided.

I gave her a quick kiss on one cheek, which was the nearest we had ever got to sex. She gave me a sharp, quizzical look, and I felt an irrational stab of guilt for my night with Amanda.

But Georgie went off to deal with Cocoa's preparation. She insisted on plaiting him and grooming him until his coat shone like the bowl of a well-used briar pipe. When we reached the racecourse and his travelling rug was off, she would comb a pattern of diamonds on each of his big, round quarters.

I piled everything else I would need into the box, topped with the water tank, tossed a spare hay net on to the Luton, and gave Sharon a few instructions for the other horses.

I lowered the back of the lorry, and Georgie led Cocoa from his stable, across the yard to the lorry ramp.

I watched with interest and some concern. Cocoa was a notoriously bad loader, but I knew Georgie would resent the suggestion that she was less capable than anyone else of dealing with him.

Halfway up the ramp, Cocoa decided that he did not want to go into the lorry. He reared and took a few clattering steps backwards, tugging Georgie on the end of a halter rope. His front hooves crashed down again, a few inches from her feet, but she hung on, while Sharon and I closed in behind him. The horse backed down further, a hoof slipped off the side of the ramp and he began to panic.

When half a ton of not very intelligent, fit horse makes up its mind not to do what you ask, it can be a frightening experience. Four flailing, uncontrolled iron-tipped sledgehammers can kill. Georgie knew that. But she barely flinched. She still held the rope which was clipped to his headcollar, and tried to relax the animal.

Sharon and I backed away, while Georgie came down the ramp with Cocoa.

'It's okay,' she said calmly, as much to the horse as to us, 'I'll walk him up again.'

But first, she reached up her hand and gently patted his sweat-darkened neck and spoke soothingly to him. After a few moments, the animal was no longer fretting, and was ready to be led up again.

It was a fine demonstration by Georgie of gifts I did not know she had, and I was impressed.

When she had tied his headcollar to a ring on the inside of the box, I walked up quietly to put the partition across.

'Well done. I should have warned you he can be a very tricky loader. I've never travelled him on his own before and normally I put one of the older horses on first, so he doesn't mind following.'

Georgie smiled. 'He's just a bit of a baby.'

I smiled back. 'He certainly responded to a dose of womanly compassion,' I said.

Georgie was not sure if I was being genuine. She squeezed out past the partition. 'Yes, well, it has its uses,' she muttered. We both jumped off the ramp and together heaved it back up and dropped the clips into their slots. Georgie went to her car and took out a Barbour and a wicker basket with a bottle and a flask sticking out of the top. I, of course, had forgotten to make any provision for food and drink.

'Thanks,' I said gratefully, and clambered up into the driver's seat of the lorry.

At forty miles an hour, it was a two-hour drive to the race meeting. We trundled up through the Herefordshire and Shropshire hills, cocooned against the cold outside in a stuffy little cab that smelt of horse sweat and the remains of last week's cigar.

I no longer suffered from the cement-mixer guts before a race that had afflicted my early days of race-riding. While I was not over-confident about Cocoa's chances today, I felt that if he was in a good mood when we got there, he was fit and talented enough to win.

For the first few miles, Georgie and I talked sporadically. Although I wanted to, I could not bring myself yet to tell her about Bill. I became increasingly guilty as we talked instead about the horses and their training programme. She was interested and knew a surprising amount. She was, essentially, a country girl, and had ridden ponies almost as soon as she could walk. Although in five years of living in London she had spent less time in the saddle, her affection for the animals was still strong. I knew that she did not come racing with me only for the pleasure of my company.

There was a lull in our conversation and, after a while, I glanced at her and plucked up my courage with a deep breath.

'Georgie, I've some bad news for you. I had thought you'd
have heard it by now, but you obviously haven't.'

She picked up my tone of voice and glanced at me in alarm.

'What?' she said quickly.

'About your father.'

'Bill?'

I nodded. I'm afraid so.'

'But what's happened?'

'He's been . . .' I stuttered. 'He's dead.'

'Oh my God! Poor old Bill. I was going to see him next week.
I spoke to him on Wednesday. When was it? Last night?'

'No. I'm afraid it was Wednesday night or early Thursday
morning. The police aren't certain.'

'The police? Why the police? How did he die?'

I gulped. 'He was murdered,' I almost whispered.

Georgie let out one big howl, them lapsed abruptly into
silence, staring at the road ahead through tearful eyes.

I did not speak for a while as I felt her grief. After a mile or
so, I said, 'I'm sorry. I wish I hadn't had to tell you. Obviously
no one thought to tell your mother; but I can't understand why
no one told you. You're his only next of kin.'

Georgie shook her head. 'No I'm not. Legally, I'm Dad's, my
stepfather's daughter.' She turned to look at me. 'How did you
know about it?'

'The police rang me the next day. I'd seen Bill on Monday. I
feel terrible. I think it was a suggestion of mine that got him into
trouble.' I knew I had to tell her all the bad news at once. I
would be doing her no favours by letting it seep out in dribs and
drabs. 'He had left something with his lawyers, to be given to
me if he ever died a violent death. It was a picture, with instructions to restore it. When I got the lining off the back, there was
a note saying that if someone had killed him, it was probably
Clive Drury.'

Georgie did not say anything at first. I glanced at her. All the
colour had drained from her face. Then she blurted, 'But for
God's sake, Archie! How? Why? How are you involved?' Her
eyes were wide with horror. 'Why should Drury do that? My
God! I wonder if Dad knows anything about it. I mean, he's
Chairman of Drury's company.'

I had already forgotten how shocked I was when I had realised that what had happened was murder. It was not the sort of thing that normally came near the lives of people like us.

'There's no question of that,' I said. 'Of course Drury didn't do it himself, and I doubt that he'll ever be charged. He was probably three or four moves away from the actual killing. The police may suspect him, but I'm certain he did it.'

I told her almost everything: about the Stubbs in Drury's house, about my asking Bill if he could get it, about the few documents Bill had left in the small Victorian painting.

'I'm sure Bill had been expecting some kind of a showdown one day. He left instructions for the lawyers to give me the picture six or seven years ago. Frankly, the bumph in the picture proves nothing. I presume that was Bill being deliberately obscure; partly, I suppose, because he didn't want to give too much away if it was opened by the wrong person before he died, though I don't know why he should have worried. The picture and the letter telling me to "restore" it were always kept apart by the solicitors.'

I told her that I was in no doubt that Bill had tried to get the Stubbs by blackmailing Drury; it was precisely the sort of scam he liked.

'I can't believe it,' Georgie said when I had finished. 'I can't believe that my poor old father would do this kind of thing. But why did you ask Bill to get the picture?'

'I didn't, not intentionally,' I protested. 'I wanted to know if he knew anything about it, and then next thing I knew, he was planning to get it. He didn't know that I knew Drury had it. I never dreamed it would get so out of hand. I didn't know that Drury was an out and out hood; for God's sake, he's a very big man in Lloyd's; he's got several vast businesses, he has peers of the realm on the boards of his companies.'

'My stepfather will have to resign!'

'Not yet. Whatever you do don't tell him about this yet. The police may not be able to feel his collar, but Bill asked me to see that justice is done. And believe me, I'm going to. But if Drury finds out that I know what I do, I won't have a chance.'

'You don't mean he'd kill you too?'

A week before, if someone had suggested that I might be murdered, I would have laughed at the absurd idea. Now, I was not so confident.

'I doubt he'd go that far,' I said. 'But he'd start covering his tracks. I promise you that I'll let you know when I think I can nail him, and then you can tell your stepfather.'

'You'll let me know!' Georgie exploded. 'You don't think I'm going to let you handle this on your own, do you? He was my father, for God's sake! Have you told anyone else about all this?'

'No.'

'Not even the police?'

'No.'

'Why not?'

'Because as far as I can see, they haven't a cat in hell's chance of making a charge stick. And Bill asked me not to.'

'Why?'

I sighed. 'Because any serious investigations into Drury will implicate Bill in innumerable dodgy scams in which he was also involved. It so happens, I had a long talk with Bill when I last saw him, and he told me a lot of things he had never told me before. It's bloody lucky in the circumstances, because he hadn't left me much else to go on. The thing is, above all, he didn't want you to know or be embarrassed by what he'd done. I told him I wouldn't tell you, but I have to now, and I think you understand and won't think any less of him.'

'Of course I don't! He could have trusted me. I knew how useless he was, but I still loved him.'

She was, I saw, already handling the events with a strength that did not surprise me. And though at this stage I had only the vaguest of ideas about how I was going to go about dealing with Drury, I was more than glad of her promised support.

'It's also occurred to me,' I said, 'that if the police started sniffing around Drury, it'd be a lot harder for me to get at him. From now on, I'm going to avoid arousing their suspicions about him, at least as far as anything to do with Bill is concerned, and I'm making it my personal mission to see that he gets his come-uppance.'

'Good.' Georgie looked positively bullish now. 'I'd love to see Clive Drury suffer for this. I've always disliked him intensely. So has my stepfather, as a matter of fact, but he's not a strong man, and he said he needed the money, which is balls.' She turned to me, as determined as I to see her father's death avenged. 'I'll take a few weeks off work. I'll give my notice in if they don't like it. I've got to help somehow, and I'm sure I can find out a lot you wouldn't be able to.'

Georgie, though upset, was not one to brood unproductively. She bombarded me with questions about Drury, most of which I could not answer. At one point, I saw her looking at me with an odd, speculative frown.

'What's the matter with you?' I asked.

'I saw Amanda Drury last week.'

I concentrated on the road ahead, a dead straight stretch of wide bypass.

'Oh, yah?' I said non-committally.

'You went to bed with her last weekend, didn't you?'

'She said that?' I exclaimed in astonishment.

'No. But you did, didn't you?'

I did not reply. I did not know why I should have been denying it. Georgie had no claims on me; we were, as they say, just good friends. It should not have been any of her business, and yet, I knew that it was.

'I shared a flat with Amanda for two years,' Georgie said quietly. 'I know her very well, and I know that after she's slept with a man, she talks about him in a different way.'

'In what way different?' I said to delay admission.

'Sort of victorious. She's a scalp-hunter.'

'She does seem to have had a lot of practice,' I said by way of oblique confession.

'Not that it's got anything to do with me,' Georgie went on hurriedly, sorry that she had now extracted the truth.

'No,' I agreed. 'But it didn't happen on my initiative. I told you on Sunday morning that Clive Drury had asked me to go and see him about some picture deal. I knew then that there would be more to it than that. In fact, all he wanted was the Consul, for Damian. I turned him down, of course, but he stormed off in a huff, and Amanda appeared. I was already quite drunk by then, and anyway, I was fascinated by Drury. I've never met anyone so ruthlessly determined to get what he wants. So, she offered me dinner, I thought she might tell me more and I stayed.' I shrugged. 'Amanda's the sort of girl who gets more attractive as you get more drunk.'

'I thought all women were like that,' Georgie said.

'Not you. You couldn't get more attractive.'

66

'Don't give me that crap!' she said angrily.

'Well, it's true. But, look,' I said with a change of tone, 'don't let's talk about this. I didn't plan it, and in view of what's happened since, I'd rather it didn't happen again. If you and I are going to work together on Drury, let's eliminate anything that could make it harder for us.'

'Agreed,' said Georgie. 'And anyway, I'm sorry; whatever you might have done with Amanda is none of my business.' She gave me an ambiguous smile. 'Poor old Bill,' she added, with a catch in her voice. 'That's who matters now.'

Chapter 5

The first race was due off in ten minutes and the racecourse car parks were full by the time we arrived.

It was an intermittently sunny day, cold but not too windy, and people had come out in strength from the western towns of the Black Country, as well as the market towns and the thousands of farms that scattered the East Shropshire plain.

We trundled on round to the lorry park and found a space among the disorderly scatter of boxes and trailers. Cocoa's race was the fourth, over an hour away, but Georgie and I had a lot to do. We jumped down and clambered through the small groom's door in the side of the box to take a look at him. He had not travelled well. Steam was rising off him like a hot bath and he was still fretting.

'I'll put his sweat sheet on and walk him for a bit,' Georgie said, 'and then you'd better go and declare.'

We lowered the ramp. Georgie led the moody-looking Cocoa down and we took his rug off. He was dark with sweat, and on his neck was a thin film of creamy scum.

I grunted. 'Doesn't look too good. Still, we've got an hour.'

'You get off to the secretary's tent. I'll have this chap in a better mood soon.'

'Okay,' I nodded, grateful in the circumstances for Georgie to take over. I wound my way between the other lorries towards the tents where officials would be officiating with testy self-importance.

'Archie!' The voice came from a large, gleaming black lorry with a pair of crimson stripes along the side. I glanced back and saw Damian Drury hanging out of the door of a lavish groom's room that took up half the carrying capacity of the vehicle. 'Come and have a quick one,' he invited.

I hesitated. 'Thanks, later. I'm just going to declare.'

I caught a flash of doubt in his eyes as I waved and carried on. I had not wanted to see Damian until the racing was over. I had to think very carefully about what I was going to ask him, and right now, I was beginning to feel an unavoidable pre-race tension.

I dealt with the formalities at the secretary's tent, and bought a race-card for Georgie. I took a look at the bookies' prices for the Maiden, placed a tenner on a friend's unraced horse at 25/1 and started to walk back to the lorry around the outside of the compound.

Once again, I heard my name being called. This time by a woman. I turned, and saw Amanda grinning at me. She was wearing an aggressively urban outfit: a long fawn, light-weight mac was blowing open around her legs to reveal a tiny black jersey mini-skirt. On her feet was a pair of flat-soled designer bother boots. I tried to cover my surprise and irritation at seeing her. As far as I knew, she had no interest in racing – I had never seen her at a meeting – and somehow Georgie's show of loyal strength had made me regret our encounter of the previous Sunday.

But vanity, and an honest appreciation of what we had enjoyed together, drew an answering smile from me.

'Hi,' she said. 'Damian said you might be here, so I thought I'd come and see you perform.'

'Again?' I asked.

She laughed. 'I wasn't watching last time. What time's your race?

'It's the fourth, at two o'clock.'

'Are you riding the horse that my father wanted to buy?'

'No, not today.'

'He's still desperate to get it. I think Damian's going to try and talk you into it.'

'So do I. He'll be wasting his time.'

'But you must come and have a drink at the box.'

'I've already seen your brother in his rather vulgar wagon. I'll come over after my race.'

She looked annoyed. 'I don't think I can stand and watch horses all afternoon among this boots and Barbour brigade.'

'So,' I shrugged, 'sit in your car and read the *Tatler*.'

'Thanks.' She stuck out a small pointed tongue and waggled it at me. 'In case I don't hang around, my father's having a sort of racing party next Tuesday. Why not come along? It might annoy him.'

'He hasn't asked me.'

'I have and that's good enough.'

'Okay,' I said. 'Where is it? Gazeley?'

'Of course not. In London.'

'I can probably make it. But I'll see you later anyway. I've got to go and get my horse ready.'

I could see her considering whether or not to come with me. Fortunately, she decided not to.

'Bye,' she said abruptly and turned to walk back towards the stewards' tent.

When I reached the lorry, I had been away for twenty minutes. I found Cocoa hitched to the side of the box. He was placid and almost dry now, while Georgie was applying the finishing touches to his coiffure.

'Well done,' I said in admiration.

'Thank you, sir,' she said in what she thought was the voice of a Herefordshire groom.

'And I'll see you in the hay-loft later,' I said, carrying on the charade.

'No you bloody won't,' she said in her own voice. 'Now, this animal looks as good as he's ever going to, so you'd better win.'

I scratched the horse under his chin. 'D'you hear that, Cocoa?'

Later, I sat in the changing room, waiting to be called up for weighing. The nine other jockeys were in moods as various as their experience. The old campaigners like myself put on a half-convincing display of bravado. The younger ones, in their first or second season, were quiet and pale. Damian Drury, due to ride a novice horse that was out-classed in this Restricted Open, scarcely opened his mouth until I sat down beside him.

'You're riding the animal that dumped you last week, aren't you?' he said.

'He didn't dump me. I fell off.'

'These fences are a lot trickier.'

'What's your plan, then?' I asked, not expecting an honest answer. Rather to my surprise, though, I got one.

'Just to hang on and hope I don't bloody fall off.'

71

'Very wise,' I said.

'It's all very well for you. You haven't got a despot for a fucking father.'

'No,' I replied, keeping the irony from my voice.

'Look, we won't talk about it now, but I've got a proposition to put to you later.'

The clerk of the scales was calling us up now. I stood up.

'I look forward to hearing it.'

Georgie and the other grooms were already walking the horses around the parade ring. I gave her a grin as I walked in with the other riders. Then I saw Amanda, leaning against the rail by the exit down to the track, looking moody at the sight of Georgie leading my horse.

I did not return her glare, and it was only when I was mounted and about to leave the paddock that I heard her.

'Good luck, Archie, you shit!' she hissed.

I tried to ignore it and headed down towards the course. Passing near the bookies' stands, I heard a shout of, 'Evens – Bill's Flutter.' Evidently they thought as little of the opposition as I did.

I walked my horse through the gap in the railings on to the course and hacked down to the start.

I had not noticed it while we were among the crowds by the paddock, but as I cantered the half mile round to the start, I heard the faint click of a loose plate on my horse's near hind.

I cursed my carelessness. I should have checked. It was the foot that had slipped off the back of the ramp when we had been loading Cocoa at home.

I reined back to a trot that would be less likely to loosen the shoe still more. I had to decide whether to turn back now and find the farrier, or go on down to the start and have him summoned there. I decided to go on. If the starter did not know what was happening, he was quite likely to send them off without waiting for me.

I carried on, while the other runners cantered past, until I pulled up by the flat-topped trailer where the starter and two bowler-hatted stewards were waiting to send us on our way.

'I'm sorry, sir,' I shouted from the now excited and prancing Cocoa, 'I've got a loose plate. I'll need the farrier.'

All three men looked annoyed, as did two other jockeys within earshot. Ten minutes walking around at the start could make a lot of difference to a horse's mood and performance.

A mounted runner, a member of the local hunt whose event this was, was despatched back to the tents. I dismounted and led my horse away from the rest of the field, to a chorus of groans and light-hearted abuse.

A few minutes later, a small red van was speeding down the course towards the start. It came to a halt beside the starter's trailer, and a burly man in his early twenties leaped out. Modern technology had not affected the need for a blacksmith to be a fit, strong man, especially if he was prepared to deal with unknown, excited thoroughbreds. From the passenger door a woman, almost as burly, jumped out.

The farrier went round to the back of his vehicle, opened the doors and began to pull out an anvil and a box of tools. He was about to dive back in for a selection of shoes.

'It's okay,' I shouted, leading Cocoa towards him. 'He's still got it. It's just loose.'

The farrier grunted. 'Bring him 'ere then.'

I led up the horse and pointed to the faulty shoe. Without any hesitation he firmly grasped the leg, spun round with his back to the animal, and held its fetlock between his thighs.

'He's spread it,' he said. 'He'll need another. Bring me the box of shoes!' he yelled at his female assistant. She dumped the box next to him, and he picked out a light-weight, aluminium shoe that looked about the right size.

Cocoa began to get impatient. Though he could not lift his inside back leg as long as the smith was holding the other, he paddled with his front legs and dragged the man backwards for a few feet.

'Hold the bugger still,' the farrier yelled angrily at me.

'Sorry.'

I took a firmer hold on the reins and wished Georgie were here with her calming influence. Cocoa settled for a moment and, deftly, the farrier pulled a claw hammer from his belt, and hooked off the loose plate and the nails that secured it. With a pick he scraped an accumulation of turf and muck from the inside of the hoof. The beefy woman handed him a file twelve inches long and he quickly scraped it across the naked hoof to remove any rough edges. He tried the shoe he had selected against the hoof, grunted in satisfaction and dropped the horse's back leg.

Cocoa, glad to have two back legs again, immediately reared. I
lost my hold on the reins and thought I had lost him completely
for a moment, but I managed to grab them before he could run
off.

'You better hold that fucker a bit 'arder if you want a ride,'
the blacksmith said over his shoulder from where he was noisily
hammering the shoe to the right shape.

Feeling thoroughly inept, I desperately tried to get Cocoa
under control. I cursed my bad luck again. This was taking as
much out of me as the horse.

But I held him, and the blacksmith, without a second glance,
grabbed the appropriate leg, and grasped it between his thighs
again. In his mouth were half-a-dozen clenches – square-section
blacksmiths' nails. The woman handed him the shoe and he
clamped it on. It was a good fit, thank God. He pulled his
hammer out, and quickly knocked the clenches through the shoe,
into the nerveless wall of the outer hoof, and out the other side,
an inch up from the edge. With a quick twist, he bent off the
protruding points, gave the shoe a couple more whacks, and put
the horse's foot back on the ground with evident satisfaction.

'That'll stay put for a while,' he declared. 'And I 'opes you
ride 'im better than you holds 'im.'

Justifiably censured, I mumbled my thanks as the farrier's
strong right arm legged me back into the saddle. I checked that
my girth was still tight and trotted over to the starter.

'Ready, sir.'

'About time,' he snapped, and turned to the rest of the field
circling impatiently behind the start.

'All right, jockeys. Try and form a straight line. We're running
behind now and I don't want to have to call you back.'

I rode round and joined them, nodding my apologies to no
one in particular. Cocoa had sweated up a bit, not as badly as
in the box, but he was definitely becoming nervous. I pulled him
into line with the others. He started edging sideways past the
start. He knew what was coming and he wanted to get on with
it.

'Get back number eight!' the starter yelled. 'You've held us
up enough already.'

Reluctantly, I wheeled my horse right round so that he was
facing the wrong way. I carried on wheeling him, and was halfway

back, a couple of lengths behind the field, when the starter yelled, 'Okay!' and dropped his flag.

It was not a fair start, but I could not really complain. Anyway, Cocoa was thoroughly relieved that we were on the move and was level with the rest of the bunched-up field in half a dozen strides.

I had not, like the rest of the runners, had a chance to show him the first obstacle. It was a fairly low, plain fence. Nevertheless, I brought him back a couple of lengths behind the next horse, so that he would have a good view of it.

He saw it and I felt him lengthen in his eagerness to reach and jump it. We were well-placed; his stride was just right. He took off and flew it with a foot to spare.

He landed galloping, keen to get on to the next one.

At least, I thought, he's enjoying the job. Unless someone gets in the way to upset him, we won't have any jumping problems.

Now, it was a question of pace.

Cocoa was not a quick horse by National Hunt hurdling standards, but he had as much speed as any other good horse on the point-to-point circuit. What was more, he had a lot of stamina.

The ground, as I had found earlier on a quick walk along the track, had dried overnight from heavy to soft. Cocoa's rather ill-bred large feet gave a bigger surface area to support his weight, so he would not sink into the turf as much as another, finer-footed animal might.

The race consisted of two and a half circuits round a left-handed course of a mile and a quarter. Though a Restricted Open Race could be fairly competitive, the really good proven horses were not eligible. I reckoned that as long as I stayed within ten lengths or so of the leaders at this pace for the first two circuits, I could take advantage of Cocoa's relative speed in the final stages of the race, picking off the leaders as it suited me. I settled him down at the back, always able to take the shortest way round the course.

The fourth fence was an open ditch, an obstacle for which Cocoa had sometimes shown a dislike, but he saw it and accepted it. He took off half a length too early. I held my breath for a moment, but he cleared it with an enormous leap, gaining a length on the horse in front. The field was still well bunched, so

I eased him back as gently as I could; I did not want to fight him and waste his energy.

When we passed the finishing post for the first time, we were lying a comfortable last. I heard a voice in the crowd yell, 'Kick on, Archie!' and ignored it with a smile.

Swinging left, away from the crowd, I had to pass two horses that were labouring badly. They were too unfit, and if the riders had any sense, they would pull up before they did some serious physical damage to them. I leaned forward and gave Cocoa a pat. He was warm and sweating, but no more than he should have been after a mile and a half. He was still seeing his fences and, most of the time, seeing his own stride. At the fence before the post, which would be the last next time round, neither of us could make up our mind when he should take off, and we ended up paddling through it. He pecked, but I was ready for it. I leaned right back. Instinctively, I took one hand off the reins and threw an arm out behind me to commit the jockey's cardinal sin of style by 'calling a cab'. But I stayed on board.

It frightened me, but Cocoa did not seem fazed at all and, as we galloped on past the winning post for the second and last time, I realised I had to take more care about helping him to judge his stride. We were still only eighth. There were a few more desperate yells from punters who had backed me, and obviously thought I had no hope. They could not have been regular racegoers if they thought the positions over a mile from home had anything to do with the final placings.

But I did decide that it was time to kick on. I shortened the reins a little, and squeezed Cocoa's flanks with my legs. Happily, he lengthened his stride and we passed two horses before we reached the next fence, another open ditch. Cocoa pricked his ears and stood right back off it and we landed in front of the next horse. We were lying fifth now, and the two leaders were going away. I gave Cocoa a quick touch with my stick, just to let him know we meant business, and he responded again. Over the next four fences, we passed the next three horses and then, I noticed with some satisfaction, Damian Drury on his young horse.

Cocoa was still pulling and I began to feel that particular elation that occurs when you know you're going to win. I was two lengths away from the leader with two more fences to jump.

The jockey in front had his whip out as we swung left to take the second from home. I pointed Cocoa at the left-hand side of the fence, planning to get upsides the leader on the inside as we landed.

As we left the ground a little behind him with a good big leap, I saw that the other had fumbled it. He had caught his back legs on the lower, thicker part of the brush and, angled to swing to the left, he pecked, just as I had done earlier. But he did not recover. The horse and his rider came down right in front of us.

Even in the air, I felt Cocoa stiffen in alarm. Most horses do not like to tread on other horses, or their riders for that matter. But there was not much we could do. Cocoa's hooves hit the ground trying to swerve left and he came crashing down on his shoulder.

As I carried on another eight feet through the air, I thanked my guardian angel that my feet had left the stirrups. I hit the soft ground with a hard thump.

But I was lucky. I rolled well, and clear of the course. The rest of the field, led by Damian Drury, had seen what had happened and took the fence to the right. I was on my feet in a few seconds, and so were the two horses which had fallen; they had decided to carry on. The other jockey was lying in a heap, groaning. I glanced at the rump of the riderless Cocoa taking the last fence, cursed the horse which had brought me down, and went over to help its rider.

I had been racing long enough to be philosophical. The bad news was that we had fallen; the good news was that we were still in one piece. But I was honest enough with myself to know that it should not have happened. When you are going as well as I was, you do not take a chance by following the horse in front so closely; and we had definitely been going to win. It was likely that next time out in similar company, we would.

The other jockey had only been winded. I helped him walk back to the changing room where the doctor had a look at him and declared him shaken but undamaged.

I went back down to the course to find Georgie leading Cocoa back.

'You okay?' she asked.

I nodded.

'Thank God you rolled clear.'

'Yes,' I agreed. 'Is Cocoa sound?'

'He seems to be,' Georgie answered, and ran ahead to lead him into a trot for half a dozen paces.

He was moving easily and straight. I nodded my head in satisfaction as Georgie came to a halt and waited for me to catch up.

'What a shame,' she said. 'He was going so beautifully. He only made one mistake as far as I could see, and you were going to win.'

'I know,' I agreed ruefully. 'I haven't looked yet but I presume Damian won?'

'By default, jammy little sod.'

'Don't you like him either?' I asked.

'No, he's a spoilt brat. By the way, his sister didn't seem very pleased to see me leading you round. She gave me a very unfriendly look as we came out, and she didn't seem too pleased with you either. She must think that whatever happened last weekend meant rather more than you did. Or did she?'

'Maybe. I don't know. I've said all I'm going to say about that. But I do have to go and have a word with Damian. With luck she'll have gone by now.'

'Why do you have to see him?'

'He said he wanted to speak to me, presumably about the Consul, but I might be able to find out more about his father.'

'Don't for God's sake make it too obvious. The last thing you want is Clive Drury suspecting you know anything.'

'Sure, I'll be careful.' We took Cocoa back to the box. I changed out of my racing gear and told Georgie that I would go along to Damian Drury's box.

She nodded moodily. I smiled. 'Amanda won't be there. I won't be long.'

I found Damian helping his groom to sponge down his horse. He had not changed yet and still looked gleeful at his recent win.

'Well done, Damian. I bet you didn't expect that.'

Damian grinned sheepishly. 'That's the way it goes.'

'Sure,' I conceded, 'some of my best wins have been behind falling leaders.'

Damian abandoned the scraper with which he was taking surplus water off his horse's flanks. 'Come into the box and have a drink,' he invited, leading the way up the steps into the front section of the lorry.

78

I followed him up. The so-called groom's quarters were fitted out like a state-of-the-art American motor home. All the woodwork was solid oak. The upholstery was in a heavy, modern tapestry. One side was fitted out as a small kitchen, with hobs, ovens and fridges. A tall wardrobe with its door open revealed Damian's change of clothes hanging, neat and well pressed. Beneath it, stuffed into a large canvas bag, was the rest of his racing paraphernalia beside an old Round-Up weedkiller flagon with 'Hoof Oil' scrawled on it.

Damian opened a fridge and took out a bottle of '84 Dom Perignon worth at least half the prize money he had just won.

'I always bring one along, just in case,' he said. He even had a set of clean champagne flutes in a rack. He filled two and handed one to me.

I nodded his good health and took a sip. It was better than a cup of cold tea.

'Has Amanda gone?' I asked.

'Yes,' Damian grinned. 'She went off in a huff. I hadn't realised you two had got it together.'

'It depends on what you mean by got it together. Anyway,' I went on, 'what did you want to talk to me about?'

'Sit down,' he said.

I lolled comfortably in the deep upholstery, but Damian sat on the edge of his seat looking tense. I regarded him, I hoped without expression, and studied him closely for the first time.

He was stockily built and not much more than five foot eight, but he probably had as much trouble as I doing even the generous weights of amateur racing. His features were not without character, but there was a wary, cowed look to his eyes. In his thick, black eyebrows and chunky jaw he was very similar to his father of whom he was altogether a more compact version.

'Look,' he began, 'I know my father tried to persuade you to sell Caesar's Consul. I told him you wouldn't, but I said the only way he might succeed was to wrap it up as part of another deal.'

'So I gather.'

'I don't blame you. You want to win as much as I do. You've got your reasons, I've got mine. I want to tell you about mine. I enjoy all this well enough, but frankly, my main reason for doing it is because it's the only way I can keep my father from persecuting me. He's a fucking monster,' Damian said bleakly.

'So why not just move out and go your own way?' I asked, assuming it was the thought of his father's money that would not let him do it.

'Good God! Do you think he'd leave it there? He'd make my life a misery, wherever I went. I tell you, he's got no feelings for anyone. I know behind his back everyone still says how uncouth he is. They think that the richer he gets, the more civilised he should become. Frankly, exactly the opposite's true. Now he thinks he's immune to the law. As far as he's concerned, money can buy everything. He's made up his mind that I'm going to win the championship.' Damian stopped.

'Even if he has to buy it, you mean?' I asked.

'Precisely,' Damian nodded. 'And Caesar's Consul looks invincible. So if he can't buy him, he'll stop him.'

'I didn't know it was as bad as that.'

'Well take my word for it.'

'Why are you telling me? Don't you want to win?'

'Yes, I do, though I'm not obsessive about it like you, which probably means I never will. And I'd only like to do it on fair terms.'

'There are no such things. The man with the longer purse is always going to have an advantage. He can field more horses and, on the whole, he can buy the best.'

'Of course, but at least that's all above board and open, and it's no guarantee.'

'No, thank God, or I wouldn't stand a chance.'

'And why are you so concerned about it?'

'I love racing, and I enjoy winning.'

'It can't just be that. Somebody told me there was some old rivalry between you and the Prideaux-Jameses.'

'There's that, too,' I admitted.

Damian refilled our glasses. I took the opportunity to delve into other areas.

'Tell me, Damian, what does your mother have to say about your father's despotism?'

'Ma? She's a spent force as far as he's concerned. I don't think she ever had any influence over him. He married her because she looked the part, and gave him a bit of class. Since then he's completely terrorised her into thinking whatever he tells her to. She'd never admit it, but I'm not sure that he didn't use to beat her up. There were times when we were younger when he'd yell at her for hours, then she'd stay in her room for a few days, seeing no one. Poor woman, sometimes I think she wants to let it all out, but she daren't.'

'Was your father married before?'

Damian hesitated. 'Yes, I think so. He's never spoken about it, but I once saw a letter in his office from a firm of solicitors confirming that they had bought a house on his behalf for a Doreen Duckett. Dad used to be called Duckett, though for God's sake don't tell anyone I told you. She could be a sister I suppose, but not his mother; she died in the early 'fifties, I think. But he would never tell us anything about it.'

I wanted to ask more, but I did not want to arouse Damian's suspicions. Besides, I did not think he knew much more. It would have been helpful to know where Doreen Duckett lived.

'Where was the house?' I asked.

'Somewhere in Lewisham, I think. Why?'

'I just wondered. It seems so incredible that he might have had another family and not told you about it.'

'It's typical of the way he treats people, I'm afraid.'

'Look,' I glanced at my watch, 'I'd better get back; I've left Georgie Henry with the horse. You've got two or three good horses now. You stand a good chance of getting near the top this season, but if I have a fall, and get put out of action, you've got the rides on the Consul.'

Damian did not try to disguise his excitement. 'Christ, that's bloody good of you. Why should you do that?'

'I don't know, really. In a way, it would be poking your father in the eye.'

'Yes,' Damian nodded. 'Because he'd have to be grateful to you. He'd hate that.'

'That's what I thought.' I said as I jumped down from the box. 'Mind you, I intend to stay in one piece.'

Chapter 6

On the way home, darkness fell and, in the warmth of the cab and the glow of the Cuban cigar to which I had treated myself, Georgie and I talked about Clive Drury and how he could be dealt with.

Her eagerness alarmed me. I had vaguely, rather weakly, intended that she should be some kind of confidante, rather than a co-conspirator. But she had at least as much right as I to want justice for her natural father, and she made it clear that she would not be happy until justice had been done.

Although, on the face of it, Georgie was a more or less archetypal Sloane Ranger, she was more intelligent and better educated than most of that type. She had a good degree from Exeter University, and worked now as a junior editor at a small publisher. She had no need of the salary, but she claimed that the job gave some structure to her life. Though she was honest and direct, she was not entirely naive. Her good looks, and her money, meant that she was used to being pursued, and I had witnessed her adeptness at deflecting pursuers in a firm but not unfriendly way.

Now, as she talked, I found myself taking her seriously and, for the first time, seriously fancying her. The determination with which she approached our task showed a new side to her. In the headlights of oncoming vehicles, her brow wrinkled and her shapely, set chin revealed a character I had not seen in her before. She was, to me, in these circumstances, as attractive as I had ever seen her.

She had two friends, she said, who might be able to help us. I would meet them at Temple Ferris the following weekend. One was a journalist, and the other a dare-devil young Irishman, trained as an actor but more interested in real-life drama.

'How can they help?' I asked.

'I don't know, but there may be a way we can use Sean to catch Drury out, and Jamie Lloyd-Jones works for the *Sun*; he's used to digging around for any muck which may stick to the rich and famous.'

'Okay, but don't tell them anything about this until I've met them. I'll try to work out a plan this week. I'm going to a party at Drury's in London on Tuesday. That might yield something.'

'Did he ask you?'

'No,' I admitted. 'Amanda did.'

We arrived back at the farmhouse and unloaded Cocoa. He seemed to have travelled better this time and ambled into his stable, heading straight for the bucket of dampened sugar beet and oats that Sharon had left for him.

We checked the others, and all was well. I invited Georgie in for a drink and some early supper.

'I suppose that means I'll have to make it,' she said.

'Would you?' I asked. 'At least it would be edible then. I'll open a bottle.'

Georgie bustled around my kitchen and, as if by magic, produced a bowl of succulent *gnocchi* in a delicious sauce made up of various bits and pieces she had found.

I uncorked a bottle of Barolo to underpin the meal, and sat drinking the first couple of glasses while she cooked.

'God, you're useless!' she said.

The heavy Italian wine warmed and mellowed me. I stood up and walked across the kitchen to wrap my arms around her waist from behind. I touched the back of her neck with my lips.

I felt her tense at this first advance I had ever made.

'Food is all you're getting from me this evening. You can satisfy your other urges with Amanda,' she said with husky brusqueness.

'I told you, Georgie, that was a one-off.'

'Was it? Well I dare say you know a few more Amandas.'

I gave her a squeeze and released her with a philosophical laugh. 'Yes, but I'm trying to give them up.'

Georgie turned and looked me straight in the eye. 'Let me know when you have.'

I could not help grinning, and, as we ate, I could sense a new, warm intimacy between us. I did not make any more suggestions, or advances, and when she announced after two pots of strong coffee that she was going to go back to Gloucestershire, I did not try to dissuade her. I walked out to her car and gave her the customary peck on both cheeks.

I watched the lights of her car disappear down the lane, frustrated but confident that patience would yield a rich reward.

As I went back into the house, my thoughts returned to Clive Drury and the ways in which a man of his wealth, influence and connections could be damaged by someone of such meagre resources as myself.

Clive Drury lived in one of those vast Chelsea houses that you do not know exist until you have been invited to them. It was hidden behind a twelve-foot wall of ancient brick.

One of a pair of high black gates was open, with a security man checking the guests as they entered and walked up beneath an awning to the front door. The house had been built for a northern duke in what, two hundred years before, had been an area of intensive market gardening which supplied the needs of the great city a mile or so down the river.

Now it allowed all the convenience of living in London with the privacy of a small country manor. It was a beautiful house, and a man like Clive Drury ought not to have been living in it.

I told the doorman who I was. I thought Amanda might have withdrawn her invitation, in view of her sulky performance at the races the previous Saturday. But evidently my name appeared on the doorman's list. He ticked it off and nodded me through.

There were sixty or seventy people gathered in a large drawing room. I recognised a cabinet minister, the rector of the RCA, a recently knighted actor and several well-known racehorse trainers. Immaculate waiters handed round glasses of champagne or offered to fetch any drink the guests wanted.

I asked for a whisky and soda, and a voice behind me said, 'Quite right, Archie. I find too much champagne makes one fart.'

I turned to find Harry Winchcombe.

Harry was an ex-cavalry officer, a year or two older than myself. His father was a member of the Jockey Club, and Harry had been an enthusiastic, though not too successful, amateur rider. Now he was the manager of a small Sussex racecourse. He was famous for his coarse joviality and a prodigious appetite for dumb, decorative women.

'I'm not interested in the causes of your flatulence, Harry,' I laughed, 'though I'm sure it always made you go faster when you were racing.'

'Yes, I think it did.' He glanced around the room as he spoke. 'Hhm,' he grunted, 'the crumpet around here is rather senior tonight; a wide selection of high-mileage models.'

'And a few of those have already had their clocks wound back,' I remarked.

'Yes,' Harry grinned, and returned to racing. 'I see you keep falling off. The repulsive Prideaux-Jameses will catch you up if you don't learn to stay on.'

'Our host's son is still ahead of them, though God knows he doesn't deserve it. He only won on Saturday because I was brought down.'

'You mean the drab little Damian?' Harry nodded in the direction of Damian Drury, who was standing on the other side of the room, talking to one of his father's trainers.

'Yes, though I suppose one shouldn't be too hard on him. I don't think he enjoys it that much, but he's not a bad jockey, and from what he told me, his father terrorised him into racing; preferably winning.'

'Drury Senior's a fairly revolting specimen,' remarked Harry.

We looked a few yards to Damian's left, where our host was holding court with the politician and his tired-looking wife. He was bestowing his approval with a slow nod of his large head. His jaw and his thick, black bushy eyebrows jutted out from his face. He boomed with laughter as his eyes swept around the room, and briefly narrowed as they spotted me.

'He doesn't look too chuffed to see you, Archie.'

'No,' I agreed. 'His daughter asked me, and I don't think she's too pleased with me either.'

'You haven't been sniffing around there, have you? She suffers from seriously weak knicker elastic.'

'I don't think she ever wears knickers.'

Harry laughed. 'I wouldn't mind a crack at it, but I wouldn't want to get on the wrong side of Clive Drury. I should think he can play very rough. Anyway, I got the impression Amanda was into rough trade.'

'Thanks.' I acknowledged the jibe. 'It's more a question of anything to annoy her father, I suspect. Have you had any dealings with Drury?' I asked, taking the opportunity to concentrate on my purpose in coming to this party.

'A few. In fact, I'm surprised he asked me here. I was largely responsible for persuading the owners of my course not to sell it to him.'

'I'd heard he was prowling around looking for crippled race-courses to buy.'

'Only in the South of England. He's spent a fortune putting down the all-weather track at his course, and I think he just wants to buy up all the opposition to close them down because people aren't taking his seriously enough.'

'Good God, that's a bit over the top. After all, his course can only be a tiny fraction of his investments. What are the finances of yours like at the moment?' It was a second-eleven jumping course with no more than fifteen days' racing a year.

'Not good,' Harry replied gloomily. 'My bosses are hopping at the moment. We've just spent a pile of money re-turfing and re-seeding. As you know, grass grows well in our part of the world, and I've had thousands of gallons of fertiliser flung at it, but it's going backwards. It's all going brown and dying.'

'Have you had the soil tested?'

Harry nodded. 'Yes, I'm waiting for the results.'

As he spoke, Amanda appeared beside us. I ignored the gleam of triumph in her eyes as she stretched up to exchange greeting kisses.

'I am glad you could come, Archie.'

'Are you?' I asked.

'Of course I am,' she almost purred. 'As long as I don't have to share you with half the Sloane Rangers in London.'

'Are you referring to your old flat-mate?'

'The Honourable Jolly-Hockey-Sticks Georgina. Even you won't get your leg over that.'

Harry was looking on at this conversation with glee.

'Talking of leg-overs, Mandy, can you tell me who that delicious-looking piece of junior crumpet is who's just walked in?'

'I'll do more than that; I'll introduce you to her,' Amanda said. 'Anything to keep your groping hands off me.'

She led him away across the room. There was an excited,

fatuous smile on his face. I grinned to myself and turned to the group beside me.

I had not seen them come in. There were three of them. Two were tall and thin, with lanky hair that tended to fall across their faces. They were brothers, not twins, but they behaved like twins; they knew there was strength in numbers. They both had the habit of constantly flicking back their blond hair with an arrogant tilt of the head, allowing them to look down their long, beaky noses with a permanently unpleasant sneer on their small mouths.

It was an expression I had known and detested for nearly twenty years. My adolescence at school had been made a misery by Richard and Robert Prideaux-James.

'Good Lord, Dick, do you see what I see? It's Archibald Beast.'

I looked into the two pairs of eyes, and knew I should turn and walk away. These people were not worth my pity, let alone my hate. But they held a horrible fascination for me. I longed to see them writhe with humiliation, preferably inflicted by me. It was a juvenile obsession, but it was an obsession.

'Ah, Pinky and Perky, the pantomime horse,' I declared.

'You creep,' uttered Robert. 'You couldn't even stay on a pantomime horse.'

'I wouldn't know, but if you were the arse end of it, I'd give it a good hiding before I came off.'

'Don't be so fucking cocky, Beast. You've had your share of flukes for this season. If Damian Drury can beat you, I can't see that we're going to have much trouble. We've been saving our good horses till now.'

We all knew this was nonsense, but it did not seem worth challenging; there would be plenty of chances to do that on the racecourse.

'I hope you've got someone good to ride them.'

I had noticed the third member of their group, whom I did not know, becoming embarrassed. He was short and swarthy with dark brown eyes. He was not English or, I thought, Irish. I turned to him, ignoring any reaction from the Prideaux-Jameses.

'We haven't met. I'm Archie Best.'

The man looked relieved that normal social behaviour had been re-established. The brothers were momentarily put out. They had evidently overlooked his presence, and thought better now of pursuing their hobby of baiting me.

The dark man shook the hand I had offered him. 'I'm Michel de Mosnay.'

I knew his name at once. He ran the Mount Edward Stud in County Waterford, where three of Europe's most expensive stallions stood.

The Prideaux-Jameses flicked their hair out of their eyes and said, 'We'll see you later, Michel,' and pointedly turned to walk towards Clive Drury.

'I hope not,' Michel de Mosnay said quietly to their departing backs.

'Did you come with them?' I asked.

'I'm afraid I did. I have been staying with their father.'

That was understandable. Sir Cyril Prideaux-James was a perfectly affable man and an influential owner. He also held a quarter of the shares in Mount Edward's top stallion.

'You find the sons less palatable than the father then?'

He laughed. The question did not need answering.

'That was a strange conversation you were having with them,' he said. 'You sounded like schoolboys.'

'That's about right. I was at school with them and they've always brought out the worst in me, however hard I try to ignore them. It must sound terrible. But what brings you to Clive Drury's then?' I went on.

He shrugged. 'I was in London, arranging a new syndication, and he asked me. He has ten shares in Tomahawk.'

'Has he, by God? I had no idea.'

Tomahawk had been the star young stallion for his first covering season. He had had a tremendous three-year-old racing career which culminated in his winning the Prix de L'Arc de Triomphe. After that, his owner had taken a large and popular gamble in having him trained on as a four year old, when he had obliged in the Eclipse, the King George and Queen Elizabeth, and the Arc for a second time. He was Europe's number one horse when he had been retired to go to stud two years before. He had been syndicated, in other words his ownership had been divided into forty shares, with a value of twelve million dollars, and Clive Drury had a quarter of them.

It probably looked like a good investment at the time, but two factors had subsequently taken the gilt off shares in Tomahawk.

One was general to the bloodstock breeding business as a whole. Now that the big influx of Arab owners had their own proven mares and stallions, they were tending to breed most of their own young stock, rather than buy it in the big public auctions at Goff's in Dublin or Tattersall's in England. The recent recession had seen many of the traditional buyers tightening their belts and the heady days were over for every type of bloodstock breeder. Sending a top mare to be covered for a hundred thousand pounds had begun to look a distinctly risky proposition, and the rate card for all stallions had been heavily modified, downwards.

Added to this, in the case of Tomahawk, not all the choice mares he had covered in his first season had got in foal. This could, of course, have been the fault of the mares, but the proportion of failures was high enough to be ominous.

Reports of his first foals that had been born, yearlings now and due to be sold that autumn, were not encouraging. Of the twenty-five, there were none rumoured to be outstanding. The chances were that most breeders who had used Tomahawk would not be sending mares back to him – certainly not at his original tariff – and his capital value now was probably a quarter of what it was when he had been syndicated.

His buying shares in Tomahawk must have been one of the worst investments Clive Drury had ever made. He must have been kicking himself and, even harder, anyone else he thought he could blame for it.

I smiled at the thought, and an idea began to take shape.

'He can't be too chuffed about that,' I said to the Frenchman.

'Excuse me?' he answered.

'I said that Drury must be feeling a bit unhappy about his investment.'

'Of course he is not happy. But,' de Mosnay shrugged, 'that is normal with bloodstock. He was offered shares in better, cheaper stallions, but he wanted to own the star. For me, I would never buy into an unproven stallion.'

De Mosnay was paid simply to run the stud. It did not make a great deal of difference to him how much owners were prepared to pay to have their mares served by his charges.

I continued talking to him for a while about the other horses on his stud and prospects for the autumn sales. It would be a long time, if ever, before I would be making use of the services of the

Mount Edward Stud, but it was always useful to know what was going on.

We parted with his inviting me to come and look at the stud any time I liked. And I invited him to meet me after the Foxhunter Chase on Gold Cup day at Cheltenham, but I resisted the temptation to tell him to meet me in the winners' enclosure.

'Make sure you beat those two skinny bastards,' he said in his French-inflected stable-lad English, nodding at the Prideaux-Jameses.

As I looked around, thinking about rejoining Harry Winchcombe, who was tucked in a corner with the piece of junior crumpet he had spotted, I felt a hand squeeze my buttocks.

'Hello, Archie Beast,' Amanda said in my ear.

'You've been talking to the Prideaux-Jerks.'

'Yes,' she made a face. 'They're sucking up to my father. I think they're trying to fob him off with a couple of donkeys for Damian. Would you believe my father's impressed by their kind of brainless snottiness. I think he's fascinated that such idiots manage to stay rich. He wants to see you, too,' she added.

'He didn't seem remotely pleased to see me when I came in.'

'Well, he's changed his mind. Come over and deal with him now, then we can get out of here and go somewhere a bit more exciting.'

I thought of Georgie, briefly, then I thought of the advantages of staying on good terms with Amanda, and I looked at the dimpled cheeks, and the pouted invitation on her lips.

'Okay,' I said.

Clive Drury was Mr Amiable now.

'How are you, Archie? Good to see you. I didn't know you were coming until Amanda told me. I gather you're taking her on to dinner afterwards. Look, I want you to go ahead and get those two pictures for me. My secretary will send you formal instructions and terms tomorrow.' He raised his hand, as if anticipating my objections. 'No strings, though I'll always be glad to make you an offer for Caesar's Consul, when you're ready.'

I did not know what he was up to, but I nodded my agreement, and said I looked forward to doing the deal. The exchange of a few more inconsequential remarks completed the conversation. We said goodbye and shook hands. Amanda tugged at my arm to lead me towards the door.

'Hang on a minute,' I said, 'I must have a quick word with Harry Winchcombe before I go.'

'Don't be long; I'm feeling very horny.'

I reluctantly admitted to myself that I was too, but I found Harry and dragged him away from the girl he was almost eating by now.

'I'm off. I just wondered if you'd mind letting me know the results of your soil test, when you get them.'

Harry looked puzzled. 'Sure, but why?'

'I'll let you know. See you.'

Amanda wanted to go straight to her own house, a few streets further down the King's Road.

I wanted to take her to dinner, somewhere noisy where we would not be too noticed and I could ask her a few questions.

She suggested without much subtlety that we went back to her place to work up an appetite first. I was tempted, but I guessed we would not get out again until all the restaurants in Chelsea were closed. And I had to be up early next morning to get back for my race in Herefordshire.

'No,' I insisted. 'You must eat first. I don't want you suddenly feeling like a bite at the wrong moment.'

We went to an Italian restaurant where the food was passable and cheap, and the tables crowded and noisy. There were a few people we knew there, but, thankfully, none who were likely to inflict their presence on us.

Amanda sat opposite me and ploughed her way happily through a pile of *taglierini*, stopping every so often to stretch her hand beneath the small table to grasp my excitable genitals.

I tried not to drink too much wine, and to concentrate.

Casually, I asked, as I had done Damian, 'How does your mother put up with being married to someone like your father?'

'Ma? She's all right now. He hardly notices her. He yells at her occasionally if things aren't going well in business. I suppose he jumps on top of her in bed now and again, though he usually relies on a few tarty mistresses for that sort of thing. She gave up trying to influence him years ago.'

'Was he ever married before?'

Amanda laughed. 'Yes, and he's dead ashamed of it. But no one's allowed to mention it, on pain of death. I wish I could find

92

out who she was and threaten him with revelation. I'd have him by the goolies then.'

'Haven't you any idea?'

'No, though I imagine it must have been some poor little East End girl. He must be paying her to keep her quiet.'

'Or he's scared the hell out of her,' I suggested.

'Or that.'

'Do you know if she had any children by him?' I asked.

'Some big cockney half-brothers? That'd be a laugh, but I've never heard anything like that. Why do you want to know?'

'Your father is so awful that he's rather fascinating. I don't think I've ever met anyone as ruthlessly self-serving.'

'You should meet a few of his cronies, then. And some of the most upright-looking toffs are the worst of the lot, but I suppose they're brought up to be a bloody sight more subtle about it.'

I probed a little more, but did not gain much beyond the idea that Amanda could be a willing and useful ally in the right circumstances.

We sat around for a while after dinner, drinking sambucca, the potential after-effects of which I deliberately weakened with large intakes of fizzy San Pellegrino water. But we did not linger too long – Amanda was becoming impatient – and by half-past ten we were in the bedroom of her small but immaculately converted early-nineteenth-century workers' cottage in a highly fashionable Chelsea cul-de-sac.

Amanda put some soul music on the CD player, poured two large armagnacs and pulled her clothes off with a few deft movements. She lay on the bed, her back propped against a chintz headboard, to watch me undress.

I removed my clothes more decorously than she had, but the sight of her waiting, warm, naked body on the bed denied me any control over the surging in my groin. I lowered my trousers as nonchalantly as I could and kicked them to one side. My underpants proved trickier. As I unhooked them from an uncompromising erection and slid them off my legs, Amanda gurgled.

'My goodness! He's been putting on a lot of weight. It's going to take an awful lot of exercise to get that back to normal.'

* * *

93

I did not know what time it was when I woke, but I knew I wanted to leave.

Judging from the absence of traffic noise from the King's Road a hundred yards away, it was about three. I could feel Amanda's soft buttocks against my thigh, and there was a momentary twitch in my cock which nearly made me change my plans. But I talked myself out of it. Amanda seemed to be sleeping deeply and it would be easier to go now, without disturbing her.

In the darkness this time, I managed to gather up all my clothes without waking her and let myself out of the bedroom. I dressed by the light of the street lamps in the small drawing room. I fumbled around with three locks on the front door and let myself out into the chilly silent night.

My echoing footsteps sounded so loud I thought that I might wake Amanda, and I quickened my pace up to the main road. I found my car where I had left it near her father's house. I had to scrape a thin layer of frost from the windscreen and prayed that the old car would not let me down.

After a couple of reluctant tries, it burst into life and I set off through the empty streets towards the M40.

From Perivale to Oxford, the needle on my speedo did not drop much below a hundred and ten. Within an hour of leaving London, I was dropping off the Cotswolds outside Gloucester. It was only the small Herefordshire lanes beyond there that forced me back to a more pedestrian pace. At a quarter to five, I turned into the no-through-road that led only to my farmhouse and my two neighbours.

This is where we came in.

I saw the stock lorry in which Caesar's Consul was being abducted, intervened, and ended up being walloped on the back of the head.

I was left lying senseless at the side of the lane.

Chapter 7

When I next opened my eyes, the scene before me was lit by the beginnings of gloomy, grey daylight.

For a moment, I could not think where I was. The last thing I remembered, with some pleasure, was lying beside Amanda, her big breasts across my chest. Then the journey and events that had intervened came groggily back to me.

I shivered in the damp morning air and turned my head painfully to see what had happened. The lorry was gone, and my car, with a nasty gouge down one side, was lying in the ditch.

I shook my head violently in an attempt to clear it; this made things worse. But I had to get myself together, and see if the Consul was still at home. Then, with a sinking heart, I heard the sound of a lorry rumbling down the lane towards me.

When it came round a bend into view, I breathed a sigh of relief.

The vehicle stopped a few feet short of where I was lying. I saw a pair of wellington boots emerge from the cab and walk towards me.

'Bloody hell, Archie. What you doing there? Had a few too many last night?'

I lifted my head and smiled with a wince.

'Morning, Harold. I was trying to stop someone stealing the Consul.'

'Bloody 'eck!' the farmer exclaimed. 'Has 'e gone?'

'I don't know. I was walloped on the head about five and I've only just come round. What's the time now?'

'Half six.' He leaned down and grabbed me under the arms. 'Come on. I'll take you back.'

'No, don't worry about me. I'm sure you've got other things to do.'

I was on my feet now, stretching the pins and needles out of my legs.

'Bollocks. It's only a few old ewes for market. I may as well get fuck all for 'em next week as this.' He helped me towards his lorry, and by the time I reached it I seemed to be functioning normally. 'All I was worried about was gettin' away from the market in time to see you ride the Consul at Gazeley. D'you reckon you can?'

'Provided I've still got the bloody horse.'

We clambered up into the cab. Harold put the motor into reverse and careered recklessly backwards up the lane for the four hundred yards or so to the entrance to my yard. With skilled abandon, he backed straight through the gate, then jammed on the brakes with a jerk, unconcerned about his bleating passengers.

I leaped out. There was no sign of the Consul in the yard. His stable door was open. I ran across, looked in and almost fainted with relief. He was standing passively, his quilted rug a little askew, his headcollar rope trailing around his front legs, tugging the last few strands from his hay net. I flung my arms around his neck and rubbed my cheek against it. He carried on munching, evidently quite unfazed by his outing.

Harold came in more slowly. 'He looks ready for a race. I'm not so sure about you, though. D'you give him a feed on race days?'

'Yeah, a few crushed oats and a bit of hay.'

'Right. We'll do that later. Let's go inside and get you sorted out. You better ring the police.'

I nodded and let go of my horse with a pat. I came out of the stable to find the sun feebly trying to penetrate the clouds above the hills to the east. The blackbirds and thrushes were attempting a little early spring song. I took in a couple of large lungfuls of air.

'Okay,' I said. 'Let's get some coffee on.'

Harold, with more brandy than coffee inside him, left when Sharon arrived at half-past seven. He had decided that there was still time to get to market and get his ewes sold before coming on to the races. Such was his enthusiasm by now that he was planning an alarmingly large wager on me and the Consul. I pleaded with him that, if he had to do it, to leave it until a moment before the off.

Sharon came into the kitchen, wide-eyed and puzzled by all this early activity.

'Cor! You look bloody terrible,' she said with her customary lack of finesse.

I had not told Harold who I thought was behind the attempted kidnapping of my horse, and I thought it wise not to tell Sharon either, but I told her what had happened since I met the lorry coming down the lane at five that morning.

'Hell, man, who'd do that? It's got to be someone who's riding against you today. Let's look at the entry.'

'It may not have been. Someone might have wanted him for a ringer for another race. God knows who it was.'

'What do the police say?'

'Not much. It was dark. I couldn't even tell them what make of lorry it was, let alone a number. And he'd have been gone an hour or so before I told them. They're coming up here, but . . .' I shrugged, and I meant it. I did not think they would discover much; and at this stage, I did not want them to.

'What were you doin', gettin' back at five o'clock on a race day?'

'I'd been in London. It was probably a mistake, but there it is.'

'Well, you go and get some sleep. I'll do all the horses, and I'll wake you when the police come.'

'I think I've drunk too much coffee to get any sleep now, but I'll have a bath and see what happens.'

A small red-faced constable arrived from Bromyard shortly after eleven. Sharon had to shake me a few times to rouse me from where I slumbered in a bathrobe on my bed.

I had a quick cold shower before going down to see him, feeling almost human.

He told me that he was called Jim Lewis, and, not surprisingly, that he had no news of the lorry. I tried him on a sketchy description of the driver, but that produced no result.

'Have you any idea who it might have been?' he finally asked me. 'A rival, maybe, or someone with a grudge?'

'Obviously I've thought about that, but no one in particular comes to mind. It's not as though we're talking about Derby horses here. There's no big money involved in point-to-pointing. And while I'm not claiming universal popularity, I don't think anyone loathes me enough to go to this amount of trouble.'

'And you were due to ride the horse today?'

'Due to? I *am* riding him today, and with a good chance of winning.'

'Could it have been one of the other jockeys?'

'I doubt it, but here's a list of the runners and riders.' I shoved it across the table to him. 'You could always come to the races and have a look at them.'

'I don't know if the station sergeant would agree to that; sounds too much like pleasure.'

'Well, anyway, I don't think it was any of them.'

'I'm sorry we haven't come up with anything yet, sir, and I'm afraid there's not a lot to go on. But we'll make some more enquiries, and you let us know if you think of anything.' Constable Lewis stood up. 'And best of luck this afternoon. At least you've still got the horse; that's the main thing, and no one was seriously hurt.'

'No, not seriously, though I'm still a bit sore.'

'I wouldn't take any chances with a smack on the head like that. Why don't you get someone else to ride your horse?'

'Ah, well. Riding the animals is the whole point of it, as far as I'm concerned.'

'Look after yourself, sir. We'll be in touch, then,' he added doubtfully.

'Thanks,' I said, and showed him out.

When he had left the yard in his small white police car, Sharon came back in.

'Did he have any news?'

'No,' I said. 'But I didn't expect him to. Now let's start getting this animal ready.'

At a Wednesday point-to-point meeting, there are always fewer spectators than on a Saturday, but most of them, having taken the trouble to sneak off from the farm or slipped away from work for the day, know what to expect.

It came as no surprise to anyone that Caesar's Consul won the Open Race, least of all the bookies who, by the off, had marked it at three to one on, if they were prepared to take a bet on him at all.

But I was euphoric. If, at half past six that morning when I came to with a crashing head and serious doubts as to whether or not I still had the horse, anyone had told me that I was going to win, I would have accused them of outrageous optimism.

Sharon came out on the course as we trotted back from the finish. She clipped a rope on to the Consul's bit and led him proudly back to the winner's spot in the paddock.

As she led him, she patted and nuzzled him. 'Well done, Consul, you lovely boy. You jumped beautiful.'

'What about me?' I asked from his back.

'You? The state you're in, all you had to do was sit on him. He done all the work.'

I laughed. She was right. I was already utterly exhausted. I had been approached when I arrived to ride another horse in the maiden, but was talked out of it by Sharon. 'Thank God I didn't take that other ride. I don't think I could even get my leg over now.'

'That'd make a change,' she grinned.

When we came into the paddock, there was a flutter of applause and a few cheers. Before I slid off the Consul's back, I looked around for Clive Drury. He was listed on the race-card as a steward, but I had not seen him earlier, so I guessed he had ducked out of officiating at this particular meeting in his own park. That ought to have been very surprising.

His wife gave me the cup. 'Well done, Mr Best,' she said graciously. 'My son was hoping he might win today.'

Damian had run well into third place.

'I can't always fall off to let him through,' I said lightly, while I wondered if it was possible that Damian knew what had happened during the night.

Sharon and I were drying off the horse by the lorry when Jim Lewis, the policeman from Bromyard appeared, in plain clothes now.

He was wearing a flat cap and a waxed jacket. He could have passed for any Herefordshire farmer taking a day off.

'Hello, Mr Best. That was a good ride. I even ventured a small bet on you myself.'

'Do they encourage you to go gambling while on duty?'

The policeman laughed. 'No, but I'm not on duty. I got the

afternoon off, but I came to do a bit of crime prevention, like. I reckoned if I could find out who tried to pinch your horse last night, we could discourage him from trying again.'

'Did you find anything out?'

'No. I had a good long look at all the jockeys and their connections. None of them seemed surprised or annoyed to see you there. Far from it. As far as I could tell, they were all resigned to you winning.'

'The bookies, what about the bookies?'

'No. Most of 'em had you marked at odds on before they'd started taking any money. Anyway, there's never enough at stake in point-to-points for them to bother with nobbling.'

He asked a few more questions, about security at my yard, then left with a quick tug on the front of his cap.

'Bloody useless,' Sharon said scornfully when he was out of earshot.

'Well, at least he's trying; in his own time too.'

And at least he's not succeeding – I thought to myself. The last thing I wanted now was Clive Drury being alerted to suspicions harboured by the Bromyard police.

The next day I drove to London. I avoided most of the central traffic by heading south of the river and coming back across Tower Bridge, to park in one of the small streets in Wapping.

Fifteen minutes' brisk walk brought me to the new Lloyd's building, looming with confident, arrogant modernism between its pompous Victorian neighbours.

I asked one of the anachronistically attired 'waiters' the way to the offices of J J Stewart, brokers and members' agents.

It was just before one and Johnny Stewart was expecting me.

I already had a woolly idea of what went on in Lloyd's, but, never having had the required capital to become a member, I had never had its arcane workings explained to me in detail.

In the knowledge that Lloyd's of London had provided the bedrock to Clive Drury's fortune, I thought it wise to find out more about its workings. I had flicked through my address books to find someone I knew close to the centre of this mystifying institution. And I had soon come up with one.

I had first met Johnny Stewart, scion of a Scottish land-owning family and enthusiastic follower of jumping horses, in my early

days at Oxford. He was clever, witty and articulate. He had made
the decision that if he was ever to keep a roof on his family home,
he would have to spend a few years in the City making money
before settling down to the dubious pleasures of the Highlands. A
happy mix of intelligence and charm had suited him admirably for
the curiously personal way in which Lloyd's works.

Johnny greeted me with a firm friendly shake of his hand and a
quizzical look.

'So, what brings you here?' he asked. 'I take it you're not
thinking of joining.'

'Is my continuing impecuniosity so obvious?'

Johnny glanced at the threadbare edges of my old cashmere
coat. 'Yes. Perhaps you'd better turn professional.'

'Not much call for six-foot jockeys,' I said. 'Anyway, you're
right, I don't want to join. But for reasons I won't bore you with,
I need to know a bit about how this place is run. Not the full
degree course, more a short foundation course.'

'Well, I hope you've got good reasons, because it could take a
while.'

'I said a short course, please.'

'Okay, as long as it takes to eat the lunch you're going to buy
me.

'Broadly speaking,' Johnny began, 'Lloyd's works like this. You
have assets that are earning for you in the normal way; shares
producing dividends, property producing rent or whatever. You
can earn additional income from those assets by using them to
underwrite other people's insured risks. In other words, if you
were worth a million quid, you'd be in a position to pay out a
million quid claim. Simplistically, through your working underwriter, you could say to a Greek shipowner, "Okay, your ship's
worth a million pounds. If it sinks, I will pay you a million pounds.
And you pay me, say, five per cent of your ship's worth for taking
that risk." That, as you probably know, is called the premium.
Now to put all your eggs in one basket would be foolish, so you
spread the risk by becoming one of maybe twenty members of a
syndicate who between them can insure risks of twenty times that
size, but they split it up between dozens of different risks, which
are, in turn, split up between twenty or thirty different syndicates.
Are you following so far?'

'Yes,' I said. 'As far as I can see, what you're saying is that Lloyd's is like a giant bookmaker's. If I own a ship, I say to you, "What price will you give me on my ship sinking next year?" to which you reply "Twenty to one, Gov." and I think, "That's a pretty good price, I'll have some of that." So, even if I lose my ship, at least I've won my bet.'

'That's not quite how we like to put it, but that's essentially it. Our actuaries are constantly making books on all the various types of risks people ask us to cover. Right, there are twenty-five thousand individual "names", that's to say, members of Lloyd's, and they all have to be looked after in various ways. A members' agent does that. He advises them on what syndicates they should join and so on. Very often, of course, a members' agent might also be involved in running a syndicate, but he wouldn't, if he was an honourable man, simply push all his names onto it; that doesn't look too good if the syndicate doesn't perform. Okay?'

'Yes,' I nodded. 'People who are taking out insurance presumably pay their premiums at the beginning of the year. That's put into the syndicate's kitty, claims are paid from it and the members divi up the balance at the end of the year.'

'Quite,' said Johnny. 'Though longer-term risks can complicate the issue. Suppose you're an American doctor and you've insured against clients suing you for incompetence, and a leg which you mended three years before goes wrong again as a result of your treatment and the punter comes looking for redress, the premium you paid in the year you treated him covers you. But in simple terms, what you say is right.'

'Okay. What happens to all the premiums before the divi up?'

'The working members of the syndicate – that is, the people who sit in the Room downstairs and actually decide what risks are to be taken and at what rate – can invest for the benefit of the syndicate, until such time as their dividend is due.'

'And that, presumably, can be a great deal of money?'

'Oh yes. Obviously, there are rules that restrict the extent and type of investment, but there's a fair degree of latitude. Sometimes, a syndicate's management may decide to insure against some of their own losses, quite frequently with foreign or off-shore parties who are prepared to underwrite these second-hand risks.'

'So whoever manages the syndicates has control over vast amounts of premium income for quite a while.'

'Within certain bounds, yes.'

'And one man could control several big syndicates, like, for instance, Clive Drury?'

Johnny nodded. 'Like, for instance. Clive Drury. What's your interest in him?'

'If I told you Drury had done a close old friend of mine a great personal disservice, would it surprise you?'

'Not a lot,' Johnny laughed.

'Why? What's his reputation in Lloyd's?'

'Apart from the fact that he's still considered altogether too flashy by many people, including myself, there's nothing specific that can be levelled at him. He's one of the most successful underwriters in Lloyd's. He makes a lot of money for his names. He has a couple of members' agencies as well. His influence is widely felt; and this discourages overt speculation.'

'It would be interesting to know how much scrutiny his activities here would stand. He's in a spot of trouble elsewhere.'

'That you've had a hand in?'

'Yes. I won't go into details, but I wondered if you'd mind delving more deeply into Drury's performance here. If you could dig up some dirt, it would go a long way to supporting my other efforts.'

Johnny looked at me with surprise. 'You've really got it in for him, then? You should be careful with a man like that. I don't suppose I can help much. Drury's an old hand and if he has misbehaved himself, which is perfectly possible, you can be sure he's been very subtle about it. I'll see what I can do, but I'll have to tread very carefully.'

To my frustration, Johnny was not prepared to elaborate more than that, but at least he had agreed to look, and I now had a better idea of how Drury had had access to such vast funds over the years, and why, as Bill had hinted, he liked to shuffle his profits around the world; there would normally have been substantial tax liabilities on the kinds of profits he had reputedly made over the years.

We finished lunch with a couple of large, old armagnacs which I could ill afford, but I thanked Johnny Stewart, and promised I would be back to pester him again for information.

'I wouldn't advise digging too deep into Drury, though,' he warned. 'It is common knowledge that he has a very short temper.'

The time check on Jazz FM gave four o'clock as I crossed back over Tower Bridge towards Lewisham.

I had looked up Ducketts in the London telephone book and found four in the Lewisham area. Armed with this information and a bogus solicitor's letter requiring a signature before certain funds could be released, I had studied the A to Z and worked out a route that covered the four addresses.

The first two were occupied by old women who would willingly have owned up to being Mrs Doreen Duckett if there was a bit of money in it, but they could not prove it. Protective of their own interests in case there was a chance they would still be in the running, they were reluctant to suggest the whereabouts of any other local Ducketts they knew.

There was no one in at the third address, but the place was so squalid and dilapidated that I thought even Clive Drury would not allow his ex-wife to live there. I asked a neighbour who confirmed that it was occupied by a single old man, when he was not in the betting shop in the nearby shopping precinct.

The fourth address, in Airedale Avenue, a tree-lined and substantially gentrified street, produced a studious-looking woman of thirty or so. She was, I guessed, a schoolteacher or a social worker. She invited me in and the titles of the hundreds of books that filled her shelves suggested I was right.

I explained guiltily that I was looking for a Mrs Doreen Duckett, aged about sixty, who had come into some money. I showed her the letter, which she accepted at face value.

'My first name is Deirdre. For several years, I've had letters for a Mrs D. Duckett at Airedale *Road*. It's about a quarter of a mile from here, so I've always re-directed them and posted them back. I think the Post Office sorters must do it almost automatically, and I do receive quite a lot of post,' she added with a touch of self importance. 'Did you have an address there?'

Knowing that I did not, I consulted my list and shook my head. 'No. Perhaps I should try it. Can you remember what sort of letters they were?'

'I don't suppose I ought to tell you, but I can't see any harm. They're usually postcards, from all over the place: Morocco,

Wales, Salisbury. From a son or daughter, I should think,' she admitted.

I thought of the birth certificates in the picture Bill Beecham had bequeathed to me: John Arthur and Diane Marlene. They must be in their late thirties now.

Deirdre Duckett went on. 'One doesn't feel so bad reading postcards, don't you think? I mean, if they were very private, they'd put them in an envelope.'

'Oh yes,' I agreed, 'postcards are traditionally for public consumption. Well, thanks very much for your help,' I said, turning towards the door. 'With luck, this will be the right Mrs Duckett, and you will have done her a considerable service.'

'I am glad,' she said. 'So many of the people round here in are such dire straits these days – with all the cuts.'

I walked down her front path and let myself out of the small wrought-iron gate. I was thankful that I had not found a space to park outside the house. My Mercedes was a hundred yards down the street, out of her sight.

The A to Z quickly revealed the whereabouts of Airedale Road, and I headed off, excited and optimistic.

I easily found the house. It was ordinary-looking and semi-detached, built, probably, in the late 'twenties. It was a patchy neighbourhood, with houses ranging from the neat and well-kept, like this one, to the downright neglected, with old bangers in the front gardens. I drove on and parked round a corner. I walked briskly back, and pretending once again to consult some papers, strode confidently up the short, empty parking area.

I rang the bell beside the sunburst-glazed door and heard an electronic triple chime echo within; but nothing else.

I tried again and waited with growing frustration. I felt sure this was the right house. According to the period over which the mail had been misdirected, this Duckett had lived here for some time, and there was a telephone line to the house, so she was either ex-directory, or the phone was not in her name.

After the third ring and wait, I gave up. I considered asking neighbours about this Mrs Duckett, but decided against it. They might alert her and, possibly therefore, Clive Drury to my interest.

I drove back into London feeling reasonably satisfied that I had made progress which I would be able to follow up next week.

I had to go to the house sale in Stow-on-the-Wold next day, so I was planning to head back home. I thought that first I would drop in and have a drink in a small Chelsea pub that was habitually used by several other picture and antique dealers. I might be able to get an idea of what sort of turnout was expected at the sale.

Though it seldom surprised me to run into people out of context, I had not expected to see Amanda Drury in this pub. But there she was, wearing a skirt that barely covered her crotch, sitting on a stool in a way that all but advertised her lack of underwear.

She was surrounded by three eager, already drunk admirers. She was laughing and encouraging them in such a way as to let them all feel they had a chance of getting off with her, which for all I knew, they had.

She did not see me at first. When she did, her discomfort expressed itself in guilty aggressiveness.

'Oh, look,' she said to her gang of admirers, 'it's the phantom fucker. Starts a job and never finishes it.'

The three men looked at me and laughed uncertainly.

'Well this is no fucking phantom, Mandy,' one of them declared, clutching his genitals in his tight jeans.

'Hello, Amanda,' I nodded. 'I'll see you.' I left the pub quickly and pointed my car thankfully towards home.

Had I known that half the dealers in England were going to be at the sale in Stow, I would not have gone. There were only four or five interesting pictures, and those of us who had come were prepared to pay over the odds to justify the journey. Evidently I needed less justification than the others, and left empty-handed after an almost wasted day. Not entirely wasted, though.

Another disgruntled picture dealer sought me out in the temporary bar that had been set up to keep the dealers hanging around.

'You knew old Bill Beecham quite well, didn't you?' he asked me.

'Sure. I was an old friend.'

'He didn't have too many of those. He could be bloody offensive.'

'Only when confronted with bullshit.'

The other agreed. 'Which is most of the time in this business. Do you happen to know if he still had his Irish connection?'

I looked blank. 'I didn't know he had one.'

'You must have done. He made a lot of money – oh – twenty years or more ago, coming up with lost pictures from ruined Irish stately homes. It was beginning to look a bit dodgy, so he stopped before anyone was made to look silly.'

'Were they authentic?'

'I think the first one or two were, as a matter of fact, and he didn't want to give up such a useful source. After that he relied on very high quality Sexton Blakes. The provenances were convincing enough to persuade a few experts to put their names to them. But some were beginning to grumble.'

'He certainly didn't do much of that kind of thing in recent years, as far as I know,' I said.'

'Not directly, but half a dozen "lost" pictures have shown up over the last ten or fifteen years, usually coming back from the States, not through Bill. I always assumed there was a connection. I tackled him about it once because I had a punter who didn't give a toss where I found his pictures.'

'I know the type,' I agreed.

'And I asked Bill if he might have a crack at finding this one for me. He just stared at me with those bleary eyes of his and said, "Dear boy, that would be like looking for an antique dealer in heaven." But he knew damn well what I was getting at.' The dealer shrugged. 'I guess, even if he had told you, you wouldn't be likely to tell me, but if you ever think you can find the odd missing item, do let me know.'

'Sure.' I laughed, as non-committal as I could be.

I left the sale, collected a cheque from a gallery in Stow which had unexpectedly sold a picture I had left there on sale or return and drove the few miles down to Temple Ferris.

I was far too early for a weekend guest. But, I thought, what the hell? Georgie wouldn't mind, and I wanted to see her before the house filled up.

If Lady Walford was annoyed by my early appearance she did not show it. Georgie, she said, was in Cheltenham getting a few things. Did I want to go and have a look at the mares and foals that had recently come back from stud?

I enjoyed inspecting these fine specimens of English thorough-bred. Each mare's breeding, and that of her foal at foot and the one within her were on a label outside each box. They were mostly from famous, classic bloodlines. I always found it a pleasure to look at the two-week old progeny of sometime classic race winners, and speculate about what they would or, probably, would not achieve.

I noticed that none of the foals were by Clive Drury's Tomahawk and nor had any of the mares been covered by him this season. Lord Walford may have been a close business associate of Drury's but he was obviously not prepared to waste his money on a disappointing stallion, just to please its owner.

While I was in one box, leaning down to examine a nice filly foal by Dominion, I heard the stable door being unbolted. I was still on edge and suspicious since the events of Wednesday morning, and I straightened myself and spun round as a youngish man, late twenties or so, closed the door behind him.

He was about five-nine, well-built without being stocky. He wore jeans and an off-white Aran sweater. Bright, inoffensive blue eyes shone from a friendly, good-featured face below a mop of dark brown hair. There was a disarming innocence in his manner.

'Hello,' he said.

I nodded. 'Hello.'

'You must be the fearless Archie Best?' The voice had humour and a soft Irish lilt.

I was still, unreasonably, suspicious.

'I am.'

'I'm Sean Grady, friend of Georgie's. I'm staying here too.' He held out a hand.

I took it with relief. This had to be the actor Georgie had spoken of. 'She mentioned you,' I said.

'They've some incredible fine bloodstock in this place,' Sean said, inclining his head towards the mare and foal I had been looking at.

'Yes,' I agreed. 'Are you involved in this racket at all?'

'No. My father wanted me to be; but I was too much of a coward. I'll hunt a bit, if I'm guaranteed some docile old brute that's disinclined to break out of a trot and knows where all the gates are. But you can't hurt yourself by looking at the animals. I love to see them about the place.'

'Georgie told me you're an actor.'

'Sure. Mostly the theatre of life at the moment. Fee-paying jobs are a little scarce right now,' the actor said light-heartedly.

There was an outburst of barking from the yard outside, followed by some shrill cursing. Georgie's head and shoulders appeared over the stable door.

'Hi,' she said. 'I'm sorry I wasn't here when you arrived. You two have introduced yourselves, I take it?'

'Sure.'

'Great. Come back to the house when you're ready. If you behave, you might get a drink.'

Over the next half-hour, another three weekenders arrived: Jamie Lloyd-Jones, a tabloid journalist whose appearance and manner defied all the stereotypes; and two girls, both old schoolfriends of Georgie's and, as is often the case, with little in common now besides memories of erstwhile feared mistresses and loathed schoolfellows. But they helped create an easy atmosphere for the three males of the party who had never met before.

I collected my tattered suitcase and Georgie showed me to a bedroom of great size and decorative elegance.

'Good lord,' I exclaimed, 'are all your guest-rooms like this?'

'Of course not. This is the best.'

I hoped the indication this gave me of Georgie's priorities was not false.

Lord and Lady Walford ate dinner with us with an air of affable tolerance. Lord Walford, with a famous but ultimate harmless tendency to flirt with all his stepdaughter's friends, displayed a charm and general knowledgeableness of which I had not suspected him from our previous short encounters. I judged that he was more shrewd than he liked to let on. I speculated about his involvement with Clive Drury.

After dinner I touched on this as lightly as I could. I asked him how he had come to be on the board of the public company which Drury headed. His answer was revealing, and possibly reassuring.

'He bought up the Lloyd's members' agency I had been with for years. Later, when he was looking for snob-appeal on the board of the main holding company, he invited me on. I agreed because I thought it would give me a chance to keep an eye on him. I contribute very little, but I listen.'

'Interesting chap, Drury,' I said innocently. 'I'd like to know more about him. Thanks to your suggestion, he's asked me to get him some paintings.'

'It wasn't my suggestion. He approached me and asked me if you were any good. If you want to know more about Drury, somewhere I've got a very thick book of cuttings on him which my secretary has always kept updated. You're welcome to have a look some time.'

I did not think that this would tell me much, but I thanked him, and said I would like to see it, perhaps over the weekend. After that, he pointedly steered the conversation back to racing.

In many respects, it was a comfortable, old-fashioned sort of house-party; we were not expected to dress for dinner, the women did not leave the dinner table for the men to guzzle port and tell unseemly jokes, and there was a Dire Straits record playing in the billiards room where we all went to play snooker.

Bearing in mind Georgie's suggestion that Sean and Jamie might well prove helpful in my campaign against Drury, I used what opportunities I could to assess their usefulness. I was encouraged by both.

Jamie was an impressive type. He was still young, only three years out of my college at Oxford, but he had deliberately launched his journalistic career at the bottom of the market, so, he said, that he could understand what the average man considered news. The argument was in some ways flawed by the low esteem in which his editor held his readership, but he was honest enough about it to make me believe him. He seemed well-equipped to wheedle stories out of sources who might have resisted the traditional toe-in-the-door, grubby-mac reporter. He had also used some audacious subterfuges to get close to a story. He had, Georgie told me, presented himself as an Anglican vicar, a tax inspector, a new-age hippy traveller and a Member of Parliament.

Sean Grady displayed a surprising knowledge of English literature, outspoken liberal politics, and a deeply persuasive manner.

Even as I sat talking and joking about other things, I was seeing roles for both of them, and I was impatient for a chance to sound them out.

None came on that first evening, but next morning I woke early with a good clear head, and drew back the curtains of my bedroom to reveal an idyllic view, enhanced by bright early spring sunshine. Despite the decorous brush of lips on cheek that had been all that Georgie had allowed me the evening before, I was feeling confident, not only of her support, but also about her ultimate response to my growing interest in her.

In a thoroughly positive frame of mind, I dressed and went downstairs. It was half-past seven, and there were noises from the kitchen, I presumed from the housekeeper and other staff I had seen around the house the day before.

I poked my head round the door, with the intention of begging some orange juice or coffee, and found Sean sitting at the table, munching toast and reading the *Independent*.

'Papers already?'

'I drove up to the garage on the Fosse Way to get them,' Sean answered through a mouthful. 'I've made some coffee. D'you want a cup?'

'Thanks.' I sat and drank a well-made cupful, while Sean read snatches from the paper. Then he said, 'I'm going to take a walk down to the lake; see what fowl it harbours; maybe get a few shots.'

I was surprised by this.

'You didn't strike me as the type who enjoys killing our feathered friends,' I said.

Sean shook his head with a smile and pointed at a camera with a powerful-looking lens beside him.

'Ah,' I said. 'Do you mind if I come?'

'I'd be delighted.'

We crept, at Sean's suggestion, around the downwind side of the lake. It was in a dip about a quarter of a mile from the house. On the far, west bank, an earlier Walford had planted a stand of aspens, tall and delicate, not yet in leaf. Half the perimeter of the four acres of water was taken up by rushes, from which came encouraging rustles.

When a few teal had emerged, and then several rare species of winter-visiting ducks, Sean snapped away eagerly.

'I was giving his lordship a bit of stick last night for allowing his friends to shoot across this lake. It's criminal that these little, innocent creatures should be slaughtered the way they are,' he whispered.

I was inclined to agree and waited until he had seen all he expected to. After twenty minutes, we started back towards the house. 'Let's take the long way round by the paddocks,' he suggested.

Here was the opportunity I had been waiting for.

'Georgie said you might be interested in helping me with a problem I have,' I started casually.

'Did she now? What was that?'

'It sounds a little more heroic than it is, and my motives aren't as altruistic as they may appear, but I want to see a big man – a very big man – get his comeuppance for crimes for which it's unlikely he'll ever be charged.'

'Great! I'm all for that. But you don't strike me as being a vigilante type.'

'I'm not but, among other things, this man recently killed, or rather had killed, one of my oldest friends – Georgie's natural father, Bill Beecham.'

Sean gave me a sharp, querying look. 'What's that? Is old Lord W not her father, then?'

I shook my head. 'It was her idea to ask you to help, so I guess she must have expected me to tell you about it. Bill Beecham was an eccentric, tricky old bugger. He was an old friend of my father's, and I knew him well. It was only when I started seeing a bit of Georgie at the races that he told me she was his daughter. Hardly anyone knows because Walford adopted her when her mother married him. Georgie was about two then. Normally, she always refers to him as her father, but she knew Bill, and was naturally fond of him, despite his moodiness. It sounds a bit melodramatic, but Bill left me a posthumous note, telling me who had murdered him, and asking me to make sure the man gets his just desserts.'

'And that fine body of men, the English constabulary, won't get him for it?'

'Bill didn't want the police involved. There are rather a lot of things he's done which he's not too proud of that might have come out in an investigation. He didn't want Georgie or Lady Walford embarrassed by it all. Anyway, the police haven't got much of a chance. It was a virtually untraceable contract job. The visible motives are obscure, and the man has friends in the highest of places; the Home Secretary comes to his parties.'

'My goodness. And you want to take this fella on?'

'I do. And with some discreet help, I think I can.'

'And how do you think an out of work Irish actor can help?'

'I have a plan, not complete yet, but I think your skills could be very helpful. It could be a little injurious to your health, though.'

'And me a terrible coward. You'll have to tell me who yer man is.'

'Clive Drury.'

There was a silence, then Sean gave a low grunt.

'Hhm.'

'Do you know him?' I asked.

'I know very well who you mean. An ogrish sort of a fella, fingers manipulating furiously in any number of pies. He and my father almost came to blows once.'

'That's interesting. How was that?'

'My father's in the meat trade in Ireland, and England. As a matter of fact, he's one of the Mister Bigs, one of the honest ones. Drury has a large piece of one of his rivals.'

I remarked on the coincidence.

'Not really,' Sean replied. 'You maybe don't know just how many things Clive Drury is involved in. Anything where there is big international money and movement, he likes. As far as I know, he's never made an honest move in his life. So, if you're targeting Drury, I'm on.'

We agreed to meet shortly. I did not want to put a half-baked scheme to him, but I also thought he might have a few ideas of his own. We had reached the house by now, and went back in to find the rest of the party in the dining room tackling large plates of bacon and eggs. We willingly joined them.

'Where have you two been?' Georgie asked.

'Birdwatching,' I replied.

'You must be having a good influence on him, Sean. Archie has a reputation for being a strictly action man.'

I ignored the gentle jibe.

'Talking of which,' Georgie went on to me, 'Jamie wants to go hunting. I said you'd take him. There are a couple of fit mares in the yard, if you'd like to, or would that be too much of a busman's holiday for you?'

'No, I'd like to,' I replied.

'Thanks, Archie,' Jamie said. 'The thing is, I'm not all that competent, so I may need someone around to catch a loose horse.'

Pleased at the suggestion that gave me an hour or two's private talking time with this other potential ally, I went out with Georgie to tack up the horses.

'I thought,' she said, 'that you might be able to use this

opportunity to sound out Jamie on helping you with Drury.'

I laughed. 'Good girl! That's exactly what I was thinking. I've already had a chat with Sean. He'll help, and I've got a plan where he could be the ideal man. You were right, by the way, both of them could be useful.'

'Don't sound so surprised,' Georgie said. 'I'm not one of your dunder-headed bimbettes.'

'But you've got the body of one,' I said, unable to resist a quick squeeze of her hips as she bent down to buckle a girth.

'Don't do that,' she said between gritted teeth. 'I might kick.'

Chapter 8

The horses on which Jamie Lloyd-Jones and I were mounted could both have walked away with prizes in any country show. They were fine examples of threequarter-bred English hunters. Lord and Lady Walford hunted them only occasionally with the North Gloucestershire but they were kept fit throughout the season.

In luckily well-fitting, borrowed hunting coats, we rode out of the Walfords' spotless yard and hacked a mile and a half to the village. Two dozen other mounted followers were already there, including an old man in a pink coat who was Master. Hounds and huntsmen had not arrived, but the landlord of the pub was rushing about, handing glasses of mulled wine and sausage rolls to anyone who wanted them. Jamie, at this unenergetic stage of the day, was happily playing the part. For a self-confessed inexperienced horseman, he looked remarkably confident. He was having no difficulty handling his double bridle, his whip, a large glass and a lighted cigar. I thought perhaps he had been under-rating his abilities.

Georgie drove down to the meet with the other two girls and Sean Grady, who ran an appreciative eye over the horses and hounds gathered there.

After we had moved off to the first covert and quickly found a fox, it became clear that Jamie had been over-modest. He and his mare took the two small fences on the way with tidy fluency. When we started to run, we both found ourselves constantly on the point of barging into the backside of the Master's horse, as he checked and dithered at every turn.

Fortunately, in the small world of point-to-pointing, I was well enough known to have any minor transgressions tolerated, and by association, so was Jamie. We were more or less invited to go on, and managed to extract the most from this first short run. A two-mile gallop across upland sheep pasture, several stone walls and one good hedge brought us up to the next covert. But the day was warming up, and scent was rising too fast for hounds to keep a good line, and the young vixen we were hunting won a reprieve that day.

Georgie, Sean and the others arrived in a Land Rover. We chatted while the hunstman cast his hounds through the small wood. Any foxes that there might have been had gone to ground. There was a discussion with the Master, and a decision to move off to another covert.

Jamie and I said 'Goodbye' to our foot followers and set off behind the Master. Hounds searched fruitlessly through two more coverts.

'This is all we'll get today,' I suggested. 'It's too bloody warm. We may as well hack back now.'

Jamie looked disappointed. 'This is the first day I've had for five or six years.' So we carried on. I understood the optimism that always persuades you that you could be lucky and get a run when you least expect it.

But after an hour, Jamie had to agree that I had been right. We were four or five miles from Temple Ferris now. It was a beautiful day and we headed back feeling quite content with our uneventful morning.

I had not, within earshot of other people, touched on what I most wanted to discuss with Jamie. Now I had the chance.

'Have you ever had cause to sniff around Clive Drury, in a professional capacity?' I asked.

'No. Not really. There have been the odd rumours, but nothing substantial. You can't take chances with a man in his position. He'd have Carter-Ruck onto us like a pack of wolves, unless we had absolutely irrefutable evidence.'

'What sort of rumours?'

'I promise you, nothing worth bothering with. Vague connections with dodgy Colombians, a whiff of suspicion about pictures he's bought and sold over the years; rumblings of discontent from Lloyd's names in his agencies and syndicates – but that's normal these days now a few heavy cash calls are being made. Certainly nothing for us to get stuck into.'

116

'What about his family?'

'Amanda the Queen of Tarts and dead-beat Damian? Nothing of note there, until Mandy gets laid by a peer or a soap star.'

'Not that family,' I said. 'His other, first family; the Ducketts.'

Jamie turned to look at me sharply. 'Never heard of them,' he said.

'Well, they exist. There's an ex-wife and some kids. I've been to their semi in Lewisham.'

'Good God! Tell me more. Why are you so interested, anyway?'

Knowing how hard it is for reporters to keep a secret, especially one which they think their readers might like to share, I had decided not to tell him too much. 'I've had a few dealings with Drury recently,' I said vaguely. 'And I've come to the conclusion that the man's a villain; it would be a public service to put him in his place.'

'You've obviously got your reasons, but there are plenty of people who wouldn't disagree. But most of what we've heard has been from anonymous tip-offs and is too unsubstantive. Tell me about this family.'

I told him what I knew – though not by whom and why the information had been given to me – about a Mrs Doreen Duckett who lived somewhere in Lewisham, and my visit there the previous Thursday.

He was gratifyingly impressed.

'Shit! We could have some fun with that.'

'That's what I was hoping. I'm too much of an amateur to make the most of it. But I should have thought if you could track down one of the children, you'd have a tale to tell. I'd guess that one of them is some kind of hippy or dope-head, anyway, a serious embarrassment to his father.'

Jamie tried to grill me for more details, but I had given him all I had on the subject of Drury's family. By the time we rode back into the Walfords' yard, he could barely restrain himself from going straight back to London to pursue the story.

We had not been expected back for lunch and there was an informal sort of meal taking place. Georgie had invited a few local friends as well, and there were a dozen or so people sitting around the table.

After lunch, Georgie organised a walking tour of the estate, in which, to my surprise, everyone wanted to take part. I excused myself and, finding Lord Walford, asked him if I could take him up on his offer to let me see his Drury cuttings.

He led me to his study, pulled two big albums from a shelf and put them on his desk.

'There you are. Help yourself.'

I thanked him and he left me in the quiet room, with only the resonant ticking of a handsome wall clock for company.

The albums were arranged chronologically and I started with the earliest.

There was very little from Drury's first days at Lloyd's and nothing from before that. Most of the early cuttings were from the Lloyd's Log and financial pages, dealing with Drury's acquisition of Beecham's. They did not add much to what I already knew.

I leafed my way through, and the printed references to Drury gradually became more frequent. It seemed that he had soon realised that a high profile in public charities paid dividends in creating a good image. And those charities that he had chosen to espouse, presumably for their newsworthiness, must have benefited greatly from his organisational skills and financial acumen. The quid pro quo was that he was presented in a glowing light of philanthropy. As I read, I shook my head at the hypocrisy of it all.

As Drury's business empire expanded during the 'seventies, and he became involved in commercial activities outside the world of Lloyd's and insurance, the papers apparently began to take consistent notice – largely benevolent. In fact, working my way through the second book, I realised what a formidable opponent he was going to be. He had taken every public opportunity to win friends and influence people. And I was not in much doubt that privately, less noble inducements had been employed.

He was widely quoted as a City guru on many topics. He was pictured with government ministers of both hues. Amanda's coming-out party had earned a full column on the *Mail* gossip page. Even his son's entry into point-to-point racing had not gone unremarked.

Feeling daunted by the strength of the platform he had built for himself, I flipped back through the first book again. This time I noticed a few cuttings loose at the back, tucked inside the cover. I pulled them out and unfolded them.

None of them mentioned Clive Drury, but when I started to read them, my blood froze.

They were reports of the accidental deaths of various people, over a period from 1959 to 1965. There was no obvious connection between them. Clearly, Lord Walford thought there was. Seeing these reports, which had appeared unsensationally in small corners of local papers, made me more acutely aware than anything I had been told of just how dangerous and ruthless Clive Drury had been. And how much he had to answer for besides the murder of Bill Beecham.

I decided not to talk to Lord Walford about these particular cuttings. I wondered if he had even remembered they were there. In any event, I did not want to arouse his suspicions over Bill's death. He would have been certain to go to the police about it and he was in a much better position than I to make them take him seriously.

I debated whether or not to tell Georgie. I did not know how alarmed she would be, and I did not think it would help, so I chose not to. She and I did not have a chance to talk alone until late in the afternoon when everyone else was discarding their green wellingtons and Barbours. We were in the stud office in the yard, ostensibly looking up the breeding of a mare.

'Now you've had a chance to talk to Sean and Jamie, what do you think?' she asked me.

I nodded. 'You were right. They could both be useful and seem to be willing, especially Jamie.'

I told her about Mrs Doreen Duckett and my hunch about the offspring.

'Great!' she said. 'I can hardly believe it. He'll hate that getting out.'

'Yes, won't he?' I grinned.

Georgie, in a pair of loose-fitting old Levi's and a baggy sweater, seemed to me then as attractive as she ever had. She wore no make-up and her hair was a mess from beneath which her eyes glowed. I wanted badly to reach my arms around her and squeeze her to me.

Instead, I told her about Amanda.

'I think I might have lost Amanda Drury as an ally.'

'Good,' said Georgie. 'Why?'

'I saw her in a pub in London on Thursday evening surrounded

119

by a bunch of oafs and she was very unwelcoming.'

'Why was that? Had you stood her up, or turned her down or something?'

'Something like that.'

'Well don't tell me the details, please. I'm afraid that she and I don't have much mutual sympathy any more. And if you think you've now got my permission to corridor creep and leap into my bed, forget it.'

'What an extraordinary idea,' I exclaimed.

'Hmm,' Georgie raised an eyebrow at me with the hint of a smile.

I drove back to Herefordshire the following evening to find the horses still there, a note from Sharon, who had stayed for the last couple of nights to watch out for the possible return of the rustlers, and several messages on the answerphone.

Judging by the collection of empty bottles, Sharon had not spent the weekend alone. I did not mind; I was quite happy to have a member of the SAS acting as an additional security guard.

Most of the messages were mundane requests or instructions, but I was pleased to hear Harry Winchcombe's voice in a state of high excitement, asking me to ring him back as soon as possible.

I dialled the number he had given.

'Hello?' he answered from his Sussex farmhouse.

'It's Archie Best.'

'Great! Thanks for calling back. It's about my turf.'

'Have you had the results of the tests already?'

'No. I phoned the lab. They should have something for me tomorrow. But I was thinking that if there was something wrong, it must be the fault of the chaps who seeded and fertilised it.'

'Your groundsmen?'

'No. It was much too big a job for us to handle ourselves. I'd had a circular from some outfit I'd never heard of, offering to quote for seeding and spraying and so on. I contacted them and a few other firms, and their quote for fertilising was half the others, so I gave them the job. I rang them a few times last week after I saw you at Drury's, and I couldn't get any reply, not even a machine. Well, after a couple of days, I thought this was pretty odd, so I drove to the address which they'd originally given me. It turned out to be a dilapidated shed on some waste ground outside

Portsmouth. It was all locked up. I got a look through a window but I couldn't see much. I found the farmer whose ground it was on, and he said he'd rented it to a couple of chaps for a month and then they'd just buggered off, disappeared completely. They'd paid their rent for the next month, so he wasn't worried.'

'What did he say they'd been doing there?' I asked.

'Apparently they kept a couple of tractors and a pick-up there, and a few attachments, you know, seeders and fertilisers, which they took off somewhere most days. It was during that time that they did my job, but that only took a week, so they must have been doing some others. I phoned a few course managers round here, and one of them had used them, and was having similar problems to us. And, did you read the *Post* on Saturday?'

'No.'

'There was a report that they've been having turf problems at Brockhurst Park, too. I haven't been able to get hold of anyone there yet to find out if they used the same geezers. What do you think?'

'I think it's very likely,' I answered.

'But you were obviously suspicious about something when we talked last Thursday. What do you know about it?'

'I'm not sure yet. But the results of your tests might tell us something. Ring me as soon as you've got them.'

'Okay. Then for God's sake, if you can tell me more, I've got to try and get myself off the hook with my board. They're blaming me for all this. If the grass is dead, the course will be worthless. It would take at least five years before new grass gives enough cover to race on. We're barely breaking even as it is, and there are plenty of other buyers sniffing round since Drury walked away.'

'Look forward to hearing from you then.'

We said goodbye, and I put the phone down with a smile.

Later, when I thought he would have got back to his Belgravia flat, I rang Sean Grady to arrange a meeting as soon as possible.

He wanted to come out to my place, which suited me, and he was prepared to come the next day.

Sean arrived the next morning when I had just opened the formal instructions Drury had promised. I was authorised to find and buy on his behalf the two Fernley paintings, up to a total of three hundred and fifty thousand pounds the pair. I groaned to myself;

that was not going to be enough, even in the current market. He must have known that. And there was supposed to be fifty thousand in the deal for me. I thrust it to one side as Sean walked in with a cheery 'Good morning'.

He sat opposite me at the table in my shambolic kitchen and looked at me eagerly.

'You've a scam worked out, then?'

'Yes. It'll take all your acting skills and a lot of bollocks to make it work, but if we bait the hook right, I think we could land Drury in a lot of shit.'

'Say on,' Sean grinned.

Two days later Sean and I were in his flat in a Lowndes Street block which was occupied mostly by foreign diplomats. 'Not mine, my father's,' he said, catching me looking around, calculating the cost of the furniture.

We were going to test a tape-recorder I had borrowed from Jamie Lloyd-Jones, and see how best to conceal it in Sean's clothing.

'The big bastard didn't take much persuading,' Sean was saying. 'He's obviously quite used to dealing with low-life types.'

'What did you say to him, exactly?' I asked.

'Not a lot. I couldn't get through to him at first, but when I told one of his minions that I wanted to buy his shares in Tomahawk and I would only speak to him about it, I was put through in a flash.'

'They're obviously trained to know his priorities,' I remarked.

'Sure. I told him I had a proposition to put to him regarding the stallion. He asked who I was, and I said I couldn't possibly tell him at this stage and surely he realised that. I tried to get him to meet me somewhere near Gazeley, as we hoped, but he wasn't having that. Don't worry, though, I'll get him there, or somewhere out in the open for the next meet.'

'Are you happy about going to his house?'

'I'm shitting bricks, but then I always do before the curtain goes up; after that, I'll be cruisin',' Sean smiled with reassuring confidence.

'You're sure he won't recognise you from anywhere?'

'Sadly, I've not worked anywhere where he would have been likely to see me. I can't imagine him going to any of the North

122

London fringe productions I've been in; I don't have the impression he's all that interested in experimental theatre.'

'You'll have the advantage of his very willing suspension of disbelief. I had a discreet word with Michel de Mosnay who runs the stud. He says Drury is desperate to get out of his position in Tomahawk before the animal's value falls even further. He should be easily tempted by any scheme that will get him all his money back.'

'We shall see.'

'I'm looking forward to it. By the way, I'm planning to hang around, out of sight near the house, to see if I can photograph the two of you together.'

'Don't be stupid,' Sean's eyes blazed. 'For a start, there's no way he'll be talking to me out in the street, and a shot of me going in proves nothing. Besides, if he catches the merest glimpse of you, he'll know something's going on. You'll have your chance for the shots at the next meet, I promise you.'

I agreed reluctantly. Jamie had acquired from one of his colleagues a thousand millimetre lens that was normally used for snapping inaccessible celebrities in compromising circumstances or the Princess of Wales in a bikini. I was looking forward to using it; and I was less confident than Sean about his ability to persuade Drury out for a second meeting.

We strapped the small German tape-recorder on to Sean's belt and plugged in the tiny button mike. We tried using it in several different positions and circumstances until we were getting the best result.

'Does Jamie often use one of these things?' Sean asked.

'Apparently. It's less obvious than a notebook and a stub of pencil.'

'He's a little civilised for a gutter journalist. I suppose that's how he gets away with it,' Sean observed.

'Yes, and he's going to be very useful over this. Mind you, there are a few scoops in it for him. But what's in it for you, Sean?'

He smiled. 'The chance to do my father a bit of a service, and a bit of adrenalin.'

'At least Jamie's paper is paying most of the expenses.'

'My father would, too, if we could tell him what we were doing.'

'So, tell him after we've done it,' I said.

* * *

123

For over an hour I sat alone in a large brasserie in the King's Road. It felt like a day. I could not concentrate on the newspaper in front of me or the banal conversations of the people jostling around the tables beside me. I had had four cups of cappuccino by the time I saw Sean stride jauntily into the place.

I leaped up and waved him into a chair.

'Christ, you've been a long time. I thought he must have sussed you.'

'No chance!' Sean beamed confidently. 'The thicker I laid it on, the more he lapped it up. He's over the bloody moon. He's certain he'll get all his three million back now. He seems to treat the whole insurance business like a game with marked cards.'

'He's been doing that for thirty years. How else do you think he's made so much money? What did you tell him?'

'Hang on. Let me get a bloody drink first. I didn't have a drop while I was with him.'

I waved an arm for a waitress, who eased herself disdainfully off a bar stool to come over and take my order for two beers.

'Why did it take so long?' I asked Sean while she was fetching them.

'I took twenty minutes coming here. I wanted to be sure he'd not put a tail on me.'

I had not even thought of that. I would have to sharpen up.

The girl returned and clattered two bottles and glasses on to the marble-topped table.

'Had he, do you think?' I asked Sean.

'No, but he might next time, now he thinks he knows who he's dealing with.'

'So, what did you tell him?'

As soon as Sean had rung the front doorbell, it had been opened by a silent blank-faced man who was clearly expecting him. He was shown into a room which sounded from his description like the drawing room where the party had been held.

Drury got to his feet from a large chair where he had been reading some kind of report.

'Good evening, Mr . . . ?'

Sean had chosen to fortify his Irish accent for the meeting. 'You won't need to know my name, Mr Drury. Let's just say that I represent a powerful and influential group of Irishmen.'

Drury, towering over Sean, glared down at him. 'Now look here,' he growled. 'If you've come here to mess around, you can leave now.'

'I've come here to talk to you about Tomahawk. You know and I know that you want to get rid of your shares in the animal and right now you'd not expect a third of what you paid for 'em. Our proposition values him higher, and if you want to, you'll hear it on my terms or not at all.'

Drury's expression conveyed that he was prepared to give a short hearing. He offered a drink which Sean declined. His taciturn minion closed the door and stayed a few feet behind Sean.

'It's alone we'll talk.' Sean hardened his eyes with the words, and Drury curtly nodded the other man out of the room.

Drury did not beat about the bush. 'So, what's your proposition?'

'Not so fast, Mr Drury,' Sean said. 'I want to be quite certain of what it is I'm dealing with. Can you show me documentary proof of your ownership of shares in Tomahawk?'

'Of course I can. It's registered at Weatherby's.'

'I'll be needing to see that. Can you also show me policy documents relating to the insurance of the animal?'

'What's that got to do with your buying shares?'

'Nothing at all. I need to know how he's insured. Can you tell me that?'

Drury seemed unwilling. 'My insurance arrangements have got bugger all to do with you.'

Sean shrugged. 'If it's abusive and evasive you want to be, I'll be leaving now.' He turned towards the door.

'I have insured my interest in the horse against death,' Drury said.

Sean turned back. 'At what value?'

'The price I paid, three million dollars.'

'What about theft?'

'Too rare to be worth it. It's only happened once.'

'But nevertheless, after Shergar, a lot of people do insure against theft, do they not?'

'Certainly. We've underwritten several policies ourselves, willingly.'

'Well, you'd better get someone else to underwrite yours.'

Drury's slow smile signified his appreciation of Sean's proposition. 'How much?'

'Ten per cent.'

'Don't be ridiculous,' Drury exploded. 'The animal's not worth a light to anyone else. If you think I'm going to subsidise a bunch of Paddy hoodlums to the tune of three hundred thousand for a job I could get done myself, you're dreaming.'

'That kind of talk is very . . . unwise. You've your own health to consider. And have you had a better offer?'

'I haven't the slightest doubt, since you mention it, that there are several parties who would do it for a quarter of that.'

Sean looked at him without blinking. He shook his head slowly. 'They'd not dare,' he said quietly.

Drury stared back, trying to assess what he was dealing with. After a quarter of a minute, he turned to cover his uncertainty by topping up his drink.

'All right. You've put your proposition to me. I'll let you know.'

'We'll be wantin' thirty grand before we start. I'll ring you tomorrow to tell you where to bring it.' Sean turned on his heel before Drury could answer. As he let himself out of the room, he heard Drury bellow half-heartedly, 'Hold on!'

Sean shut the door behind him, and was out of the house and the high black gates before anyone could stop him.

I was disappointed.

'So he hasn't actually said he's going for it?'

Sean grinned and put a hand on my arm. 'There's no question about it. First, he's very greedy, and this is the only way he has of saving his investment, and secondly, he'll be too shit scared to turn us down. It was great! It was one of the easiest roles I've ever played but, by God, it got the adrenalin going!'

I could not believe it had gone so simply. 'Well, I hope you're right.'

'I'll go to the lav, and get the cassette out for you. You have a little listen to it later.'

We had another drink before leaving the bar separately. I had arranged to meet Jamie Lloyd-Jones at his house in Fulham. I found my car clamped in Park Walk. I cursed and kicked it a couple of times and hailed a cab.

Jamie answered his door, bubbling with excitement.

126

'Hi, Archie. How are you?' He did not wait for an answer. 'Your lead has turned out to be very fruitful.'

'Good. Just let me ring my declamping service. I've got to get it done tonight, I'm due in Sussex early tomorrow.'

'Go ahead,' Jamie invited with good-natured impatience.

When I had done that, agreeing sourly to the hundred pound fee, I was able to concentrate on Jamie's news.

'You've been to Lewisham?' I asked.

'I certainly have. And I found Mrs Duckett.'

'You're sure it's the right one?'

'No question.'

'What's she like?' I asked, catching his enthusiasm.

'A skinny, haunted-looking woman of about sixty. She was very shy about talking to me, and obviously I didn't want to stampede her into going to Drury in a panic. I'd decided to use your first story about a legacy from an Australian Duckett, except I said it only applied to male heirs. It's amazing how people will buy that kind of story: she accepted it completely, but she was still adamant that they were the wrong Ducketts. I said that was possible but I had to check it out, and it was essential she told no one about it until I had done that. She became very cagey then, but finally admitted to a son of thirty-nine called John. She said she hadn't seen him for months, but she'd had a card from him around Christmas.'

'Great! Where from?'

'The bad news is that he seems to be something of a vagrant. I suppose he's some kind of new-age traveller, you know, a hippy in a converted bus. The good news is that the card was from Wales, which narrows it down a little.'

'But these people move around, and it's ten weeks since Christmas,' I said. 'It might take a hell of a time to trace him. But it'd be well worth it.'

'You're not kidding, and I don't suppose they do move much in winter. And even if they do, they leave quite a trail behind them. I could come up and stay at your place, and use it as a base while I try to track him.'

'You think that's the best thing to do?'

'Sure. I don't want to print anything until I've got the whole story, so that Dury can't injunct us or anything.'

'I've got copies of the birth certificates, the marriage certificate and Drury's change of name by deed-poll, come to that.'

'How the hell did you get your hands on them?'

'I'll tell you another time. There should be a daughter too, Diane.'

Jamie shook his head. 'She didn't mention her. And I wasn't pressing her on daughters.'

'Having got this far, it shouldn't be too hard to find her as well.'

'The more the merrier. By the way, I got the impression that she had not told the offspring about their father. I asked about him, and she said she had been a widow since the early 'fifties. She was utterly convincing, so she's clearly in the habit of telling the story.'

'Drury must have terrorised her into keeping her mouth shut. I'm surprised he's let her survive; she could be a terrible liability to him. Did she seem to be looked after?'

'The house inside is comfortable enough; new furniture and carpets, plenty of electronic gadgetry and expensive crappolata. I think you must be right, she knows that if she ever stepped out of line and blew the whistle on him, he'd get rid of her,' Jamie said.

'Are you certain she didn't suspect anything?'

'Yes. I don't think she'd have told me a thing if she had.'

'So, what do we do next?' I asked.

'When are you coming back from Sussex?'

'Tomorrow night, then I'll have to get back to Herefordshire.'

'Fine,' Jamie said. 'I'll see you there tomorrow evening. It'll be late, though. I've got a couple of pieces I have to tie up here before my editor lets me swan off for a few days.'

He suggested that I stay the night at his house, and I went back to Chelsea to rescue my car before meeting him for dinner at a bistro in Parson's Green. He had been looking at maps of central Wales, and planning forays to Hay-on-Wye and Macchyntleth, both important on the itinerant hippy circuit.

Over dinner we went through the possibilities, and what the discovery of this second, abandoned family could do to Clive Drury. I also told Jamie about the progress Sean and I had made.

Jamie looked alarmed. 'Look, don't get too close to that man. I'm sure he can be a ruthless bastard when he needs to be; and he's got a lot of strong connections on his side. I'm not saying he's above the law, but he's a great deal less susceptible to it than most of us.'

Chapter 9

Just after nine next morning, I walked into Harry Winchcombe's office beneath the old, peeling grandstand of the racecourse he ran. He leaped from behind his desk and grabbed my hand.

'Am I glad you could come! I've had the results of the soil test, and there's a strong smell of rat about it all. I really ought to take it to the police.'

'You haven't yet, have you?'

'No, but you must tell me why you didn't want me to.'

'I will. I already have a strong hunch what's happened, but let's go and visit this barn your seeders rented. Bring the lab report with you; you can read it to me on the way.'

Harry nodded, grabbed a folder from his desk and followed me quickly out of the office to the patch of crumbling tarmac where I had parked my car.

When he had aimed me in the right direction for the M27, I asked him to read me the report.

It was quite straightforward. Beyond the normal constituents and trace metals of Sussex loam, there were high proportions of herbicidic compound.

'You know what that is, don't you?' Harry asked.

'Yes. Reach behind your seat. There's a plastic can there.'

Harry grappled in the back and found an empty plastic container which I had put there.

'If you look at the back of the can, you'll find a list of ingredients.'

Harry spun it round, and nodded as he read. 'Yeah. This looks like the stuff, no doubt about it. It'd wipe out a forest if you sprayed it on thick enough. How did you know?'

'I've used it myself, so I know the symptoms. I was reminded of it the other day, strangely enough, by Damian Drury.'

'He was talking about it?'

'No, but I noticed that he keeps his hoof oil in an old Round-Up can. It started a chain of thought.'

'I told you, old Drury has to be a prime candidate!' Harry said. 'He'd love to see us smaller southern courses out of action because the Jockey Club would be forced to make more use of his all-weather track.'

'Yes. It seems out of all proportion but I'm beginning to think that Clive Drury hates losing his money so much, he'd resort to anything, and there's no doubt that so far his Equitrack just isn't paying its way.'

'Well I think we ought to take the results of this test to the police and let them follow up these chaps.'

'Believe me, Harry, if Drury was involved, it would have been at arm's length, and he certainly wouldn't get his own collar felt for it.'

'What does that matter to you, though?'

'I've got my own reasons for seeing Drury personally humiliated and banged up for this.' I did not want to involve Harry in the whole story, so I took another line. 'We've got a far better chance of seeing a conviction if we wait until I've dug up so much evidence that even his cabinet chums can't ignore it. And with a criminal conviction against him, you'll have no trouble getting a civil judgement for compensation.'

Out of the corner of my eye, I saw Harry gaping incredulously. 'But Archie, Drury's a big, so-called respectable businessman; you make him sound like the Krays.'

'That's not far off.'

'But for God's sake, what chance have you got against a man like that? What about these fellows who rented the place we're going to? They could be really heavy! I hope to God they're not there.'

I laughed. 'You're a bit chicken for an ex-soldier.'

'I always felt quite safe inside a tank – a more substantial tank than this one,' he added.

The fierce south-westerly that had been blowing all morning decided finally to release the rain it had been threatening. My wipers were working overtime as Harry directed me off the motorway outside Portsmouth, through a rusting gate and along a rutted cinder track. The unfenced land on either side had the air of being reluctantly cultivated by someone who was expecting much bigger dividends when the planning authorities decided that the expanding city could not do without it.

The track ended between two ex-military, concrete sectional buildings, each about sixty feet by twenty.

'Which one were they using?' I asked.

Harry pointed to the one on our left.

We left the warmth of the car for a howling wind and rain outside. Neither of us had brought any kind of wet-weather clothing and we made a quick dash to the double doors at the far end of the building.

We had nearly reached them when we saw that one was ajar. We stopped at the same time and glanced at each other apprehensively.

Harry turned and headed down the lee of the building towards a window. I followed. It was less noisy and windy on this side.

'We'd better check if anyone's there,' Harry half whispered.

I cautiously edged my head towards the grimy panes of glass. The first thing I saw was a lighted, naked neon strip bulb. Beneath it was parked a Land Rover with a trailer hitched on to the back. There was a man bending down behind it, lifting a full plastic sack from a stack of a few dozen. He heaved up the twenty-five-kilo bag and dumped it with others already in the trailer. He straightened himself to stretch his back, and I saw the man's ruddy features. The last time I had seen them, I had woken up a few hours later with a vicious headache; they belonged to the lorry driver I had stopped in the act of stealing Caesar's Consul.

I pulled my head back sharply.

'There's someone in there,' I whispered above the wind to Harry. 'He's the man who tried to take my horse last week. If he sees me or my car, we're stuffed. I'm going to get out of here now. You stay and try to see everything he does. I'll dump the car somewhere and wait for you near the gate.'

Harry did not look too keen on the plan, but he accepted it. I set off at a run, ducking beneath the other windows, around the far end of the building to my car. I started it up, fatuously trying to do it quietly, and prayed that the wind would cover the sound. I backed until I thought I was well out of sight of the building's few windows, swung the car round and headed the four hundred yards along the track to the road.

I turned right towards the motorway until I came to the next gateway and drove in. I found myself in front of a fine, old farmhouse, ill-kept and carelessly patched up in parts in a way that would have gravely upset Pevsner. There was a broad, densely weeded sweep of gravel in front of the house which could be seen from the road. I drove on down a track that followed the side of the house, and turned into a tumbledown yard at the back. It had occurred to me that the place might belong to the owner of the barns. The man loading the trailer had looked as though he had at least another ten minutes' work, so I walked up to the back door of the house and rapped on a dirty reeded glass panel.

After a few moments, it was opened by a stout, scruffy man of fifty or so. He was in shirt-sleeves and there were wet socks on his feet. He had evidently been caught out in the rain too.

'Good morning. I wonder if you can help me? Do those old army sheds over there belong to you?' I asked.

'Yer,' he nodded.

'Oh good. Could I have a word with you about them?'

'What about them?'

'I wondered if I might rent one.'

'Oh-ah. You'd better come in then.' He opened the door a little wider and invited me in with a nod.

'I'm rather wet, I'm afraid.'

'Don't matter. Come on in so's I can close the bloody door.'

I stepped over the threshold into a broad, flag-stoned passage. The man, whom I took to be the farmer of the surrounding land, led me into his kitchen which was stiflingly hot from a large Rayburn. My nostrils were filled with the smells of frying, damp clothes and nicotine.

'There's two sheds. Which one was you interested in?'

'Are they both available?'

'They will be in about ten minutes. I 'ad some tenants in one, but they're leaving. They're just clearing out the rest of their stuff and bringing the keys back to me.'

They – I thought in panic. There must have been two of them. Maybe the other had seen me, or my car. I fervently hoped that they would not drive round to the back of the house as I had done.

132

I tried to react normally. 'I'd like to look at both sheds in that case. Could I wait until they get here with the key?'

''Course you can. Have a cup of tea, or'd you rather have a scotch?'

'Tea'll be fine, thanks.'

I sipped the sticky liquid for a few minutes, talking to my host about his farming activities, which seemed as minimal as possible on his remaining hundred acres. He told me that he had been watching the hi-tech industrial parks creeping ever nearer, and this had proved something of a disincentive to efficient farming, if that had ever been an option.

At a faint sound of wheels on gravel, he got to his feet. 'That'll be them now with the keys,' he said, and there was a knocking on the front door.

'Could I use your lavatory?' I asked hurriedly, 'I haven't stopped since breakfast.'

'Help yourself.' He jerked a thumb towards a door in the front hall of the house.

I found the lavatory in a cloakroom full of old army coats, discarded boots and two shotguns. I opened the window which gave on to the front drive and sat on the wooded lid, hoping to hear the Land Rover start up and drive away again. After five minutes it did. I made a bit of noise with the hard loo-paper and pulled a rusty old chain before going back into the kitchen.

The farmer was sitting back in his chair with a pair of keys on the table in front of him.

'There you are,' he said. 'You can go and have a look at them now if you want.'

'Fine,' I said, picking up the keys. 'I'll bring them back in half an hour or so, if that's okay.'

'Take your time. They're not too tidy, mind, and they may be letting in a bit of rain with this bloody wind.'

'Right. Thanks very much. I'll see you shortly.'

I hoped that the previous tenants, having handed back the keys, were well on their way. Harry would be getting impatient by now.

I started the car and drove out of the yard. I was relieved to see from the Land Rover's tyre marks that it had not been driven anywhere near the back. I swung my car out into the road, and sped back to the track up to the sheds.

This time, I parked on the far side of the second building and made my way cautiously to the doors of the recently vacated shed. The doors were padlocked now. I listened at the crack between them, but could hear nothing above the wind. I wondered where Harry was sheltering, and walked across to the other shed. It was shut but not locked. I listened again, crept round the side to look into a window, but could see nothing of the gloomy interior.

I went back and opened one of the doors a crack. There was no reaction from inside, so I opened it a little more and slipped in.

Harry was lying face down and motionless, a few feet inside the door.

As I dropped to crouch beside him, I saw a patch of his hair, matted, sticky and crimson, on the back of his head.

I let out a gasp. 'Harry?'

I had not expected a reply. I pulled off the sweater I was wearing, and put it beside his head so that I could roll him over. I moved him as gently as I could until he was lying on his back. His eyes were closed and he was breathing. That was something.

I had never been confronted with such gory results of deliberate violence and my instinct was to panic. With an effort, I forced myself to work out what my next moves should be.

Harry's clothes were soaking wet. I guessed that he must have been attacked when he was still outside, then dragged into this shed. They must have known who he was, so he was lucky still to be alive, or maybe that had not been their intention.

Despite Harry's condition and my first instincts, I knew that involving the police was out. It would alert Drury to the fact that I was on to him and stymie my campaign.

Pulling myself together, I ran out to the car and drove it as close as I could to the front of the shed.

I opened the car's nearest rear door and went back in. I lifted Harry's limp body by his armpits and dragged him across the floor, out to the car. I heaved him on to the back seat, found a dusty old blanket in the boot and flung it over him.

I remembered just in time to go back and get my sweater, which was stained with blood now, and wrapped it into a ball to make a pillow to put under Harry's head. I closed the doors of the shed, and leaped into my driving seat. I knew I was breaking a few cardinal rules of first aid but I drove back down the track with as much care as I could to avoid jerking in and out of the ruts.

First, I went back to the farm, parked in front of the house and ran round to the back. The farmer eventually answered my hammering. I thrust the keys at him. 'Thanks. I've had a look; I'll let you know.'

He shrugged, unconcerned, as I turned and almost ran back to the car.

Once more out in the road, I headed for Portsmouth, trying to cook up a story as I went. I did not have a clue where the hospital was so I aimed for the centre until the words 'Accident and Emergency' began to appear on the signposts.

Harry looked terrible.

A rectangular shaved patch on his head was decorated with a six-inch gash and a dozen neat little cross-stitches. He looked like one of Dr Frankenstein's less successful creations.

But at least his eyes were open, and he was almost smiling. The nurse was in the process of changing his dressings, and had objected strongly when I burst my way through the curtains.

'I'm sorry,' I said, 'but Sister told me he had come round, and I just wanted to see him before I leave.'

Harry blinked his appreciation. I gave his arm a squeeze and said, 'Harry, I've got to go, but I'll be back as soon as I can. Sarah should be here soon, and she's going to stay nearby for a few days. Keep your end up and don't worry about a thing. It's all under control.'

I chose to detect a weak grin on his face, and left the hospital a great deal more optimistic than when I had arrived.

I had no problem convincing the emergency staff that Harry had slipped off the edge of a boat in the marina and cracked his head on a steel stanchion. It would not have been the first time they had had semi-nautical accidents of this sort to deal with. And it was clear that it was a blunt piece of metal that had caused the damage.

I had telephoned his parents' house in London – not knowing which girl was his most current – and spoken to Sarah, his sister. She had volunteered to come at once and, with her driving habits, I thought that she would be there in not much more than an hour.

I had also told her the yachting version of the incident, at which she expressed some surprise in view of Harry's frequently expressed loathing of the sea and anything to do with it. But she did not question it.

I arrived back in London at two. Still wincing at my hundred pound declamping bill from the day before, I cruised around St James's Square several times before a thoughtful old biddy in a silver-blue Daimler and a bit of a trance nearly backed into me as she vacated a four-hour space.

I acknowledged my luck and considered it a good omen. It was, to the extent that I saw the man I was seeking almost the moment I walked into the St James's Oyster Bar.

He saw me too – he habitually gazed around a room and its inhabitants, whoever he was talking to, and his sharp eye fuelled a prodigious memory for people, places and pictures.

On this occasion he was alone, flipping through a sale catalogue. He arched an eyebrow and beckoned me over with a wave of his long fingers.

'Archie, dear boy, you look a trifle windswept.'

I had replaced my blood-stained sweater with a tatty old jacket. My hands were still grimy from manhandling Harry and I had not put a comb through my hair since waking at Jamie's house that morning.

'Are you prepared to be seen speaking to me?'

'Prepared?' He made a quick moue with his small lips. 'I should be thrilled if you would join me for a glass or two of this overpriced Chablis. Some of the best, prettiest pictures I ever bought I found in the nastiest frames and in the most filthy of conditions.'

I sat down without replying. It was wise not to encourage Lucien Hart (Lucy to his intimates; the Beating Hart to his detractors).

'I was looking for you, Lucien.'

'I suppose it's only my knowledge you're seeking?'

'I'm afraid so. I have a contract to buy a pair of Fernleys, and I thought you might know where they are.'

'Which pair?'

I described them, and their known history.

'I do know,' Lucien said with satisfaction. 'And they're a long way from here.'

'The States?' I guessed.

He smiled. 'Jolly big, the United States. Five per cent will narrow your field of search considerably.'

'But that's half my commission,' I protested.

'Half a commission's better than none.' Hart poured some wine from his bottle into a glass in front of me and took a sip from his own.

I smiled. Hart did a deal like this, sitting in this bar, several times a week. It must have been one of the easiest ways on earth of earning a quarter of a million or so a year, But he did not achieve it by being soft.

'Two and a half,' I said lightly. 'Or I look elsewhere.'

'You should do more of your own homework, and then you wouldn't have to give anything away. Would you like a few molluscs? They might make you look less gloomy.'

'Only if you agree to two and a half.'

Hart put his head on one side and dropped his chin while keeping his eyes fixed firmly on mine. 'I can see this is going to be a very expensive luncheon.'

The name of the current American owner of the Fernleys came as a surprise to me. Not because she was not a well-known collector of this sort of painting, but because she was frequently in England anyway, to watch her chain of steeplechasers perform. With luck, she would be in the country now, or very shortly, for the Cheltenham National Hunt Festival which took place the following week. But prising pictures out of her at the bargain prices Drury had stipulated was going to present a major challenge to my negotiating skills. Maybe Drury thought I employed more scurrilous methods than I did.

With rather more Chablis inside me than was wise, I found my car unmolested by traffic wardens and drove west out of London.

I had to get back home to meet Jamie Lloyd-Jones later that evening but Lambourn was on the way and, with luck, there I would find Nicholas 'Nosey' Parker, trainer to, amongst many others, Mrs Arthur Arlington III.

Nicholas Parker's sobriquet related to his facial features, and in no way to his social demeanour. It was apparently one of his attractions to them that he was completely uninterested in his owners or their business. He refused to talk about money with any of them, and left that all to his chubby wife while he concentrated on training horses.

I had had several rides and a few wins for him in amateur races, and though he was not good company, I could not deny his skilful dedication.

As I parked outside his small but handsome house, I decided it would be more productive to talk to Jeannie, his wife. I found her, as usual, sitting at the kitchen table, roaring with laughter down the telephone. She made a couple of suggestive jokes to her listener, laughed again, reminded him to send a cheque next day, and put the phone down with a thump.

'God, what a wanker!' she declared. 'Hello, Archie. What do you want? If you've come for that jock-strap you left here last time, you're too late. It's been washed and Mrs Williams has been using it to polish the silver.'

'Oh, no!' I pretended to look crestfallen. 'It's really hard to get them my size.'

'Balls.' Jeannie laughed.

'Quite,' I said.

'Look, I'm busy. If you just want to boast about your wedding tackle, go out and do it to one of the girls; I'm a bit old for fairy stories.'

'I wanted to know if Bambi Arlington was over here yet.'

'Good heavens, why? She's got bags of boodle and old Arthur's extremely deceased, but I'd have thought she was a bit of a challenge, even for you.'

'I don't know where you got the idea that I want to get my leg over anything with tits. I'm really quite fussy these days. I'd just like to have a quick chat with her about something, that's all.'

'She doesn't want any of her horses ridden by amateurs this season,' Jeannie said brusquely.

'It's got nothing to do with horses, and it's got nothing to do with you either. I just wanted to know if she was here yet, and as I was passing, I thought you might be able to tell me.'

Jeannie, having administered her 'Hands Off' warning, nodded affably. 'She checks into the Connaught on Sunday night. She's having lunch here on Monday. Do come; we could do with some help. Nosey only talks to her about horses and I think she finds it rather hard going.'

'Sure. That'd be great. Is Nosey in?'

'Yah, in his office, up to his ears in entry forms.'

I left the kitchen and walked across the yard to the trainer's lair, next to the tack room where he could keep a close eye on everything.

I knocked and walked in. Nosey turned and peered at me down

his long beak. He looked back down at the schedules on the desk in front of him.

'Have you got a ride in the Foxhunters?' he asked without preamble.

'Of course I have, Nosey: the Consul.'

'Waste of time. We're declaring The Dealer.'

'So I assumed,' I said. 'He should come in the first nine.' There were only nine expected to run.

Nosey ignored this. 'Look, if you want a chance of a win, let me know.'

'I will, thanks.'

'What are you doing here, anyway?'

'Just looked in to say hello.'

'Oh? Well, keep in touch.' The trainer turned his attention back to the pile of forms, and I left, without any sense of insult.

I arrived back at Stone House Farm after dark. As always before going into the house, I checked the three horses, and noted that Sharon had padlocked all the stables, including Jasper's, which was something of an overkill. But I was pleased that she was as concerned as I about their security.

On the kitchen table was her customary rambling, misspelt account of the day's events, or in this case, non-events. Both the racehorses had worked well and Jasper was desperate for a day's hunting; could Sharon take him on Saturday, if Georgie was going to groom me?

I smiled at this prospect, and played my phone messages.

Jamie had rung to say that he would be with me about nine, and my mother wanted me to call her back.

I dialled her number. After a couple of rings, she answered.

'It's Archie.'

'Oh good. Is everything all right?'

'Yes,' I said as easily as possible. 'Why shouldn't it be?'

'I've been worried about you. You haven't been home much, and I don't like you doing business with that ghastly Drury.'

'Why not?'

She hesitated. 'I've just always thought there was something very nasty about him.'

'Well, there is, lots. But I'm aware of that, and for God's sake, Mother, I have to make a living.'

'Just be careful, dear,' she said quietly.

'I will. Now, are you coming to Cheltenham on Thursday?'

'Do you want me to?'

'If you want to.'

We had this discussion every year. My mother still hated to see me ride, but she wanted to be around in case something happened. She did not care in the least whether I won or not.

'Yes, though I can never actually watch you.'

'Fine. I'll arrange lunch for you in someone's box.'

'Thanks. Let me know the details soon, won't you?'

I assured her that I would not forget, as I had done once several years before. And, although she had not told me anything I did not already know, I said goodbye with a slight increase in my misgivings about my ability to handle Clive Drury.

Chapter 10

It was just after ten in the evening when Jamie Lloyd-Jones shot into my yard in a convertible BMW. He hammered on the seldom-used front door and breezed in with two camera bags slung round his neck and carrying a pigskin suitcase.

I commented on the photographic kit.

'You'll have to help out with that,' Jamie said. 'I really didn't want to bring along one of our snappers at this stage. They're not very subtle and they get in the way. Besides, I haven't told my editor too much about this gig yet.'

'What have you told him?' I was concerned that even a whisper might get back to Drury.

'To be perfectly frank, absolutely nothing, but fortunately, he trusts my judgement.'

'Good. I hope he's right.'

I showed Jamie up to my sparsely furnished but picturesque spare room.

'The windows aren't entirely wind-proof,' I apologised. 'And you'll probably need more blankets.'

'Don't worry about me,' Jamie said, 'I'm used to sleeping rough.'

We talked for an hour or so before going to bed early, and woke to a blustering, drizzling sort of a March morning which did nothing to quell our keenness for the hunt. We had already started to plan our strategy over breakfast when Sharon arrived at half past seven.

Jamie looked at her appreciatively as she went out to the yard. 'Scope for a bit of naughtiness there, I should think.'

'Her boyfriend's in the SAS,' I answered.

141

'I think I'll leave it alone, then,' Jamie nodded. 'Right, let's get the maps out and decide where to start.'

'Don't bother. A group of six or seven hippy coaches have been parked in a lay-by outside Hereford for a couple of weeks. We'll try them first. They may have come across John Duckett or know of some of the other current sites.'

'Right. You'd better leave the questioning to me. You keep out of sight with the cameras ready in case we get lucky first time out. I'll have to turn up on foot, so it doesn't matter what car we take. You know the roads; do you want to drive?'

'Sure,' I said, wondering how Jamie was going to go about communicating with the new-age travellers.

'I'll go up and change.'

He had not shaved for a day, but when he came back downstairs, he had somehow contrived to look as though he had not done so for several weeks. He was wearing a pair of what had once been black needle-cord jeans, split at the knee and thick with grime. On his feet he wore a pair of decrepit trainers with the soles half off. An ancient denim jacket with an ill-painted sunrise on the back was slung over a T-shirt of indeterminable colour. His longish hair was mussed up and much greasier than it had looked twenty minutes before, and there was a small earring in one ear. He was frankly unrecognisable as a suave young journalist.

I laughed. 'I should think your mother would love to see you now.'

'Look, man, don't hassle me. I'm, like, a free spirit now. I just need a tepee and a weekly giro.'

'Do you think they'll talk to you?'

'Sure,' Jamie said in his normal voice. 'I'll play it by ear. These guys are so unused to anyone approaching them unaggressively that all their inclinations will be to trust me.'

'What a duplicitous shit you are,' I said.

Jamie shrugged. 'It's part of the job, like being an actor or a barrister, or a second-hand picture dealer, come to that. Anyway, how do you know that I'm not sympathetic? I rather envy them their freedom.'

'Oh, well, I'm sure that'll help. Shall we go?'

I drove us down into Hereford, and along the old Roman road that skirts the northern edge of the city. Halfway along, on a patch of wasteland earmarked for some road-widening project for the next century, a small cluster of brightly coloured, graphically decorated buses and trucks were arranged in a corral. Within the circle, a fire was burning and several children and long dogs scampered around it. Jamie ducked his head down as we cruised by. After two hundred yards, he said, 'Okay, go round this corner and wait.'

I did as he asked, pulled up and switched off the engine. Jamie climbed out, clutching a well-worn khaki webbing kit-bag which he slung over his shoulder. He nodded farewell with a shake of his greasy locks and shambled off towards the encampment.

I switched on the radio and waited.

About an hour later, Jamie reappeared. He opened the passenger door and flopped on to the seat. He turned to me with a vague smile.

'All right?' I asked.

He nodded. 'Yeah, fine. Nice people.'

'Oh, God, you're stoned already.'

Jamie giggled. 'Just a bit. They had some amazing grass.'

'At least I suppose that means they believed you.'

'As a matter of fact, I didn't tell them any lies. I just said I was looking for this geezer so that he could denounce his fat-cat capitalist father.'

'Did they know him?'

'They thought so.' Jamie nodded again and gazed into the middle distance.

'Well, where is he?' I asked testily. I did not care in principle if Jamie wanted to smoke a bit of dope, in fact, I enjoyed it myself from time to time, but it was going to make the task of finding John Duckett very slow if he got stoned every time he found a group of travellers.

'Don't worry about a thing. I'll find him. Let's head out to the mountains.' He waved in a vaguely westerly direction.

'Is that where he is?' I asked.

'Sure.'

Doubtfully, I turned the car back on to the Roman road and drove towards the distant profile of the Black Mountains.

It was an easy drive out towards Hay-on-Wye. There was little traffic on the flat, straight road that followed the Wye valley, past Clive Drury's mansion at Gazeley Park.

143

When we reached the small market town, just over the Welsh border, I thought it would be wise to get Jamie straightened up before we continued our search for Drury's son. I suggested we find something to eat and a cup of coffee while we planned the next move.

He agreed, and we found a small cafe, full of earnest, bookish types, displays of organic carrot cake and the smell of fine fresh coffee.

Hay's function as a market town had been largely superseded over the preceding twenty years by its emergence as the country's, if not the world's, greatest centre for second-hand books. This had caused the establishment of a sub-culture quite alien to the surrounding hill-farmers. Painters, writers, and a few musicians found the atmosphere sympathetic, and the sporadic appearance of bands of modern travelling folk went almost unnoticed.

The travellers came for the wealth of magic mushrooms that were to be found in autumn on the slopes of the mountains above Hay. And some of them lingered in sites by the roads that ran up the river valleys towards Central Wales. The sight of Jamie, slouching in his tattered, dirty clothing, raised not an eyebrow.

The first impact of the grass he had smoked had worn off. Jamie admitted that he had not had any for some time, and it had affected him more than he had expected. 'I wish I'd bought a bit from them,' he added wistfully.

'Try and restrict yourself next time, or you'll forget what the hell you're supposed to be doing.'

Jamie agreed, and he tried to focus on our next move.

What we should do, he said, was to carry on up the Wye valley towards Builth Wells. The travellers in Hereford thought that John might be with a group up there. Their directions, or Jamie's interpretation of them, were vague, but I felt that a few enquiries as we reached the area would probably find them.

It turned out that no enquiries were necessary. We spotted the vehicles in what had once been a siding of the disused railway line. Once again I cruised by. But this time, I had to go on a quarter of a mile before Jamie thought it safe to get out.

He wandered back down the road, and turned into the lane which led to a bridge across the course of the old railtrack.

I hoped he was together enough to deal with John Duckett if he found him.

I turned on the radio again, and soon found myself being shaken awake by Jamie. This time, he was more coherent.

'I haven't found him, but these people have seen him recently, and they said he was making for a place by the Teifi, on the other side of the mountains. There's a farmer there who puts up with them, for a small rent.'

I looked at my watch. It was after midday. It could take another couple of hours to find them, and the same to get back to my house that evening.

'Okay, let's go.'

The damp, buffeting wind of the morning had blown the clouds from the tops of the hills and died since morning. It was a fine, clear spring day; a perfect day, as it happened, to be driving the deserted hill roads of this empty part of Britain. Jamie, still in a thoughtful, aesthetic frame of mind, became almost lyrical, and I found it hard to believe that he was normally a highly successful, rhinoceros-hide scandal seeker. He talked about this for a while, castigating himself and all his colleagues for their profession. I hoped that he was not on the point of experiencing a Damascus Road flash; not before he had tracked down John Arthur Duckett and pulled all the elements of his story together.

As he talked, I felt pangs of guilt over Harry Winchcombe's condition, and hoped that it was improving. My mind, despite the tranquil sunlit scene around us, was whirling with thoughts of Sean's meeting with Drury the following day, and I was frankly dreading the consequences when Drury started tracing the cause of his impending troubles back to me.

After we had topped the Cambrian watershed, to the sight of empty hills rolling westward to the Irish sea, Jamie turned his attention to me.

'What spurs you on, Archie, if you'll excuse the equestrian metaphor?'

'Normally, nothing particularly spurs me on. It's more a question of being inexorably sucked towards the future by some great vacuum cleaner.'

'That sounds nasty, and, if I may say so, rather disingenuous. You're obviously fanatical about winning your races. I read in the racing pages that you're the likely favourite for the big hunter chase at Cheltenham next week, as well as the amateur championships, and you don't get to the top of any tree – even amateur ones – unless you're slightly fanatical. And you seem very determined to score over Drury.' He turned and looked at me with surprisingly bright eyes.

I nodded. 'Yes, I want to win races; I want to win the championship, at least once.'

'Why?'

'Mostly just because I want to win it, but I've given myself a few other incentives to justify it.'

'What are they?'

'I won't bore you with them now; there isn't a story there. And as for Drury, I can't wait to see him thoroughly stuffed. There's a very big story behind that and I promise you'll be the first to get it.'

Jamie was too experienced to protest. 'What are you up to with that chap, Sean Grady?' he asked. 'Why did you want to borrow the camera?'

'Like I said, you'll be the first to know.'

The sense of reaching our goal became more marked as we wound down off the mountains towards the small river which drained their western slopes. I felt like a hound closing in on its quarry, and I sensed Jamie gearing himself up to resume the role of new-age traveller.

We reached a village which straddled the Teifi. I found a small Post Office and went in to ask if anything was known of a local band of wandering hippies.

The woman behind the counter made a face. 'Are you from the social, then?'

'Yes,' I said.

'Good. It is absolutely disgraceful. Some of them comes here for their dole, yet they wouldn't do a stroke if you asked them. I 'ope you put a stop to it.'

'Can you tell me where I'll find them?' I asked non-committally.

She gave directions to a farm three miles upriver, and wished me luck.

We followed the river as it bounced and scurried through rocky gorges and meadows. I glanced across at Jamie. He seemed intent on preparing himself for his role and had, perhaps unconsciously, adopted a hunched, defensive posture.

'How do you want to play this?' I asked.

'Drop me out of sight. If I'm not back in half an hour it'll mean I've found him. He may be hard to persuade and I'll have to stay there for a while, certainly tonight. I'll ring you tomorrow and tell you the score.'

'That sounds a bit over the top. You don't want to hang around there all night do you?'

'As a matter of fact, I think I do. I'm beginning to see a really tasty feature piece – "The Legacy of the Sixties; What happened when Flower Power shrivelled and died?" '

It seemed he had his guilt-feelings about his job well under control now.

'That's a bit deep for your rag,' I said.

'Not if there are a few pictures of degenerate, horny-looking women.'

'But what if none of them are horny-looking?'

'Curiously, they quite often are, in a grubby sort of way. But if they're not, we'll just rub a bit of dirt on a few page three hopefuls.'

'Are you sure you won't just end up getting totally stoned?'

'No,' he laughed, 'I'll be careful.'

We saw the encampment on the edge of a marshy meadow. There were at least twenty vehicles, and a collection of bend-overs – tents made from willow branches, bent in semicircular hoops and covered with polythene.

'Are you happy about staying the night in one of those?' I asked.

'It won't be much less comfortable than your spare room,' Jamie said. 'And if John Duckett is there, it's going to take a while to establish some kind of rapport with him. I've got to be prepared to muck in with them.'

'Muck in sounds about right.'

'Don't be so blimpish.' Jamie started to climb out of the car. 'Okay, if I'm not back in half an hour, I'm hanging on there and I'll ring you tomorrow.'

'I'm riding in a race, and before that I may have to make contact with Sean, but leave a message on my machine if I'm out. I'll make sure I get it. Best of luck . . . and don't get too stoned.'

Jamie grinned. 'Not *too* stoned.'

I had pulled up about half a mile beyond the travellers' camp. Once again, I resigned myself to waiting, hoping that Jamie would be lucky this time. I was still not sure that this scheme would really work, and even if it did, how much impact it would have. But I felt that it might contribute to an overall sense of persecution that would make Drury commit indiscretions and force him out into the open.

I watched Jamie saunter down the road like some anarchic vagrant. He had a good ear and was quick-witted enough to pick up on the mood and jargon of these self-marginalised people. And though they were not dangerous, I admired his guts.

I waited forty minutes, to allow for any hitches, but Jamie did not reappear. I started the car, and headed off up the valley to take the mountain road east towards Rhayader and England.

I stopped at a small hotel, which was Rhayader's grandest, to use a telephone. I dialled the Portsmouth hospital and asked for Harry Winchcombe. After a while, I heard him.

'It's Archie,' I said. 'How are you?'

'Better since they shoved me into a side ward.'

'Is Sarah there?'

'Yeah, she has been.'

'How's the head?'

'I'm so dosed up that I haven't a clue. I can't feel a thing.'

'What do they say?'

'I can probably go home in a few days. But did you get my message?' His voice had a panicky edge to it. 'I don't think my troubles are over. I've had an anonymous card. It says "Get well soon, and don't forget, indiscretion can seriously damage your health." Doesn't take much to work out who sent it.'

He sounded almost desperate now.

'For God's sake; whatever you do, don't go to the police yet,' I urged him.

'But Archie, these guys are serious. I think they meant to finish me off last time.'

'Okay. I'll come and get you when you're ready to leave, and we'll take you somewhere out of the way until I've finished my job. Please don't panic or we'll never get the bastards. And don't tell anyone else what happened.'

'All right,' he murmured reluctantly, 'though Sarah was pretty astonished that I should have been attempting to sail.'

'Just keep your pecker up. I'll be in touch and get down to see you as soon as I can. Ring me at home if you've got any problems.'

'Sure,' he said, resigned.

We said goodbye, and I hoped he would have the resilience not to spoil by panicking what little progress I had made.

Then I dialled Georgie's number in London. There was no reply, so I tried Temple Ferris. She was not there either, though expected. I left a message for her to ring me and tell me if she wanted to groom for me the next day.

A short, russet-faced man in a flat hat was twitching behind me, anxious to use the phone. I did not want my next conversation to be overheard, so I offered it to him. He grasped it gratefully. There was a guilty, remorseful look in his eye and a strong whiff of whisky on his breath. He dialled and when his call was answered, he issued a passionate declaration that he was never going racing again, followed it up with a few meek grunts, and tottered out to continue his journey from Ludlow racecourse to whatever West Wales valley he inhabited.

When he was out of the less than private hallway, I wished I had allowed myself to be beguiled by the various salesmen who had attempted to sell me car phones over the last few years. Cautiously, I rang Sean Grady in London.

He answered right away. 'Where have you been?' he asked curtly, 'I've left three messages on your machine. Is it working?'

'Yes, but I'm not at home. What's happening?'

'I've fixed it for tomorrow morning – ten thirty.'

'Where?'

'I'll tell you when I see you. I'll be at your place at about nine, okay?'

'Fine. See you then.'

I trembled slightly as I put the receiver back. If Drury had agreed to turn up with thirty thousand pounds for what he thought was a bunch of Irish terrorists, he was surely going to cover his back. If Sean slipped up, he could be in a lot of trouble. For the first time, the real danger came home to me, and I wondered if I was mad to be trying to deal with Drury, aided only by three amateurs, who had probably never hit anyone in anger, and one of whom was a gently nurtured young woman.

Darkness fell as I drove along the empty roads which swept along the valley floor between the Radnor hills. My doubts about my ability to deal with such a formidable foe as Drury did nothing to relieve my nervousness about my race the next day.

I had to win it to keep my place in the championship, but I

dare not take any risks, with Caesar's Consul running in the big Foxhunters Chase at Cheltenham the following Thursday. Both Robert Prideaux-James and Damian Drury were riding in the next day's race, and they would both be trying their damnedest on animals they did not have to save for Cheltenham. It would in any case be a competitive open race, on a good, fast course on the west bank of the River Severn in Gloucestershire.

The prospect of winning this season's cup, though better than ever, had been pushed into second place for me by Bill Beecham's death and his posthumous plea for justice, but I had been so committed to it over the years that I simply could not let it go now. Besides, I did not want to arouse anyone's suspicions by behaving in a way which would be considered out of character. So my campaign for these insignificant racing honours would have to continue alongside the more serious campaign in which I was engaged.

Sharon had her feet on the kitchen table. Her boots were off, and she was cleaning tack. Opposite her sat a short-haired, deeply tanned man of about thirty and impressively gorilla-like proportions.

'Hello, Arch,' Sharon greeted me as she carried on her cleaning. 'This is Ian.'

The ape-man thrust out a large fist, and smiled with a glint of hard, aquamarine eyes. 'Hello. Sharon didn't know what time ye'd be back, so I said I'd wait with her,' he said in undulating Glaswegian.

'That was good of you,' I answered, uncertain whether or not he had intended to convey that he was doing me a favour.

'Georgina phoned,' Sharon said, 'and she's going with you tomorrow. Will it be all right if I hunt Jasper?'

'Of course. Have there been any other messages?'

'That's the only one I've took, but the light's been flashing all day.'

I turned to the machine and wound it back.

Sean's messages, each more testy than the last, were interspersed with Harry's, which was even more panicky than the conversation I had had with him, and one from Amanda Drury, announcing that she would be dropping in on her way to Gazeley that evening.

'Has she been yet?' I asked Sharon.

'No.'

None of Sean's or Harry's monologues had been specific, but their tone was obvious.

'Ye sound as though you've got a few problems,' Ian remarked. 'Sharon told me some villain tried to pinch your horse, too.'

'There's a connection,' I conceded.

'Let me know if ye need any help.'

I looked at him for a moment; his unmoving, dispassionate eyes; the bulky biceps and pectorals that showed through his T-shirt on which was printed, 'I Don't Give a Saddam'. There was no question; he was a professional, where my team and I were not even apprentices.

'No,' I said reluctantly. 'It's not something you could get involved in, not if you're in the Regiment.'

He shrugged. 'That dinna worry me. I'm out in two months; starting m' own security business. Anyway, it doesna' matter. Ye look as though ye can look after y'self.'

'I could maybe do with a bit of advice, though.'

'Sure,' he gestured generously.

'Is there any chance you could come here about nine tomorrow?'

'When your friend Sean's coming? I'll be here.'

'He was going to help me to take Jasper to the meet,' Sharon said.

'He still can,' I said.

Sharon looked as though she doubted it, but said nothing. I guessed that the two of them had already discussed what little she knew of recent events. She finished soaping and polishing a set of rawhide stirrup leathers and swung her legs off the table. 'Well, that's done,' she said with satisfaction. 'We'd better be off now, Ian.'

Ian stood up, and said to me, 'Ye tell me all about it in the morning, okay?'

'Thanks. I will.'

They carried the tack out with them and I heard them drive off in Sharon's car. I did not want to overvalue the help Ian might be able to give, but I was very relieved to have this possible recruit, even if only as advisor.

I had not eaten anything since wholemeal scones in Hay that morning, so I made myself a couple of ungainly Marmite sandwiches and went up to run a bath. It had been a long, strange day, but at least I was making progress.

I sank into the bath, and had almost fallen asleep when I heard a loud hammering on the back door.

I had forgotten Amanda's threat to call in. I considered ignoring her, then reluctantly clambered from my bath and wrapped a robe around me. Still dripping, I opened the door to her.

'Caught you on the job, did I?' she asked with a strained grin.

'No,' I said without expression, while I wondered how I had let myself succumb to such unsubtle charms.

'Well, can I come in, then?'

I opened the door wider to let her in. She burst through it as if taking possession. I said nothing, but closed the door and followed her through to the kitchen.

'Christ, this place is a hovel,' she said, glancing round.

'You don't have to stay.'

'What are you being so snotty about? You had a serious sense of humour failure when I saw you in London, but I thought that was just because you were jealous.'

'Well it wasn't.'

Amanda walked across to me and stretched up to clasp her hands together behind my neck. One of her legs made a gap in my robe, and snaked between my thighs. Her hips began a rhythmic thrusting against mine.

'I know how to cure you of pompous bullshit,' she muttered, and for a moment I almost wanted to be cured, but the telephone saved me.

It was Harry Winchcombe. He sounded terrible; my heart sank.

'What's happened?' I asked.

'One of those men has been here.'

I was about to ask him for details when I remembered Amanda. 'Hang on, I've just got to deal with something here,' I told Harry, and put the receiver down beside the phone.

I turned to Amanda, who was looking at me uncertainly.

'Sorry, something's come up. You'll have to go,' I said without a lot of charm.

'It's okay,' she said. 'I'll wait.'

'No, you won't. You can't.'

I walked to the back door and opened it for her. She stood and glared at me venomously for a moment, then, without a word, she marched out to the yard and did not look back. When I had heard the car start and move off, I closed the door and returned to the phone.

'Was it one of the men who attacked you?' I asked Harry.

'Yes, the big one.' The one I had not seen.

'What did he do?'

'He'd come looking for me. I wasn't in my room; I'd just been down to the hospital shop to buy a book. When I reached the end of the corridor, I saw him slipping into my room. Thank God he didn't see me; I went and got a nurse; she and a porter slung him out. I told them that he was a chap who had a grudge against me, and they agreed to move me to another room for tonight.' He paused and added apologetically, 'Then they rang the police.'

'Oh, no,' I groaned.

'It's okay. I stuck to my story about a disgruntled ex-employee and gave him a bogus name, but, Archie, he'll be back, I'm certain of it. The police are going to keep a look-out tonight, but I'm supposed to stay here for a few more days.'

'All right. You'll just have to sign yourself out first thing in the morning and get Sarah to drive you to London, but for God's sake make sure you're not followed. I'll arrange for you to stay in Sean Grady's flat for the time being.'

'Who the hell's Sean Grady?'

'He's helping me, but Drury and his men know nothing about him. Try and find a way of leaving the hospital without being seen.'

Harry sounded doubtful. 'I'm still not feeling too good anyway, with all the drugs they've given me.'

'Give me a number where I can reach Sarah, then. I'll tell her what's happened and she can arrange it.'

Harry sounded unconvinced of the value of this move as we said goodbye, but I judged that Sarah was well up to the job and dialled the number Harry had given me with reasonable confidence.

She was in, and she was quite willing to do things the way I suggested without asking for too many details. I told her I would come to London on Monday and fill her in then. I made her promise that whatever happened, she was to keep Harry out of sight in the Lowndes Street flat, and not to go to the police.

She agreed, though obviously burning with curiosity now, and I tried to sound as though I knew what I was doing.

Chapter 11

I slept badly. Visions of Drury pursuing and cornering me dominated my dreams. By morning, it was only the knowledge that Ian Jack was arriving shortly to add his strength to my amateurish efforts that stopped me from caving in and handing the whole thing over to the police, even though their grounds for feeling Drury's collar were still scanty.

Sean turned up in a gleaming new Range Rover a few minutes before nine. I had just started to tell him about our new military advisor, when Ian and Sharon drove into the yard in an ancient and scabrous Land Rover.

The soldier shook Sean's hand, and the Irishman glanced at me with a slight nod. I had decided anyway to trust Ian. Although my judgement of character in the past had often proved regrettably erratic, I was sure that Sharon was a hundred per cent loyal, and she and Ian gave all the appearance of being thoroughly committed.

A pot of coffee had finished percolating, and I swept a stack of unopened bank statements and brown envelopes to one side of the kitchen table. We all sat down, and I gave Ian almost the complete story. He took it all in, though his head and eyes did not move, and he did not speak until I had finished.

'This guy sounds a bit outa your league, if you don't mind my saying so,' he commented. 'And why are you so determined to deal with him; what's it to you?'

I told him that it was loyalty to Bill Beecham, and a desire for justice. He looked unconvinced.

'Well, whatever your reasons, I think you're right that the police won't be able to touch him yet. You do have to get him out into the open. Whether this business of revealing his other family will help, I don't know, but if you can get him mixed up in defrauding his insurers, and pin the sabotage of the racecourses on him, you'd be giving them enough to go on. Then you'd better back off pretty damn quick. You're already part of the conspiracy in the eyes of the law.'

I was relieved that a cool-minded outsider took that view. 'The point of the press campaign,' I added, 'is to expose him for what he is. I've also got someone in Lloyd's digging into his early activities to see what skeletons are in that closet. This is all ammunition in a campaign to denigrate him in the eyes of his grand friends.'

'Well, maybe that'll help, but lots of people in high places have skeletons in their closets too, and I shouldn'a think they're that keen to encourage that sorta thing.'

'But it'll make him jumpy; maybe panic him into doing something rash.'

'He doesn't sound the panicky type,' Ian said.

'His social standing is his weak spot; he's hypersensitive about it. An attack on that could just get him to react irrationally,' I said, wanting to justify Jamie's task.

'I think Archie's right,' Sean backed me up. 'And, as you say, it can't do any harm.'

'Okay,' Ian said. 'But let's concentrate on what you're doing today.' He seemed naturally to have assumed command. 'Show me on the map exactly where you've arranged to meet Drury.'

Sean unfolded the OS 1:50,000 map of the area and with a biro put a dot on the north bank of the Wye. 'Drury's got two miles of fishing on this bank. It would be a perfectly normal place for him to be meeting someone, to discuss a let or something. That's why I brought a Range Rover. We'll get some tackle out and handing over a bag of money and checking it should be a piece of cake. It's right out in the open – not a busy place but very visible, so if we are seen, it'll not look as though something dodgy's going on. It also gives Archie a good chance to get some close-up shots, and of course I'll be wired. He agreed to it anyway. I said it had to be out this way because I was heading straight back to Ireland.'

'He must have been getting bad advice or ignoring it then.' Ian had been studying the map as Sean talked. 'How are you going to approach the meet?' he asked.

156

'Straight down this track from the main road.' Sean indicated a white line that left the road and curved through a quarter of a mile of woodland before crossing flat, open meadowland to the river.

'If he's got any sense, he'll probably assume you're going to put someone into those woods. He must've thought of the possibility that the whole thing's a straight con.' Ian sat back in his chair. 'As a matt'rafact, the whole thing's a totally amateur job, on both sides. I think I'd better help stack the odds in your favour.'

Sharon, who had not spoken, looked pleased, but concerned.

'D'you think you should, Ian?' she said. 'You'll be drummed out the Regiment if you're caught.'

'I won't be caught,' he laughed. 'Don't you want me to help your boss? You go and chase your wee fox, and don't worry.'

Sharon accepted this with unexpected meekness. I thought that, probably, she had been hoping all along that her boyfriend would throw his considerable weight – in physique and experience – behind us.

'Right,' Ian went on, 'let's get this straight, then. The object of the exercise is to convince Drury that you're going to steal his horse, so's he can claim the insurance. He's bringing you thirty grand up front. You're going to record and photograph him in the act of handing over the money. Then what?' He looked at Sean and me.

'We use that as evidence of a conspiracy to defraud,' I said.

'I would'a thought the police'd want more than that. You really need him to make the claim.'

'But that would mean actually taking Tomahawk from the stud. That really is out of our league. I think if he's confronted with the tapes and shots, we'll have him by the balls and on the run.'

'Sounds uncomfortable,' Ian said drily, 'but hardly the lethal blow.'

'I know it's not perfect, but I'm certain we can establish his connection with the racecourse sabotage, and, of course, we'll have the use of his thirty grand for a while.'

'For a while! D'you mean you're going to give it back to him?'

'No, to the police.'

Ian shrugged. 'Well that's your business. I'll not charge you for my help – and by God you're going to need it.'

Ian, Sean and I went minutely over our ramshackle plan. Ian

157

pulled it into a more workable shape, taking into account a dozen factors Sean and I had not. He would look after any back-up Drury had in place in the woods. He told us that we must assume Drury would have Sean followed, and that if Sean could not shake them off, he would have to press on as if he was intending to go back to Ireland. He had told me the way I should take my shots, and how Sean should go about the handling of the money. To him, it was a routine sort of an activity, and some of his calm rubbed off on us, but not enough to completely quell my seething guts as we prepared to set off separately for our different positions.

Sharon seemed sorry not to be part of it now. I gave her instructions for Georgie, who was due in half an hour's time, and left her moodily plaiting my impatient hunter.

It was half past nine when we left my house. Sean had arranged to meet Drury at eleven. We pulled out of my yard in a convoy and headed across the small hills to Hereford. There I parted company with the other two to take a route south of the Wye to my position on the opposite bank from the meet.

Ian was going to station himself in the woodland through which Drury and Sean would have to pass. He aimed to park a mile downstream, where the woods curved down to the riverbank, and work his way on foot towards the track. If, as he expected, Drury had a man, or men, in those woods, he would deal with them. I had not asked him how. And I was reluctant to ask him specifically if he was armed.

Sean would drive openly down to the rendezvous, to reach it half an hour before the appointed time.

I was guiltily grateful that I had the easiest job. I was in no doubt that Drury would not think twice about using violence if it provided a simple solution to a problem.

After seven or eight miles, I parked my car on the road, as close as I could to my spot by the river. I made my way down to the bank, keeping low in a drainage ditch alongside a tall hawthorn hedge. By ten fifteen, I was in place in a clump of scrubby alders and young sycamores, twenty feet above the fast silent water. I checked my map. I had a clear view of Sean's meeting place. I took the camera from its bag, set it on a tripod and fixed on the long, thousand millimetre lens. Peering through it, the far bank was six feet away.

The next fifteen minutes passed at the pace of a Boycott test innings. I could not relax and every sound made me start. I could scarcely believe that the first of our impromptu plans to bring about Drury's decline and fall was about to reach its high point. I was so nervous that I doubted my ability to handle the camera; I wondered at what point Sean's stage fright would desert him.

When I saw him driving slowly into view in the dark green Range Rover, I felt as if the starter in a race had dropped his flag, and all my apprehension fled.

I put my eye to the camera to focus on the vehicle where it had stopped. I could see Sean clearly through the windscreen. He was looking relaxed, smoking a cigarette, with his left arm slung over the back of the passenger seat.

I changed the lens to a wide angle and took a couple of shots to set the scene. I had just finished and was refocusing the telephoto lens when Drury appeared in a mud-spattered Mercedes. He was alone. I began to take my shots. He pulled up a few yards away from Sean's Range Rover and got out. He walked towards Sean, who did not deign to open the door until Drury had reached him.

Drury looked positively affable, and ready to shake his co-conspirator by the hand, but he was not offered the chance. Sean climbed down from his seat, flung down his cigarette and ground it into the earth.

There was a brief exchange, after which Drury leaned into his car and pulled out a briefcase and a fishing bag. They both got into the Range Rover.

They spoke for two or three minutes during which I got some clear shots of Sean examining the contents of the fishing bag, nodding and putting it on his lap. Drury left the car, looking less affable than when he had arrived, but apparently satisfied. He went back and got into the Mercedes.

I could hear the Range Rover start up, and watched Sean swing it round and bounce back along the track towards the woods and the main road.

Drury's car remained silent and motionless.

I breathed again, as if for the first time in ten minutes. So far, so good.

But I was going to have to wait until the afternoon's racing was over to hear if the rest of the operation had succeeded.

I waited another quarter of an hour, until Drury started his car and disappeared after Sean. If, as we assumed, he had put a tail on Sean further up the road towards Wales and Fishguard, he would not be in any hurry to follow and would be returning to Gazeley to carry on a normal Saturday morning. It was even likely that I would see him later, taking the credit for any races Damian might be lucky enough to win. Though, I was determined, Drury Junior was not going to win mine.

I packed up the camera and almost ran the half mile back to my car. I dropped off the film at the house of a discreet photographer who had agreed to develop it for me himself. I also stopped at a phone box and rang Sean's flat.

Harry answered the phone with a mumbled 'Hello?'

He had, he assured me, got away from the hospital without being detected. He had not even risked signing himself out. Sarah had brought her car to a doctor's space by a back entrance. Harry said his sister had taken elaborate precautions to make sure that no one was following them. They were certain that they had not been spotted by Drury's man.

I tried to convince Harry that he would be safe where he was, but agreed to move him somewhere else early the following week. He suggested France.

I put the phone down, trying to sympathise with Harry for the hammering he had taken. I leaped into my car and was back at my house by twelve.

Georgie had everything ready. We loaded the Consul and set off at once for the races.

'Well?' she asked as we started down the lane, 'how did it go?'

I had not had a chance to see Georgie to tell her the plans I had made with her two friends. It was just a week since we had all been staying at Temple Ferris, but, reviewing it, it had been a hell of a busy week.

'Great, I think. I'm sorry I haven't had a chance to tell you before what we were doing, but it's all happened so fast. How did you know what was going on today?'

'I didn't. Sharon just told me you'd gone off with Sean and her soldier, and it's obvious that you've been up to something.'

'You're right,' I nodded. 'We've set Drury up to defraud the company that insures his shares in Tomahawk, and as far as I can tell, he's bitten. We photographed and recorded the whole thing this morning. Sean convinced him that he was part of an IRA unit, wanting three hundred thousand to kidnap the horse. Drury handed over the first thirty thousand this morning, but I won't know if it's really worked until Ian meets me at the races. He should have met up with Sean by then.'

'He's coming there?'

'Yes. It seemed the best place. We can talk there without being noticed. And if Drury comes, I want him to see me there.'

'But what are you going to do with the money? You can't just hang on to it.'

'When we've got all the evidence together, we'll take it to the police.'

'But I thought the whole idea was not to go to the police, like Bill asked.'

'That's the whole point of setting Drury up. Bill's name won't come into it. It'll be one scam of Drury's which we can be sure Bill wasn't involved in. What we're doing is everything we can to get Drury in deep shit without having to bring Bill's murder into it. Destroy his reputation; get him banged up for an entirely fresh crime.'

'But, Archie, it sounds dead risky to me. What if he realises it's you?'

'Yes, well, that's the downside. But so far so good.'

'Has Jamie been helping as well?' Georgie asked.

'Oh, hell!' I cursed myself.

'Why?'

'I forgot to see if he'd left a message for me.'

'What about? Where is he?'

I gave Georgie a run-down on all the past week's developments. Jamie's visit to Doreen Duckett and my visit with Harry to the barns in Portsmouth. At my description of the attack on Harry and his attacker's follow-up visit to the hospital, a look of horror crossed her face.

'My God,' she gasped, 'were they trying to kill him?'

'I don't know. Maybe. I hope to hell they weren't but he's the only person who could connect them to the racecourse sabotage. I'm certain they're working for Drury. Don't worry, though; Harry'll be okay for the time being, provided he lies low in Sean's flat. I'll have to move him soon, in case Sean gets rumbled, but that's a long shot. He did a great job on Drury at their first meeting. The tapes were amazing.'

'But, Archie, what will Drury do if he does discover you're involved?'

I summoned up some bravado and a confident grin. 'He won't.'

'I wish you'd never started it,' she said angrily. 'I'd never have encouraged you if I'd really thought it could come to this. Archie, you must take it to the police and drop it now.'

'No, not yet. And I didn't start this. Drury did by killing Bill. It's always been on the cards he could do the same again. But I'd blow the whole thing if I gave up now.'

Georgie pleaded some more, and in her pleading, I sensed a note that warmed me very much, but I was not going to be talked out of the action I had started.

'There's nothing impressive about persevering with it out of sheer bloody-mindedness,' Georgie persisted, 'when people's lives are at risk. If Bill's motive for telling you not to go to the police was to protect my mother and I, well, I can tell you, we'd far rather live with his misdemeanours coming to light than with someone else's death.'

'Listen,' I answered, 'until we're certain of nailing Drury, it's going to go on being risky. But we've got to get enough evidence together to convince the police that they can bang him up in the face of a legion of London's heaviest lawyers. We can do things the police can't, otherwise I'd have been more than happy to leave it to them.'

Georgie was silent for a mile or two. When she spoke again, she gave no sign of whether or not she accepted my reasons. As if the preceding conversation had never taken place, she asked instead about that afternoon's race.

'Will the Consul run all right if the ground's still heavy after all the rain we've had this week?'

I jerked my mind back to the business of horseracing.

'He doesn't like the mud too much, but I think he's got enough stamina to see off today's opposition,' I said, still not really focusing on the race.

'If you can go out and win this one, do you really think it will divert Drury's attention from the possibility of your being mixed up in what went on this morning?'

'Sure, that's the idea. And I want to win anyway, remember?'

Georgie smiled. 'How could I forget?'

Georgie had done her usual magnificent job of turning out Caesar's Consul. He looked the picture of a classic jumping horse as she led him around the parade ring.

With her dark hair blowing in gleaming strands about her lovely face and the longest legs I had ever seen in a pair of Levi's, Georgie was attracting as many glances as the horse; particularly from Clive Drury.

Drury stood in the centre of the ring with his wife and a fellow owner who looked like a financier. He had not seen me yet, but the sight of Georgie with the Consul had him glancing around for me as I approached the ring from the changing room with the other jockeys.

When he saw me come in, a few paces behind his son, he looked at me with cold, clear eyes which skewered through mine and hit me in the back of the head. I tried not to flinch, and carried on walking towards him. I gave him a quick, meaningless nod, and his face abruptly assumed a bland smile; he had not seen my fear.

'Archie,' he boomed in greeting, 'have you found my Fernleys yet?'

'I'm getting warm,' I replied lightly.

'You'll have to do better than that,' Drury said, provoked, as I knew he would be.

'And you're going to have to pay more than you think,' I added.

'I doubt it,' Drury said with certainty.

'Anyway,' I said, turning to Georgie and the Consul, who were now walking towards the centre of the parade ring, 'I've got to go and make sure your son comes no better than second in this race. You're not trying to impair my concentration, are you?'

Drury's companion laughed; Drury scowled, and started to open his mouth, before snapping it shut with a visible effort of self-control.

I turned my attention to my mount. Always, before a race, I found that I could clear my head of all distractions from riding and winning. Even Georgie's hand on my thigh after she legged me up into the saddle did not affect me. She looked up at me with big, worried eyes.

'Be careful, Archie. And make sure you win. I was watching Drury as you came in; he was giving you a filthy look.'

I gave her a quick smile as I leaned down to adjust my leathers. Like most people, my legs are of slightly different lengths, and if the saddle was not sitting exactly upright, it meant you were riding lop-sided; at the end of three miles, that would make one leg ache a lot more than the other.

Georgie led me in silence for a couple of circuits round the ring, before taking me out and unclipping her rope to release the Consul to canter down to the track and the half mile round to the start.

Robert Prideaux-James passed me on his chestnut gelding, Scud Missile. The animal had been regrettably named before the weapon had become notorious in the hands of Saddam Hussein. He looked as if he had been specifically prepared for the race. He was on his toes and his muscles stood out like iron hawsers. This gave me some cause for concern; he was known to be an out-and-out stayer and, though the Consul needed the race quite close to Cheltenham to keep his lungs clear, what he did not need was a really hard slog. If the worst came to the worst, I made up my mind that I would pull the Consul up, rather than exhaust him.

It had not rained since the previous day, and a sharp south-easterly had been taking the moisture from the top of the ground for five or six hours. It was still quite soft but not enough to slow the Consul significantly. I overtook Damian Drury, who glanced across with an uncertain smile. His horse had small feet and the softish going definitely would not suit him. Had it been my horse, I would have been tempted to withdraw him in these conditions, but I did not suppose Damian was allowed that option.

Down by the start, several other jockeys were showing their mounts the first fence which was plain and inviting. Although by point-to-point standards it was well-built, it was as soft as a dandy brush compared to Cheltenham. I joined the other runners with the Consul, and was amiably greeted by a pair of long-standing rivals. Their horses were both outclassed in this open race, but did not qualify for any of the lesser ones. Mike Thomson and Freddy Philby, like myself, owned and trained their animals on a shoe-string.

'I suppose you think you're going to hack up today,' Freddy said.

'Provided you don't get in my way when I'm lapping you,' I replied.

'Prideaux-James's looks the danger,' said Mike.

I nodded. 'He's very fit, and he'll get the trip on this ground.'

'If we can get in his way for you, we will,' Freddy offered, acknowledging the realities of his own chances.

'He probably knows that, and he won't give you the chance; but if he does . . .' I gave them a grin and turned the Consul back towards the start.

The starter got the eight of us away with a nice clean break and straight away, Scud Missile and Prideaux-James set off in front on the inside to take the first fence next to the rails. He stood back at it with almost a stride to spare, and flew it impressively. As I reached the fence, he landed and galloped on at a real good clip to the next. It was obvious that he intended to take the wind out of our sails as early as possible.

The race covered two and a half circuits of the right-handed course. For the first two, I would be quite content to stay within ten lengths of Scud Missile. The Consul liked to see another horse's backside a few lengths in front, and if he sensed that I was not constantly pushing him, he would be a lot happier.

A couple of other jockeys took another view. Damian, with his horse fighting the bit, had no choice and galloped past me after the second fence. He got to within a length of Scud Missile and managed to stay there for the rest of what was an eventful first circuit.

Freddy Philby was cruising along beside me as we passed the winning post for the second time with one full circuit to run. He looked across. 'I'm afraid I'm not going to be able to help much,' he shouted above the wind howling in our ears.

'It doesn't matter. I'm going okay,' I yelled back as we prepared to take a big open ditch going away from the crowd.

The Consul put in an enormous leap and landed two lengths ahead of Freddy's horse. Damian Drury already had his whip out as I came alongside him, now six or seven lengths adrift from Scud Missile. I could almost see Damian shrug as I pulled past him. He must have known that he would have to pull up soon; his animal had run itself into the ground.

Before the next fence, I had time to take a long glance behind me. Prideaux-James's pace had killed the race for the rest of the field. Led by Mike Thomson they were labouring already, a good ten lengths back. The Consul was going comfortably, still well on the bit, and I knew that it was only a question now of whether or not Prideaux-James had misjudged his pace. In this going, I thought there was a good chance he had, and I tucked myself tight to the rails where the good ground was.

For the next five fences, I enjoyed myself, placing the Consul as well as I could, helping him to find his stride, and relishing the sensation of flying the fences.

Four furlongs and two jumps from home, I asked him for an extra effort. He responded magnificently. He knew what was needed and stretched his legs so that they seemed to cover another yard with each stride and we took the next fence just two lengths behind the leader.

As we landed, I eased the Consul a little to the left as the course swung right towards the final fence and the home straight. The Consul pricked his ears, craned his neck and brought us alongside Scud Missile. Prideaux-James caught sight of us from the corner of his eye, then turned his head directly towards me and glared malevolently with the old, familiar sneer on his lips. I suddenly realised that he was driving his horse across the course to my side and was trying to run me out. If I had not been going so easily, he might have had a chance. But, by this time, the Consul was almost running away with me; all I had to do was let out some rein and get a neck in front.

I felt sorry for Scud Missile, who was probably wondering why he was being pulled all over the course after running his heart out on the soft ground. He certainly must have been confused and unbalanced because, until then, he had always been the safest of jumpers. But as the Consul stood off and pinged the last, Scud Missile literally did nothing about it. He hammered into the solid, lower part of the fence and crashed down behind me.

The Consul needed no help now. We galloped for home, with the race won. I felt the glow I always felt when I passed the post first, but Prideaux-James's obvious aggression had alarmed me. There had been more than just the will to win on his face as he had tried to ride me off.

Although he had won easily, Caesar's Consul had nonetheless galloped three miles in testing conditions. I dropped my reins as soon as I could, pulled him up to a walk and jumped off. Scud Missile cantered past riderless with dangling reins and mud all down one side, followed about fifteen lengths later by Freddy Philby on his floundering animal.

Georgie was already running on to the course to greet us. For the time being, it seemed, all other worries were suspended. She wore a broad, unsubtle smile of triumphant pride. She even let herself go to the point of leaping up, throwing her arms around me and kissing me warmly on the lips. I gave her a return squeeze and was ready to press home my advantage when we were interrupted by a mud-smeared Robert Prideaux-James. He had apparently decided to engage in the proverbial best form of defence by tapping me on the shoulder and smashing a fist on my chin as I turned it towards him.

I staggered with the shock of the blow, but was ready to retaliate when, fortunately, Georgie came between me and my instinctive reaction. Holding the Consul's bridle now, she placed herself between me and Prideaux-James and faced me squarely.

'Don't be such a pratt!' she yelled with unexpected vehemence. 'He knows perfectly well he was in the wrong. He's just trying to rile you into fighting.'

Prideaux-James was trying to pull her to one side to pursue this aim, when a pair of red-faced and puffing stewards arrived at a run.

'What the hell's going on?' the senior of the two spluttered.

Georgie turned to the bowler-hatted official, who recognised her. 'This man,' she indicated Prideaux-James with a disdainful gesture, 'simply came up and attacked Archie without the slightest provocation.'

'Yes. We saw,' said the other steward, with his breath recovered. 'We saw what you did, Robert, and it was absolutely inexcusable.'

Prideaux-James turned to him white with fury. For a moment it looked as though he was going to hit the steward. But he bit his lip and unclenched his fists.

'You're wrong there, sir. He jumped straight across me, and my horse had to change direction taking off.'

The bowler-hatted official was even redder in the face now.

'Don't you dare answer a steward back like that. You interfered blatantly with Best coming up to the last. I don't know what the hell you thought you were doing, but don't think you're going to ride again this afternoon. We'll have to put the question of a penalty to Portman Square after that. And you haven't improved your case by attacking the other party.' He turned to me. 'Are you all right, Archie?'

I nodded. 'Yes thanks, sir.' I tried to show how little affected I was by Prideaux-James's hard-swung fist.

The steward did not appear to believe me, but he nodded. 'You'd better get your horse away. Let me know if you want to take the matter of this attack any further. It's the sort of thing we vigorously discourage in amateur racing.'

'I'll let you know, sir,' I said, and turned to lead the Consul away with Georgie.

The stewards turned their angry attention back to Robert Prideaux-James.

Chapter 12

A large section of the crowd had witnessed what had happened. They parted to make a gangway of staring faces as we made our way towards the winner's spot in the paddock.

After weighing in I came back out to accept my trophy from the wife of the owner of the local tractor dealers who had sponsored the race. The presentation was greeted with a ripple of applause and a few shouts of 'Well done!' and 'Sock it to him, Archie!' Freddy Philby, who had had to drag his horse into the ring and second place slot, laughed. 'I'd heard there was a bit of scrap.'

'Not on my part, unfortunately. Georgie jumped between us before I could hit him back and then the stewards arrived.'

'Did P-J carve you up or something? I was too far behind to see.'

'Sure, he tried to put me through the offside wing.'

'That's bloody odd. He's a nasty bastard, but he's not usually a complete arsehole. I wonder what made him do it?'

When we were leading the Consul back to the lorry, Georgie asked the same thing.

'I don't know yet,' I replied, 'but I'll bet you odds-on that Drury is lurking behind it somewhere. He likes winning, and in this case that means Damian winning, and he's certainly up to demanding a bit of assistance. But I can't think why the P-Js should oblige.'

'But Damian hadn't a hope. He pulled up halfway round.'

'Maybe just stopping me was part of the brief. I'll grant you that sounds absurd, but Drury doesn't conform to normal behaviour where his perverted sense of honour is concerned.'

'You don't think he's found out you're mixed up with the plan to steal the stallion insurance, do you?'

'No. He'd be trying to kill me, not just knock me off my horse.'

'For God's sake, Archie, please don't talk like that.'

'I'm not that enthusiastic about the idea, either,' I said, 'but with luck, we'll have done enough soon to get him put away. I wonder if Ian Jack's got here yet. I'll have the shots I took of Sean and Drury later tonight. With the tape Sean made today and the first one in Drury's house, we might have enough.'

We reached the box and tied the Consul to a ring on the side. The ramp was down and Cocoa was looking over his shoulder. He greeted his stable companion with a whinny. I jumped up to see how he looked. He had not sweated up and seemed calm and ready for work. I was stroking his neck, murmuring private noises of encouragement at him, when I suddenly noticed Ian Jack's face above the partition on Cocoa's far side.

He grinned at my embarrassment at being caught chatting to my horse.

'Hello, Archie. Well done. I'm afraid I didna' have time to get any money on you, but it was a pretty miserable price, anyway.'

'How did your end of things go?' I asked impatiently.

'I dunno. I'm not telepathic. Sean didn't make it back to our rendezvous, but that doesna' mean much. He may have taken a while shaking off a tail. He might have to follow the thing through and take the ferry if he's still got someone behind him. Losing a tail isn't as easy as it looks on the movies, especially if they know what they're about.'

'Do you think they'd actually follow him on to the ferry?'

'With luck they'll accept he's genuine, and not bother; but they might and then he'll just have to use his initiative. His best bet would be to walk off the ferry and worry about the vehicle later. He should contact us before the ferry leaves, or from the boat. I'll talk it through with him then.'

'Okay. You'd better get back to my place now, then, in case he does phone. What happened your end of the meet?'

Ian's eyes flickered over my shoulder, and he sank back into the shadows. I turned. Georgie was at the bottom of the ramp with a bucket. As she came up, I said to the invisible Ian, 'It's okay, she's with me. She knows what's going on.'

Ian's face reappeared and Georgie gave a quick start.

'Relax,' I said. 'This is Ian who's been advising us.'

'Advising?' Ian snorted.

I gave a quick laugh, 'All right, running the show. So, what happened?'

'There was a coupla fellas I had to look after. One was a pretty harmless sort of a gamekeeper type. The other had been about a bit. But they weren't together, and neither of them saw me. I left 'em trussed up with sticky tape over their eyes and mouths. That'll let Drury know that he isn't dealing with amateurs: not all amateurs, anyway.'

'Thanks, Ian.'

'You're welcome, pal. I enjoyed m'self. How can I get into your place?'

I told him where I left the spare key. He opened the small groom's door in the front of the box, made a quick survey of what was going on outside, and dropped quietly out.

There was another race before the last in which Cocoa was entered. I helped Georgie dry off the Consul and lead him up the ramp of the box. I asked her if she would start getting Cocoa ready while I made my presence as calmly visible as possible for Drury's benefit.

On my way to the marquees around the parade ring, I found Damian Drury walking beside me.

'I was just coming to find you,' he said.

I stopped and turned to him. 'Well, you've found me.'

He stood in front of me, failing to meet my eye. 'I just wanted to say sorry about what happened.'

'There's no reason why you should. It wasn't your fault, and we won anyway.'

'Yes, but . . . It must be bloody nasty when that kind of thing happens.'

'Have you any idea why Prideaux-Pratt did it?'

He looked at me and answered quickly, 'God, no! I suppose he was just pissed off that you were going to beat him again. Those brothers hate your guts for some reason.'

'For no reason, as it happens. But you're probably right. Have you got another ride today?'

'No.'

'Are you declaring for the Foxhunters?'

'Yes.'

'See you at Cheltenham, then,' I said lightly, and left with what I hoped was an affable nod.

As I neared the tents, I spotted Drury himself, standing with a group of cronies. He was pouring drinks from a stock in the boot of his car which was parked, inevitably, in the course's prime viewing position. I deviated towards him and hailed him from a few yards away.

He turned and looked at me sourly.

'Bad luck in the last,' I said. 'Not quite the right going for your chap. Maybe if the rain keeps off, the ground at Cheltenham next week will suit Republican better.'

Republican was Damian's declared ride in the Foxhunters.

Drury did not reply at once. 'Maybe. Do you want a drink?'

'Thanks. A small Scotch can't do any harm.'

Drury poured three inches of Glenmorangie into a cut-crystal Waterford tumbler and handed it to me.

The other people gathered around Drury's fountain had stopped to witness the conversation. I took a couple of sips of the fine malt, and put the still full glass on the roof of his car. 'That's all I need,' I said. 'Thanks, Clive. I'll be in touch on Monday about your pictures.'

The other guests looked entertained as I gave Drury a pat on the back and walked on towards the stewards' tent.

An hour later, having told the stewards that I personally did not want to take the matter of Prideaux-James's attack any further, I was well on my way home with Georgie in the cab of the lorry and a state of euphoria tainted only by the threat of impending confrontation with Drury. Cocoa had performed near faultlessly and had hung on to fight out a close challenge at the finish, winning by half a length. His maiden days were well and truly over now, and he knew it. I could not deny that the fact that I now had a commanding lead in the point-to-point riders' table had evoked a certain amount of jubilant boastfulness in me, but Georgie understood. Later, when she insisted on bringing our conversation back to Drury, she primed a fresh source of adrenalin in me.

'Where's it going to go from here, Archie? Why are you doing anything about these pictures he's asked you to get him if you think he'll be arrested any day now?'

'Because he might not be, and I don't want to do anything to make him suspicious. Anyway, he's formally ordered the things, so even if he does get banged up, he'll still have to take them and pay for them, and, frankly, I need the money.'

This was the first time I had referred to that fundamental difference in our circumstances, but I had reached the stage where I wanted to be open with her.

Georgie did not answer for a moment. When she did, she was not sympathetic.

'I think I'd rather stay poor than rely on people like him for my living.'

I bridled instinctively. 'It's not being poor I object to; it's keeping my bloody horses that costs the money.'

'Why don't you sell me the Consul? Then I'll have to pay his keep; you'd have to carry on riding him of course; I'd want him to go on winning.'

I laughed. It was an absurd idea; but then, it was a kind thought – and it would infuriate Drury.

I thought for a moment, and glanced at Georgie. She was sitting on her hands. Her eyes were wide open in expectation.

'If I win next week, you can have him, but I want to take the Christie's Foxhunter on my own horse; after that, I don't think I'll mind too much. And then I couldn't possibly sell him to you at his market value.'

'I wouldn't have him for less. You must know that I've had just as much of a kick out of seeing him win this season as you've had riding him, and I haven't had any of the expenses or the worry, or the work.'

'I wouldn't say that, even if you have won a few quid for turning him out best.'

Georgie put her hand on my arm, and her tone became more serious. 'Look, Archie, we're getting off the point again. When I buy the Consul, I want you around to ride him. You must promise me you'll call off any more plans you've got for Drury, before he finds out and . . . and something horrific happens . . .' Her voice trailed away.

'I can't promise that, I've told you. Until I'm certain that he's going to pay for what he's done I won't drop it. You've been a tremendous help, bringing in Sean and Jamey, but they're committed too, now, for their various reasons, and they certainly wouldn't drop it, even if I did.' I glanced at her worried face and undisguised fear. I stretched out a hand and put it on her thigh.

'Look, at least we're getting some professional help now, thanks to Sharon.'

'Yes, Ian looks as though he knows what he's doing – like a highly intelligent gorilla. Why's he helping you?'

'Frankly, I don't really know, but thank God he is.'

As soon as we reached the yard, Georgie and I unloaded the horses and put them away with a warm feed. I looked in at Jasper who looked well after his day out with Sharon.

In the house, the kitchen was thick with smoke and the smells of cooking. Sharon had produced a large pan of near-solid soup which Georgie and I swallowed gratefully while Ian Jack talked.

'A fella phoned. I think it musta' been your journalist. He didn't know who I was and he wouldn't tell me anything. I said you'd be back about now, though; so I guess he'll try again. It was a relief to find that at least one o' you has some discretion.'

'Jamie's a hardened hack,' I said.

'Let's hope to God Sean uses his head,' Ian went on. 'He'll be on the ferry b' now. I'm worried that he won't know if he's still being followed. Some of the guys working for your man Drury are gonna be professionals. What sort of villainy did he get up to in the old days?'

'Originally, before he found his niche in the City, I don't know,' I answered. 'But in Lloyd's, he was involved with paper robbery – virtually undetectable, because people weren't even aware that they were being robbed. There was no need for physical violence. But he was prepared to kill Bill Beecham, so there's a good chance he's done it before. He came from the East End, and though he's tried hard to distance himself from it, I should think he still keeps up a few contacts there. Of course he went on to do rather better than the out-and-out street villains, so maybe it was tactful to keep in touch and pass the odd bit of business their way.'

'What I can't understand,' said Ian, 'is how he's fooled so many of these establishment toffs for so long.'

'That's simple; he was making money for them. The fact that he was tucking away even more of their profits for himself hasn't come to light yet. With the current state of the insurance market, though, everyone's getting jumpy – looking for nasties and someone to blame. It may not be long before people want to start turning over a few stones around his syndicates.'

'They sure will when all this other shit about him hits the fan.'

'That's the idea,' I said as the telephone began to ring.

I answered. It was Jamie. He sounded relieved to hear me.

'Christ,' he said, 'I thought Drury had sussed us when some gravelly jock answered the phone.'

'That was Ian. He's been giving us a hand. Are you on your way?'

'Yes. I'm down in the village. I'll be with you in five minutes.'

I put the phone down and met Ian's angry eyes.

'Don't,' he growled, 'ever use names or say more than you have to over the phone. It's hardly ever necessary, especially if you're about to meet anyway.'

'Sorry,' I said, chastened.

'It's bad enough,' Ian went on, 'having half your friends involved.' He flashed a look at Georgie.

'It was my father who was killed,' she said indignantly. 'And I'm not going to let anything out; I'm too bloody scared Drury's going to find out what you're doing as it is.'

'So long as you realise that if you tell a single other person about it, you'll be shortening our chances of getting him first.'

Sharon, awkwardly silent until then, turned to Ian. 'Don't go on about it. Georgie's not going to say nothin'.'

Ian accepted this judgement with a shrug. 'Okay, but that goes for all of you. I shouldna' be mixed up in all this anyway. It's only her's got me into it.' He nodded at Sharon, then shook his head. 'I must be mad.'

There was a knock on the door. It could not be Jamie yet. Ian saw my concern.

'Don't get so jumpy; nobody knocks on a door like that if they want to cause you grief. I'll get it.'

He walked down the short, cluttered passage to the door and was followed back into the room by the photographer I had asked to develop my film from that morning. With everything else going on, I had forgotten that he was bringing the prints up to the house. He looked at the people in the room with interest.

'What's going on here then?' he asked.

'Just planning racing strategy,' I answered quickly, and took the large brown envelope he was holding. I slipped out the sheaf of large 8″ × 4″ shots and flicked through them. 'Great,' I said, 'thanks a lot.'

'That's a hundred quid,' he answered.

'Okay. I'll send it to you.'

The photographer looked doubtful.

Ian, standing beside him, took a wad of notes from his pocket and produced two fifties. 'There you are. But before you have it, do you know who these people are?' He nodded at the photos.

'No. I haven't got a bloody clue.'

'Where are the negatives?'

'In the bag with the prints, like Archie said.'

Ian took the envelope and fished inside for the cellophane pack of negative strips. 'Did you make any other prints?'

The photographer was looking nervous under Ian's hard, blue gaze. 'A couple, yes, but they were too light.'

'You destroy them the minute you get back. If anyone else sees them or you tell anyone what you've done, you'll be ever so sorry. D'you understand what I mean?'

The man understood. He shook his head rapidly, and Ian seemed satisfied.

'Okay. There's your money, and here's an extra fifty. Get on back, and make sure I don't have to come looking for you.'

'Right. I'm on my way,' the photographer replied, and started backing out of the room. As he turned to let himself out, the door burst open. A gush of cold, wet air and Jamie Lloyd-Jones came in. The man took a surprised look at Jamie's grimy face, and brushed past him to get out of the house as soon as he could.

Jamie looked even scruffier than he had when I had left him the day before. He also looked pleased with himself.

'Will John Duckett do it?' I asked.

'Yes, I think so, with a bit more persuasion. We're going to need to show him his birth certificate, and I think it would help if you came and talked to him; told him what his father did to Beecham and all the other strokes he's pulled. And we ought to try and get some pictures of John and his common-law wife and brats, at least from a distance, in case he digs his heels in and won't come to Gazeley.'

'Where d'you say this guy is?' Ian asked.

'Halfway up the Teifi, ten miles above Lampeter.'

'We'll go up tomorrow,' I said. 'The sooner we can start putting the pressure on Drury, the better. When I saw him at the races, I was sure he hadn't connected me with the Tomahawk scam, or Harry Winchcombe's problems, but it's only got to be a matter of time before he does, and we need him totally hampered by the press, and the police too, if possible.'

The phone rang next to Ian's elbow. He moved aside to let me pick it up.

It was Sean.

'Hello?' His voice was more Irish than normal. 'Who's that?'

'It's Archie. Can you talk?'

'Not a lot.'

'Okay. I'll put you on to Ian. He'll tell you what to do.' I handed the receiver to the big Scot.

'Okay,' Ian said, 'if you've got to talk, pretend you're talking to your wife. Are you on the ferry? . . . Did your tail follow you on in his car? . . . He probably came on by foot. Do you know what he looks like? . . . You're right not to take any chances. Here's what to do. See if you can find a truck driver who'll give you a lift off the ferry – it doesna' matter where to. When the boat docks at Rosslare, go down to the car deck, get in and start your motor. A few minutes before you're due to move, slip out the passenger door and get along to the truck. Just take your bag with the money and the tape. Don't worry about the vehicle – we'll phone the ferry company and deal with that. Get your driver to drop you at the next big town out of Rosslare – Wexford or wherever – and find someone who'll let you make a copy of the tape . . . Just use your initiative, it shouldn't be hard, but for God's sake, be discreet. Put the copy tape in the post to us right away. We'll get it Tuesday morning, and that'll have to do. If they're on to you, and stay with you, you'll not get it back to us at all otherwise. If you still don't know if you're being fol-lowed, carry on down to Cork, and try and lose yourself there. It shouldna' be hard. Then make your way back, but don't come here. Ring tomorrow night, same time. Now say a nice goodbye to your missus.'

Ian smiled at Sean's reply, and put the phone down. 'Well,' he said, 'it's no perfect, but it's the best he can do.'

'Are they still following him?' Jamie asked.

'I don't think he's got a clue,' said Ian, 'but he was definitely followed to Fishguard, so we should assume he's been followed on to the boat. There's no guarantee he'll give his tail the slip on the car deck, but there's a chance. If they're on foot, whoever's following will watch him into his car, then have to go back up and walk out, to pick him up driving off. The poor bastard doesn't know what the hell he's doing, but I don't think he'll be touched, not as long as they think he's going back to meet up with the boyos to pinch the horse.' Ian made a face and rattled his lower lip. 'We'll just have to hope he uses his nouse.'

'Sean's a very resourceful man,' Georgie said. 'He'll be in his element, as long as he's got a role to play.'

'It'll be more than a bloody role if they suss him. You guys want your heads examined. Still, you're committed now. You'll have to push along your propaganda exercise and get a bit of heat on him as quick as you can. I'll come with you tomorrow and take the pictures.'

I wanted Georgie to stay that night. I had an uncomfortable feeling that the whole scenario I had created with Drury was closing in on me, and some instinct was urging me to sow my seed before it was too late.

When it came to it, though, I did not ask her to stay.

She drove off into the black, wet night in her natty little German car, and before she had reached the gate, I wanted to run after her and call her back. But I watched her tail lights disappear down the lane and thought there would be another, better time.

Back in the house, Ian and Jamie were still bending over the shots of Sean and Drury. They had come out at least as well as I had hoped. In two of them, Drury passing the bag to Sean in the car and Sean checking the money were clearly visible. They were going to be devastating, with Sean's sound-track; but we were going to have an agonising two days' wait for that – always assuming Sean could follow Ian's instructions.

Ian and Sharon left shortly afterwards. It was still only nine o'clock, so Jamie and I sat and dealt with a bottle of budget Bulgarian cabernet-sauvignon.

Next morning, a clear, bright sun, and a sharp north-easterly helped to cure our headaches. Jamie and I picked up Ian in Hereford soon after nine. He looked reassuringly bright-eyed and fit as he clambered into the back of the car.

He had brought his own camera, which, he said, was at least as good as the one Jamie had lent me, and a good deal more familiar to him.

'I paid a visit to your photographic pal on the way back last night. He'll not be any problem, but you were taking a risk, going to a stranger for a job like that.'

'I knew he was safe,' I justified.

'At least between you, you delivered the goods,' Jamie said. 'Those shots are great. I'll even be able to get you a nice fat fee for them when we run the story.'

'And then you'll be able to pay me back the hundred and fifty I had to give him,' growled Ian.

'Thanks for that, by the way,' I said. 'I'll pay you back later.'

'All part o' the service,' Ian grunted. 'By the way, I'm back to work Tuesday, so you'll be on your own then.'

'Off on some dirty mission?' Jamie asked with professional inquisitiveness.

'Perhaps.'

'Where to?'

'If I told you that, I'd have to kill you after, so I'll no' bother.'

'When you leave the Regiment, if you want to tell me anything, I could get you a hell of a deal from my rag,' Jamie said, undeterred.

In the driving mirror, I saw Ian shake his head with a smile. 'No thanks Jamie.'

Chapter 13

There was scarcely a car on the roads. Ian, Jamie and I reached Lampeter in two hours. We drove up the river valley towards the travellers' camp, and pulled up a quarter of a mile before it. Ian was going to drive on to find a higher spot to take his photographs. We had sketched out a rough strategy for getting John Duckett and, if possible, his woman and children out into the open.

Jamie and I trudged up the road in the quiet sunny morning. I was dressed in jeans and an old sweater. Jamie had not thought it necessary for me to go to the same lengths as himself; John was not expecting me to be a fellow traveller.

We walked through a gap in the hedge into the field where the old buses and horse-drawn wagons were parked among tepees and bend-overs. The sounds of children laughing and playing drifted across the meadow with the spring songs of a multitude of birds.

Several of the adults were gathered around fires or walking up from the river with buckets of water. It occurred to me that, while that sort of life would not suit me, on this fine bright morning, the attractions of the eccentric existence these people had chosen seemed plausible. This helped to neutralise any shameful prejudices that might otherwise have affected my attitude towards Drury's son.

We strolled towards one of the ancient motor-coaches, and as we approached, a tall man climbed down from it. He smiled at Jamie in friendly recognition and nodded at me without expression.

'Hello, Jim. Is this your mate who says he knows my father?' he

181

asked Jamie in a flat, London accent overlaid by a couple of decades of hippy drawl.

'Yeah,' said Jamie. 'Archie, this is John Duckett.'

Shaking hands did not seem appropriate, so I nodded, and John said, 'Come up into the bus.'

He went back up the steps into a vehicle that must have been used twenty years before by groups of tourists or old age pensioners on trips to the seaside.

The interior was clean and orderly.

'D'you want some tea?' John asked incongruously. We said 'Yes', and he filled a pair of mugs from a battered metal teapot. The tea was a pale green colour.

I took a sip. It was not unpleasant, but quite unlike any tea I had ever tasted.

'What do you make this from?'

'Nettles, like, and other stuff,' he shrugged.

I continued to sip.

Since we had first conceived the idea of tracking down Clive Drury's rejected progeny, I had been deeply curious to see what the son would be like. Somehow, I had not imagined anyone as big, or with such presence as the handsome hippy who greeted us. It had not occurred to me that Drury would have passed on those particular genes which had given him such domineering energy, but I saw recognisable signs of it in the son.

John Duckett was a well-built man of six feet or so. He looked a little younger than his forty years. His hair straggled in long dark brown locks to his shoulders and the beard which covered his face showed only a few flecks of grey. His dark eyes were clear and steady, and he was strikingly good-looking in the same way some thought his father was. It was not that his features were particularly fine, or even, but they were strong; a large jaw and a heavy brow. He was wearing jeans and a sheepskin jerkin which had been finely embroidered with naive depictions of crops and domestic beasts.

He dropped into a worn wooden rocking chair and invited us to sit on a low broad padded seat which ran halfway along one side of the coach. In front of the bench was a hand-carved elm table where the teapot and mugs stood. The sides of the vehicle were draped with Indian printed cottons and velours. It was like a tiny oriental salon.

John looked at me, prepared to be receptive, but not gullible.

'So, tell me about my father,' he said, displaying reluctant interest.

I turned to Jamie. 'How much have you told John?'

'A little, but you tell him from the top.'

I turned back to John. 'Do you ever see the newspapers?'

'No, man.' He shook his head. 'I used to, but that world hasn't got nothing to do with us. We can't touch it; it can't touch us.'

'What do you object to in that world?' I asked with genuine curiosity.

He shrugged. 'The ugliness of material greed; the acquisitiveness of people; the obsession with convention. Most people out there live in, like, a social straitjacket.'

'Your father, Clive Drury, is the living embodiment of those things. If you read the papers, you'd recognise his name. Under the guise of legitimate business, he's made and stolen millions of pounds. He is accepted now as a member of the City Establishment. He has made a lot of other rich influential people even richer, and they have, on the whole, overlooked what they would normally consider his social shortcomings. He is the single best example I can think of of greed in action. And make no mistake, you are his son.' From my jeans pocket I pulled rumpled photocopies of the birth certificate of John Arthur Duckett and of the marriage certificate of Clive Duckett and Doreen Baker. 'Do you remember your mother's signature?' I asked him as I handed them to him.

He looked at the documents with little show of emotion. 'It looks like her signature. But how do you know Drury is this Clive Duckett?'

'He had his name changed by deed-poll. That's a matter of public record. Here's a copy of the entry and both his signatures.'

John studied them and nodded.

'Mum always said my father had been killed. I never had a reason to think she was lying. We never had relatives; I never questioned it.'

'Do you ever see her now?'

'Now and again, every few years. She wasn't what you'd call a communicative person. She was always very nervous, but she was good to us. I know she hated it when I started travelling, but she seemed to understand. I just told her I didn't think I was like

183

other people, and she said, "You're not", and didn't argue.'

I pulled more sheets of photocopied paper from my pocket. They were a selection of recent press-cuttings I had borrowed from Lord Walford. I smoothed them on the table to show John. He picked them up; I had brought them to show him different aspects of the public persona of Clive Drury.

As he read them, I said, 'These pieces only tell the sort of things Clive Drury wants the papers to tell. You must read between the lines. He runs that children's charity only for the good press it brings him. He hasn't got a grain of charity in him. He's interested exclusively in Clive Drury.'

'Yeah,' John nodded slowly as he read.

Jamie stood up. 'While you're looking through that lot,' he said, 'Archie and I'll go out and find Marianne and your kids.'

'That's cool.'

Jamie and I left him immersed in the cuttings and climbed down from the bus.

'We'll find the kids, and stick with them until he comes out,' Jamie said quietly when we were out of earshot. 'We'll try and hang around near the middle of the camp so Ian can get his shots.'

'Do you think we're going to need them?' I asked.

'I don't know. John's not giving much away. He's obviously interested, but he'll have to be convinced there's a good reason for him to come out and confront his father. He's quite impressive, isn't he?'

'I know what you mean. He looks as though he could be just as bloody-minded as his father, with enough provocation.'

'That's why I thought he'd do it.'

'Which is his girlfriend?' I asked as we approached a knot of men and women gathered round an old bath tub which was propped above a blazing fire.

'That tall one, with the henna'd hair.'

'My god!' I exclaimed, 'she's amazing looking.'

'You should see the children. I think they're both his though it's sometimes hard to tell even whose mother is whose. A girl of about ten and a boy of six or seven. That's them, coming up from the river with the long dog.'

A shaggy grey lurcher trotted elegantly with his head at shoulder level to a beautiful, dark-eyed boy. Behind the dog and the boy was his sister. As they came nearer and recognised Jamie, they smiled, she with an unexpected, serene self-possession.

'Hello, Jim. Have you come back for more of Dad's grass?' she asked in a husky, placeless voice.

Her mother, hearing her, glanced up from the bathtub where she had been washing clothes. Her eyes met mine and clouded with suspicion. The children reached us. Jamie ruffled their hair and stroked the dog's long nose.

The woman left her washing and came over to us. She smiled guardedly at Jamie. 'I didn't know you'd be back so soon. Who's this you've brought?'

Her voice gave me a surprise; it was rather similar to Georgie Henry's.

'This is Archie, Marianne. He's the man who knows John's father. We've left him with a pile of cuttings.'

Marianne turned to me. 'Jim said you might want John to help you take some kind of revenge on this man. Why should he?'

'I'm not looking for personal revenge or anything like that. This man Drury, who's John's father, has caused a lot of grief. He's an evil man who tramples on anyone who gets in his way. Unfortunately, that included an old friend of mine – stabbed in a dark alley. Do you think he ought to be allowed to get away with it? I'm no moral philosopher, but I think people like Drury should be contained; don't you? Normally I'm too idle to feel the need to do anything about them. But Drury killed a harmless old man I had known and sort of loved all my life. For all I know, he's killed other people and stolen from thousands. But he's very well insulated from the law. He has a lot of powerful friends, and he never exposes himself by doing his own dirty work. He threw out his first family thirty-five years ago. He's paid John's mother enough to live on and terrorised her into keeping her mouth shut about him. I suspect that the only reason he never simply had her removed is that it might have caused some serious inquiries into her history.'

'I don't see how John can help.' Marianne said.

'He can, and so can you, by supporting him. John's father stands for everything you've rejected in the world you've left. You'd help a lot of people by showing up his rotten values. But it's up to you both.'

'Please don't encourage him,' Marianne said. 'We have a peaceful and happy life the way we are. It could change things if he got

185

involved with these types of people. He's not always stable,' she added reluctantly.

At that moment, John appeared in the door of their bus. He saw us and walked over. His children grabbed his hands as he came near to us.

'It is my father,' he said. 'It explains a lot. I think I've always been sort of aware of him and that's caused me a lot of hassle for a long time. But I'd like to talk to him first.'

Marianne looked at him. Her soft eyes were wide with doubt. 'Why, John, why? It'll only unsettle you.'

He shook his head. 'I've never been a totally calm person, you know that. And if I have achieved an equilibrium, it's because I've worked at it. This is something I've got to exorcise. I think maybe just seeing him and speaking to him, maybe only once, will do that.'

'But, John,' Jamie said, 'you won't get near him. You'd be blocked by all the protection he has around him.'

'There must be times when he's reachable; I'll wait for one.'

'I tell you what,' I said, as if the idea had only just occurred to me, 'If you turned up at his house, you and a large crowd of other travellers, you could make a camp on his land, and insist on seeing him before you went. He'd see you then, before the police or the press got to hear.'

John grinned. 'That'd piss him off, wouldn't it, if the papers got on to it?' He waved the bundle of press-cuttings. 'All this charitable crap would look sick next to the story of the man who disowned his family. Oh yeah, I like that.'

'But John,' Marianne said desperately, 'you can't bring me and the children into it if it's going to get into the papers.'

'Don't worry, your precious family aren't going to be looking for you among a bunch of dirty old hippies.'

Marianne did not answer. I saw guilt and sadness in her eyes.

Jamie pressed John. 'Drury's going to the States next Friday,' he lied, 'and because there's a big race meeting at Cheltenham, he'll be at his place in Herefordshire on Wednesday. D'you think a group of you could pack up and make it over there by then.'

John glanced around the camp. 'Yeah, some of them'll come; not the pony wagons, of course, but if we've got a good reason for giving this ugly bread-head who happens to be my father a hard time, we gotta do it.'

'He'll *have* to see you if you come then,' said Jamie, 'and you'd be doing a lot of people a lot of good. I'll tell you something else; just think about it. If you're prepared to talk to the press, it would be a fantastic opportunity to put the case for all the new-age travellers. The hacks will be on your side for once.'

Marianne grabbed her man's arm. 'You mustn't! We've chosen this way; we don't have to justify it to anyone.'

John looked at her, evidently without much sympathy for her reticence, but he said, 'Maybe. I don't know about the media, Jim, but we'll come to this place.' He looked at Marianne. 'My inheritance,' he laughed.

On Monday morning, cloud lay like a thick layer of porridge six hundred feet above the lowlands of England. There was no wind to move it from the ridges and escarpments I had to cross as I drove to Nosey Parker's yard on the Berkshire Downs.

Despite the efforts of Nature and an anti-cyclonic gloom to fill me with pessimism, I was inclined to feel exuberant about my progress towards justice being done to Clive Drury. I was also looking forward to extracting the Fernleys from Bambi Arlington. As I had told Georgie, I was confident that if I got them and Drury was already out of circulation, I would still be able to get the money for them from whoever was administering his affairs. I badly needed the commission; Drury and racing between them had left me with little time to make a living over the past weeks.

In the back corridor of the Parkers' house a trail of muddy footprints led to the kitchen. Jockeys, work-riders, grooms, vets and everyone else involved in the day-to-day functioning of a racing-stables would have been traipsing back and forth since early morning to visit Jeannie Parker at her big kitchen table. They came for instructions, for money, for coffee or a gossip. As I walked in, she looked up from a discussion with a tearful stable-girl. Relief showed through her welcoming smile.

'Hello, Archie,' she bellowed. 'Coffee? Whisky? Help yourself.' To the girl she said, 'Look, Tracy, the best thing to do when some bastard man's let you down is to concentrate on your work; throw yourself into it. I tell you what,' Jeannie sounded as though she was offering a big favour, 'I'll try and persuade Nosey to let you do an extra horse.'

Tracy looked unconvinced, but snivelled her thanks and slunk out of the room with a sideways glance at me.

'Why these girls let themselves be shat on by the nastiest little jockeys is beyond comprehension,' Jeannie said when she had gone.

'You mean it would be more understandable with the nasty big jockeys, do you?' I asked.

'With the big, amateur ones it's particularly incomprehensible because they're all such rotten jockeys. Still, I'm glad you've come. I told our Bambi you'd be here and she sounded rather pleased; but remember, no begging her for rides; we want a few more winners for her this season.'

'When is she arriving?' I asked.

Jeannie glanced at a grand old long-case clock ticking ponderously in the corner. 'About now,' she answered. 'Are you going to tell me why you're so keen to see her?'

'It's no big deal,' I shrugged. 'I want to buy a couple of pictures from her.'

'Oh, that's all right. I thought maybe you were going to try and sell a horse, and you know how mad Nosey gets if he doesn't buy his punters' horses for them. Anyway, I wish you luck with your pictures. She may look like a cuddly little lady, but she's hard as nails in business. That's how she's made her pile.'

'How do you mean? I thought old Arlington left it to her.'

'No. He had a good old pedigree, but not much loot – not by East Coast American standards, anyway. Dear little Bambi is, I'm told, a bigshot picture dealer, responsible for quite a few clever coups. She always tries to sell a few when she's over here. Clive Drury has bought a lot from her.'

I hoped that Jeannie did not notice the reflex twitch in my neck as this piece of information hit home. I would have to be very careful not to tell anyone who my buyer was. It must be sheer chance that Drury had not tried her himself for the pair of pictures he had asked me to find.

But the agitation I felt was covered by Nosey Parker walking into the room.

He nodded at me and mumbled, 'Hello.'

'Coffee, Nosey?' his wife asked.

'Something stronger,' he replied. 'I've just had a nasty shock.'

'Oh dear,' Jeannie said without any sign of concern. 'What's happened?'

'Hugh Yeovil's sold The Dealer.'

Jeannie dropped the spoon she was holding. 'Good God. His lordship must be even harder up than we thought. Still, at least we'll get the last three months' fees out of him now.'

'I don't know anything about his finances, but he's sold the horse for a hell of a price.'

'Who to? Will he stay in the yard?'

'Not if I can help it. Drury's bought him.'

'How extraordinary. We were just talking about him. Does he want to leave The Dealer here?'

'Of course he does, and he wants that little tyke of a son of his to ride on Thursday.'

'Poor bastard,' I laughed. 'If he doesn't win, his father will skin him alive. I saw him on Saturday, and he looked very cagey when I asked him what he was riding in the Christie's.'

'It's all right for you to laugh,' Jeannie said. 'It improves your chances no end.'

'Damian's not such a bad jockey,' I answered.

'The Dealer's the best available hunter-chaser in the country, but he's not an easy ride. He's wilful, and very strong, and he hates a loose-fitting jockey flopping around on top of him. It's a fucking disaster,' Nosey added with unusual foul-mouthedness. 'And I vowed that I'd never keep horses for Drury again. I did once, ten years ago, and the man's a bloody crook. He was always telling me when he wanted his horses to win or lose.'

'I imagine he's quite keen for this one to win, so at least you won't be asked to compromise your principles,' I said.

'With Damian on board, you'll beat him,' Parker said morosely.

'For God's sake, don't say that to the *Sporting Life*; I want to keep the Consul's price out a bit.'

'You having a punt on yourself then, Archie?' Jeannie asked.

'After what Nosey's just told me, I think I might.'

Parker groaned and left the room.

'I don't know what he's moaning about,' his wife said. 'He's got the favourites in the Triumph and the Ritz. Poor old Nosey, he thinks his owners think he's chiselling them if their horses don't win every time they go out, and that's after twenty-five years.'

'I'm sure you've always been able to convince them he's not,' I remarked.

Jeannie smiled, and cocked her ear to a jangling in the front hall. 'We have a guest; might be the Widow Arlington. Give her a treat and go and let her in. Bung her in the drawing room and give her a drink. You can do your bit of business with her; but don't forget, no offers to ride for her. I'd better run a comb through my hair.'

I nodded and walked through the flag-stoned hall to the front door.

Bambi Arlington was, as Jeannie had said, a cuddly little woman of fifty or so. She still carried an air of plausible voluptuousness which she deployed with dignified restraint. I had met her once, briefly. She was an avid and knowledgeable follower of English National Hunt racing, and she probably knew more about me than I did about her. She lifted her eyebrows extravagantly when I opened the door to her.

'Well, well. Archie Best,' she said in a mild, Anglophile American accent. 'Why are you doing doorman duty for old Nosey?'

'One has to make a living,' I said. 'I've been instructed to make you at home and ply you with Martini. But let me take your dead bear first.'

I helped her off with a sable coat that weighed at least a stone and showed her through to the Parkers' surprisingly formal drawing room. There was a well-established log fire burning in the grate. The silver picture frames and Nosey's more important trophies – buffed, I presumed, with my discarded jock-strap – gleamed in the light of half a dozen table-lamps. I marvelled at Jeannie's energy and eye to the details that mattered to a trainer's clients.

'Martini, then?' I asked.

Bambi shook her head. 'Nope, thanks. When in Rome. Gin and tonic.'

As I poured the drink for her, she asked, 'What brings you to Nosey's? Have you been riding much for him?'

'Not this year. I'm afraid I can only do top-weight stuff these days.'

'Well, you are a big fellow,' she said with a hint of archness. She sat down on a large sofa upholstered in a giant floral chintz.

I poured myself a drink and remained standing on the fine Afghan rug which covered the centre of the floor.

'The reason I'm here is that I heard you were coming. And I wanted to see you.'

'That's flattering.'

'Not entirely. I wanted to buy some pictures from you.'

She put her head to one side. 'Did you indeed? And what have I got that you want?'

'A pair of Fernleys: two mares of Lord Tullamore's, about eighteen twenty.'

'Devon Lass and Ophelia. I'm very fond of them. Both mares appear in the pedigree of the best jumper I ever had.'

'Arlington Star?'

'That's right. I love having their pictures on my wall. But sadly, they don't belong to me.'

I did not believe her.

'That's a pity. Who do they belong to?'

'Some little investment company in the BVIs. They rent them to me.'

'Ah,' I said. 'I wonder if perhaps you have any influence with them?'

'I might have. How much do you want to pay?'

I held my breath, probably a fraction too long. 'Three hundred and fifty thousand.'

Bambi Arlington chuckled. 'Oh, Archie,' she chided, 'I'm all for a bit of horse-trading, but not silly jokes. What cheap-skate are you buying them for? I hope you don't mind my assuming they're not for you,' she added, with a small, not too sincere smile of apology.

'I can't tell you that, Bambi,' I said lightly, covering my frustration, 'that's my living.'

I had known, and I had told Drury that we would be going in far too low at three hundred and fifty thousand. But he had seemed completely confident, and I assumed he had been doing his own homework on the market. But it was a notoriously volatile, arbitrary market, and Bambi's protestations at my meagre bid might just as easily have been bargaining tactics, particularly in view of what Jeannie had told me about her that morning.

'Archie,' she said, 'you're an attractive young man, and I'm sure people like to do business with you, but you're not going to get anywhere in the art market by trading like a gypsy at a horse fair. You go back to your buyer and get sensible instructions, and maybe I might be able to put in a word for you with the owners.'

I looked at her for a moment before answering. 'Tell me,

Bambi, how much do you know about these pictures? They don't appear in the definitive catalogue,' I lied.

'Oh yes they do,' she came back quickly. 'They're at the back in the list of works lost or destroyed. They were thought to have gone up in flames in a fire at Rostrevor Castle in the eighteen-nineties. But they didn't.'

'Who found them?'

'God, I don't know, but they're right; they're well authenticated. They're a beautiful pair of pictures; I should be sorry to lose them.'

'You could always have them copied; very few of your compatriots would know the difference.'

A completely unexpected hardness appeared in Bambi's eyes. 'I don't think that's very funny, Archie.'

'I shouldn't worry about it, Bambi. I can't offer you more,' I said quickly. 'I doubt that you'll have to part with them.' I thought of Drury's arrogance, and how impotent it would be before the week was out. There were other ways to survive. 'My punter won't budge above three fifty.'

Bambi glanced down at her drink. 'Oh well, that's too bad.' She looked up and seemed for the first time to notice the room we were in. 'My goodness,' she said, 'I wonder how Jeannie manages to keep this place so elegant. It's not as though that's her natural style.'

I laughed. 'Have you ever thought of writing gossip for one of those vicious women's magazines you have in the States?'

'People have suggested that I might have something to offer along those lines, but it really wouldn't be my style,' said Bambi. 'I don't think I could stand half the world cutting me, the other half fawning all over me, and all of them hating me.'

Jeannie was coming into the room. 'Who hates you, Bambi?' she said.

'I think it's always a little dishonest to answer a question like that; there are so many one may not have considered.'

'Well, no one hates you here, as long as the old training fees are paid on time. I'm sorry I wasn't around when you arrived. Has Archie been a good substitute?'

'He's been adorable,' said Bambi, flashing a big smile at me. 'And we've had a dear little business chat.'

'Well, you'd better have another drink. Nosey will want to talk to you about horses all through lunch.'

By the end of lunch, I was glad to get away from the contrasting bitchiness of Bambi and Jeannie. It made a great show, but two hours was enough. I left with them both wishing me luck for Thursday's race, while Nosey headed off in his battered Range Rover to saddle a runner at Windsor; a truly dedicated trainer.

I drove away towards Gloucestershire and my mother's house. I phoned on the way to tell her I was coming and was assailed by the vague sense of guilt I always felt when she gently failed to censure me for not keeping in touch more than I did, especially at a time like this.

When I arrived, she already had tea and cake on the kitchen table. Jeannie's vast cassoulet had yet to make any headway through my stomach, and I felt almost painfully bloated. I felt that if I ate another thing between now and Thursday morning, I would be putting up a stone overweight, but I gritted my teeth before sinking them into the large slab of chocolate cake my mother put in front of me.

'I'm glad you've come. I probably won't get a chance to speak to you at the races, will I?'

'No, especially if I win.'

'The thing is, there's a whole pile of Bill Beecham's stuff arriving here on Friday. Apart from a couple of nice pictures to Georgie, he's left me absolutely everything, as far as I can tell. I suppose he thought Sue and Georgie already have enough of their own. The solicitors wanted me to go to his old flat, but I refused; I couldn't bear that depressing little place when he was there, and now he's gone . . .' She shook her head with horror. 'I really wanted you to help me go through it all. I think I'd find it too upsetting on my own. Would you mind awfully coming over and helping?'

The chances were that I would not be feeling too bright that morning, but I understood what my mother was saying. There were bound to be things that would remind her of my father. There was also a chance that there might be something among Bill's papers that could help me in my pursuit of Drury.

'Sure, but I won't be that early.'

'That would be so kind of you,' my mother said gratefully as she cut another chunk of oozing chocolate cake and put it on my plate.

* * *

193

Ian Jack was waiting for me with Sharon when I arrived back at my house.

'Just wanted to wish you luck, Archie. I'll be sorry to miss the rest of the action,' he said. 'Here are my long-distance studies of Drury's hippy son and his family.'

He handed me a folder of colour photographs. I flipped through them, and was struck again by the good looks of Duckett's woman and children.

'If there are English papers wherever you're going, you should see the first results soon,' I said.

'I'll look out for them,' he said. 'Did Sean ring last night?'

'Yes. About midnight from Cork. He managed to copy the tape, and posted it from Jury's Hotel. It should get here tomorrow. He seems fairly sure that he's lost Drury's man. He still doesn't know if he was on the boat. But he'll probably wait a couple of days, then pick up the Range Rover at Rosslare and come back.'

'Tell him not to go near the car. Phone the harbour authorities and tell them he's still in hospital and the hire company will deal with it. He should fly back. He can get a plane from Cork. Even then, tell him not to come near this place.'

I nodded. Though I had my doubts that Sean would ring again, there did not seem any point in telling Ian that.

Ian and Sharon left after we had drunk to our operation, his mission to the anonymous destination and the Consul's chances in my big race. When they drove out of the yard, I was more than sorry to see him go, and it came home to me that in the three days he had chosen to help us, the whole quality of our plans and their execution had become a lot more professional.

Now, with Sean in Ireland and Jamie back in London, I felt abruptly exposed.

And in two days, I was to ride the biggest race of my life.

Chapter 14

Sean Casey did not phone from Ireland that evening, but Harry Winchcombe did, from Sean's flat in London.

'Look, Archie,' he started, 'what the hell's going on? I feel as if I've been sitting here for bloody weeks now. Sarah's been great, bringing food and papers and things; and I've made myself two and a half grand punting, but the longer I'm here the greater the chance of these people finding me.'

'It's okay, Harry,' I calmed him. 'Sean'll be back in a few days and we can move you then. There's no way anyone's going to find you where you are, so just relax, and put a big bet on the Consul for the Foxhunters.'

'It's all very well for you,' Harry moaned, 'but these buggers want to kill me.'

'Well they can't while you're there. We're making a lot of progress up here. We may get the results we want before the end of the week. But anyway, I told you, as soon as Sean's back, he'll move you.'

'When are you coming to London?'

'Tomorrow. I've got to see a few people. I could drop in when I've finished and tell you what's been happening.'

'I wish you would!' Harry sounded very relieved, and I put the phone down understanding just how threatened he felt.

I pulled a pair of lean lamb chops from the fridge, grilled them and ate them with a few leaves of spinach. Trying to keep my weight at a stone and a half below what would be normal was taking some toll on me, especially with all the abnormal uncertainties my campaign against Drury had caused. I munched the chops dolefully while I tried to catch up on the racing papers. They were mostly full of prognostications about the week's three biggest races, the Champion Hurdle – held tomorrow, the first day of the festival – the Triumph Hurdle and the Gold Cup. But some space had been allocated to the big amateur race.

Caesar's Consul featured among all the pundits' selections; one journalist – an old friend – had made much of my lead in the amateur jockeys' table. He had even managed to rake through the statistics and come up with a couple of spurious records he claimed I had broken. It was the first I knew of them, but it did my confidence no harm.

I rang Georgie when I had finished my scanty supper. She was at Temple Ferris, intending to spend the next three days at Cheltenham.

'How did everything go on Sunday?' she asked with a casualness that must have strained her.

'Absolutely fine,' I answered. 'All that we hoped. I wanted to ask you a favour. Sharon's not coming in till late tomorrow, and I've got to go to London. Could you come over and ride one of the horses for me before you go to the races?'

'Are you sure you want me to?' she asked. I could tell that she was all for the scheme.

'Why not. You ride well enough, and they're neither of them particularly tricky. They only need an hour's walk and a couple of canters. I'll give the Consul a bit of quick work tomorrow.'

'Can I ride Caesar's Consul? After all, he might be mine soon.'

'Do you still really want to indulge in that extravagance?' I asked.

'Of course I do. I only wish it could be me who leads him in on Thursday.'

'I love your confidence, and if he wins, you can lead him in anyway. In the meantime, you're sure you don't mind coming over and doing him tomorrow?'

'I'll be there about nine, so that I can make it to Cheltenham for the two o'clock,' she answered.

'I'll have left by then, but Sharon should be in by eleven. Leave her a note telling her what you've done.'

When Georgie had rung off, I thought about this enthusiasm of hers; I was finding that it reached inner parts of me that had hitherto been unreachable.

I continued to sit at the kitchen table and pulled a blank pad of paper and a biro from under the heap of mail and catalogues.

Trying to organise myself and plan my next moves, I drew up a list of what I had achieved since I had set out to nail Drury.

I had decided that as soon as the press stories broke about Drury's missing family, and Sean's tape had arrived, I should get a complete dossier together for DS Robinson. The tape, the photographs, Drury's thirty thousand pounds, a sworn statement from Harry Winchcombe and details of his stay in the Portsmouth Hospital would be, I was confident, enough for the most unimaginative policeman to go on.

I also thought it would be wise, having done this, to go and lie low with Harry until we were sure that Drury could not get back at us. I was determined to see justice done on behalf of Bill Beecham and anyone else who had fallen foul of Drury, but not to the point of martyrdom.

It was not yet ten, so I made two more telephone calls, to Johnny Stewart, my Lloyd's contact, and Lucien Hart. I reached them both and, after making brief arrangements, I put the phone down feeling that I had done all I could that night. I was contemplating a couple of Marmite sandwiches to fill the pit in my stomach, when I heard a car pull up quietly outside the back door.

I turned the yard lights on and went to the window.

A dark-coloured Bentley gleamed beside my muddy Mercedes and horsebox. I wondered why its owner should call on me at this time of night. A chauffeur got out and walked round to open the rear door on my side.

A couple of seconds later, Clive Drury emerged.

He strode towards my back door – it was the only lit part of the house. He gave a token knock on the door, and, without waiting for an answer, let himself in. He reached the kitchen a second after I had swept the notes I had been making under the nearest pile of papers.

I was standing, and attempted to look surprised and not unpleased to see him when he walked in.

'Do come in, Clive,' I greeted him with light sarcasm.

'I'm glad you're in, as you haven't answered any of my phone messages.'

I glanced at my answering machine, but nothing flashed there. I had already played all the messages, hoping – vainly as it happened – for a word from Sean Casey.

'I haven't had any messages. But, of course, I'm delighted to see you in person.'

'I spoke to someone here this morning. Anyway, I wanted to know how you're getting on with my pictures.'

'You came here just to ask me that?'

'What else would I want to ask you? Well, have you found them yet?'

'Yes, but you'll have to raise your price, I'm afraid. You want them too cheap.'

'I've told you all I'm prepared to pay.'

'Then I'm sorry; no deal.' I heaved my shoulders in a gesture of mild regret.

'What! You'll have to try harder than that. Are you telling me you don't need the money?'

I had the impression, possibly as a result of a vague suspicion that was forming in my mind, that we were playing out some kind of ritual theatre. But it was essential that I kept up my part.

'Of course I do, but the owner won't deal at that price. If you're serious, you'll have to give me a bigger budget.'

Drury contemplated this for a moment, while narrowly watching me.

'I'm not prepared to pay any more. If you can't get them, you can't get them. Frankly, I didn't think you would. You're a bloody dilettante, aren't you? Gentleman jockey, training your horses on the cheap,' he snorted.

'Not an accusation one could throw at your son, eh?'

'No. I like to see things done properly, not like you half-baked amateurs. When I play a game, I like to win.'

'Then you're rather missing the point. If you want Damian to be a professional, you'll have to buy your own trainer. Not that any trainer worth having would be bought by you.'

Drury's eyes widened angrily. 'Don't cheek me, you puppy. I've taken the trouble to try and help you. I've offered you a more than fair price for your horse.'

'Well, you won't be needing the Consul, now you've bought The Dealer.'

'Who told you that?'

'I was at Parker's yard today.'

'Yes, I'd heard. But I told that bloody Parker to keep his trap shut until Thursday.'

'I don't think Mr Parker likes you, though, and he hates taking instructions from owners – he told me.'

'The only instruction he'll be getting from me tomorrow is where to send my bloody horse. And my offer for Caesar's Consul still stands.'

'I'm afraid I've given a binding option on him elsewhere.'

'Who to?'

'They've asked me not to say.'

'You stupid bastard. You'll fucking regret that.'

'Why? Are you going to have me duffed up?' I laughed at the implausibility of it.

'Listen, sonny,' growled Drury, as he pushed a finger into my chest, 'you never bloody know. Don't say I didn't warn you.'

'No, but I might say you threatened me.'

Drury, turning to leave, roared with laughter. 'And who the hell d'you think would listen to you?'

He marched down the narrow corridor, knocking a couple of Barbours off their hooks, and kicking a pair of wellington boots in front of him.

His banging of the back door was followed by the gentle purring of the Bentley, and the sound of its wide tyres sweeping across my pitted yard.

I slept badly that night. By seven next morning, I had watered and fed my horses. When I heard the postman's van crawling up the lane, I went and waited impatiently for him at the gate. He handed me a small bundle of unattractive-looking mail, which did not include anything that might have contained a cassette.

I cursed and went inside, fuming with frustration at the unreliability of the Irish and English post. Maybe Ian had been right not to let Sean come back here yet, but it was hell relying on the Post Office for the arrival of the most damning evidence against Clive Drury that we had yet been able to gather.

I was about to leave, when I remembered that I had not even phoned the ferry company in Rosslare to tell them what to do with Sean's Range Rover.

I was doubtful that there would be anyone competent to deal with it at this time of day as I found and dialled the number in Ireland. My call was answered quickly, and within a minute I had been told that the vehicle had been collected the evening before by Mr Sean Casey, whom the hire company had confirmed was the hirer.

I put the phone down, and hoped fervently that Sean was not still being followed and that he was not going to come here. He still had not phoned, and unless he did when I was here, there was nothing I could do, so I tried to be philosophical about it, and concentrate on the possible.

At eleven o'clock that same morning. Lucien Hart was already installed in the St James's Oyster Bar, with a limp leather briefcase and a large cafetiere in front of him.

'Archie, dear boy, you're very punctual; I do so appreciate that in the young.'

'I'm not that bloody young,' I said, sitting on the bench beside him. 'And I certainly don't feel it this morning.'

'Oh dear! You must get more sleep, less fornicating and sowing of the bad seed.'

'Speak for your own seed.'

'I'd rather not. You see, I have a large wager on you in the big race. I might even break the habit of a lifetime and watch you on the television.' He pronounced the last word with fastidious distaste.

'If you don't tell me more about those two pictures you aimed me at, I'll fall off just to spite you.'

'What about them?' He raised an eyebrow.

'Are they real?'

'The catalogues say they existed once. No one actually saw them go up in smoke, so perhaps they still do. Who knows?'

'I bet you do. Tell me, did you ever know anything about my late friend, Bill Beecham, bringing pictures of spurious but just plausible provenance out of Ireland?'

'He made several spectacular and thoroughly respectable finds.' Lucien inspected his small, neat fingernails and pursed his lips slightly. 'Some of his later finds were not so respectable. But what would he have to do with these pictures?'

I stood up. 'If by chance, after a little thought, you come up with any theories, let me know.'

'There's no need to look all wild-eyed about it. As far as I know, they're right; otherwise I would have told you before.'

'And done yourself out of your cut?'

Lucien looked hurt and shrugged. 'Archie, dear, I was simply doing you a favour; it's only a little deal, after all.'

'And I am, of course, very grateful to you, Lucien.' I gave him a bogus smile, and left the bar, still no wiser, with growling doubts about the history of these pictures.

I had left my car out of harm's way in West London, and hailed a cab in Jermyn Street to take me down to Lloyd's.

Johnny Stewart also expressed surprise at my punctuality when I walked into his office at midday.

'Hope you're as punctual on Thursday,' he added.

'Who knows,' I answered vaguely, not wanting stories of my confidence to circulate among the eager gamblers that abounded in this Meccano palace. 'Thanks for seeing me at such short notice,' I went on, 'but I didn't want to talk on the phone. What have you found out?'

'I would say that there's no question Drury's been creaming off his names for the last twenty-five years. I've been through his syndicates' published accounts, and analysed the business they've been doing and setting it against the averages. I would guess that as much as ten per cent of the net premium income in all three has been siphoned off.'

'How much might that come to over the years?'

'Could be anywhere between fifty and a hundred million.'

'Shit!' I uttered. 'But how the hell could he have got away with it?'

Johnny shrugged. 'He's a very good underwriter. He's got one of the best noses in the business. He understands the odds on a risk almost instinctively. And he always seems to know what's the best value business around in the market. None of his names has ever lost, even now, so they've never complained. Also Drury has had himself appointed to endless committees. He sits on the main committee; he's been close to the last three chairmen. No one's ever suggested that he's not squeaky clean; at least, not for twenty years or so, and then it was only because they didn't like the cut of his jib.'

'Was Bill Beecham still involved with him then?' I interrupted.

'Theoretically, yes. But he had nothing to do with the insurance side by then. I think he was doing little more than running errands for Drury at that stage, and then Drury eased him out all together. There was a bit of a stink over all that, for sentimental reasons really; there'd been Beechams involved in Lloyd's for two hundred years. But nobody could do much about it.'

'And no one's thought of delving deeper into Drury's way of doing business? After all, it must have been fairly brutal, even by City standards.'

'No, though I agree, it is surprising no one's bothered to undertake the exercise that I have, despite the fact that it required a lot of guesswork and fiddling about with industry averages. But I'm told that the minute anyone on the syndicates complains or asks questions, they suddenly find that they've done just a little better than the other names for various reasons that they are happy not to go into, and they keep their mouths shut.'

'But what does he do with the money?'

'I can't help you there, but my guess is that it goes offshore; Netherlands Antilles, Cayman Islands, any of those little fiscal boltholes. They are seething with reinsurance companies of varying degrees of authenticity.'

'What can you do with the information you have?'

'Absolutely nothing, apart, I suppose, from publishing a circular and being sued into oblivion for libel. It would need a full DTI inquiry to get at the facts and what hard evidence there might be, but I'm afraid Drury is much too well placed for that to happen. Of course, if his names were to start losing money, that could change, but, as I say, he's been bucking the trend and putting in reasonable profits. He foresaw all the problems like asbestosis and American medical insurance and laid it off a long time ago. He's carrying very little nasty long-tail business now. And by pure good luck, he missed out on any really heavy claims from the hurricanes.'

'If there was suddenly a smell about other, unrelated business and activities he's involved in, would an inquiry stand a better chance?'

'Of course. You think something's brewing?'

'Yes. Get all your facts and your support together. Have an informal chat with a good silk about it and keep your eyes on the papers,' I replied. 'Of course, I'll ring you as soon as the shit's going to hit the fan. Then go straight to the Committee of Lloyd's and try and persuade them to announce that they are starting an inquiry into Drury's operation. Failing that, go to the Serious Fraud Office.'

Johnny nodded. 'I might see you on Thursday. I'll be coming up to Cheltenham.'

'You and the rest of the people in this building. I probably won't have a chance to talk, but I may be in touch that evening.'

'All right, I'll make up a complete dossier on what I've found and my conclusions. And now, on a more serious note, what are your chances in this bloody race? Who are the dangers?'

'No shortage of dangers. Clive Drury has bought The Dealer for his son, Damian, to ride. Damian may be a bit of a prick, but he's not actually that bad a jockey; and Nosey Parker has the horse in very good shape; I saw him yesterday.'

'What about Prideaux-James?' Johnny asked.

'He's got a good horse too, but it might not get the trip. He's very keen to win, but he also seems determined to stop me. I think there may be a Drury connection there.'

'Between the P-Js and Drury, you mean?'

'Yes.'

'There is,' Johnny said. 'It's common knowledge here. The whole family nearly went belly-up with last year's cash calls; they were on all the worst syndicates and writing the maximum business they could get away with, and this year has been even worse for them. The word is that Drury's bailed them out.'

'Why should he do that?'

'I don't know, but it could have something to do with the fact that that old fool Sir Cyril P-J has an awful lot of substantial assets that Drury would like to get his hands on. There's the estate in Yorkshire, for a start, with one of the best grouse moors in the country, not to mention holdings in several moribund steel works in Sheffield, and masses of other bits of property. You can be sure our Clive has helped himself to some kind of a charge over a lot of it while he sits back and watches Cyril and the boys piss through the money he's lent them.'

'That's more or less how he got Gazeley from Georgie's grand-father.' Something else occurred to me. 'Lord Walford still sits on various boards of his because, he says, he likes to keep an eye on him, so bear him in mind if you get an inquiry going.'

'I will.'

I stood up and looked down at the people milling around the square like slow-moving ants a hundred feet below. 'Thanks for your help, Johnny.'

'What? Are you going? No lunch?'

'I'm afraid not. If you want me to win the Foxhunters, don't encourage me to eat or drink. I've got to lose ten pounds in the next two days.'

'God, what an appalling thought,' Johnny said as we shook hands. 'Still, the very best of luck to you.'

'There is one other favour I'd like to ask you. Have you still got that great lump of a house near Burford your uncle left you?'

'It's more an orderly pile of stones than a house, but yes, I still own it.'

'Is it liveable in?'

'If you're used to staying in one of Her Majesty's prisons or any English public school.'

'That'll do. For reasons I won't go into, I may need a bolthole a bit off the beaten track. Not for long, a week or two.'

'How intriguing. By all means use the old dump. The woman in the Post Office has a key. I'll ring her and tell her to expect you sometime. I haven't been down since the New Year, but there's plenty of wood for the fires and the Aga. But watch out for rats and woodworm.'

I thanked him, and left to take news of the planned move to Harry.

Harry took it well.

I told him where the house was and the arrangements with the key. We planned, provisionally, that I would pick him up on Friday, after I had been through Bill Beecham's things at my mother's.

Harry fretted at the delay, but I calmed him with a report of all that had happened in the last few days.

'We're closing in on him,' I said.

'You're sounding like the commander of a Chicago dragnet,' Harry said.

'Some dragnet!' I replied. 'The plan is to hit him simultaneously with a series of broadsides from the media, the police and, if we're lucky, Lloyd's, all within a few days of each other. What I need you to do as soon as possible is to write a complete statement on the whole business of the sabotage of your racecourse. Include every fact you think may be relevant, but don't embroider or make anything up. If you can get in touch discreetly with the other managers who had dealings with Drury's men, that's fine, but for

God's sake, don't tell them where you are, or about the Drury connection.'

'God, I hate writing reports, but I suppose it'll give me something to do while I'm sitting here.'

'Listen, Harry, we're going to need all the ammunition we have to nail Drury, so don't underestimate the job.'

Harry agreed reluctantly to stay where he was for three more days, accepting my logic that if by the remotest chance he was seen by any of Drury's men, with or without me, during that time, it could blow all our plans; as well as cause serious damage to his health.

'The slightest suspicion by Drury that I'm involved with you could see us both off, so just keep cool and keep out of sight.'

I left him to get on with his job, with a firm warning not to jump the gun.

From Harry I drove down the Fulham Road to a large, lavishly equipped health club where I was a member. For the next two hours, I lost myself in the most punishing work-out I could devise, and an hour's soak in the sauna. Normally, when I was preparing for a big race, I was single-minded to the point of being boring about it. But this time, I had let everything go by the board while I had chased around the country being a cross between Sam Spade and Lord Peter Wimsey.

But the exercise and the wet heat gave me a chance to get myself together. I drove back home, determined to get the race won and out of the way, so that I could give my all to seeing Bill Beecham's death paid for in full.

John Duckett had said he would arrive at Gazeley that night, or early next morning. Jamie was coming back from London to stay at my house with one of his paper's photographers so that he would be up early for his scoop, like a lark for a worm.

I found them waiting for me back at Stone House. The photographer had wasted no time finding my fast-diminishing stock of drink, and was making headway into diminishing it still further.

Jamie, cleaned up now, and thoroughly sober, was looking on with good-natured disgust. He greeted me with relief.

'Thank God; someone to talk to with an IQ of more than ten. Doug, this is Archie, your host.'

The snapper belched, and I beckoned Jamie to follow me

through to my freezing drawing room. He was bursting with information.

'I've managed to dig up a mountain of grubby stuff about Drury. I've found a lot of talkative people who used to know him under his old name. And when I told them who he was now, they couldn't wait to tell me more. He'd done a very thorough job of covering up his tracks; he must have spent a ton of money keeping people quiet. And I've found one guy who'll swear blind his father was killed by Drury. This chap's dad used to be a partner of Drury's in an illegal bookies they ran in the early fifties.'

'What about Doreen? Did you see her?'

'No. No rush, though. I'll get to her on Thursday. I didn't want her going to Drury until the first story breaks. But I think I've found out what happened to the daughter. She went off to be an exotic dancer – in other words, a stripper – in Beirut. She left there when the troubles started and disappeared in Brazil. We've already got a lad on his way there to track her down.'

'That's amazing,' I said, impressed.

'We're professionals, Archie. We've already been and checked up that John and the motorised division of his entourage are on their way and found them trundling past Brecon.'

'Great! When will they reach Drury's?'

'They were going to camp up near Hay overnight, and they'll be setting off for Gazeley at dawn tomorrow. John's really got into the swing of it, though his po-faced girlfriend is still nagging him not to come. Fortunately, she hasn't got a chance. He's loving the idea of a self-righteous showdown with the bread-head father who jettisoned him. And he'll love the exposure; he's a politician *manqué*.'

'Sounds perfect. What about the telly?'

'I'll get my story out first, and when it's gone to press, I'll telephone my mate at ITN. They'll get a crew up there first thing Thursday morning. I'll also tell them to try and pick up a few shots of Drury at Cheltenham, for a bit of a contrast. And I've got two freelance friends who'll go anywhere with an ENG on a good tip-off. That way we'll get it fully covered.'

Jamie's photographer had been getting lonely. He lumbered into the room and flopped down beside Jamie on the sofa.

'You wouldn't believe it, but Doug's shit-hot when he's sober,' Jamie nodded at his colleague, who blinked back at him.

206

'Bloody right. But right now, I need a bit of kip,' he grunted.

Jamie stood. 'You've got it. Leave him there, Archie; he'll be all right. I'm just about ready to crash out myself. I want to be down at Gazeley in time to see them arrive. Don't want to miss the first confrontation between John and Drury.'

Chapter 15

I did not go with Jamie next morning. The last thing I wanted was to be spotted near Gazeley by any of the locals who might recognise me and report back to Drury.

Besides, Georgie had left a note for me; she had enjoyed herself so much exercising the day before that, she said, she'd be over at nine to do the same again, if that was all right by me. Which it was.

Jamie set off at seven, with Doug, the bulky paparazzo, perfectly sober now and wedged into the passenger seat of his convertible. I wished them luck and arranged to see Jamie later that afternoon at Cheltenham. I was going to the races to be seen by Drury, and to see how he was coping with the invasion of his land – and the reunion with his first-born son.

When Sharon arrived, I told her that Georgie and I would be exercising Cocoa and the Consul. She looked as though she was going to sulk, then quickly asked if she could hunt Jasper again the following Saturday; she knew when she had a strong bargaining hand.

For the next hour I fidgeted, wondering what was happening at Gazeley, and getting up every few minutes to see if the postman was coming. When he did arrive, he had a package with a Cork postmark. I grabbed it and hurried inside to tear it open.

It was Sean's cassette. I put it in the kitchen ghetto-blaster, and listened.

It was sensational.

Drury's gravelly voice, less polished than usual in those circumstances, was nevertheless unmistakeable. Sean fed him all the lines, and with every reply or question, Drury condemned himself as the willing financier of a conspiracy to defraud Tomahawk's insurers of three million pounds.

With my shots of Sean and Drury in the Range Rover, it was cast-iron.

When Georgie arrived, I was flying. I rushed her into the house to play her the tape and show her the photographs.

'We've got the bastard! We've done it!' I shouted and thumped the table with my fist. 'And with all the circumstancial evidence involving him in criminal damage to three racecourses, the police have got to charge him, however chummy he is with the Home Secretary.'

'Great!' Georgie said, mostly from relief that the business would be out of my hands soon. 'My stepfather will be delighted.'

'For God's sake don't tell him yet. Not until Drury's had his collar felt. It's quite possible he could try and do a runner if he hears what's going on in time.'

Georgie nodded.

'Right,' I said, standing up, 'are you ready to ride?'

'Sure am.'

'Let's go and give 'em a bit of welly, then.'

The cloud had lifted a little since the day before, and rested on the tops of the hills. There was still no wind; it was one of those mornings when you can hear every sound – birdsong or animal rustle.

I rode Cocoa, the more unpredictable of the two horses, while Georgie rode the Consul. As we set off up the track towards the gallop, blackbirds fled before us with panic calls. Squirrels leaped to the upper branches of the budding trees. A pheasant honked and raced up the track to take flight. Grazing sheep, spotting us only at the last moment, scattered with dopey alarm in the eerie stillness.

When we reached the high field which I used for galloping, we pulled up. The cloud still hung thick here, and we could not see the far end of the field.

'Now,' I said to Georgie, 'give him a circuit at a hand canter, then take him back up the slope beside the wood as quick as you can, just to clear his lungs. Pull him up before you reach the turn.'

Georgie nodded and grinned at me before setting off and disappearing into the mist.

She came back into view returning down the other side of

the field. She and the Consul swung round in front of me and straightened to go up a few gears.

She asked him, and he obliged with a quickening of pace and lengthening of stride.

They were almost swallowed up in the white blanket of fog when I heard the shot.

It sounded like a howitzer in the still, silent air; followed by alarm calls of a dozen birds and the noise of a vehicle starting and skidding down through the woods.

Before the echoes of the shot had died, I had gathered up my reins and dug my heels into Cocoa's side. He did not need asking twice.

We raced up the gallop as fast as I ever had, until I saw the Consul cantering riderless out of the mist towards us.

My head surged with a dozen unbearable possibilities. The thought that Georgie might be dead numbed me with horror. Subconsciously, I must have seen that the Consul was moving normally, and I did not give him another thought as I urged Cocoa on at full gallop, up to the top of the field.

My eyes frantically swept the pasture through the mist, until, with a thudding of my heart, I saw a still, small khaki mound. I raced up, leaped off Cocoa and abandoned him to crouch down beside the unmoving body.

Georgie lay on her front, hunched in a foetal position.

'Georgie!' I tried not to yell. 'Georgie?'

She did not stir.

I gazed at her desperately, racked with guilt. Nothing like this would have happened if Drury had not been provoked; somewhere, at the back of this, there had to be a connection with him.

My eyes searched the girl for signs of any wound, but found none. As gently as I could, I turned her head, still encased in a black helmet.

She groaned; my body flushed with intense relief.

Her lips quivered as she breathed deeply and moaned again.

'Georgie, can you hear me?'

She gave an almost imperceptible nod.

'Thank God,' I whispered to the silent morning. I wanted to ask her if she was hurt, what had happened, but I put a hand on her shoulder and let her get her breath. Whatever other damage she had sustained, she had been badly winded by the fall.

I became aware of the sound of a vehicle bouncing up the field towards us. I turned and the square lines of a Land Rover emerged from the mist. It pulled up a few yards away and my neighbour, Harold, leaped out.

'What the 'ell 'appened, Archie?'

'Christ knows,' I said. 'Someone took a shot at her.'

'At *her*?' the farmer said, surprised. 'More likely at the horse.'

'Have you seen the horses?'

'Oh yes. The boy's got 'em. They're fine, though there's a couple of nasty grazes on the Consul's quarters.'

'What kind of grazes?'

Harold shrugged. 'Dunno, but it could be duck shot.'

Georgie was stirring a little. I turned back to her. 'Georgie, are you hurt?'

'I don't know,' she whispered. 'I just don't want to move.'

'Shall I go back down and call an ambulance,' Harold asked.

'There doesn't seem much point, she'll be just as shaken in an ambulance as in your Land Rover up here. We'll try and lift her in a minute.'

'I can make a sort of stretcher. I've got a tarpaulin and some fence posts in the back,' Harold offered.

'Great. We'll leave her a bit longer. At least she doesn't seem to have been hit. You're probably right; they must have been aiming at the horse. What brought you up here?'

'I heard the bloody shot. There shouldn't be nobody shooting up here now, and I've been on my toes since they tried to steal your horse. There's some nasty business going on.'

'I can hardly believe it,' I said, 'so much trouble over a bloody hunter chase.'

'The boy saw him driving out the woods, down by the main road; a green Daihatsu, but he didn't get the number. Now, I'll try and put this stretcher together.' He walked round to the back of his vehicle.

I turned my attention to Georgie. 'Can you tell me what hurts yet?'

'No,' she murmured, 'but I'm sure I'll be all right.'

'Just don't try and move. We'll lift you as you are onto a stretcher, then lay you in the back of the Land Rover and get you to hospital.'

'What about the Consul? He was hit!' she gasped.

'He's fine.'

'Was it Drury?'

'I don't think so – at least, not directly, not so soon before the race, and anyway, he thinks he's bought Damian his winner; The Dealer's rated three or four points better than the Consul.'

'Oh God, Archie,' Georgie said, still breathless, 'Drury must be involved. I wish I'd never encouraged you. If he's tried this, what else will he try?'

'Look, don't worry about it. Drury doesn't know what we've been doing, and when he does, he'll be out of harm's way. If they don't bang him up immediately, he'll be under heavy surveillance until he's tried. The horse is fine; all we need to do is get you checked over. Here's Harold with a stretcher.'

The farmer had made a serviceable stretcher with his posts and canvas. He laid it down next to Georgie, and by putting all our four arms under her, we were able to get her onto it without any significant change in her position.

We wedged her on to the long seat in the back of the Land Rover and climbed in the front. Harold drove gingerly back down the field and the track to the house. Harold's twenty-year-old son was already in the yard with the two horses, and Sharon was checking them.

'Right,' Harold said when we reached the gate, 'you take her on into Bromyard, we'll stay here and check the horse over with Sharon. Shall I ring the police?'

'I suppose so, though they won't be able to do much. Don't make it sound too urgent. I know what this is all about, and if the police start asking questions in the wrong places, they could bugger up a few arrangements I've made.'

'That's up to you,' the farmer concurred. 'The boy can stay in your hunter's box with a couple of dogs tonight. There's no way we're going to let anything else happen to the Consul until he's on the racecourse tomorrow. So don't you worry, leave all that to us.'

I thanked the farmer with heartfelt gratitude, and took his place at the wheel, knowing that he meant what he said.

A thorough inspection by an over-awed young doctor, and an hour on a bed in the emergency ward revealed that Georgie had suffered from no more than severe winding and shock. Nothing was broken; there were no flesh blemishes on her. She walked out of the hospital beside me with a wan smile.

'Sorry to be so pathetic,' she said.

I put my arms around her and squeezed gently. 'You aren't. I know what it's like, remember? Do you still want to come to the races this afternoon?'

'Of course I do. But my clothes are in my car back at your place.'

'Fine; we've plenty of time to get back, change and still be there for the first race. I want to take a look at Drury. He'll be feeling very sore if a convoy of hippies has turned up, led by a son he thought he'd written out of his life. I'd like to see how much he lets it show.'

'Do you have to go near him, Archie?'

'Yes, I do. It's the best way to keep him off my scent.'

Back at the house, Harold, his son and Sharon were in the Consul's box, dressing the scratches on his nearside quarter.

Georgie and I went in and had a look at them; they were barely skin deep.

'Thank God for that,' I said. Do you think shot would make marks like that?'

'If he didn't start out with them this morning, and someone's took a shot at him, then I reckon that's what they are. But it could be anything,' Harold said. 'Them's not serious cuts. Whoever tried to shoot him must 'ave been bloody useless. He'd have been no more than ten or fifteen yards away.'

'And if 'e wanted to kill the 'orse,' added Harold's son, 'e wasn't goin' to do it with a bloody shotgun anyway.'

'Depends what shot he had,' Harold said. 'With a bit of buck shot at that range, he could have done plenty of damage, if he knowed how to shoot straight.'

'At least the Consul's all right,' Sharon said, 'but how's Georgie?' she asked, turning to her.

'I'm fine; just a couple of bruises.'

'What did he do when he was hit?' Sharon asked.

'He stumbled a little and ducked to the right. I'm afraid I wasn't balanced enough to stay with him.'

'Anybody'd come off then,' said Sharon charitably.

'Specially you,' Harold's son teased.

'Never mind that,' Harold said. He turned to Georgie, 'I'm

very glad to hear you're all right, miss.'

Sharon suddenly remembered something. 'Oh, Archie, there was a telephone call for you. A lady called Sarah Winchcombe; she said it was important and she'd wait where she was to hear from you when you got back. I gave her the number of the hospital, but you'd probably left by then.'

Harry's sister – that did not sound good. 'What number did she leave?' I asked.

'It's by the phone.'

I ran into the house feeling suddenly hot.

As I had feared, the number was Sean's London flat.

I dialled it.

'Hello?' It was Sarah, worried.

'It's Archie. What's happened?'

'I don't know, but Harry's not here.'

'Shit!' I groaned. 'Does it look as though he left willingly, or,' I tried to choose my words, 'is there any sign of disagreement about it?'

'No. Everything's the same as yesterday. The only thing is there's a tape-recorder in the hall that wasn't there before.'

'What kind?'

'Hang on. I'll have a look.'

She left the phone and came back a few seconds later. 'It's called a Euer or something like that.'

'That's the one Sean was using. He must have gone back there. How long have they been gone, can you tell?'

'It can't be long at all. The kettle's still warm and there are a couple of dirty coffee mugs they used.'

'Has Harry taken anything with him?'

'I don't know, but I'll look in the bathroom.'

She left the phone once again, to return and report that her brother's shaving things and toothbrush were absent.

This, I reckoned, was good news, but I cursed Harry and Sean for leaving when they had.

'Okay, I think I know where they've gone, but leave a note for them to ring me as soon as they get back, in case they do. Thanks for letting me know. You'd better get out of there ASAP, and make sure you're not followed. There could be someone watching the flat now.'

'God, what the hell has Harry let me in for?' Sarah asked.

215

'Relax,' I said, 'I'm just asking you to be careful, and it wasn't Harry's fault, I can assure you. At least he should be safe where he's gone.'

She rang off, not sounding happy, but there was nothing I could do about it. I was fairly certain that Harry had persuaded Sean to take him to Johnny's house, but I had not wanted to compromise her by telling her that.

Georgie had come into the room. 'What's going on? she asked, seeing my face.

I told her, and my deductions.

'Suppose they're still being followed, and they come here?' she said with panic in her voice.

'I think that's unlikely. Sean's not a fool. We've told him not to come here, and he won't. So, don't worry, I don't think it's a problem. Now you'd better get changed if we're going to the races.' I tried to sound as if everything was normal.

'Sure.' She gave me a crooked smile. 'And so had you.' She nodded at my mud-caked jacket and spattered jeans.

The first person we saw in the owners' car park at Cheltenham races was Amanda Drury. Dressed loudly in a silver-fox coat and scarlet boots, her eyes flashed below her matching fur hat.

'Fancy seeing you here,' she scowled, pointedly ignoring Georgie. 'Daddy!' she yelled towards a group of backs making their way to the stands. 'Look who's here!'

Drury turned. His face was like a thunder storm about to burst. He glared at me for a second. His wife, beside him, looked on with fearful apprehension.

I sensed Georgie stiffen beside me. I knew I had to be careful.

'Morning, Clive,' I said lightly, pre-empting him. 'Your runners in good order for today?'

'Yes, and for tomorrow,' he growled.

'Well, best of luck,' I said and, taking Georgie by the arm, swept past them with the rest of the crowd converging on the stands.

When we were in the enclosure, lost from Drury's sight, Georgie said, 'Do you think his son's arrived at Gazeley?'

'Yes. He's obviously got a lot on his mind. That's the worst I've ever seen him.'

'He doesn't think you've got anything to do with it,' Georgie said confidently, 'I'm sure of that.'

'So am I. But he's still not one of my greatest fans.'

'I suppose he simply dislikes you because you're one of the few people who doesn't seem terrified by him, and you represent a lot of the things he'd like Damian to be; though God knows why he should want his son to be a philandering shit like you,' she added, laughing. 'You must really have put Amanda's nose out of joint.'

'Yes, well, it doesn't take a lot to do that. Now,' I said, turning to the day's plan, 'I arranged to meet Jamie in the Arkle Bar while the first is being run. There's always such a scrum there, no one will notice us, and anyway, Drury will stick in his box all day, apart from going to the paddock to see his runners.'

'I can check on that,' Georgie volunteered. 'My stepfather's box is two down from him, so I can keep an eye out, and waylay him if he goes anywhere near the bars.'

'He won't; he's too worried about his image to go there. But keep an eye on Amanda for me.'

'Right,' she said.

I gave her hand a grateful squeeze. 'Look, I'll probably leave as soon as I've found Jamie, so don't expect to see me again today. Meet me at the lorry park tomorrow about midday, unless I let you know otherwise.'

She nodded.

'Are you sure you feel all right now?' I added.

She looked at me with her big honest eyes. 'Yah, I'm absolutely fine. But, please, look after yourself.'

I watched her disappear into the crowd, then found a corner of the bar near the door. I unfolded a *Sporting Life* and raised it in front of my face to avoid unwanted conversations.

Jamie arrived a little before the off. He did not approach me at first, but ordered a drink and took up a position a few feet away. Only when the race had started, and everyone had crowded to the stands or glued their eyes to the television monitors on the walls did he speak to me.

'A bull's-eye,' he said.

'Great. Don't tell me about it now, though. We've got to go.'

'Where? Why?'

I was already hustling Jamie out of the stand and towards the car parks.

217

'Sean went back to London,' I answered, 'and I think Harry talked him into taking him to the place I said we'd go on Friday. I wish to hell he hadn't, but with luck, no damage has been done. We've got to get over and check it out. There's no phone or anything there.'

'Where is it?'

'Not far; the other side of Burford. We'll take your car.'

We split up and I let Jamie get twenty yards ahead. The BMW was parked a good quarter of a mile from the stands, but only when we reached it, and were both inside did we speak again.

'So what happened? Did Drury come out when the travellers got to Gazeley?'

'He certainly did. They've made a camp down below a copse, out of sight of the house but clearly visible from the road.'

Jamie manoeuvred his car out on to the track which led away from the course, and headed for the Oxford Road.

'Drury must have been on his way here when he first saw them,' Jamie went on. 'It was perfect. He ranted and raved and was about to lay into one of the travellers when he saw Doug taking pictures. Then he went berserk; threatening us with gamekeepers' guns, prosecution and the police. He seemed to guess I was a hack, but I denied it so he grabbed hold of me and started getting rough. He's a big bugger and I was a bit worried for a moment, but I managed to blurt out before he killed me, that I'd like to introduce him to John Duckett. He stopped as if he'd been shot and fortunately, John appeared right on cue.

'It was a fantastic sight. There was the Bentley purring away, with the chauffeur at the door, in front of a collection of ramshackle old buses and trucks, and John standing his ground while Drury screamed denials at him and threatened him with every suit he could think of. When he had run out of steam, he went off quaking and said he'd sort them out this evening. But he didn't call the police, and I think he realises there's not much he can do.'

'Will John and his friends stay there?'

'Oh, yes. John's loving it. He could see he'd got his father by the balls. I've given him some great coverage and he can't wait for the telly news to get there tomorrow.'

'Have you told them yet?'

'No, of course not. I want my story in tomorrow's paper first, that was our deal, remember, and with luck, no one will pick it up before. Doug's gone back to London with his pictures and I've phoned in most of my copy.'

'Will they use it?'

'Sure they bloody will. I'd done my homework. Of course, my editor was shitting bricks about libelling Drury, but I told him about all the corroborating background stuff and documents I've accumulated and where to find them. I'd already entered it all up on my terminal. I'll call him in a minute to make sure he's got it. But I know there's enough for him to feel safe.'

The minor worries I had about Sean and Harry's flight to the country were well dampened by my elation at knowing we had struck so deep into Drury's outer casing of respectability. By this time tomorrow, the story would be being broadcast on every TV and radio news bulletin in the country, and by the next day, in every newspaper.

But Jamie turned my attention back to our current journey.

'Why are we going to this house? If Harry's there, he can't get into any trouble from Drury's heavies.'

'I just want to be sure. And I want to talk to Sean. His tape arrived this morning, and it's pure semtex. With the shots I got, you'll have a much bigger story to follow up this one with. I'm going to give it to the police, but if your paper is prepared to run the story at the same time, it'll put irresistible pressure on them to follow it up.'

'That may not be so easy. A story about an abandoned son is one thing. For a start, it's not actually a crime to disown a son, especially if you can show that you made provision for him and his mother early on. But a huge fraud conspiracy is another matter, and I doubt my paper will risk going with a few photographs and one tape-recording, however convincing they are. But it doesn't matter, Drury's influence tomorrow will have been completely wiped out. Very few politicians are going to stand up and be counted on his side, I can tell you.'

Jamie wanted to phone his newsdesk, so I took over the driving. From the grin on his face, and a lot of eager affirmatives, I gathered that his editor had checked Jamie's facts and was running the story.

'Well?' I asked as he put the receiver back. 'Is it a goer?'

'Oh yes,' he answered smugly, 'unless the Prime Minister

219

commits suicide or the Pope has triplets in the next twelve hours, I've got the whole of tomorrow's front page.'

My head buzzed at the thought of the success we had had.

We had done it! The first part of our strategy was home and dry – barring the Pope's triplets. And, despite Jamie's reservations about the value of the tape and shots to his editor, I had no such doubts about their effectiveness.

It was half an hour since we had left Cheltenham, and we were driving down the steep main street of the picture-postcard Cotswold town of Burford. We crossed the bridge at the bottom and turned off onto a narrow lane that followed the meanders of the River Windrush. After a few miles, I turned up an even smaller lane through dense broadleaf woodland.

'This is the start of John's land; you can tell from the state of the fencing. The house is half a mile up here. There's a long drive but I'll park down there. We can walk up through the woods.'

'Why don't we drive straight up?' Jamie asked.

'Because for all we know Drury's man may have followed Sean back from Ireland. I'm taking no chances.'

I turned into a track. Once the car was out of sight of the road, I stopped and we got out. We set off through the trees towards the house. I had only been there once before, shortly after John had inherited it, so we had to rely on my rusty sense of direction.

We were among tall, ancient beech trees. There was not much undergrowth and the going was easy. We did not talk, and tried to keep the sound of our progress to a minimum. After ten minutes, the handsome, weatherbeaten mansion started to appear between the trees.

'Is that it?' Jamie whispered.

I nodded. Jamie abruptly grasped my arm and pointed ahead of us.

There, on an overgrown forecourt, I could just make out a number of cars. Jamie looked at me with raised eyebrows. I shrugged; we crept forward more cautiously.

The tree species had become rarer, more ornamental as we approached the house. There was also a good spread of rhododendron, now completely out of control, along the side of the drive. We slipped beneath its concealing branches, and inched forward silently until we could peer between the leaves for a clear view of the front of the house.

There were three cars. Sean's Range Rover, which was blocked in by a brown Ford Sierra, and behind them, a green Daihatsu.

Chapter 16

My heart crunched against my ribs. My guts felt like minced meat.
I looked at Jamie; all the colour had gone from his face.

'Oh my God!' I whispered.

Jamie nodded with an anguished grimace. 'They must have
tailed him the whole way.'

'And got some back-up,' I added.

'We'll have to get the police,' Jamie said, and he started to
turn.

I caught his arm. 'No, we haven't got time. Follow me.'

Jamie looked scared. I thought for a moment he was going to
desert me.

'For God's sake,' I hissed. 'We've got no choice.'

I released my hold on his arm, to give him the choice. After a
moment, to my intense relief, he made up his mind.

'Okay,' he whispered. 'I'm coming.'

I had spent two days at this place with Johnny Stewart, a year
before. We had been discussing his plans for the house and I had
been all round it in detail. Now, creeping down the edge of the
drive behind the prodigiously overgrown shrubs, I forced my mind
back to that visit to reconstruct the lay-out.

There were several entrances to the house. I aimed for a sunken
door at the back that was reached by a flight of stone steps
and gave directly into the rear cellars. We were hidden by the
rhododendrons almost up to this door. When we were opposite it,
barely ten feet away, we stopped and listened.

The only sounds were woodland noises. I glanced at Jamie and
asked him silently if he was coming. He nodded.

We worked our way warily out of the bushes. On the wall that faced us were half a dozen windows of old kitchens and sculleries. No light showed through their dusty panes. After a few more seconds' listening, we made a quick run to the steps. Once down, we could not have been seen from the house.

In front of us was a grey painted door which might have been two hundred years old. But until recently this house had been occupied by a rich family, and even the cellar doors were of durable hardwood. Securing the door was a heavy cast-iron bolt and padlock.

'Good!' Jamie whispered. 'That should mean there's no bolt on the inside.' He fished in the pockets of his anorak. To my amazed relief, he produced a small bunch of skeleton keys. Journalistic ethics at his level were not high.

The third key did the trick. Jamie took the padlock out, put it on the ground and slid back the bolt. Inch by inch, he began to push the door. It groaned with each inch, and he stopped to listen between each groan, but nothing suggested we had been heard.

When it was open wide enough, we slipped through and closed the door behind us. The only light was from a grille a few feet away, but it was enough to let us see the stairs that led up to the interior of the house.

As far as I could remember, the door at the top of these stairs opened into a warren of back passages. Opening it would be like playing Russian roulette. This time it was my turn. I lifted the latch and pulled. The door swung back easily and silently. I listened; there was still no sound to be heard besides a tap dripping into a sink somewhere in the cavernous pantries.

I tried to quell the nausea bubbling up from my stomach and opened the door wide enough to get my head through. Submitting to the whims of chance, I poked it out.

I saw a broad, gloomy passage with a linoleum floor and pre-war cream and brown walls. We both crept out and stood, straining our ears. We did not dare speak, but after a few moments, I beckoned Jamie to follow me.

I led him along the corridor to the bottom of what had once been the servants' stairs.

It seemed to take an hour, though it was probably only five minutes, to reach the top of the second flight. Every step creaked under each of us and I was almost rigid with tension by the time we reached the top.

But our presence had still gone unheard.

One more flight of steeper and narrower stairs, and another squealing door revealed our best chance yet of delivering Sean and Harry.

I had been counting on Johnny's having done nothing about the illicit collection of sporting guns that he had shown me in the gable-end attic room.

In a corner, among discarded rocking horses, Edwardian children's prams and stacks of well-bound old books, were four double-barrelled twelve-bores, a pump-action shotgun and a Mannlicher deer rifle.

Next to them were two boxes of cartridges and .270 calibre high-velocity bullets that Johnny and I had put there on my last visit.

Jamie looked at them, then glanced at me with surprise. He spoke for the first time since we had entered the house.

'Do those things work?' he asked in an undertone.

'Yes. Johnny and I cleaned them up and did a bit of pigeon shooting last year. I had a crack with the rifle too. It's fine.'

Jamie picked up one of the guns and inspected it doubtfully.

'Look,' I said, 'if you don't want to get involved in this, I'll understand, but Sean and Harry are in deep shit. I don't know how many guys there are down there with them, but with the guns and as much surprise as we can manage, we stand a chance.'

'I'm on,' Jamie whispered back. 'If you can handle the rifle, I'll take the pump gun.'

He picked up the weapon. I opened the box of cartridges and he helped himself. He slotted eight into his magazine, and put another dozen in his pockets while I loaded the deer rifle with a magazine of five.

'We shouldn't have to fire the bloody things,' I hissed, 'but if we do, for God's sake don't aim at anyone.'

'Judging by what they did to Harry last time, they're not going to be too soft. There may be no choice.'

'Just watch out for Sean and Harry, then,' I said.

With that, I led the way back downstairs.

There were about fifteen rooms on the ground floor. Drury's men could be holding Sean and Harry in any of them.

When we reached the passage we had started from, we walked back towards the centre of the house, past the door to the back cellar, checking all the kitchens, laundry rooms and larders as we went. There were signs of occupation by rodents and insects, but none of recent human habitation.

At the end of the corridor was a wide, double-hinged door covered in green baize that had been worn away by the elbows of generations of tray-bearing servants. This, I recalled, gave into a large back hall.

Holding my breath, I cocked the rifle and grasped it as if I was going over the top of a dug-out. I gently shoved the door with my shoulder. It opened quietly. I let out a breath and waited.

For the first time, I heard voices; not words, but an angry murmur several rooms away. I pushed a little more, and held the door for Jamie. He had cocked his gun and clutched it grimly. He followed me into the hall. Without conferring, we made our way along opposite walls to an archway that led into a magnificent double-storeyed front hall.

Four rooms gave off this hall, and a heavily carved staircase curved round above our heads. Next to the front entrance, a door to one of the rooms was half open. From there the muffled voices came. I thought back to my last visit.

That room was a library and beyond it, four or five feet down a narrow flight of stairs, was a small study. It was probably the easiest room in the house to keep warm, with one window giving onto an abandoned shrubbery. That was where they had to be. I drew back beneath the arch.

Speaking as soundlessly as I could, I told Jamie, 'I know where they are. There's a very narrow entrance; we'd only get through one at a time. You go back through the cellar, and work your way round the house to the left. You'll come to a small terrace with a balustrade along the edge. When you reach that corner of the house, the window to the room they're in is a few more feet on your left. Wait there. You should be able to hear what's going on. If any of them seem like trying to come out that way, stop them. For God's sake, don't fire unless you absolutely have to. I'll give you five minutes to get there. Okay?'

Jamie took this all in. He nodded and sidled back through the green baize door with hardly a sound.

I took a deep breath, and leaned against the inside of the arch. I glanced at my watch and waited. And wondered what the hell I was doing. I had loved old Bill Beecham like a favourite uncle, but was he worth all this?

But then, there was Harry; and there was Sean. I was responsible for dropping them in this. Too late, I realised that I should have gone for the police right at the beginning.

The murmuring voices, rising and falling, sometimes abating completely, reached me still without discernible words. That gave me hope; as long as they were still here and talking, Sean and Harry were all right.

I lifted my left arm again. My hand gripped the barrel of the rifle with white knuckles. I tried to relax and checked the time. Jamie should have been outside the window by now.

I took a grip on myself, and set out across the great hall.

At the door into the library, I stopped and listened. One voice was distinct now; a hard London voice: '*Tell* me, you fucking Irish pratt.'

Another voice, incomprehensible.

Then, 'Shut up, you fucking wally.'

It was a deep doorway. I slid halfway through, so that I could see around the library. It was in semi-darkness; most of the shutters were closed. From a small opening at the far end, a light shone up. Above the fireplace was a large overmantel glass. Reflected in it, I could see part of the small room beyond and, in the room, Harry in profile, trussed to an upright chair.

Facing Harry was the man whose voice I had heard. I had never seen him before. He looked about forty, clean-shaven, hard-jawed. He was dressed like a countryman; khaki jacket and a flat tweed cap. In his right hand, aimed in Harry's general direction, he held a short-nosed revolver.

Beyond Harry, I saw the legs of someone else seated, which must have been Sean. I could not see anyone else but, from the cars outside, there had to be at least two of Drury's men.

I slipped into the library and followed the window wall round to the small opening at the far end of the room. When I reached it, I put my back to the wall beside it and turned my head slowly.

My memory had been right. There was a short, narrow flight of six or seven steps at the bottom of which the door into the small study was wide open. This did not give me much more of a view of the room than I had had through the mirror. But I could see two more men. One of them I had seen before; once, trying to steal my horse, and again, loading the trailer in the sheds where Harry had been caught.

I turned my head back and felt the sweat between my hands and the rifle. I could hear both sides of the conversation now.

From the confident aggression and East End vowels of the man in the cap I guessed he had been imported by Drury from London. He was evidently used to getting results but was finding more resistance in Sean and Harry than he had expected.

'Look,' he snarled, 'for the last time, you Paddy arsehole, if you don't tell me who the fuck you've been pulling this scam with, I'll put this gun in your gob and pull the trigger.'

When he answered, Sean sounded relaxed and bored in his natural southern Irish drawl.

'You do that, my friend, and you'll find out soon enough, and after you've found out, you'll be dead as a pound of pork sausages y'self.'

'Don't give me that crap!' his inquisitor yelled. 'Tommy followed you the whole way to Cork and back to London. You didn't talk to nobody; no one come looking for you or nuffing.'

'Yer man didn't do too good a job if that's what he told you.'

'Tommy,' the flat hat said to one of his henchmen, 'did you see anyone or not?'

'Well, no.' Another London voice, nasal and whining. 'He didn't see no one to talk to. He's made a few phone calls, though.'

'You stupid dickhead,' the other jeered, 'why didn't you say so before?'

'You didn't give me a bleeding chance. And he was in the hotel for a bit when I couldn't see him,' Tommy went on, 'but not long, Fred, I promise yer. There's no way he met up with any IRA geezers.'

Sean laughed, 'No, of course not.'

'And,' Fred resumed his interrogation of Sean, 'what the hell have you got to do with him?' I guessed he must have been referring to Harry.

'Like I said,' Sean answered, 'we've a mutual interest in race-horses. He reckoned your boss would like our plan; and he was right. Drury's very keen to lose that horse, and you're making it difficult for us to get on with the job. He'll not be too pleased with you, when I tell him what's held things up.'

'Don't be such a pratt. Why d'you fink he put Tommy onto you? He knew there was a good chance you was pulling a stroke. And he'll be wanting his thirty grand back.'

Fred, the man with the gun, was sounding near the end of his short tether. It was clear from the rising pitch in his voice that he was not going to put up with Sean's story for much longer.

The other men did not carry any weapons that I had seen in my quick glance. I reckoned that the red-faced countryman was out of his depth, and Tommy, the other cockney, sounded fairly harmless.

I put the rifle to my shoulder and swung round to face down the stairs into the room. I aimed the weapon directly below Fred's neck.

'Drop it, or you're dead.'

My mouth was dry as a desert, and the words rattled huskily from my throat.

Fred turned towards me with his eyes blazing. And as he turned, he lifted his right arm.

I squeezed the trigger. I shut my eyes but my arms held steady.

The high-velocity cartridge exploded with a roar. Through numbed ears, I heard an astonished, angry bellow of pain. I blinked my eyes open.

I had hit Fred in the shoulder.

The impact hurled him on to his back. The gun dropped from his hands.

The ferret-faced Tommy lunged for it, picked it up and swung round towards me.

Before he was halfway through his swing, my first shot was echoed by another from the window, and a third from the revolver as Tommy jerked forward with a grunt.

I glanced back at Fred, writhing on the floor, and then at Harry.

Harry had been hit by Tommy's stray bullet. He flopped forward where he was tied in his chair, coughing and retching; a small trickle of blood oozed from the corner of his mouth.

Jamie was smashing the window with the stock of his gun. He pushed through the splintered wood and crashing glass.

I descended the stairs cautiously, covering the one uninjured member of Drury's team. The red-faced man was glancing at his own shotgun, propped against the dusty desk.

But Jamie had seen him too. He was in the room now aiming the pump gun straight at the man's stomach. 'Don't even think about it!' he yelled.

I turned my attention back to the others. Sean, impotent in his chair, was gazing at Harry in horror.

'Jesus!' he hissed.

I looked into the panic-stricken eyes of the uninjured man. 'Give me your knife.'

'And do it slowly,' Jamie said, jerking his gun.

The man delved into his jacket and produced a large pocket-knife.

I took it from him and cut Sean free. He leaped up, flexing his limbs, and helped me to cut Harry loose and lay him on the floor.

'Tie these bastards up,' Sean said, 'starting with him.' He grabbed the petrified countryman, spun him round and, putting his foot on his behind, sent him sprawling on his face.

With the thick nylon cord that had secured him and Harry to their chairs, he tied the man's hands and feet. Jamie and I continued to cover the other two, who were both groaning quietly on the floor. I reached down, picked up the revolver and put it in my pocket.

'We'll need some more cord, Sean. There'll probably be some in the Daihatsu outside.'

Sean regarded his handiwork on his captive and tightened a couple of knots. 'Okay,' he said, getting to his feet and running up the stairs through the library.

Jamie looked at me, pale but collected. 'Harry's in a hell of a state. We're going to have to get him to hospital. What shall we do with this lot?'

'There are some wine vaults under the front of the house, separate from the others. There's only one way in and there used to be a safe so it's got an iron door to it. We bung them in there and worry about them later.'

'But they're in pretty bad shape, Archie.'

'Yes, but they're not dying. And if we take them to hospital, Drury'll get to know about it.' I had a sudden thought. 'My old vet lives near here now. He'll deal with them without bothering about formalities.'

'A vet?' Jamie asked.

'Don't worry, the principles are the same.'

Sean careered down the stairs into the room with more cord.

While Jamie stood by with his pump gun, Sean and I trussed up Fred and Tommy. Fred grunted with pain as we moved him. Tommy screamed; he had a nasty wound in his lower back. I nearly weakened in my resolve not to take him to hospital yet. But that would have been disastrous, and I had meant what I said to Jamie: the vet was as capable of dealing with him as most doctors.

We carried them one by one to the cellar door. There was a heavy iron bar across it, but no lock. I swung it open and felt my way down the stone steps into the pitch darkness.

When all three were in, we banged the door shut and dropped the bar back in place.

'Okay,' I said, 'I'll go and fetch the vet. Jamie, you take Harry to Oxford in the Range Rover now. You'll have to try and cobble up some story about how he was hit. Sean and I'll put their cars out of sight then go back to my place in your car.'

'You'd better give them some food,' Jamie said.

'Right,' I agreed.

We carried Harry outside and laid him on his injured side as comfortably as we could in the back of the vehicle. He had been hit just below the ribs, and there was no exit wound. But he was still conscious and aware of what was happening.

'Harry, you'll be all right,' I said. 'Jamie's taking you to hospital. They'll sort you out.'

I had no illusions about the seriousness of his condition, but at least he was alive.

Jamie drove away grey-faced. He had never met Harry before in his life, but the knowledge that he could almost as easily have been hit himself had shaken even his journalistic stoicism.

Sean stayed at the house to put the Sierra and the Daihatsu in one of the garages while I ran back to Jamie's car and went to look for the vet.

I had known the vet well, and for a long time. When I found him on a call, fortunately only a few miles from his surgery, and sketched out the circumstances, he agreed to come at once.

He went straight to the house, while I made a detour to a village shop and bought food and candles, still doubtful about what I was doing with our prisoners.

But – I convinced myself – it was only for a couple of days, and it was no more than they deserved.

Driving back over the Malverns an hour or so later, it seemed incredible that it was still only five o'clock on a fine spring evening with the sun going down in a blaze in front of us.

Sean talked continuously. It was, I supposed, an antidote to the shocks he had experienced at the afternoon's events.

He felt pathetically guilty, too. It was all his fault, because he had failed to see that he was being followed.

'Thank God,' I remarked, 'that they didn't try to stop you earlier. I'd never have known then.'

But Tommy, the man tailing him, must have had specific instructions not to stop him. Sean had gone to his bank and deposited Drury's thirty thousand before picking up Harry. He had spoken to his father on the phone in Ireland, and having told him what he was involved in, his father had advised him not to touch Drury's money and had transferred five thousand to Sean's account to help with expenses.

'Where did you make that call?' I asked, worried.

'From Jury's in Cork, but don't worry, there's no way I was overheard, and I didn't need to mention any names; my father knew exactly what I was talking about; he was damned happy about it, too. He's coming across with details of a few more of Drury's strokes, very willingly, I can tell you. When I went to the flat, Harry absolutely insisted I get him out to that place. He was scared shitless, and I didn't see it could do any harm. He'd written the statement you asked him to, so I deposited that in the bank on our way out. We'd only been at the house about a quarter of an hour when those fellas arrived but we never heard them coming. Tommy must've phoned through to get that other hard bastard over to help. He's close to Drury, Fred is, I'm sure of that from the way he was talking.'

'I've never seen them together,' I said, 'but I guess he must have been one of the guys that Ian Jack dealt with when you had your meet with Drury. Anyway, that's three of his men out of action, and Drury won't know where the hell they are. He's been at the races most of the day, and before that, he was a little tied up trying to stop fifty trespassers camping on his land.'

'Fantastic!' said Sean. 'What's the story there?'

I brought him up to date. The story would not break until Jamie's paper was published next day, when it would be too late for the morning TV to do much. But when the cameras did get there, all hell would be let loose at Gazeley, and the story of Sean's taped conversation would follow hot on its heels.

'The police will have the tape and shots too. We'll need to get

Harry's statement to them. Shit,' I said suddenly gloomy, 'I hope the poor bastard makes it.'

'For God's sake, Archie, it isn't your fault.'

'Of course it is. If I hadn't made him follow up the people who wrecked his course, he'd still be sitting in his office, blissfully unaware of the whole thing.'

'Or he'd have been sacked for incompetence,' Sean said.

'He'd probably prefer that to a bullet in his guts.'

My yard was full of cars: Sharon's, Harold's, his son's pick-up and a small police car.

Jim Lewis, the constable from Bromyard, was visiting in response to a call from Harold earlier in the day.

'Someone's causing you a lot of trouble, sir; first trying to pinch your horse and then shooting at it.'

'Yes,' I said. 'Have you found out anything?'

'We haven't got much to go on. And though it's a serious business trying to kill animals, no harm's been done so they haven't sent anyone out from Hereford. Your neighbour's given me a description of the vehicle that drove away after, but no number,' he shrugged. 'It's your big race tomorrow, isn't it?'

'That's right.'

'There must be a connection. Haven't you got any ideas?'

'I might have after tomorrow; I'll let you know.'

The policeman took a couple of statements, then left, apologising for his ineffectiveness, and promising to follow up what he could.

Sharon, Harold and his son were enjoying themselves. As far as they were concerned, nothing was going to stop the Consul getting to Cheltenham next day, and all of them were going to stay that night.

So as not to complicate things, Sean and I did not tell them what had happened at Johnny's house. I had not told the policeman about the green Daihatsu, which I was certain was the same one that had been seen that morning, and I saw no purpose in telling the others.

I rang the hospital in Oxford and enquired about Harry Winchcombe. A nurse took the call in his ward. Before she would tell me anything, she wanted to know who I was and my relationship to Harry. I said I was his brother, Charles Winchcombe, and crossed my fingers.

'We've operated and he's stable, but I couldn't say more than that,' the nurse offered.

'Just tell me how serious it is. What are his chances?' I pressed, impatiently.

'Not too good,' the nurse was replying, when the phone was taken from her.

A male voice asked, 'Who is this, please?'

'Charles Winchcombe, why?'

'We've already spoken to Charles Winchcombe in France. If you're a friend of Harry Winchcombe you'll . . .'

I put the phone down. My hand was shaking.

First, for Harry; and then, because, with the police at his bedside, there was a chance they might extract the whereabouts of Johnny's house and our temporary prisoners.

Sharon, watching while she had been chatting to Harold, said, 'What's the trouble Archie?'

'Nothing. Just a friend of mine who's ill in hospital. It doesn't sound too good.'

'That's a shame,' she said, and carried on discussing the possible identity of that morning's attacker with the farmer. She had not forgotten my instructions not to tell Harold about our other activities, or her boyfriend's involvement in them.

Sean and I had listened to the radio news on the way back from Gloucestershire, and there had been no mention of Clive Drury. I turned on the television to see if they had anything yet.

Towards the end of the bulletin Clive Drury was mentioned, as the owner of the horse that had won the Queen Mother Chase at Cheltenham that afternoon.

I exchanged a smile with Sean. That was going to be the last piece of favourable news about Clive Drury for a very long time. Sharon saw, and winked.

It was not easy to sleep that night. I finally became unconscious some time after the BBC World Service 4 am News had started on the radio beside my bed.

Three hours later, I was awake with the worst dose of pre-race nerves I had ever experienced.

I knew that I had my best chance yet of winning this race, one of the biggest of the amateur chases. Winning this and the jockeys' championship with the number of wins I had already managed to clock up that season would provide me with the high point of my sporting ambitions. And, less admirably, the thought of seeing the Prideaux-Jameses publicly beaten by someone they had never made any secret of loathing gave an added sweetness to the prospect of victory.

And today, the public humiliation and, with luck, the beginnings of the process of justice would be meted out on Clive Drury.

As far as that was concerned, events were now almost out of my control and I was going to have to work hard to separate the panic this caused from the normal misgivings I felt before a big race, where a jockey's cool judgement and steady nerves were almost as important as a horse's talent and fitness.

I heaved myself out of bed and glanced down at the yard through my window. The first thing I saw was the Consul's head and neck craning over the top of his stable door.

At least, so far, I had a horse to ride. Harold's boy was already up and about. He came into view carrying a bucket of water and a hay net. I opened the window and yelled, 'Don't give him that! Just a few rolled oats, and not too much water. Better still, wait for Sharon and let her do it.'

The boy nodded and plodded back towards the feed-store.

I dressed quickly and went downstairs. Sharon was there already. 'Harold's just gone home to see about a few things,' she said, 'he'll be back in a minute. He's coming in the lorry with us to Cheltenham; he thinks we might be hijacked,' she added with a laugh.

'There's not much chance of that,' I said.

'How d'you know?' she asked.

'Because Sean, Jamie and I locked up three of Drury's men yesterday afternoon, and I'm sure that one of them was here yesterday morning. Another of them was the fellow who tried to pinch the Consul the first time.'

'But Drury might send someone else.'

'He'll have other things on his mind this morning; and I don't think he ordered anyone to shoot at the Consul. But anyway, I can't come in the lorry with you and you could do with some help.'

'Why aren't you coming, then?'

'I'm going over to Gazeley. I want to see what's happening there. Jamie's story'll hit the paper this morning. Let's see if the telly's picked it up yet.'

I turned on the television. It was the business news. A reporter was talking about the condition of the stock-markets. I held my breath. Then it came.

'Revelations about the early private life of Clive Drury, the insurance market leader, have sent ripples through Lloyd's of London. Allegations in the story published in the *Sun* this morning have already evoked denials and the threat of libel writs from Mr Drury. But the ugly scenes yesterday at Gazeley Park, Mr Drury's Herefordshire estate, have already given rise to further questions about his business activities. Clive Drury also has substantial interests in a number of private and public companies in the food and leisure sectors.'

The report was accompanied by library pictures of Clive Drury with the Princess Royal at the opening of a new children's home; and Clive Drury receiving a racing trophy from the Queen Mother.

The item was over.

It had said little, but more than enough to satisfy me.

I rang Johnny Stewart at his flat. He was wide awake.

'It's Archie,' I began.

'I've just seen it,' he said before I got any further. 'I'll take my stuff to the Fraud Squad immediately. The barrister I saw said they were far more likely to act quickly on it than the Committee.'

'Okay. Tell them to get in touch with a Detective Sergeant Robinson at West End Central. He'll be getting a whole lot more information from me later this morning.'

'Okay. It's amazing how much the media are making of this hidden family of Drury's.'

'I think a lot of people have been wanting to catch him out for a long time. They'll extract all they can from this one, and hope that it shakes out a few more.'

'It sounds as though they won't be disappointed.'

'They won't,' I said.

'For God's sake, ring me if you have anything new that could help this end. I won't be coming to Cheltenham; I'll be following up the Drury investigation. So, best of luck, and try not to fall off; I've got a monkey on you.'

I put the phone down. My head felt like a ping-pong ball on a fountain. I had to grab hold of my thoughts and try and get them into order.

Then Jamie rang from his car.

'I'm at Gazeley,' he said breathlessly. 'It's mayhem here. There are already three television news crews. And every paper in the country has sent someone as far as I can tell. Have you seen the story yet?'

'No, of course not. They don't deliver papers up here. I'm on my way over. I'll get one on the way. It made the telly news,' I added.

'I know. My news desk told me. People are already digging up any shit they can find. This thing's worked better than you could have dreamed.'

'I'll be down there soon, then I'm going to meet the London police to give them the tapes.'

'Fine. I'll run our story tomorrow. The police won't be telling anyone else about it.'

I rang West End Central, and asked for Robinson's home number. He had already left for work, so I rang the station back and left a message for him to meet me at Cheltenham, without fail, and prayed that he would think it worth coming.

After that, I ran out of the house clutching a briefcase containing all my evidence and leaped into my car.

I picked up a copy of the paper from a garage on the main road, and glanced at it long enough to see the front page.

'TYCOON'S TIFF WITH LONG LOST SON.' And a picture of Drury looking demented with his finger thrust at John Duckett's face.

I laughed as I hurtled through the town and out towards Gazeley.

Jamie had not exaggerated. I was struck by the irony of a group of half a dozen policeman standing at the main park gates, protecting Drury from the newsmen baying for his blood.

Through the park railings, John Duckett's encampment of battered buses and painted lorries stood incongruously among the ancient oaks and parkland cedars.

I drove back down the main road, and turned up towards one of the side entrances. Here too, there was a gathering of the more enterprising media people, and more policemen blocking the way.

I found Jamie talking to a camera news crew and drew him to one side.

'What's happening?' I asked.

'Drury's sent a sidekick down to say that he will sue the employers of anyone who puts a foot on his land, and he's asked the police to shift the travellers.'

'Are they going to do that?'

'Not without a lot of resistance, and they won't want to be seen siding too obviously with Drury. Me and Doug want to catch Drury leaving this place.' He pulled a battered copy of the local OS map from his pocket. 'Which way do you think he'll leave?'

'I suppose that depends on how many people there are at the various gates. But the most obscure is this one.' I showed him a small lane that emerged onto the main road about two miles away.

'We may as well wait there then. I think he'll try and go to Cheltenham today, just to show his face, so I'll come along there afterwards. Any news of Harry?'

I blinked. 'My God, I've hardly thought of him this morning. When I phoned last night, they didn't sound optimistic, but then a copper came on the line and I hung up.'

'I'll ring now from my car,' Jamie said. He dived into his vehicle and emerged a minute later, looking grim.

'He's alive, just.'

'Oh hell! I'll go and see him after the races. I'll just have to risk the police.'

'For God's sake, Archie, tell the police about Drury's men; let them deal with it. We were completely justified in what we did, but if one of them gets worse, we'll be in big trouble. I'll try and get another reporter on to it.'

'No, don't! Not yet. Please.'

Jamie shrugged. 'Someone else'll probably get there first then.'

'If they do, they do. You've got your first-hand version to write in a couple of days, but I don't want my connection known. Not until Drury's out of the way. You've got the tapes and the shots. What more do you want?'

'All right, all right. Try and get me on the mobile phone if you've got any more news, okay?'

I nodded, went back to my car and pointed it towards Cheltenham.

Chapter 17

Detective Sergeant Robinson stood in the Tote hall of the Tattersall's stand, staring up at the prices displayed on the television screens. In a trilby and mackintosh, he did not look out of place. Beside him, also studying the screens, was an older man, who turned and spoke to Robinson. Robinson's eyes left the screens and swept round the hall until he spotted me. He gave me a nod and I walked outside into a melee of people heaving in all directions.

When I found a less populous place behind a tobacco kiosk, I stopped and waited.

Half a minute afterwards, I was joined by Robinson and his colleague, whom he introduced as Chief Inspector Waller. Waller, with gold-framed spectacles, neat silver hair and some kind of club tie, looked more like an accountant than a policeman. He did not look particularly friendly, either, but at least they had taken me seriously enough to respond to my message.

'Well, Mr Best, Sergeant Robinson convinced me you wouldn't be wasting our time,' Waller said.

'Good. I won't,' I answered, and unclipped the briefcase I had brought with me.

'Don't get anything out here,' Waller warned hurriedly. 'Tell me what you've got first.'

'It's about Clive Drury,' I said. 'Sergeant Robinson asked me to let him know if I heard anything.'

'In connection with the murder of Mr Bill Beecham,' Robinson added.

'No. I'm afraid not,' I said quickly. 'Nothing to do with that. But I told you Drury wanted to do some business with me.'

'Over a horse?' Robinson asked.

'Yes, and some pictures. I like to know what I'm dealing with and I've come across a few things that will interest you.'

'Clive Drury, eh?' said Waller. 'He's getting a lot of attention today.'

'Yes,' I agreed. 'What I've got here is a recording of him meeting someone whom he believed was a member of an Irish terrorist organisation, and subsequently meeting again to hand over the first instalment of a payment for stealing one of his horses. I also have photographs taken of him at that second meeting.'

'And why should he want the IRA to steal one of his horses?' Waller asked flatly.

'Because he has it insured for a great deal more than it's worth.'

'And how did you come by these tapes?'

'That's a long story. But with the shots, they provide incontrovertible evidence that he was up to his neck in a conspiracy to defraud the insurers of his stallion.'

'Was it a genuine conspiracy?' the inspector asked.

'No.'

'Just a con, then?'

'No. The money he paid has been lodged intact in a bank. It will be delivered to you tomorrow together with a detailed statement from the manager of a racecourse which was deliberately sabotaged by one of Drury's companies.'

'This is all very interesting, no doubt. But we have difficulties with *agent provocateur* cases; especially when perpetrated by civilians.' He removed his spectacles and gave them a polish. 'I imagine that there'll be a lot of fanciful theories about Drury's misdeeds doing the rounds now. But I understand from Sergeant Robinson that you wanted to talk about William Beecham's murder.'

Waller's manner was horribly deflating. He was somehow managing to make my revelations look like so much gossip. But I did not have time to debate.

'I apologise for misleading you, then. I just needed to be sure I was getting this material to someone who had already expressed an interest in Drury,' I said with growing impatience and disappointment. 'If he had anything to do with Beecham, you'd never be able to prove it, so I'm suggesting you concentrate on this.'

I pulled my tapes and envelope of photographs from my brief-case, ignoring Waller's injunction. 'Look, take the stuff I've got here, and listen to it.'

Angrily, I thrust the envelope and cassettes into Robinson's surprised grasp, and walked away from the two policemen as fast as I could without actually breaking into a run. I knew my way around Cheltenham racecourse, and lost them almost immediately. From a balcony overlooking the paddock, I watched them below me, looking around. Robinson, still clutching my evidence, seemed to be getting some stick from the inspector. I cursed his superior's stodgy resentment.

But, I consoled myself, he could not possibly ignore all that I had given them.

Or could he? My heart sank. Surely we could not have gone through all that for nothing? Or was it possible that Waller had instructions to stonewall any suspicions about Drury?

I closed my eyes in frustration. We might just have to rely on Jamie's paper to break the story, and force it out into the open.

It was easy to get out of the enclosures and to my lorry without bumping into Waller and Robinson. When I reached it, Sharon and Harold were sitting in the cab drinking tea.

'Any problems?' I asked.

'No. And the horse is fine,' Harold answered.

'Georgie came looking for you,' Sharon said. 'She said to say that she'll be in her father's box, and she'll look after your mother when she comes.'

'Okay. I want to go and quickly walk the course from the third last to check the ground at the bottom turn. Start getting him ready and take him up to the course in half an hour or so.'

I went back through the seething masses of racegoers and hardly noticed them. Usually, I was very affected by the excitement and bonhomie of the Festival Meeting, but this year, the first time I would be riding, I could not focus on it all.

But I made my way down to the bottom turn. There was plenty of time before the runners came out for the first race – the Triumph Hurdle – to walk a few yards along the course that I would be riding forty minutes from then.

There had been a good drop of rain during the night and there were sticky patches close to the rails, even though the course had not been used since December. The New Course was always kept fresh for the last day of the Festival meeting to provide good and even ground for the world's premier steeplechase. There were, not unsurprisingly, quite a lot of professionals who were unable to see the sense in letting a bunch of amateurs churn up the ground only an hour beforehand.

I walked a few hundred yards of the soft turf to get the feel of it, but my heart was not really in it. Still not able to concentrate, I walked back up to the stands to see Georgie and my mother in Lord Walford's box.

My mother greeted me with a worried frown, habitual on these occasions.

'You will be careful, won't you?' she pleaded. 'And don't forget; you're coming to see me tomorrow to look at Bill's things. They've already arrived, but I simply don't want to open them on my own.'

'I won't forget,' I promised, and realised that I would have to deal with this problem as fast and as tactfully as possible next morning.

A lot of well-wishers interrupted further private conversation with my mother, and attempted to offer me drinks which I did not want.

I helped myself to a glass of water and a couple of cheese biscuits which immediately tried to resurface. Then it was time to go and change.

I walked out of Lord Walford's box and straight into Clive Drury's path.

He was steaming down the corridor like a warship, pushing in front of him a bow-wave of palpable fury. Where yesterday he had been thunderous, today he was quaking with rage.

He glanced at me as he passed, but did not acknowledge me.

The immediate cause of his anger became apparent at the entrance to the members' enclosure. A cluster of frantic reporters, brandishing notebooks, tape-recorders and lightweight video cameras was milling round, trying to find ways of homing in on their prey.

But the gatemen stood their ground; whatever their private thoughts about Clive Drury, they would protect his privacy as long as the job was within their remit.

I pushed my way through the gang of hacks and found Jamie

Lloyd-Jones and his photographer on the outer edge.

'Why aren't you in the scrum with the rest of them?' I asked.

'They're not going to get anywhere,' Jamie said, 'and we've already got our morning's scoop. You were right about his way out of Gazeley. We were the only people there. I stood in the way of his car and he wound down the window and screamed abuse at me while Doug fired away with the Nikon.'

'I just saw him inside. He was looking very savage,' I said.

'I'm not surprised. He's going to be crucified. You may have thought we had something on him. Well, so do a hundred others. The stories are flooding in; most of them unusable as yet, but enough to leave him covered in shit.'

'You're going to have to try and get our fraud story into your paper. I arranged to meet two London coppers here earlier. I gave them copies of the stuff but they weren't too impressed; at least, the boss wasn't.'

'That's going to make it tougher,' Jamie groaned. 'We've got to be very careful; Drury's already blasting off writs like a Gatling gun.'

'For God's sake, you must use it!'

'Of course I'll try, but it's not the end of the world if we save it till later. The Serious Fraud Office have confirmed that they're instigating an inquiry into the reinsurance activities of his syndicates, and that'll do as much damage.'

'Any news of Harry?' I asked.

Jamie shook his head. 'I phoned the hospital but they wouldn't tell me a thing.'

'I'll ring tonight and go tomorrow,' I said.

An announcement over the loudspeakers reminded me that I was supposed to be riding in the next race.

'Hell, I'm late! I'll try and see you after the race.' I hurried off towards the jockeys' changing rooms.

'By the way, good luck,' Jamie called after me.

By the time I was changed and weighed – by some miracle, only a pound overweight – I did not even feel like going for a hack, let alone racing three and a quarter miles around Cheltenham. As if they were in another world, I heard the other jockeys nervously joking with each other and I reflected how amateur steeplechasing brought together the oddest collection of participants.

I knew most of them, at least by sight; a middle-aged Yorkshire farmer, a sporting Guards officer, an Irish playboy, and an American banker among the regulars.

There were only nine of us and with the possible exception of Damian Drury, we had all been drawn here by the incomparable thrill of riding flat out over Britain's most demanding steeplechase course.

The list of runners and riders published that morning read:

2.50 THE CHRISTIES FOXHUNTER STEEPLECHASE CHALLENGE CUP

Owner	Trainer	Age st lb
1 ACACIA QUEEN		11 11 9
Mr J Bidwell	(T Paton)	Mr D Dudley-Smith
	(Bicester)	
2 AIR TROOPER		13 12 0
Mrs J Angus	(Mrs J Angus)	Mr M Thomson
	(Berkeley)	
3 BEAMISH		12 12 0
Sir Richard Westcott	(M Westcott)	Capt M Westcott
	(VWH)	
4 CAESAR'S CONSUL		9 12 0
Mr A Best	(A Best)	Mr A Best
	(Ledbury)	
5 MOTOWN		8 12 0
Dr E Elliot-Powell	(F Philby)	Mr F Philby
	(N Herefords)	
6 SCUD MISSILE		12 12 0
Sir Cyril Prideaux-James	(R Prideaux-James)	Mr R Prideaux-James
	(Cotswolds)	
7 SHRIMP		13 12 0
Mr R Savary	(P Savary)	Dr R Halper
	(Zetland)	
8 THE DEALER		10 12 0
Mr C Drury	(N Parker)	Mr D Drury
	(Vine & Craven)	
9 WATAMU		8 12 0
Mr S O'Sullivan	(R Price)	Mr M Powell
	(Surrey Union)	

The Dealer and Scud Missile were the horses I thought would be my biggest dangers. Motown was good, but he still lacked experience at this standard. Air Trooper, Shrimp and Beamish were able but past their best.

Darren Dudley-Smith and Mark Powell, riding Acacia Queen and Watamu respectively, were probably the best jockeys. They were both only twenty, fearless and eager and Mark was certainly good enough to turn professional one day, given the right opportunity. But neither would win today without divine intervention.

In the changing room, Damian Drury was sitting on his own, more worried than usual and attracting a few sympathetic comments from his rivals. There could be no one in the country now who had not heard about his father's problems.

Robert Prideaux-James sat languidly smoking, from time to time glancing at Damian with contempt, and at me with angry loathing.

Mike Thomson and Freddy Philby were both riding reasonable prospects compared with the mounts they had had the previous Saturday. They joined me as we walked out to the parade ring.

'What are you going to do if P-J goes out front like he did last week?' Mike asked me.

'Watch him pull up after the first circuit, I should think. I've just been down to the course, and it looks quite testing.'

'My God,' Freddy said as we saw the horses being led in. 'Old Nosey's got The Dealer into some sort of order.'

I looked across and reluctantly agreed. 'It's lucky Damian's riding him,' I said.

'Poor bastard. I think he'd rather go to hell than ride in front of this crowd, with all the stick his father got in this morning's news,' Mike said. 'Did you see it, Archie?'

'Yes. I always thought there was something suspect about him.'

We parted company to go to our respective connections. I only had Georgie and Harold, who was making the most of this chance to stand in the famous ring.

A few yards away I noticed that Nosey Parker stood without his owner. That would please him.

Sir Cyril Prideaux-James and his other son, Richard, both wearing regulation battered trilbies and ancient binocular cases, gazed dispassionately at the runners being walked round by the self-conscious grooms.

Georgie drew me to one side. 'Archie,' she said, as Caesar's Consul strode by, led by a beaming Sharon, 'are you all right? You're looking very pale.'

I smiled. 'I feel very pale, but I'll be okay once we're off. I only wish to hell nailing Drury hadn't clashed with this race.'

'Just concentrate on the race,' Georgie urged. 'You don't have to do anything more about Drury; everyone's saying he's had it. If you beat Damian, that'll be another kick in the teeth for him.'

I grinned at her intensity. 'You only want me to win so you can hold me to my promise.'

'Bloody right,' she said. 'I can't wait to lead him in.'

The bell rang for jockeys to get mounted and the parade ring suddenly burst into life as connections scurried off in search of their horses.

Sharon had turned the Consul in under the large digital number board. By the time we reached them, she had already undone the leather roller and pulled off the paddock sheet. The Consul looked magnificent, even if I did think so myself. The dapples were just beginning to show through on his sides; his dark coat shone like a fresh conker. The Dealer was not going to have everything his own way.

I checked the girths and surcingle, pulled down the irons and asked Georgie to leg me into my three-pound Australian saddle. She squeezed my thigh as we turned away.

'Good luck, Archie.'

I looked back and thanked her with a small wink. 'I'll need it.'

There was no parade for the Foxhunters', and we followed the rest of the runners out of the ring, along the tarmac road beside the trade stands. Both sides of the road were ten deep with punters and racegoers. From the voices in the crowd, I guessed at least half of them were Irish, a lot of whom, with no home runners to cheer, seemed to have tacked on to my chances. They were bellowing encouragement as if I were an old friend.

A few small butterflies flapped wildly inside my stomach as the adrenalin began to trickle through my arteries.

When we were out on the course, Sharon wished me luck as she unclipped the lead rope and gave the Consul one last big pat on his neck before we cantered off up in front of the stands.

We turned with the rest of the field just above the famous winning post and headed back down towards the three-and-a-quarter-mile start below the tented village that sprang up at Festival time.

Galloping downhill on a fresh horse is normally a prescription for getting run away with for amateur jockeys. A few of us were struggling not to let it happen, including me. I could not think of a more embarrassing place to get carted than in front of the enormous Cheltenham crowd.

Without warning, Scud Missile came bolting past me, out of control, with Robert Prideaux-James looking as though he was trying to pull a rapist off his mother.

I laughed so hard, I almost lost my grip on the Consul. I was still laughing when Scud Missile was eventually yanked into a big circle at the bottom of the course by the two-mile start.

'I'd have paid good money for that to have happened,' I said to Freddy as we turned our horses to look at the first fence.

Freddy grinned. 'God doesn't repay debts with money, Archie. Serves the bugger right for what he did to you last week.'

We made our way back behind the starting tapes to join the others and we all had our girths checked for the last time while we waited for Scud Missile to trot back to us.

'You should have had a couple more Shredded Wheats for breakfast!' I called over to Prideaux-James when he reached us. He tried to ignore me and turned away muttering under his breath.

The assistant starter walked over and pushed two fingers under Scud Missile's girth, then called to the starter, 'All okay!'

The starter ducked under the running rail and climbed the ladder to his rostrum. There was no need for him to call us into line. We were all ready.

'Right! Come on!' he shouted. At the same time, he pulled the lever to release the tapes.

Freddy Philby and Motown went on straightaway to make the running up the middle of the course. They were closely followed by Air Trooper and Shrimp. Freddy was going a good racing pace and I was happy to tuck into fourth place on the rails.

When we had settled over the first two fences, I turned to see where Robert and Damian were. I had not expected to see Damian in front of me because the one chink in The Dealer's armour was stamina; he just might not get home on the soft ground in a truly run race. But I had expected Robert to be making the running. With luck, being run off with at the start had made him change his plans.

I had to crane my neck right round to see Damian sitting immediately in my slipstream. Robert was a good six lengths adrift of the rest of the field.

For a circuit, I was happy to stay where I was. Apart from getting a bit close to the fence on top of the hill, and pecking slightly, the Consul did not put a foot wrong.

After point-to-pointing, riding at Cheltenham was like playing football at Wembley when you are used to playing in a car park, and that sense of occasion was not lost on the Consul. He felt as strong as ever and was, for the most part, jumping brilliantly.

We headed out away from the stands for the final circuit and the time had come to make my move and give the race a bit of edge. As we ran slightly downhill to the first fence along the back, I caught hold of the Consul and made him lengthen his stride. He got himself into gear and stretched out his neck as he realised that the race was on.

The three horses in front of us took their time at the next fence while the Consul pricked his ears and flew it; we passed all three in mid air and landed galloping towards the water. It was a supreme sensation, to be going well on a really good horse, on a great course, with no one else in sight.

The Consul loved to be in front, and so did I. Not just out of vainglory; in amateur races, the biggest danger was not usually the fences, but the other jockeys, and now they were all behind me.

At the second open ditch I heard the crack of breaking timber and the jangle of stirrup irons as someone fell behind me. But I did not waste time looking back. I could sense some of the others chasing me and over this distance, at this pace, I had to give the Consul all the help that I could.

We pinged the last plain fence on the far side and crested the rise before the left-handed turn towards the top of the course and the fence where the Consul had pecked first time round.

It was the worst fence on the course, and over the years I had watched dozens of horses fall at it. Placed as it was on the brow of the hill, it gave the impression as you jumped it that you were going off the edge of the world. A lot of horses crumpled on

248

landing because they momentarily lost concentration.

Remembering that last time we had met the fence on a long stride, I kept a tight hold and made the Consul get in close.

It was the wrong decision. As we lost speed, his mind wandered. He crashed through the fence, just above the marker rail. We came out the other side with the Consul almost on his knees. His head was tucked in between his front legs, still sliding forward. Two horses came by me as the Consul struggled beneath me to regain his balance, and I struggled even harder to stay on top of him. It seemed to take forever, though it must only have been a couple of seconds, before his head suddenly sprang up in front of me, he got up on his toes and we were on our way again.

I grappled with my foot for a lost iron as we raced off after the others. When I had found the stirrup, I realised with a jolt in my guts that the Consul's bridle was half pulled off over his right ear.

He began shaking his head with the irritation of it. The head band was across his ear and eye, but there was nothing I could do about it. His neck was stretched out galloping and I had no way of reaching his head. There were just three more fences. He was still going well, so I gave him a good sharp crack on the shoulder to take his mind off the bridle. We had lost a lot of ground and he could worry about his head after he had done his galloping.

As we raced downhill to the third last, I had him back on overdrive, and although Freddy and Mark Powell were still in front of me, I had their measure. I decided to pull wide of the field in case one of them fell and brought me down. As I did so, Robert Prideaux-James came cruising along outside me. Before I could think what he was doing, he leaned across and pulled the Consul's bridle off with his left hand. I could do nothing about it except scream abuse at him as my anger momentarily got the better of me. But I forced myself to concentrate on the job in hand. The next fence was almost on us and I reckoned as long as I kept the bit in the Consul's mouth, I would be all right.

As he stood off to jump the fence, I prayed that he would not put a foot through the dangling leather. By pure good fortune, he did not and we galloped on round the bend into the straight. Prideaux-James on Scud Missile stayed with me and together we swept past the two leading horses to take up the running.

In spite of the ground and three miles of Cheltenham's gruelling contours, both the Consul and Scud Missile were going strongly. I was amazed that Scud Missile was still with us; he had galloped a good half mile further than the Consul before the race had even started. Maybe I had misjudged the pace and should have kicked for home earlier. I urged my horse on to try and sap his rival's strength.

Now there were only two fences and three uphill furlongs to run. Ten strides off the second last fence, my worries about Scud Missile were banished as Damian came up on our inside with what looked like a double handful. I picked up my stick and drove the Consul as hard as I could while Damian and the Dealer went a length up on us.

The fence came up right on our stride pattern, and I could feel the Consul straining to stay with The Dealer and keep in front of Scud Missile. All the exertion he got from me, he doubled. He had forgotten all about the hanging bridle and was concentrating every ounce of his energy into getting us through the mud up the long hill towards the last fence and the winning post.

When we reached the last, I flung him into it without looking for a stride. He left the ground outside the wings with his front legs stretched out, straight as arrows in his effort to make the distance. I heard his back legs scrape through the brush, but we made it.

Scud Missile had tried to go with us, but realised too late that he could not make it. He put down right at the last moment, crashed into the fence and turned a complete somersault before slamming into the ground.

I pushed on with fast-ebbing strength. I had my stick up though I was too weak to use it with any force. But the Consul plugged on up the hill. The effort to get back to The Dealer and the will to beat him were almost entirely his own. It was not until we reached the end of the temporary running rail that I really thought we could get there. The Dealer's stamina seemed suddenly to desert him. His legs stiffened up and he began to wander. Damian went for his whip, but it made no difference.

With a last colossal surge of strength, the Consul changed legs and stretched his neck. With his head and bridle almost on the ground, the great horse carried us forward, past The Dealer, and two strides further, past the post.

We had done it!

He had done it.

The tension that had hardened every muscle in my body left me at a stroke and I collapsed back on to my saddle while the Consul cantered on. There was nothing I could do to pull him up, but by the top of the run-in, he had slowed to a trot.

I took the chance to swing off his back and pull the bridle back on so that I could lead him in.

Damian trotted up to me. On his face was a wide smile.

'Bloody amazing,' he gasped. 'I don't know how you got over the last few fences with that bridle dangling.'

I nodded weakly. 'Bad luck. I thought you were going to win.'

I held up a hand to shake his; and after a moment's hesitation he took it.

'Your father won't be pleased,' I could not help saying.

'Good! Serve the bastard right!' Damian said. He turned his horse back towards the entrance to the enclosure and trotted down to meet his groom.

My groom – the Consul's future owner – was running up the course towards me. I led the Consul down to meet her.

'My God, Archie!' Georgie shouted when she was near enough, 'That was amazing! We all thought you'd had it, going into the last with no bridle. It was a sensation, everyone was going mad.'

'They noticed, then, did they?' I asked.

'Of course,' she puffed, reaching me and taking hold of one of the Consul's reins. 'It was a brilliant piece of riding.'

I shook my head. 'I didn't know what the hell I was doing. It was the Consul who did it.'

The crowd were bellowing their congratulations as we made our way through them to the winner's place in the parade ring.

When we were in the ring, I relinquished my hold and let Georgie lead the Consul to his spot.

Harold and Sharon were waiting there with rugs, ready to remove the tack.

Sharon was almost speechless as she kissed first the horse and then myself. Harold's smile reached from one side of his trilby to the other.

I went inside, weighed in and came straight back out again to receive my trophy to a heartening burst of warm applause. Some unruly instinct made me grab Georgie and kiss her in front of tens of millions of television viewers, which evoked another round of applause.

251

After I had changed, glowing with the achievement of a long-nursed ambition, I was prepared to push all other thoughts from my mind and throw myself into the celebrations that Lord Walford was arranging for me in his box.

I had to pass Clive Drury's box to reach the Walfords' and I stopped as I heard Drury's unmistakable voice raised in anger. The door was slightly ajar. I peered inside. There were just two men, down at the front of the box; Drury and Robert Prideaux-James.

They were concentrating too hard on each other to notice me standing just outside the door. I ducked back out of sight and tried to listen.

'What the hell did you want to get involved in a cock-up like that for?' Drury hissed.

'What do you mean? It was your plan.'

'What the hell are you talking about?'

'Fred told me. He said you were piling it on The Dealer and I had to make sure of it.'

'Jesus, what the hell's going on? As if I hadn't got enough problems with all these fucking hacks.'

'You're not the only one with problems. I had ten grand on him. He'd have bolted up if he hadn't hit the front so soon.'

'I saw that; I'm not bloody blind. That's what Nosey said. I wash my hands of Damian.'

'At least you've got this other son to take his place,' Prideaux-James remarked with dangerous flippancy.

There was a silence. Then Drury snarled, 'Get the hell out of here. You and your snotty family have just lost a lot more than ten grand. I'm calling in my loans.'

'Hang on, Drury.' I thrilled to hear a desperate whine in Prideaux-James's voice. 'I was only joking. Obviously I'll do anything I can to help.'

'Just get out of my sight and tell your pathetic father to start packing all his scruffy old suits. I've done you people enough favours.'

'Archie? Come on, everyone's waiting for you.'

Georgie's voice echoed down the corridor.

I froze for a second. The voices in Drury's box stopped abruptly. I pulled myself together and strolled towards Lord Walford's box. As I turned into it, I caught a glimpse of

Prideaux-James glaring nervously along the corridor.

I ignored him and walked into a thunderous reception from the forty or so people gathered in the room.

Half an hour of back-slapping, questioning and theorising followed. Everyone wanted to congratulate me, tell me how much they had won, and how my bridle had come off.

Even my mother, with tears in her eyes, kissed me and congratulated me warmly.

'Now you've won this race, darling, why don't you give up, while you're ahead?'

'I promise I'll think about it,' I said.

I had already thought about it, but I did not want to spoil anyone's fun.

The fun went on for hours. I watched the Gold Cup from the box but could barely remember seeing the other three races on the card. I was happy enough to let myself be carried along with this celebration of the Consul's greatest win.

I found myself a few hours later at Temple Ferris, where the party had swelled to a hundred or so. I was answering the questions about my win in a happy haze, like a robot on dope. That seemed to satisfy most people. And every time thoughts of Clive Drury tried to enter my head, I successfully repelled them.

Later – it must have been after midnight – Georgie found me and whispered, 'Come on. I'll drive you home.'

Chapter 18

In Georgie's car, I tilted the passenger seat until I was almost flat on my back. I gave the driver's leg a squeeze and fell asleep.

When we reached Stone House Farm, I woke feeling almost human and fairly sober. The sky had cleared to reveal a bright moon. The yard and house were deserted. Georgie read me a note that Sharon had left: celebrations were being held down at the village pub.

'What's the time?' I asked Georgie.

'A long way past closing time,' she said. 'You're not going anywhere.'

'What about you?' I asked.

She ignored the question. 'You've had a hell of a day. You should go to bed.'

'Okay,' I said, and walked towards the stairs. I paused on the first step. I turned to look at her.

'Go on,' she said impatiently.

I carried on up the stairs to my bedroom.

I did not turn the lights on. The curtains were open and the silver-blue moon lit the room.

I pulled my clothes off and dumped them on a chair. I climbed into bed and waited.

An owl screeched outside. Light from downstairs shone through my open door but there was not a sound to be heard in the house.

Against all my instincts and wishes I was half asleep when I heard the first creak at the bottom of the stairs. Instantly, I was wide awake with my pulse racing.

I saw her clearly at the doorway in the moonlight. She stood for a moment, looking towards me. But the top of the bed was in darkness and my eyes were half closed. Though I wanted to hold my breath, I forced it in and out with a sleeping rhythm. I hoped she could not hear my heart thumping.

It seemed hours that she stood there; maybe it was a minute or two, but I was on the point of giving in when she came across the room.

Through widening eyes, I watched as she deliberately undressed and cast each garment aside as if she were discarding it forever.

For a moment she stood in only a bra and scanty knickers.

She reached behind her back, unclipped the bra and let it drop to the floor. The nipples stood proud on her big round breasts as she bent forward to slide the panties down her long legs. The dark triangle at her pubis showed bold against the creaminess of her skin in the moonlight.

I held my breath and cleared my throat. I could not help it any more than I could halt my growing erection. Georgie heard and took two quick steps to the bedside. She lifted the covers and slid in next to me.

'Hello,' I murmured. I wrapped my arms around her and began to caress her chilly limbs.

She gave a quiet laugh.

'What are you doing?' I asked.

'Getting warm.'

'And then?'

'Well, I thought you deserved a better prize. You can't do much with a silver cup.'

With long, gentle fingers, she stroked my back, my buttocks and thighs. From there her hand took a slow and tantalising wander until she touched the pulsing, fleshy baton at my groin.

I almost recoiled at the excitement of her fingers finally reaching this part of me. I must have been waiting for it, wanting her, more than I had realised. She wrapped her fingers around my cock and I had never felt so hard in my life.

While her hands searched my body, our mouths and tongues were each locked in deep, greedy colonisation of the other; questing, thrusting deep into warm soft private places – until my lips left hers and searched down her neck and shoulders and armpits to the big, succulent breasts and nipples. I ran my tongue around the fleshy hillocks until they filled my mouth.

My hand was between her thighs. I tried gently to part them.

256

'Open Sesame,' I muttered. The magic worked. Her legs spread wide to let my hand travel up to the soft, silky curls and the private portal they guarded.

Within the well-primed warmth, my fingers found the tender spot and she murmured her encouragement.

'I want you inside me,' she breathed later.

She gasped a small moan as I glided into her all-enveloping warmth. Her fingers lightly searched across my skin and gently squeezed until every nerve-end in my body was burning.

Later, much later, from deep inside her, our climax came. Our bodies pulsed and fused with a quivering intensity that left us limp and blissfully weak.

But we did not sleep. Her capacity to arouse was instinctive and unfailing. And a totally new experience for me.

When the first light of the spring sun showed through the windows, we made love again. At last, though, I rose from the bed feeling as fresh and vital as if I had slept for a week.

But the lingering euphoria of the night could not quieten the guilty, urgent thoughts crowding my mind. With great reluctance, I gave in to them.

Harry was ill – worse than ill – and I had not even bothered to ring the hospital the evening before to discover his condition.

Sean had gone back to Johnny Stewart's house to check on our prisoners and keep them fed. He was going to stay there until we told the police about them next day – our final piece of evidence to confirm Drury's involvement in the conspiracy and Harry's shooting. Sean and I had argued about leaving Drury's men there, but I had persuaded him that they had to stay, at least until the net around Drury was so tight that he could not move.

Jamie was trying, I hoped, to have the story of Drury's conspiracy revealed to his five million readers.

I had to make a plan.

First, I wanted to see Drury face to face.

I thought, in the circumstances, that it was unlikely that I would get him on my own if I rang and asked for an appointment.

But I did think that if John Duckett demanded a one-to-one conclave, he would agree.

I had promised and therefore I would go to my mother's house to look through Bill Beecham's personal effects, but after I had seen John Duckett and Harry.

I made coffee for Georgie and myself.

I took it up to my room and marvelled at the sight of Georgie, more relaxed and, frankly, happy than I had ever seen her, lying on my rickety bed.

She smiled at me in a way that reached in and warmed me. I did not want to tell her that Clive Drury was still on the day's agenda, even though she probably knew.

'Angel,' I said, with no self-consciousness, 'I have to go. Shall I see you tonight?'

'Sure,' she said, with a small smile. 'If you come back to Temple Ferris, you'll find a warm supper.'

Something more mundane occurred to me. 'Can I take your car? I suppose mine's still at Cheltenham.'

She nodded. 'Oh, all right,' with overstated annoyance. 'I'll drive home in your lorry, but you take it back tomorrow, okay?'

'It's a deal,' I said gratefully.

'Just promise to look after yourself,' she said.

And I promised, sincerely.

A little after eight, I drove away in Georgie's over-powered Golf. Each breath through my nostrils bore her scent and carried me back to the joys of the night before.

I was still in a state of bewildered euphoria. The suspicion that Georgie was something exceptional had been growing in me for several weeks. Finding out that I was right was like winning the Foxhunters all over again, but more unexpected.

But I knew I had to finish the job I had begun with Drury. I felt that it was now a formality. The damage we had already caused was probably enough to finish him. But I still wanted him to answer publicly for the other deaths he had caused early in his career. The only smudge on my optimism was Harry Winchcombe's condition.

First, though, I drove to Gazeley.

I parked Georgie's car on the main road, a few hundred yards beyond the gates.

It was a simple matter here to clamber over the stone walls of the park and pick my way through the meadows to John Duckett's encampment.

He and his family were up and about, busy collecting firewood and water, quite at home in the handsome park.

John greeted me equably. 'Hello, Archie,' he said. 'You wanted a showdown between me and Drury; you've got it.'

I laughed. 'What do you think? You've got him almost grovelling already.'

'If he wasn't such a complete bastard, I'd feel sorry for him. D'you know, I got, like, a real buzz from finding a father, and I sort of want to reach him, show him what matters, but he's too fucked up.'

'Beyond redemption,' I agreed. 'I want to talk to him, but I think the only way he'll see anyone is if he thinks it's you and you're prepared to let him off the hook somehow.'

'That's right, man. But we won't get anything besides money from him. So,' he made a guilty grimace, 'we may as well make it hurt.'

'Sure,' I agreed. 'But I can cause him a lot more aggravation. I want you to do me a favour. Will you send a message up to the house that you want to meet him, this evening at five?'

'So that you can turn up?'

'Yes. But if you talk to him after me, you might find him a lot more repentant.'

'A geezer like him isn't going to repent whatever you tell him. But that's cool; I'll get him to come.'

'Great. Tell him to come to the old stone barn at the home farm. No one lives there since he kicked out the last tenant. And tell him to come alone.'

John smiled. 'We'll make sure he's alone.'

I left Gazeley, puzzling over John's motives. I was certain that he did not want to extract money from his father simply so that he could spend it. I guessed he recognised that as being the only way to make Clive Drury suffer, and he was right.

From Hereford, I drove straight to the Oxford Infirmary.

I gave a false name to the ward sister, but that did not allay the suspicions of the detective constable who was standing guard outside the private room in which Harry had now been put.

'Mike Thomson,' I said I was, gambling confidently on the fact that the policeman was not a point-to-point punter.

'What's your relationship with Mr Winchcombe?' he asked.

'I'm an old friend,' I said.

'In the racing business?'

259

'Yes,' I said truthfully, 'an amateur.'

The policeman looked at me without expression. 'His sister's with him. I'll ask her.'

He went into the room, taking care to close the door behind him. I prayed that Sarah would recognise Mike Thomson's name and use her head when she saw me.

She did not blink when I was shown in. For a moment I thought Harry was going to blow it for me.

His eyes turned to me in vague recognition. He groaned faintly before relapsing into a vacuous silence. Even if he knew my name, which I doubted, he was not going to say it.

Harry looked terrible. He seemed already to have accepted that he was going. His sister gazed at him with sad certainty.

The swathed body was linked up to a battery of drips and blood bottles; electrodes fastened to his thorax and head passed messages to a screen above his head.

'Harry?' I asked quietly.

His eyes were wide open, but they were closed to me. He was staring blankly at a spot a few feet above him.

'What can they do?' I asked Sara.

'Not a lot. The bullet went through both lungs.' There was bitter accusation in her voice. It was obvious from her attitude that she was desperate to quiz me on what had happened. My gratitude for her discretion increased.

A nurse appeared at the open doorway. 'I'm sorry,' she said, 'you'll have to go now.'

Sarah rose, still looking down at her brother.

I took a deep breath. 'Goodbye, Harry,' I said, trying, for Sarah's sake, not to sound as if it was my last goodbye.

I left the room and waited outside.

'I'll need your address, sir,' the policeman said.

'Sure,' I answered, 'why?'

'We like to know why people have been shot, sir. We may have a murder inquiry on our hands.'

I nodded. 'The news on the radio said he'd just been left in casualty. Didn't anyone see who brought him?'

'They were very busy. He was dumped in the waiting-room. Some of the public gave us a description, but people don't take much notice, do they, when they've got their own problems?'

I left a fictitious address, and hoped that no one would follow it up, or Mike Thomson, for at least forty-eight hours.

I drove out of Oxford towards Bibury. It was already eleven, but I had decided to go to London after seeing my mother. I had to pick up Harry's statement and convince Inspector Waller of its worth, along with the information I had given him the day before at Cheltenham. Now that I had had time to reflect on our conversation, I was seething with frustration at the cold water he had tried to pour on my theories of conspiracy and sabotage.

Both the DTI and the Serious Fraud Office, when pressed hard, had confirmed that as a result of information received, they intended to launch investigations into Drury and all his business interests. This had to have some bearing on the way the information I had given the CID would now be treated. In just two days, Drury's credibility as a sound and respectable force in the City of London had been wiped out, and I wanted to push home that advantage.

My mother was waiting anxiously when I arrived.

'You said you'd be early,' she chided.

'I know; I'm sorry. But I can't stay too long. I have to go to London and be back in Herefordshire by five.'

'For God's sake, Archie, you can't possibly. And you did promise me. There are masses of things to go through here.'

I glanced at my watch; it was already half past eleven. I had, as usual, been overoptimistic about my journey times.

'Okay,' I said, 'don't get in a state. I'll sort it out somehow. Now, where are Bill's things?'

My mother led me through to her seldom-used dining room. It was crammed from floor to ceiling with stacks of cardboard boxes. Even the table was piled high with them. I groaned to myself.

Where the hell was I supposed to start?

'Do we really have to do this now?' I pleaded guiltily.

'Archie! You promised.'

I forced myself to be stoical about it and show willing. Having lived alone for so long, my mother was unused to seeing her plans interfered with by anyone else's. Once she had decided that a job was going to be done, she would panic until it was done.

'All right; all right,' I said and lifted the nearest box. 'Let's do them one by one in the drawing room.'

I carried the box across the hall into the cluttered room, warm and unchanged in its furnishings since I had been a boy.

I set the box down and sat on the ancient sofa. My mother perched opposite me on an upright chair. I undid the cardboard flaps while my mind wandered back to the house near Burford, barely fifteen minutes away, where Sean was acting jailer to three of Drury's henchmen; and to Drury himself and the meeting I hoped to have with him that evening.

My heart sank as I pulled out the musty old contents of the box and thought of the thirty or so more in the dining room.

This first one contained old theatre programmes, race-cards, odd woven leather buttons, shirt-collar stiffeners and a few letters written in the same hand. I glanced through these.

They were, I deduced, from Bill's cousin in the South of France. They were censorious and dismissive in tone, discouraging Bill from visiting the house in France, turning down the suggestion that, as one of Bill's trustees, he might encourage the release of some capital.

They made sad reading, even as I skimmed through. I wondered how pathetic had been Bill's letters that evoked these responses.

I described the contents of the box to my mother, and she listed them on a sticky label. I put the eclectic bunch of documents back in the box, and she stuck her label on it.

In the circumstances, this task was going to be a terrible waste of time and I wondered if my mother would be satisfied with one box.

'Well,' I said brightly, 'not much to upset you. Shall we do the rest another time?'

'But you've only been here ten minutes, and you promised.'

I tried to disguise my annoyance, and went back to another box.

The next two contained sale catalogues, heavily annotated; attempted drafts at what I assumed to be journalism about the art market, witty and well written but, to the best of my knowledge, never published; a thick pile of large paste-board invitations to deb dances in the early 'fifties; and various press cuttings about pictures which had been sold. At a cursory glance, there was no obvious common factor, so I assumed they were simply pictures in which Bill had had a part in selling.

I carried in the fourth and – I had decided – last box.

I lifted out a pile of buff-coloured loose-leaf folders, dog-eared and faded with age. They were not labelled in any way. I hoped they would fall into a single simple category for my mother's listing purposes.

I opened the top folder. Inside was a quantity of neatly mounted press cuttings, dated and sourced where necessary and occasionally underlined with a comment in the margin in Bill's spidery writing.

I had no difficulty finding the common factor in this batch of cuttings; it was Clive Drury.

Like Lord Walford's they covered every public aspect of Drury's life, business and social, everything from his second wedding in 1959, which must have been a great deal smarter than his first, to his purchase of a controlling stake in the Hiberno-Iranian Meat Company in 1989.

There were gossip stories about holidays he had been on; South American connections; lavish star-studded parties he had given; important pictures he had bought and sold; winning racehorses he had owned.

This was the public persona of a hugely successful, slightly racy tycoon. Some of his friends and pastimes may not have been in the best of taste, but they were not illegal. Any biography derived from this source would have been an anodyne work.

I finished the file, and forgetting the time and my earlier plans, dived into the box for the next.

This contained a series of typed memos and handwritten instructions from Drury to Bill Beecham from 1957, when Drury had bought Bill's family firm, to 1962, when they ceased abruptly. This, as far as I could recall, was when Drury had dispensed with Bill's services at the firm.

The instructions involved for the most part the purchase of hundreds of pictures and high quality thoroughbreds. The cryptic element to them was the consistency with which the sellers appeared to be obscure off-shore companies, Lichtenstein Anstalts, Panamanian Trust Funds or other similar depositories of untraceable ownership.

I grabbed back the first file from my mother and went to the dining room to find the box with the picture cuttings.

Here I found a connection. Most of the pictures and horses that Drury had instructed Beecham to buy had been sold shortly afterwards – usually for a substantial profit.

Suddenly I was struck with a sense of *déjà vu*: the Fernleys, Bambi Arlington's BVI company, the bargain price Drury expected to get them for.

What I could not see was why he did it. I was sure that it was not only for the profit.

I went on to the next file to see if that would tell me more. It covered another aspect of Drury's business.

The pieces of paper here appeared to have been torn out of some other record book. They were details of reinsurance business placed by Drury's various syndicates with offshore underwriters. As far as I could tell, on their own, they signified nothing, but in conjunction with Johnny Stewart's findings, they could tell another story. I decided that I would get these up to him at the first opportunity.

When I next looked at the time, it was after one, and I realised that I was not going to London today – not if I wanted to keep the appointment I hoped John Duckett would have made with his father by now.

That meant I would not be seeing Waller either. I grabbed the next folder in the hope that it too would contain further compensation.

There were three sheets of paper in it. They were photocopies of a badly typed, uncorrected report, dated January 1961 and entitled, 'THE MAN WITH THE MIDAS TOUCH – The Rise and Rise of Clive Drury'.

The piece began as if it were standard sycophantic puffery on behalf of its subject. It was written, after all, at a time when the first really big new self-made millionaires were emerging from lean post-war times and were a source of great public fascination.

But after the first two paragraphs, the tone changed. The writer claimed that although Drury made respectable profits for most of his client names, and large legitimate fees for himself, he had systematically topped up his own earnings by retrospective reinsurance with a string of offshore insurers which, it was claimed, were owned by Drury.

His offshore profits were repatriated in the form of bloodstock and paintings – high-value items subject to volatile market forces and, therefore, legitimate-seeming personal profits at a time when Capital Gains Tax was not levied.

He worked with two of the most successful underwriters in

Lloyd's, who were deeply implicated and took their cut in pictures, horses and other easily encashable commodities.

His clients were not, of course, the only victims of his cheating. The Inland Revenue were clearly missing out on their cut of these overseas profits. The writer suggested that the only reason Drury's activities had not been revealed from within was that he operated a reign of terror throughout his organisation, and no one dared whisper a word.

This allegation was backed up by the mysterious death the previous year (1960) of a senior clerk at Beecham's. The clerk, the writer contended, was about to spill the beans, and much of the information for this piece had sprung from that source.

I read the whole thing twice, utterly transfixed. It was, even by today's standards, pure dynamite and had obviously been intended for publication. Along the bottom was scrawled a handwritten note, which I took to be an editor's, demanding that unless the writer could provide a hundred and fifty per cent substantiation, he should burn the piece at once.

Under the note, and almost totally obscured by it, was typed the author's name.

I squinted at it until I could make it out.

When I realised what I was reading, my body was suffused with horror and appalling fury at the unequivocal confirmation of something I had suspected, at first only vaguely, then more insistently, since my last meeting with Bill Beecham.

I could not lift my eyes to meet my mother's. To disguise the confused rage that threatened to engulf me, I lifted the last sheet of the document. Underneath was another press cutting.

It was the report, similar to one I had read in Lord Walford's library, of a hit-and-run killing in Chelsea in January 1961. This report, unlike Lord Walford's version, named the dead man and was illustrated with a studio photograph of my father.

For a moment I was paralysed with rage at the horrific irony. The man I had been pursuing for the last month was also my father's killer. I buried my face in my hands to try and hold my head together.

'What is it, Archie?' my mother asked in a small whisper. She had been silent throughout the time it had taken me to read my father's condemnation of Drury; she was aware that this box contained a more significant legacy than the others. Now she realised that I had found what she had been dreading. 'It's to do with your father, isn't it? And Drury.'

I looked up at her bleakly and nodded.

'I knew it,' she said. 'I knew that he and Bill had been planning something just before he died. My God!' she uttered bitterly. 'Bill must have known all along.' She began silently to weep.

I stared at the photo of my father, and vowed that Drury would pay, would bleed for the thirty years of misery he had caused my mother.

The resolve stung me into action.

I stood up and handed the papers to my mother. 'I started my campaign against Drury for Bill; I'll finish it for my father.'

I went to the kitchen and picked up the phone.

I rang Temple Ferris first. Georgie was called to the phone.

'Hello,' she said, with a warmth that made my spine tingle.

'Hello,' I was more brisk. 'I need your help.'

'How?' She understood that this was no idle request.

'I'm at my mother's. I'm going to have to go as soon as possible, but I don't want her left on her own. Will you come over?'

'Of course.'

'Thanks, Georgie. I'll tell you what I can when you arrive.'

We said a simple 'Goodbye'.

I rang the detective, Robinson. It was two o'clock. He was at lunch and could not be found. I asked for Waller. He answered brusquely.

'Yes, Mr Best?'

'Look, I've been going through Bill Beecham's things at my mother's house, and there's a pile of information about Drury that you ought to see, now.'

'Concerning what?'

'His early business activities.'

'I've had the Serious Fraud Office round here this morning. Is there anything for them?' He actually sounded interested.

I breathed a sigh of relief. 'Yes, I told you, masses. I can't bring it down. You'll have to get someone out here as soon as you can.'

'Okay Mr Best. Tell me exactly where you are.'

I told him the best way to reach the house and hung up.

Back in the drawing room, my mother was gazing at the photograph of her late husband.

'What can I get you?' I asked.

'Just tea, please Archie,' she said quietly.

I made a pot and put it down beside her. I poured us both a cup and sat opposite her.

'He won't get away with it, Ma, I promise. Because of what's happened over the last few days, he's in big trouble anyway, but I'll make damn certain he answers for this too.'

'Were you responsible for all the terrible publicity he's been getting, then?' she asked.

'You must have guessed that,' I said. 'Bill left me with just enough to start the job. He knew the connection with my father's death would come out. It must have been hell for the poor bastard, knowing all that time, and too bloody weak to do anything abut it.'

'I expect he thought, by leaving it to you, something would be done; he was right, but what risks have you taken, Archie? I knew you were up to something with Drury, and I told you to take care. Your father told me what a pig he was thirty years ago. Can't you just leave it to the police now?'

I nodded untruthfully. 'I've just rung them. They're on their way here from London. I'm afraid you'll have to let them go through all these things of Bill's. There's just one thing, though. Bill didn't want me to go to the police about Drury killing him. He wanted to avoid the embarrassment for Sue Walford and Georgie. So I'm going to take this cutting out.' I slipped the report of my father's death out of the file, folded it and put it in my pocket. 'Other than this, they'll need every lead or bit of evidence they can get.'

I did not tell her about the other call I'd made until Georgie arrived half an hour later.

I left them, my mother and my new lover, in the comforting surroundings of the small room. My mother did not question my going, other than with her eyes.

'I'll see you both later,' I said.

Chapter 19

Georgie had brought my car from Temple Ferris. I climbed into it and set off for home.

There were not many people I knew well or trusted enough to lend me a weapon, but Harold, my neighbour, was one of them.

When I arrived at his house and asked to borrow the rifle I knew he had been licensed to keep for the last twenty years, he did not think twice about the consequences to himself if I was found using it.

'You're up to your neck in this business with Drury, aren't you?' he probed.

He had a right to know. 'Yes. I can't tell you about it now. But I will.'

'That's okay, Archie. He sounds a right bastard, and I hope to hell he gets his dues.'

'He will, don't you worry.'

I reached Gazeley Park at four o'clock. The meeting with Drury was scheduled for five, but I needed to check that John had been able to fix it.

I found John outside the gates of the park giving an interview to a Sunday tabloid, the sister paper to Jamie's.

He was sitting in the journalist's car. I left them to it and made my way along the park walls until I could climb over to the camp.

The numbers in the camp had swelled. Drury's threats of injunction and eviction had patently failed, and the travellers were making the most of the park and unaccustomed favourable treatment from the media.

I soon found John's common-law wife, Marianne. She was no more welcoming than she had been when I first saw her in the camp by the Teifi.

Hurt and betrayal showed in the dark blue eyes below her mop of henna'd hair.

'You've damaged our life, you know. You and your slimy journalist friend,' she said to me in her soft voice. 'Money always damages lives. Do you know what these people have been giving John for his interviews? Thousands, thousands of pounds. What do you think that'll do to us?'

'Tell him to give it away,' I said.

'You know it's not that easy. And there is something – not much – but something of his ghastly father in him.'

'Listen to me,' I said impatiently, 'that ghastly father has caused misery to a lot of people, and I had to risk upsetting a few more to see that he paid for it. If you can't handle it, that's your fault, not mine. What are you running away from, anyway? There's nothing positive in isolation from the rest of society, whatever its faults.'

I was losing control. Why should this self-righteous woman blame me for John's disloyalty to their eccentric standards? Drury had killed my father; John was Drury's son; there was an unseverable connection.

At that point John sauntered back to the camp.

I walked to meet him. I wanted to talk to him without Marianne.

'Did you fix the meeting?' I asked.

'Yeah, man. No sweat. I got one of the farm geezers to go and find him, and the message came back that it's cool. The geezer was worried though. Some of the other people working on this place have gone missing and Drury . . . my father,' he grinned, 'has totally lost his cool about it.'

'He hasn't lost them for good,' was all I was prepared to admit. 'Let me get this right, then. Drury will come alone to the barn, without anyone else, to meet you?'

'Yeah.'

'Right. I'll get there earlier, and wait out of sight. You be there to meet him, so he doesn't smell a rat and do a runner. Then I'll have my talk with him. Okay?'

'Yeah. But he may not come. He's dead paranoid. He's screaming down the phone all day up there. The hack I've just been talking to says they've started an investigation into all his shit. He

270

says he's going to be crucified. And all because I came on the scene.' John was clearly proud of his achievement.

'Do you feel anything for him?' I asked.

'Only hate. I never knew I had a father, and I didn't care much, but to find out I have and he's such a shit-head makes me really angry.'

'I never knew my father; and I've regretted it all my life,' I said quietly.

I left my car in a lane which ran along the northern edge of Drury's estate, taking the rifle with me. From there, I could make my way to the barn under cover of woodland. I reached the clearing which surrounded the deserted farm and its buildings and listened for any sounds of approach. I heard none, and made a quick dash across to the high double doors which were the barn's only entrance.

It was a large, red-brick Victorian barn, not ideal for modern agricultural purposes, but with enough height for two vast grain bins to have been installed.

These were twenty feet high and thirty feet long, still full to the brim with the last season's crop of oil-seed rape, waiting, no doubt, for a rise in the price before being sold.

I closed the door behind me and looked for a place to wait out of sight.

A wooden staircase led up the side of the bins to a platform constructed on the eaves which overlooked them. I ran up and found a clutter of old equipment and a few dozen plastic cans of Round-Up herbicide stored there. Not much light would reach it from the doors, and I had a good view of them. I sat down with my back propped against a pile of hessian sacks and unzipped the gun-slip.

I slotted five rounds into the magazine and rested the rifle on my lap to wait.

I heard the sound of a diesel engine approaching the farm. John should have been here by now. He was not. But he would not be coming in a vehicle.

Would Drury stay if his son was not waiting for him?

The motor drew up close to the barn and the engine was switched off. I heard the door slam and one set of heavy footsteps coming to the doors of the barn. With a long creak, a door swung open and the lower part of the building was flooded with light.

Silhouetted in the doorway was Clive Drury. He took a few steps inside and looked around.

'John?' he growled. 'Where the hell are you?'

Drury's gaze swept up towards me. I held my breath and did not move. He looked keenly into the shadows before his eyes moved on. I held my breath, but he had not seen me.

To myself, I echoed his question to John. I did not know if Drury had left anyone in his vehicle. It was John's task to make sure we were alone.

But where the hell was he?

Drury was already getting impatient. He stamped outside and bellowed into the surrounding woodland.

After a while, he came back in and shouted into the depths of the building where I was lurking.

'If you don't show yourself, I'm leaving. I haven't got time to fuck about.'

I got to my feet with the rifle trained on him.

'Don't leave, Drury,' I said. 'If you move, I'll blow your head off.'

He turned and peered up into the eaves to see me.

'Who's that? Best?' He was nonplussed by my appearance. 'What the hell are you doing here? What's this got to do with you.'

'I told John about his parentage,' I replied.

I began to walk down the stairs, with the gun trained on Drury. For once he seemed out of his depth.

'Is this the first time anyone's pointed a gun at you, Drury?' I asked as I reached the bottom.

Drury recovered himself. 'What are you playing at? You're out of your league, Best.'

I walked up to him. He flinched, but I thrust the end of the barrel at his throat.

'Get back against the wall,' I snapped.

Drury did as I asked.

'I'm out of my league, am I?' I said. 'You're going to go down, Drury, you're going to be pulled for every stroke you've ever pulled, for everyone you've ripped off.' My voice was rising. 'And for every poor bastard you've had killed.'

Drury's eyes slid sideways towards the door. I increased the pressure on his throat with my rifle.

'You're not going anywhere, Drury.'

'You're talking crap!' Drury screamed back at me. 'And I'll have you destroyed for it!'

'That's more like it, Clive. That's the old Duckett they remember so well in Catford. You'll have me destroyed. Like you've had Harry Winchcombe destroyed.'

'Is he dead?' Drury said with alarm, before he could stop himself.

'Probably. A nasty little gofer of yours shot him in the chest. Tommy, remember him? And Fred and the other bastard who tried to steal my horse?'

'That was their own idea,' Drury blurted, 'and Prideaux-James's. He and Fred had their houses on Damian in that race when they knew I was going to buy The Dealer. And Damian would have won, if the little prick hadn't weakened.'

'I couldn't give a toss about your efforts to make Damian a sporting gent or whatever the hell you were trying to achieve,' I sneered. 'But I am concerned about the syndicates you've ripped off for years; I'm concerned about hundreds of dodgy pictures you've sold, and horses you've bought from yourself to get the money you've ripped off back into the country; I'm concerned about the family you dumped, the racecourses you've destroyed trying to boost your own crummy course. And I'm concerned about Harry Winchcombe's life.'

Drury began to gargle as I pushed the gun deeper into his throat and my voice rose.

'Shut up you bastard!' I yelled into his face. 'I haven't finished yet. What about Bill Beecham? You made his life hell and then you had to kill him too because at last he had the guts to tell the world about you and your bloody greed. You're vermin, Drury, and you're going to be wiped out like vermin.'

'You don't know what the hell you're talking about,' Drury hissed. 'You're a nobody, aren't you? You're like Bill Beecham, aren't you? You hate people who've made a success of their lives. You think you're so fucking superior. People like you are two a penny; nobody's going to take you seriously. You'll never walk away from this, I promise you.'

He stopped to draw breath, and gulped as I pulled the bolt back on my rifle.

In the split second it took me to do it, he saw a chance. He scraped his neck across the end of the gun barrel, jerked himself sideways and made a dash for the stairs up to the eaves.

If he thought there was a way out, he was going to be disappointed.

I strolled across the barn. I could not see him now, but I could hear him scrabbling about like a rat in a trap at the far end of the loft.

I slowly climbed the stairs and picked my way through the shadows and stacks of farm paraphernalia that cluttered the dark space at the top.

I did not intend to kill Drury, but it would do him no harm to think that I did. I could no longer hear him. I stopped where I was, halfway to the end of the loft.

'Drury, you can hang around as long as you like back there. I don't care how long I have to wait.'

There was no reply.

I waited. After a minute I addressed the shadows again.

'Drury, there's no way out except past me.'

Silence.

Suddenly, a few feet in front of me and six feet above, there was a crash of splintering wood and a thump as Drury landed on the timber floor. I could see his dark bulk. He must have managed to scramble up to one of the smaller collar trusses. I thanked God for the woodworm.

I stepped forward and prodded the rifle into his side. Abruptly, we were bathed in light from a naked bulb dangling from the roof-ridge. I guessed that John had arrived.

Drury was gazing up at me, red-faced, badly shaken and very scared.

'Why are you doing this?' he growled.

'Why do you think?'

'There has to be more than just Beecham.'

'Until today, there wasn't. I wanted to see you go down for Bill Beecham. I loved him like a father because I never knew my father. Today, I found out why. You knew him. But he knew too much about you.' I gazed into Drury's black eyes. 'So you had him run down in the street, like a stray dog.'

Drury blinked. 'Fuller?' he muttered. 'Edward Fuller? But he didn't have a son. I'd have known. You're lying.'

For a moment of bitter euphoria, I could not answer.

He had admitted it! Plainly, without remorse, just as a matter of fact, he had admitted that he had conspired in my father's murder. My finger reached for the trigger. I closed my eyes.

'This is the police!'

The voice echoed up from beyond the grain-bins.

I heard footsteps clattering up the stairs but I could not take my eyes off Drury.

'He didn't have a son when you killed him,' I said urgently, 'but he was about to marry my mother, and she was already pregnant – with me!'

Drury closed his eyes. Then, with a speed that belied his bulk, he rolled out from under my gun, lashed out at my legs with his feet, caught me off-balance and sent me sprawling among the Round-Up cans.

But I still had the rifle in my hands.

I lifted myself, and put the gun to my shoulder. Through a red mist of passionate anger, I wanted to see Drury dead – for my father, and for my mother.

I tried to find him in my sights. He had been headed off by someone at the top of the stairs.

He veered to his left; crashed through the wooden hand-rail above the mountain of black seed in the great iron clamp.

He disappeared over the edge with a startled yell, watched with amazement by Jim Lewis, the Bromyard policeman.

I staggered to my feet and ran up to the broken rail. I looked down into a pair of protruding, panic-struck eyes. Drury was floundering like a drowning man. His face was scarlet with effort and terror. He was eight feet from the side of the bin, up to his waist in the shifting rape seed. He could do nothing to reach the side.

Even as I watched, he sank, struggled wildly, and sank deeper.

'For God's sake!' he yelled, 'get me out of here!'

I glanced at the policeman; I wondered vaguely what Lewis was doing here, but my concentration was on Drury.

'Get a rope!' I yelled.

The policeman turned and clattered down the stairs.

In the few seconds I had been looking away from him, Drury's shoulders had disappeared. Just his head and one arm were above the surface of the rape. He looked at me not believing what was happening.

275

'I'm going to drown! Get me out,' he pleaded.

The rape seed was at least fifteen feet deep where he was, and he would sink until he reached the concrete floor. The black sea surged around him as he began again to struggle furiously.

'Hurry, for Christ's sake,' I shouted towards the front of the barn.

'There's nothing down here!' the policeman yelled back. 'I'll have to look in his car.'

Drury gave a terrified, gargling scream as the seed reached his chin, then his mouth. His one free hand still waved frantically. I looked around for a pole, a length of wood – anything long enough to reach him.

I could find nothing at first, and searched in panic towards the back of the loft. There, with intense relief, I found a coil of orange binder twine. I grabbed an old iron bolt lying nearby. As I ran back to the edge of the bin, I tied the bolt on to the end of the twine to give it enough weight to throw down to Drury.

But Drury had gone.

A single hand showed above the surface, where the seed still surged with an apparent energy of its own.

For a few seconds I was immobile with macabre fascination; it seemed to me incredible that an inanimate heap of tiny grains should so easily have swallowed up Drury's vigorous bulk.

As I stared at the spot where he had been, the hand slipped beneath the surface. Through a haze I heard Jim Lewis running back across the barn and up the stairs. He stopped and gaped at the mound of black seed.

John Duckett was behind him, clutching a coil of blue nylon tow-rope which he began to unwind.

'Bloody heck!' the policeman gasped. 'Where did he go?'

John glanced at him. 'He's still there, you fool. We'll have to get in and drag him out. Where was he?' he yelled at me.

I pointed to a spot where the seed still shifted.

John wrapped one end of the cord around his waist and tied the other to the railing post. 'Just don't let me go under!' he yelled, and plunged in before I could stop him.

I grabbed the slack rope, made a couple of turns around the post and pulled it taut.

'Don't move!' I yelled at John. 'And spread your weight. It was struggling that dragged him down.' I turned to the policeman.

'Get some help, and an ambulance. Then get hold of Inspector Waller on Bibury 3579; tell him what's happened.'

The policeman looked at me doubtfully, then at John lying spreadeagled across the surface of the black lake, groping into it with his arms up to his shoulders. He knew there was nothing else he could do for Drury.

'Right. Bibury 3579 – Waller,' he said and ran back down to his car.

It took an hour, with two augers and a convoy of tractors and trailers to empty the bin of its seven hundred and fifty tons of rape seed.

I was beside Waller and Robinson as the first sign of Drury's head appeared, followed by his torso in a checked suit dusted black.

'I never saw anyone drowned in oil-seed rape before, Guv'nor,' Robinson observed.

'Not a pretty sight,' the inspector answered as the body rolled over.

Drury's white face was contorted with terror and the struggle for breath.

Two local police dropped into the bin and heaved the corpse free.

It had taken ten minutes' persuasion and ten minutes' heaving on my own to get John Duckett out. Now, with the same rope wrapped under the dead man's arms, and four policemen pulling, the mortal remains of Clive Drury were heaved out and laid on the loft floor in a matter of seconds.

A doctor – superfluous – and a pathologist were already standing by. They knelt to make their preliminary examination.

'Right, Mr Best. Now we have a body, you and I had better have a chat.' Waller gestured me down the stairs in front of him.

I was in trouble.

Failing to report a shooting – Harry's; obstructing the police in their investigations; unlawful detention of three men, two of whom were victims of further unreported shootings; conspiracy to defraud.

I could not stop myself from grinning as the detective inspector spelled it out.

'You haven't got much to smile about, Best.'

I shook my head.

It was only thanks to Drury's own action, taking off and crashing through the railings as he had, and Jim Lewis's first-hand evidence, that I was not facing a charge of murder.

The anger was past now. The relief was intense. Drury had brought about his own death.

There had been only a few brief seconds when I had positively wanted to kill him myself; and it might have been more satisfactory to see him in court, answering the innumerable charges that could be brought against him. But as far as I was concerned, this would do.

Sean had been relieved of his custodial duties over Drury's three men. Waller had got the local police there as soon as I had told him about them.

Jamie Lloyd-Jones was on his way; Georgie had called him in his car before she had followed Waller from my mother's house to Gazeley.

Now she was waiting outside the barn in her car.

'You've had quite a week, haven't you, Mr Best?' Waller was saying. His tone made me glance at him. There was the hint of a smile on his grey face. 'It's very lucky for you that the local constable was on the scene when the deceased, er, deceased.'

I could not argue with that. 'I know. But why the hell did he turn up here?'

'He's a thorough chap. After the shooting incident up at your place, which you also omitted to tell *us* about, he was following up ownership of every green Daihatsu in Herefordshire. There was one registered in the name of this estate. One of the farm-workers told him he'd find Drury up here.'

'Well done, Constable Lewis,' I said.

'We all do our best,' Waller agreed. 'Right, I've got a lot of clearing up to do here. I won't be needing you again today. Come in to Hereford police station tomorrow; they may want to charge you. Of course, if you don't, we'll come and get you, all right?'

I left my car where I had parked it three long hours before. I drove Georgie back to my house in her car.

Her relief at the abrupt end to my pursuit of Drury showed in every gesture, every word she uttered. Even the prospect of my being arrested and charged did not worry her.

'The judge will understand,' she said, 'I'm sure, and I'll stand bail for you,' she offered brightly.

'Thanks a lot.'

'Archie,' she said, 'I think I understand everything that went on. Except why Drury asked you to get those pictures.'

'I don't know. You'll have to try the ouija board. I don't suppose Bambi Arlington will admit it, but I'm fairly sure the Fernleys were wrong'uns. Maybe Drury was going to have me pulled for trying to sell him Sexton Blakes.' I shrugged. 'Who knows? Shame about the money though.'

'Well, you're not so hard up now. I'm buying Caesar's Consul, don't forget.'

'Ah,' I said, 'I've been thinking about that.'

She turned and glared at me.

'Archie, you swine! You promised! We had a verbal contract. You can't go back on it.'

'Well . . .' I started.

'Never mind "Well"! If you welsh on the deal, you're going to need a good lawyer.'

I glanced across at her angry, grinning face.

'All I need right now,' I said, 'is a hot dinner and a very warm woman.'

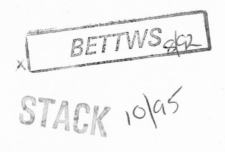